WHAT BECAME OF US

Annie, Ursula, Manon and Penny. They'd been friends at college, close friends – and on that last, apparently perfect, Oxford afternoon they'd drunk champagne and tried to imagine what the future held in store.

Now, they meet again – same place, and another glorious summer. But Penny is no longer with them, and for the other three, this is a time to confront the reality of their lives. During the course of one highly-charged weekend, old passions are revived, love newly found and long-held secrets revealed.

For Nick

Acknowledgements

Many thanks to Toby for the cupboards, to Connor for some of his best lines, to Becky for all the enthusiasm and earrings, and especially to my gorgeous husband, Nick, for his unwavering support and good humour.

What Became Of Us

by

Imogen Parker

Magna Large Print Books
Long Preston, North Yorkshire,
BD23 4ND, England.

British Library Cataloguing in Publication Data.

Parker, Imogen
    What became of us.

    A catalogue record of this book is
    available from the British Library

    ISBN   0-7505-1697-6

First published in Great Britain 2000 by Corgi

Copyright © Imogen Parker 2000

Cover illustration © Tony Mills by arrangement with Swift Imagery

The right of Imogen Parker to be identified as the author of this work has been asserted by her in accordance with sections 77 and 78 of the Copyright, Designs and Patents Act, 1988

Published in Large Print 2001 by arrangement with
Transworld Publishers Ltd.

All the characters in this book are fictitious,
and any resemblance to actual persons, living or dead,
is purely coincidental.

Magna Large Print is an imprint of Library Magna Books Ltd.

Printed and bound in Great Britain by
T.J. (International) Ltd., Cornwall, PL28 8RW

PROLOGUE

June 1982

The women were wearing black. The sombre solidity of the colour in the shimmering sunlight stopped him in his tracks, as if he had been floating and was suddenly grounded. He took a deep breath and began to walk towards them.

'Find the Parks and head for the river,' his sister Ursula had instructed.

She and her friends had that morning finished their finals and were still dressed in the gowns the University required examination candidates to wear. A picnic was spread out in the dappled shade of a huge weeping willow whose branches canopied the river.

He recognized Ursula before he was close enough to distinguish her features because her finger was stabbing the air to emphasize a point she was arguing. Next to her, a tall blonde was lying on her side, her head propped up on her arm, and only just enough buttons done up on her blouse to keep her decent.

As he came into earshot, he heard his sister saying, with a note of disapproval in her voice. 'You'll no doubt be famous.'

To which the blonde replied, 'And you'll probably be Prime Minister, God help us!'

Ursula frowned, then caught sight of him and waved.

'Roy, over here!'

For one excruciating moment, all four female faces turned in his direction. Then Ursula stood up, took his arm and marched him the last few paces.

'Girls, this is my brother, Roy. Roy, this is Annie...'

The blonde languorously pushed herself up to sitting and held out a bottle.

'Have some champagne!'

He stooped and took the neck of the bottle, not knowing quite what to do with it.

'...and this is Penny,' Ursula continued.

Penny was fair and neat, and her dimply smile made him feel a little easier.

'Have a cup,' she said, looking into the picnic hamper and taking out a paper cup in one hand and a clean plate in the other. 'Are you hungry?'

'Not half,' he grinned at her.

'And that's Manon over there.' Ursula pointed at the girl with long black hair who had her back to them and was dabbling her feet in the river.

'Penny will be doing something really worthwhile,' Annie took up their conversation again.

Penny shot him a sympathetic look understanding how embarrassing it must feel to be thrust into the midst of their intimacies.

'And Manon, what will Manon be?' she asked, as if trying to hurry the conversation to an end before embarking on a subject that could include him.

He stared at a Japanese-style footbridge a little way downriver and pretended not to listen.

'Manon will be a *femme fatale*,' Annie declared loudly.

The silence that greeted her announcement made the air feel thick with shock.

After a few seconds, the dark-haired one stood up. Her legs were slim and bare and brown.

'Don't go ... she didn't mean it,' Penny began to protest.

'It's OK,' Manon's voice had a slight foreign accent, 'I've got things to do.'

'But Roy's only just arrived,' Ursula said.

'Tell Manon not to go,' Annie ordered him, half joking, half earnest.

He shrugged his shoulders, not understanding what was going on.

'Don't go,' he said.

Manon's eyes were pale green and he was suddenly aware that she was very beautiful and he was staring. He felt the blush rising from the collar of his shirt and looked away back towards the arc of bridge.

When he looked again, she was walking away, and everyone seemed to breathe again.

'You and your mouth,' Ursula scolded Annie.

'I didn't think...' Annie tried to defend herself.

'Well, that makes a change!'

'Come and sit down, Roy,' Penny urged, trying to make him comfortable.

'Yes, come and tell us what you think,' Annie said, drawing her knees up to her chin. She was wearing black tights and there was a ladder all the way down one leg.

'About what?' he asked, crouching nervously a few feet away from them.

'We were trying to guess what will become of us.'

7

PART ONE

Wearing Black

Chapter 1

July 1999

'Cinderella?' asked Annie, twirling to look at herself from the side.

The men didn't seem to know whether she wanted them to agree or vehemently disagree.

'An ugly sister?' she asked.

'*No!*' This time the denial was immediate.

'More a touch of *Liasions dangereuses*,' Maurice suggested.

'Really?' Annie smiled at herself. 'I don't look fat, do I?'

'Absolutely not!'

Annie glanced away from the huge mirror above the mantelpiece in her living room, and back again quickly, to catch out the reflection in case it was cheating.

The effect of their afternoon's work, she couldn't help thinking, was rather stunning, but you could never be sure. Some years before there had been a series of adverts in women's magazines trying to get girls to train as mental health nurses which had shown a picture of a painfully thin woman looking in a mirror and seeing herself reflected back fat. The shout-line was something like 'She thinks she's fat' and the idea was that as a mental health nurse you would be able to help the patient to see herself as she really was. Annie's own particular neurosis was the other way around. She could get all dressed up, look in the mirror and think she looked not bad at all, really rather slim, thin even, only to walk past a reflecting shop window moments later and see the milky reflection of a whale on legs.

Even that, you could put down to angles. Worse was when some prat at a party snapped you with a Polaroid camera and the rest of the guests gathered round before you'd had a chance to destroy the evidence, chorusing:

'Oh, Annie, that's *so* good of you!'

And the very worst thing was when a similar picture appeared in *OK!* magazine.

'Annie McClintock enjoying herself at a party to celebrate...' the caption would read.

They always said *enjoying* when the camera caught you without a chin.

'Not fat at all,' Maurice assured her.

He had a big soft powder brush in his hand. He had put a lot of white powder in the elaborate hairstyle he had created, and now he wanted to powder the exposed part of her bosom.

'But why?' Annie asked him. 'Is my skin blotchy?'

'Not at all.'

'Uneven skin tone?'

'No, no. It's just part of the styling...'

Not for the first time that afternoon, she wondered whether it had been such a good idea to ask Maurice, the make-up artist on her show, if he would do her the great favour of helping with her look for the producer's fortieth birthday party. Maurice had arrived with a friend of his called Danny to do the styling.

'It's about the total look,' he had replied, when Annie asked him what that actually meant.

'But I've picked out the dress already,' she protested, wondering whether she was taking the whole business of fancy dress too seriously.

Sometimes, when she was up early enough, she caught a programme on television after the breakfast news called *Style Challenge*. Willing victims found themselves in a BBC studio being made over. The stylist's role was to pick out cheap chainstore imitations of couture for them, but oddly the contestants very rarely ended up wearing the garments that had been chosen for them.

What happened to the cigarette-leg pants from Principles? Annie would call out, as the contestant paraded about in a long skirt from C&A, almost invariably looking far older and fatter at the end of the programme than she had on arrival.

'How do you feel?' the host would ask.

'Great, really fantastic, I can't believe it!' the famous-for-fifteen-minutes would respond breathlessly.

'You look like shit!' Annie would shout.

It was one of the benefits of living on your own, being able to converse with the television, although slightly worrying, in other respects.

'Are you sure that this colour isn't too bridal?' Annie said, giving herself another long hard look.

She had set her heart on wearing a dress with a hooped petticoat, and the ivory silk had been the only one left in her size. Usually there was a choice of dark green satin or red and black tartan taffeta too, the costumier had explained, but there was a run on them that weekend because of a ball to launch a new range of cosmetics called Scarlett.

'Not with the beauty spot and the lipstick,' Denny chimed in.

He said it just a little bit too quickly. What he meant was that it did look a bit bridal but not exactly demure. A tarty bride. Oh, to hell with it. Annie looked at her big plastic watch: the mini-cab had already been waiting downstairs for ten minutes.

'You're not going to wear that?' Maurice asked, aghast.

'Can't go anywhere without a watch,' Annie told him, following his line of vision to her left wrist.

'But the look...'

'Maurice, I'm not appearing in a costume drama, I'm going to a party. The watch adds a certain ironic touch, don't you think?'

'If you say so.'

'You've both been darlings.' Annie said, kissing each man on the cheek. 'Make sure you finish the champagne!'

She picked up the little drawstring evening bag that had come with the outfit, and flicked it over her shoulder, trying out a coquettish smile on the two men.

They both smiled back indulgently.

'You don't think I'm overdressed?' she asked, opening the front door of her flat.

14

'Not with the watch,' Denny offered.

'I was joking,' she scolded him.

You hardly wanted to spend a couple of hundred hiring a dress, then whatever Maurice and Denny were going to charge for the hair, face and styling, and not look overdressed, did you?

Five hundred pounds, Annie estimated. Minimum. Still, it was fun to go really over the top once in a while. She was sick of black, black, black and all the other dark colours that promised to be the new black but somehow always ended up in her wardrobes tried on, but swapped at the last minute for the real black. There weren't many single items in her wardrobe that had cost five hundred pounds, but there were thousands of pounds' worth of brown and navy items never worn, so in a way hiring a dress was a bargain, if you looked at it like that.

Gathering up her skirts she picked her way down the two flights of stairs to her front door. Lucky that the party was in a boathouse on the Thames, and not at some grand ballroom where you had to make an entrance down a staircase. She loved the feeling of acres of rustling silk swishing round her legs, but she was slightly nervous about tripping herself up.

She looked at the party invitation in her hand. It was engraved, on thick white card, and at the bottom the instruction urged in bold italics,

'Wear something you've always dreamed of wearing!'

Chapter 2

The mangetout came from Zimbabwe. Ursula rinsed them under the cold tap. She wondered whether they were trimmed in Zimbabwe too. She imagined an African woman with a basket on her lap topping and tailing the pea pods with a sharp knife. What would she think of a woman who was too busy to prepare her own vegetables? She tipped the flat green pods into the wok and watched them sizzle, seeing them now as a symbol of failure.

Barry had just come in from work.

'I'm doing a stir-fry,' she told him, as he kissed the top of her shoulder in greeting.

'Fine.'

'Good day?' she asked.

'Not bad. He got off.'

'The rapist?'

'Yup.'

Ursula sighed. It was good for Barry's reputation to get an acquittal, but she wasn't so sure that the verdict was good for the women who would come into contact with the defendant.

They had a rule never to discuss their cases at home.

She picked up the plastic tray and looked at the price per kilo on the label.

'I was just thinking how decadent I've been buying prepared vegetables. And they're ludi-

16

crously expensive.'

'Saves time though,' Barry said, picking the *Guardian* up off the kitchen table. 'And gives someone employment,' he added.

That made her feel a little better.

'I'm just going to watch the news,' he said.

'Not vegetables again!' her older sons Christopher and Luke chorused as she ferried bowls of stir-fry on trays into the living room.

'There's chicken in there too,' she said.

'I'm not hungry,' George, her three-year-old stated categorically.

Barry did not look out from behind the paper. She wondered why it was that George allowed his father to sit reading peacefully, but would charge the paper like a toreador's cape if she so much as glanced at the television listings.

'I'm going upstairs to sort out something to wear for tomorrow,' she told the room.

No-one replied.

Her bed was covered in clothes like a stall at a church jumble sale. She couldn't decide. All her smart clothes were black, but they were her work clothes. The only other garments she seemed to possess were track suits, leggings and jumpers, and a couple of huge over-bright dresses she had bought for weddings and the christening of her goddaughter. Weddings and christenings were the limit of her social life these days. And funerals, she thought; increasingly funerals.

She tried a couple of outfits on. They were gratifyingly big, but wouldn't do.

17

There was nothing that said what she wanted to say. Nothing that said: here I am, grown up. I know that I will never be beautiful, but I have discovered that you need not have the mousy hair you were born with, and I have learned the wonders of foundation, lipstick and contact lenses. I am slim.

'I don't know what on earth I'm going to wear.' She wandered into the bathroom where Barry was now giving George his bath.

'Why don't you go and buy yourself something new?'

'It's tomorrow,' she said impatiently.

He glanced at his wet left wrist, and then at the watch that he had taken off and placed on the side of the sink.

'There's time. The shops are still open. Treat yourself. Put it on AmEx. I'll pay.'

'No...'

'Why not? Go on...'

She thought of the heap of sombre clothes on their bed.

'Will you get the boys to bed?'

'Of course I will.'

'Mummy, you're not going to be away too long, are you?' George asked as Barry squeezed a spongeful of warm water over his shoulders.

'No, I'm not going to be away too long.'

She watched as he flopped onto his front and tried to swim. His body was almost as long as the bath. Without her really noticing, he had changed from a toddler into a little boy.

'Is that a whale in there?' she joked.

'No,' he said firmly, sitting up again, 'it a boy.'

18

Barry laughed, and so George laughed too, understanding that he had said something funny, but not why.

'You're not going to be away so long?' he asked again, not yet able to distinguish between so and too.

'No, not long at all. I'm just going to buy a dress.'

'No, I mean tomorrow,' he said impatiently, as if she had deliberately misunderstood him.

'Just one night.'

His face crumpled dramatically. The little boy changed back into a baby.

'You will look after Daddy?' she asked quickly, trying to get a distracting question in before he began to howl.

'No,' he said, 'I'm too young. Chris and Luke can look after Daddy. I don't feel very well.' He put on a sad little voice.

It was pure emotional blackmail. She wished she had not put the idea of looking after into his head.

'You'll be able to go to football with Chris and Luke and Daddy,' she suggested.

Normally, Barry took the older boys to football while she looked after George on Saturday mornings. She was well aware which option he would prefer, given the choice.

'Football!' he shouted as Barry picked him out of the bath.

'Go on,' Barry told her.

'I'm going,' she said, but was somehow unable to tear herself away from the comforting domesticity of the steamy bathroom.

'Why can't I come with you?' George asked, as Barry began to towel his hair dry.

'Because it's a grown-ups' thing.'

'But Saskia and Lily are going to be there. They're little girls.'

'Well, that's different.'

'Why?'

'It's too far to take you, I'm afraid. It's a long way.'

'Not too long...'

'No, not too long.'

'Not so long...'

'Oh, for heaven's sake!' said Barry, kindly.

She left them to it.

'Half an hour before bathtime,' she said, putting her head round the door of the older boys' room.

'Oh Mum, it's Friday!'

'OK, an hour, then.'

Neither looked up from the computer game.

It was still sunny outside. The unexpectedness of starting the car and pulling out of their drive at this time of day made her feel as if she were playing truant. She immediately thought of Liam and wondered if he was still working. Of course not. Friday evening.

At the traffic lights at the bottom of their street, she fumbled in her handbag for her mobile phone and stabbed out a number. It rang two, three times, then clicked onto voicemail. She was not going to leave a message. She was not. She took a deep breath, cut off the call. The traffic lights changed to green. Just as well.

The mobile rang when she was trying on a turquoise dress. The first ring always made her panic. Barry had bought her the phone to make her worry less about leaving the children, but every time she heard its annoying half-melody ring, or the same signal coming from another phone in someone's else's briefcase, her heart missed a couple of beats as she frantically searched for the handset in her capacious hand-bag and stabbed the answer button assuming it was an emergency.

'Yes?'

'Did you ring me?'

Liam's voice was smooth and resonant and could make the simplest sentence suggestive.

She giggled like a besotted teenager.

'Yes,' she admitted.

'And I was just thinking about you...'

'It must be telepathy,' she said.

'Just what I was about to say!'

They both laughed.

She looked at herself in the changing-room mirror, trying to suppress the sensation of arousal that twitched between her legs. How could he do this just by talking on the phone.

'I'm shopping for something to wear this week-end,' she told him.

'Can I come along and see you in your under-wear?'

He crept up on her as she flipped through a rack of own-brand dresses in House of Fraser and led her to the designer section. She had only dared to venture to this part of the store recently and had not yet been brave enough to try anything on. A quick glance at the price label was usually enough to make her walk briskly away. She had enough money now to buy whatever she wanted, but the grip of childhood poverty was hard to unclench. She could not bring herself to buy something whose price she would not dare tell her mother.

Liam's body was so close she could feel his breath on her neck. She turned round. He was holding a sleeveless black dress in front of his face. She stared at the large, powerful hand gripping the hook of the silky padded hanger.

'I don't want black,' she said, affecting indifference, but she could feel her cheeks flaming to betray her.

'I've never seen you wear anything but black,' he said with a slightly disconcerted expression as he put the dress back on the rail.

He had only ever seen her dressed for work. He did not know the person that slopped around at the weekends wearing big jumpers and walking boots for their hikes in the country. Would he like her looking like that, she wondered, looking like a mum?

They wandered round the shop close together, brushing against each other. The outfits he suggested were not at all what she would have chosen, but it made her feel sexy trying them on, her newly slim figure alien to her as she came out of the changing room and twirled in front of him, trying to read his judgement in his eyes. She wavered for a long time about a suit in a shade of pink her mother would call shocking. She did not recognize herself in it. It made her look like a different person, like the sort of person who would wear shocking pink, she thought. But she was not quite ready to be that person yet.

Instead she chose a linen dress in a kind of pale stone colour to wear under a navy jacket during the day and on its own for the evening. It was still a departure for her, very plain and elegantly understated, and nobody more than a size 12 would look nice in it.

As she handed over her AmEx card, she wondered how she would explain her choice to Barry if he were to notice that her taste had suddenly changed. She would not let him pay as he had offered. Or perhaps she should, in case he suspected. There was nothing to feel guilty about. Nothing to suspect. She had done nothing, she told herself, except try on a few clothes with a friend.

'So you're going to Oxford all on your own?' Liam said in the car park as she put the cardboard carrier bags into the boot of her car.

'I won't be on my own,' she said, 'I'll be with old friends.'

'Of course you will,' he said, holding her eyes as he slipped a miniature carrier bag with the store's logo on it into her shoulderbag. Her hand went automatically to retrieve it. He caught her wrist.

'Uh-uh,' he said, shaking his head, 'not to be opened until tomorrow evening, when you're wearing the dress.'

Then he turned and walked away from her. She

23

knew that she had approximately ten seconds before he reached his own car in which she could shout, or run after him and ask him to meet her in Oxford, and he would come. But she stood immobile, her hand clutching the small package in her bag. He got into his metallic grey sports car and roared out of the car park, leaving her standing beside her car gawping.

She wondered if she had just missed her last chance. Liam was not an unreasonable man, but he would not let her dither much longer.

Even thinking about an affair terrified her. It was just not like her. If one of her friends, even Barry, were asked to come up with three adjectives to describe her they would choose words like reliable, organized, she thought, and perhaps clever, or intelligent. The words adulterous, deceitful, dishonest would simply never occur.

Chapter 3

The toilets at the Compton Club were not the most convenient place to perform a pregnancy test. From the slam of the doors and voices outside the cubicle, Manon could tell that there were at least three people waiting. The minute the test took to work felt like an hour, and then when she saw the result she did not believe it. Her condition had nothing to do with the flimsy plastic wand in her hand, but she stared at it as if it were somehow responsible: first angry, then ridiculously grateful, and then preoccupied by the purely practical question of what you were supposed to do with it afterwards. She did not want to throw it away. Wiping the wand with toilet paper, she tried to get it back into the slim cardboard box it had come from, then impatiently shoved the whole lot back into the flimsy Boots bag.

A queue had already formed at the hat check desk, and with his usual vigilance, Cosmo, the club manager, had noticed her absence. As she passed him on the stairs she saw his eyes check the plastic carrier bag in her hand. She mouthed sorry at him as she wriggled past the line and ducked under the stable door, almost upsetting the saucer of tips. He nodded at her significantly. The only qualification for being the hat check girl was being there, and she was running a risk by taking an unscheduled break. If she wasn't careful, Cosmo would have an excuse to promote her to front desk, as he was always offering to do, and although the money was better she did not want the job.

Manon liked the tiny room halfway up the stairs where she sat and watched London's media world go by. In winter, the smell of wool, cigarettes and perfume that damp coats released as they steamed gently over the radiator, reminded her of her mother's cupboard at home where she had hidden as a child and felt safe. In summer, she enjoyed brief proprietorship over tissue-wrapped designer clothes that nestled inside Day-Glow cardboard sale bags. At Easter, someone had asked her to look after a rabbit in a basket tied with yellow ribbon, and recently a celebrity mother had handed over her sleeping baby while she gave a press conference in one of the function rooms upstairs. The only thing that people never seemed to check in was hats. With tips, the money was enough. She got by. She liked the anonymity of it. She had no responsibilities except to sit there.

She dealt with the queue. People seemed to be looking at her oddly. She realized it was because she was smiling. She could not help it. She had a secret, a tiny secret that no-one else in the whole world knew about. Her secret was her companion. For the first time in a very long time she did not feel alone in the world.

During the lull, when after-work drinkers had departed and diners were taking up their tables in the restaurant, Manon picked up the splayed paperback beside her and tried to concentrate but the words would not keep still. She was excited. She could feel her heartbeat in her chest. All her senses seemed to have woken up, and still she was smiling, even though there was nobody around to smile at. She read a page twice, realizing that she had still not taken in what it said, and then a voice made her jump. She had not heard the street door opening, or the footsteps on the wooden stairs.

'Hey, baby.'

'Frank...'

'Can you look after this for me?'

He handed her a tied bunch of flowers that looked and smelt like a clump of summer meadow. There were cornflowers, dandelions, pale green ears of wheat and field poppies, the petals miraculously staying put when instinctively she touched them to discover if they were real. The florist's label was the same as the one that had been attached to the last bouquet he had bought her – a hundred roses packed together in a hemisphere, the colour graduating from velvety black crimson at the circumference to a single rose at the centre so delicate a pink it was almost white and smelling as she imagined heaven must smell. She hated it when flowers died, she had told him then, wanting to put him off buying another bouquet. She much preferred to see them growing in a field. And so he had brought the field, which was typical of the way he misunderstood her.

Why, he would sometimes ask her. Why won't you accept things from me? Why won't you let me buy you some decent clothes or get you a proper job? Because of the way you're looking at me, she would think, because you think I can be bought. But she never replied, because it was pointless to argue with him. He was good at arguments, but he would never change what she felt. It would not be enough for him to hear that she did not want wild flowers to die for her, or ruby earrings in a blue Tiffany's box tied with white silk ribbon. He would argue that her position was illogical. But it wasn't about logic.

'You're very thoughtful this evening,' he remarked.

'Yes. I mean, thank you.' She looked into his eyes, wanting to see something different there, some depth she had not understood, some vulnerability he had previously kept hidden, but he looked just the same. He was so confident in his good looks that his face was almost two-dimensional, like the square-jawed face of a cartoon hero.

'See you later?' He made the question sound like a command.

'Sure.'

She saw that he detected the waver in her voice. He stood there as if he would not move until she had given him a more acquiescent response.

At the foot of the stairs, the street door opened with a welcome draught and a crowd of PR girls clattered up the stairs. They were dressed in corsets and bloomers like whores in a saloon and they were all laughing. The air around them was smoky and sharp with recently drunk cham-pagne. One of them produced a glass flask.

'Have you tried Rhett, for the man who gives a damn?' she asked Frank, squirting the perfume in his direction.

Frank sniffed.

'What's it supposed to smell of?' he asked.

'The indefinable appeal of the rogue,' they all chanted together.

'Well, fiddle-dee-dee!' Frank said.

The girls shrieked with laughter.

He turned back to Manon, clearly pleased with his wit. She handed him one half of a pink cloakroom ticket. She was about to pin the other half to the paper around the bouquet when he leaned over the counter and took the pin from her hand and fastened the ticket onto the shoulder strap of her flimsy black dress. He stood back, as if admiring a brooch he had bought her.

'I'll pick you up later.'

He glanced at the giggling saloon girls with a mischievous smile that drew them in and somehow made Manon's shocked expression appear humourless. Carefully, she unpinned the ticket, but for several minutes after he had disappeared upstairs to the bar, the sensation of humiliation remained, and the place where the ticket had been burned like a brand on her shoulder.

Chapter 4

Roy was standing in the empty living room. It had taken little time to clear the house. In just a few hours the removal men had filled the pantechnicon with possessions accumulated over years, and driven away. Only minutes later, he was finding it difficult to picture what had been there, which cushion on which sofa. The room seemed suddenly cool as he wondered whether he was capable of building a home again, and whether his children, who were waiting outside in the car, would find him lacking.

He walked around the ground floor trying to judder himself out of the immobilizing panic that could descend so quickly. Then he ran upstairs, checking the bedrooms one by one and closing the doors behind him.

Each room was a memory box of his adult life so far, each was filled with its own ghosts of laughter and searing pain. The house had been altered, decorated and changed in the seventeen years he had known it, but without furniture and fitments, with the curtains down and the colourful rugs rolled up and on their way to storage, it looked more like it had on the day he had first visited it, the day he had come up to meet his sister Ursula out of finals.

Then, the fireplaces had been blocked and a typically Seventies gas fire, a narrow box of plastic wood with a fibreglass waffle stood in each room with a meter beside it. Manon was the only one of them who'd worked out how to cheat the meter, he remembered with a slight guilty smile as he closed the door on the tiny room which had been hers.

'Don't tell the others,' she'd whispered to him, and he never had.

Not even Penny.

He could not remember what the large room at the front had looked like then. Perhaps he had not seen it then, he thought, closing the door so quickly he almost smacked it into his nose, or perhaps what had happened there in recent times obliterated anything that had gone before.

His daughters' room had been Annie's then. She had papered the walls with a collage of black-and-white photos of movie stars torn from a remaindered book. An Indian scarf shaded the lampshade on the central light-fitting. He remembered peering in, sniffing the combination of French cigarettes and strong, spicy perfume, thinking how sophisticated his sister's friends were.

Now it was decorated with a frieze of Flower Fairies the girls had been reluctant to leave. He had promised them another in the new house, but he did not know whether he would be able to deliver it. He wished he had paid more attention on those interminable trips to Homebase.

Roy closed the bedroom door and then the bathroom, trying to picture how that had been then, but there hadn't been an upstairs bathroom then, he remembered, only one downstairs, through the kitchen. He could recall the coldness of the kitchen lino on the soles of his bare feet, as he tiptoed through in the middle of the night for a pee, terrified of waking one of the women.

His daughters were in the car, strapped into their car seats, each holding a brand new Barbie doll. He'd resisted the purchase for a long time, disapproving of the American plastic dolls, and had felt a sense of defeat as he finally handed over his credit card to pay for them. He didn't know whether he was buying them as bribes, or simply to distract his daughters from the trauma of leaving their home. Either way, he knew that he should have found the energy and words to explain why they were going, rather than covering up with toys that millions of pounds of advertising made them think they desired. But seeing their happily absorbed faces through the back window of the old Volvo, he felt that the dolls could not be doing them too much harm, or perhaps they were relieved to be leaving too.

'OK. Have you said goodbye enough?' he asked them, climbing into the driver's seat.

'It's only a house, Daddy,' Saskia told him.

'In fact, I've said goodbye a thousand times,' Lily added.

'Don't be ridiculous,' Saskia admonished her younger sister.

'Loads of times,' Lily qualified. 'Are we going to move into our new house today?' she asked, as he flicked on the indicator and tried to pull the car out of its cramped parking place in one revolution of the steering wheel.

'Not today. Soon. We're going to be staying with Grandma and Grandpa for a little while.'

'Oh.'

'It'll be a bit like a holiday, until we move to our cottage,' he suggested.

In the rearview mirror, he could see Lily's lip quivering. These days, she was very inclined to cry when denied precisely what she wanted. It was wearing.

'Manon's going to take us punting tomorrow,' Saskia reminded her, and her younger sister's face brightened instantly.

'Is she?' Roy looked in the mirror. It was the first he had heard of it. 'On Sunday, we're going to have lunch with your Auntie Ursula and Annie.'

'Oh!' Lily's lip began to quiver again.

'Annie always brings us nice presents.' Again Saskia knew exactly what to say.

She was only five years old, but already she was just like her mother, Roy thought.

At the end of the street, he wound down the window and looked back as if the house would disappear when the car turned out onto Walton Street and he would never see it again.

Suddenly, he wished, like Lily, that they were going to move straight into the cottage he had made an offer on. But there had been something wrong with the survey which involved estimates and further negotiation. He hadn't wanted to lose the sale of the house in Oxford and have to start all over again, so he had agreed to complete on the sale of the old house before exchanging contracts on the new place. Their furniture had gone into storage. Technically they were now homeless.

He remembered somebody telling him once that moving house was the second most stressful human experience after death of a close relative.

He wanted it to be over so that they could start their new life.

Chapter 5

'*Wear something you've always dreamed of wearing...*'

The words slid across the bottom of the card, then up slightly, so that there were two exactly similar instructions joined together like an ink blot, then they shrank back on top of one another. Annie looked up, caught the cab driver's weary expression in the rearview mirror, and realized that the taxi had come to a standstill.

'Oh, that was quick,' she said, as clearly and brightly as she could. She never knew whether she should talk to the back of the taxi driver's head or to the reflection of his face in the mirror.

He switched on the interior light.

'Twelve pounds.'

Resentment at the implication that she was too drunk to read the meter mingled with relief that the figure was 12 and not 72 as she had momentarily feared.

The drawstring on her evening bag had become wrapped round her wrist, cutting off both the blood supply to her arm, and access to her purse. After a moment's struggle she felt a surge of blood to her fingers and the bag falling into the rustling mass of her dress. Panicking slightly, she gathered a sheaf of the dress over her arm and heard the purse slip with a dull thud onto the rubber floor of the taxi. The hoop of her petticoat seemed to have a life of its own. Just as she thought she had it under control it snapped up in her face.

'Do you want a hand?'

The driver's voice sounded considerably brighter at the wonderful view she had afforded him of her cleavage as she groped around on the floor.

'I'm fine,' she called.

Eventually, her hand touched her purse and she grabbed at it as if it were live and would wriggle away if she relaxed her grip.

With all the dignity she could muster from a kneeling position on the floor, Annie released the cab door and manoeuvred her hoop through the doorframe and then herself, first to sitting, then suddenly to standing slightly surprised on the pavement. She couldn't decide whether to tip the driver extravagantly, or not at all.

'Come on, love, it'll be daylight at this rate,' he said with barely disguised mirth.

That did it. She thrust a five and ten pound note through the window at him and told him to keep the change, hoping that he would drive off feeling rotten for being so impatient with such a generous passenger.

'Walt a minute. Aren't you the one from...'

'No,' she said, walking as steadily as she could up the steps to the front door of the stucco-fronted house.

There was often a purely practical reason why clothes went out of fashion, she thought, and it probably wasn't just coincidence that complicated crinolines had disappeared with the invention of the motor car.

Wear something you've always dreamed of wearing.

Why, Annie asked herself, in the chilly damp dawn air, as she tried to fit the key in the lock, had no-one else's sartorial fantasy stretched further than a leather miniskirt?

Everyone else was wearing something little and black, except one woman who had a short lavender nightie under a beaded cashmere cardigan. There had been no hiding place. The dress took up about a quarter of the space in any room, and it was impossible to skulk around surreptitiously near the food table without brushing through the dip or carrying trays of mini pizza along in her wake. But the worst thing was not the sheer bulk, nor the impossibility of joining in the disco, but the backhanded compliments from the other guests:

'I do so admire you for taking all the trouble... I just didn't have time... It's so difficult when you've got kids...'

It had made her feel as if she had nothing better to do than while away hours in fancy dress shops and twirly chairs having her hair and face done.

At least no-one had been cruel enough to say 'Miss Haversham, I presume' to her face.

Still, she thought as her key finally slipped into the lock, at least the evening had provided the setting for the Christmas special of her show which she should have delivered several weeks before.

In one of those moments of blinding truth that she sometimes had when drinking excessive champagne, Annie wondered whether she had subconsciously decided to go to the party in the ridiculous dress just to give herself something to write about. A cliché about life imitating art or the other way around hovered tantalizingly just beyond her metal grasp.

Wearily she hitched up her skirts and made her way to her second-floor flat.

There was a third of a bottle of champagne left on the mantelpiece. She picked it up to drink it from the neck. A stream of it missed her mouth and trickled over her powdered bosom. She watched the delta of rivulets funnelling towards her cleavage, knowing that she was too drunk to get the dress off before the champagne met the boned bodice.

There were so many blinks on the answerphone that she lost count twice. She pressed playback, then went into the kitchen to get some water. Standing staring at the door of her fridge, she could hear the familiar rhythm and chirpy tone of her mother on the first message, and the second, and the third. The Evian was as cold as a mountain stream and felt like liquid silver in her throat. The messages went on, and so did her mother's voice.

Finally the tape came to an end and Annie returned to the large living room deliberating whether to press playback again and listen properly, but she couldn't bring herself to. She picked up the remote and pointed it at the CD player.

When *Bat out of Hell* had first appeared she had played it so often her mother had said she would wear it out. Then there had been a gap of almost twenty years when she hadn't listened to it at all, she couldn't think why not. The previous Christmas, she had fallen on a CD of *Meat Loaf's Greatest Hits* in a promotional bin in a service station with the same pleasure as you have when you recognize an old boyfriend and can't immediately remember why you ever split up. 'Heaven Can Wait' was one of those smoochy songs she never understood the words to but sang along anyway, knowing from the dramatic harmonies that it must be meaningful.

Feeling suddenly clear-headed and creative, Annie picked up her office chair she had sat in while Maurice did her make-up and tried to carry it back into her office. A sound like a strip of wax being ripped from a depilated leg alerted her too late to the fact that she had trodden on her dress.

Annie thought of the cheque for two hundred pounds she had left at the costumier's as a deposit, briefly entertained the notion of tearing the rest of the dress from her body, but decided that it would be too sad a parody of the way she had imagined ending the evening. But she could not work out how else she was going to get it off without help. The hoop made it impossible to sit on the chair. Defeated by the logistics of her environment, and suddenly exhausted, Annie sank sideways onto the sofa in her office, and after a few moments the cathartic singalong with Meat Loaf changed to heavy snores.

Chapter 6

The club closed at three in the morning. Most Fridays there was a Perudo game in the top bar that started around midnight. Sometimes the men would ask Manon to join in; others, they would wave her away like an unlucky talisman. It depended on who was playing and how much they had had to drink. Often the challenge of beating her would prove too much for them to resist. Tonight she did not want to play.

The incongruous wheat and tissue paper

bouquet lay on the floor next to a laptop in a nylon Prada bag that someone had forgotten to pick up. She wondered whether it would offend Frank more if she left the bouquet, or if she took it without saying goodbye to him. She decided to leave it and let him think she had forgotten it. Flaky was a word he often used to describe her. She wanted to slip away unnoticed, but Cosmo saw her draping the last two uncollected jackets over her counter.

'Frank was asking for you,' he told her.

'I've got to be up early...'

He gave her a long look, a curious mixture of respect and disapproval, which made her think that he probably knew she was Frank's mistress.

'See you tomorrow, then?'

'Evening off. I swapped with Kitty.'

'Course you did. Monday then. Take care.'

For a second, his hard eyes softened and his look sent a shiver of alarm through her body. She had seen it many times before on men's faces. She had always assumed that Cosmo was gay, asexual, or simply too professional to notice her in that way. Perhaps he had sensed that something about her tonight was different. She picked up her Boots carrier bag and scuttled off down the stairs.

It had been a hot day, but a breeze had cleared the skies and the night air puckered her skin beneath the flimsy cotton dress. Most of the Friday evening crowds had gone home, but the all-night cafés were still busy, and groups of people stood on the pavements licking ice-cream cones. Others crowded round minicab booths clamouring to be driven in unmarked, unlicensed cars, by drivers who could barely speak English. She liked the buzzy cosmopolitan feeling the streets of London had at this time of night.

Manon walked across Cambridge Circus and along the darkened stretch of Shaftesbury Avenue where it was suddenly quiet. Apart from the occasional scream of a distant police siren, the only sound was the squeak and flap of the flat Moroccan slippers she was wearing. She found herself wondering whether if someone were to chase her she would be able to outrun them in these sandals, and her chest tightened with un-ease. A black cab roared past. She tried to breathe through the rush of anxiety, wondering why she was frightened walking through the familiar, empty streets.

Back at the flat, she wrapped her head in a towel and took a bath, lying swaddled in the warm water until the light outside the window turned from black to grey. She pulled out the plug with her toes, then stood up, surveying herself in the long mirror on the back of the bathroom door looking for signs, but there was no visible difference. She took another towel, stepped out and dried herself, then took another look at her long, slim body. Two teardrops of blood dripped as ever from the knife that pierced the scarlet heart on her left thigh. Her tummy was flat and brown and the silver ring in her navel glinted in the bathroom spotlights. On her shoulder a bluebird tried to fly away, trapped for ever in the tattoo she had always regretted. She unwrapped her towel turban, releasing long almost-black hair that reached to her waist. She stared at her face in the mirror, wanting to scare away the look of serene calm that seemed to have settled upon her. She snapped off the light with the light pull, fled to the bedroom, pulling the top sheet on the bed right over her head, then after a minute or two emerged again to lie in semi-darkness wondering what the hell she was going to do.

There was nothing in the square, high-ceilinged studio flat, apart from the dress flung over the chair, to say that it was hers. It belonged to a friend of a friend of Annie's, someone whose link with Manon was so tenuous she could not remember quite how the connection worked. In her mind, she pictured a family tree with wiggly lines instead of straight ones and gaps everywhere, but although she did not know him, she felt warmly towards the owner for allowing her to inhabit his space, and for getting her out of Annie's flat where she had been staying after her return to England.

At the time, Annie had just bought her place in Notting Hill, and although she had made the offer of her spare room completely genuinely, Manon knew that she had not really wanted her there any more than Manon had wanted to be there. If that intuition had required confirmation, it had come later in the year when a running theme in the new series of Annie's show was the central character's struggle to get rid of a friend who outstays her welcome.

The owner of Manon's studio was on an indefinite posting abroad and wanted someone who would be prepared to go at a moment's notice but wouldn't mess the place up, who would pay the bills and get in a plumber if the pipes froze, in return for living there on a peppercorn rent. Oddly, Manon seemed to be the only person like that around. When she had last been in England, she would have known hundreds of people who would have leapt at such an opportunity, but now she knew none. People in their thirties owned their homes, and anyone who desired a *pied-à-terre* in central London was so rich already that they could buy one and decorate it as they wished. When she had left the country, the people she had known were students, or recent postgraduates. Now they had second cars and secretaries, kitchens with extractor hoods over the oven and cappuccino machines, and, sometimes, children. She had nothing to show that she had existed in the intervening years except a few tattoos and a slim volume of short stories she had written. It was as if she had been in a time warp.

In the whitening light of dawn, Manon told herself that if you were going to bear a child, you needed to have done all that. It was a bit like the tables of conjugations and declensions in Latin that you had to learn before you could read Catullus. You could not have a baby without first doing the homework: finding somewhere permanent to live, a proper job, income and all of that took time. Her reason said it was impossible.

And yet part of her knew from seeing Saskia and Lily growing up that the only thing that

42

children could not do without was a mother. For a second, she allowed herself to imagine introducing her baby to the little girls – bending down to their level, her arms cradling a bundle of cellular blanket, the wonder on their faces, and Lily's delighted surprise when the baby's tiny hand gripped her inquisitive finger.

The feeling of well-being that the image gave was seductive.

No. It was not possible. No.

On Monday, Manon decided, she would ring one of the numbers on the posters you saw on the tube escalators, the ones which emphasized the word abortion as advice. It would be quick. It was not a baby yet, she told herself, vaguely remembering the pictures of embryos that they had drawn for O level biology, comparing the size at the various stages to pieces of food, from speck of salt via kidney bean and plum, to curled up body the size of a melon.

She wished that she was not going up to Oxford. The reunion, which she had been dreading, would be worse now. She could already feel the chill of barely concealed hostility from her contemporaries as she walked into Hall.

But she had to go because she had promised Saskia and Lily that she would take them punting beforehand.

Anyway, they probably didn't perform abortions on weekends, but now that she had made the decision, she wanted to have it done as quickly as possible.

She could not have a baby.

It wasn't really a baby yet, she told herself. Nobody announced a pregnancy until twelve weeks because it could so easily miscarry. It wasn't really a baby. At this stage, it wasn't even the size of a grain of rice.

Chapter 7

'Mummy, Mummy, Mummy...!'

The voice in Ursula's dream became a voice in the house calling her, and she was out of bed and standing up before she had worked out which of her sons it was. George. Blearily, she put on her dressing gown and switched on the landing light so that she could see into his room without dazzling him.

'What is it, love?'

'I seed pictures in my eyes.'

He was sitting up in bed in his pyjamas, rubbing his eyes. She sat down and drew his head to her chest, patting him soothingly on the back.

'There, there, Mummy's here. What did you see?'

'I seed clowns.'

George was afraid of clowns. She didn't know why, but whenever he saw one on television, or in the local shopping centre making balloon animals for the children during the school holidays, he would cling to her like a limpet.

'There aren't any clowns, darling. It was just a dream.'

'Clowns won't hurt you,' he said, repeating what she always told him.

'I wouldn't let anything hurt you.'

'Mummy, clowns are not really clowns, are they?'

It was an interesting existential question, she thought, because clowns were, after all, only people dressed up as clowns.

'You're right,' she agreed, 'clowns are not really clowns.'

'Mummy, you're not going to leave me?' he asked, only half awake.

'Go to sleep now,' she whispered.

His breathing quietened against her chest. She laid him back down and tucked the blankets around him.

'Which one?' Barry asked when she returned to bed.

'George.'

'George?'

Their youngest son usually slept soundly. Luke was the one who sleepwalked and until recently had regularly wet the bed.

'He's not keen on me going to Oxford tomorrow,' she explained. 'I think it's some sort of subconscious blackmail.'

'I'll get up if he wakes again.'

'Thanks,' she said, appreciating the gesture, but knowing that she was always the first to wake. A moment of fear blossomed and died inside her as she pictured Barry sleeping through a crisis while she was away, but fire was the only thing she could think of that might not alert one of the boys, and she had renewed the batteries in the smoke alarms recently. Gradually, her heartbeat returned to normal, but she felt wide awake now.

'Can't you sleep, little bear?' Barry's voice said next to her.

Little bear had been his affectionate nickname for her from the moment they were introduced and he discovered her name was Ursula. That was long before the existence of the children's book which they had read so many times to the boys. He used the endearment rarely enough for it still to make her feel warm all over. She nestled into his side.

'How did you know I was awake?' she asked him.

'I can tell.'

'Do I snore?'

'Not usually, but there's a different quality to the breathing.'

She was surprised he noticed such things.

'It's not the first time you've been away since George was born, is it?' he asked.

'On my own, I think it is,' she said.

'I suppose you're right,' Barry acknowledged, after giving the question due consideration. 'We all went to the funeral, didn't we?'

She had been thinking the same thing. It unnerved her that their minds were so used to each other that their thoughts often followed the same route.

'I don't know why,' she said. 'It was ridiculous to drag the boys all the way there.'

'Solidarity,' Barry said, a warm hand seeking and finding hers under the duvet.

'Yes,' she said, finding it comforting to lie talking in the dark.

He rolled onto his side and put his other hand on her waist, tentatively.

'Barry, I need to sleep. I've got a long journey in the morning,' she said, in answer to his unspoken question.

'Of course. Sorry.' He turned away again immediately.

The air was filled with his disappointment.

'Don't say sorry,' she said irritably.

'Well, what am I supposed to say? You never seem to want to any more.'

'I do ... it's just...'

It's just that I can't stop thinking about having sex with someone else. It's just that I feel guilty because I'm imagining that Liam is doing it with me, not you.

'Oh, I can't have this conversation now,' she said impatiently.

That sentence, she realized, made it inevitable that they would. Now she had acknowledged it as an issue, something to be discussed. If she had let it go then his regret and her guilt would have seemed trivial after sleep.

'It's just that I'm tired. I'm so tired,' she turned onto her side and put her arms around him, trying to backtrack, 'I'm sorry,' she whispered into his nape.

'It's fine,' he replied flatly.

'It's not fine,' she protested, touching his chest with her fingers. She did not want to go away for the weekend with a bad feeling in the air. He rolled over to face her again, his erection brushing

47

against her thigh. She let him make love to her, and once they had started, they were so used to each other that the familiar rhythms of pleasure took over. It was more like a happy memory for her than an act in which she was participating.

'I love you,' he said in the moment of exhausted closeness just after she had come.

The space in which she was meant to say 'I love you' back gaped between them.

'Mummy, Mummy, Mummy...'

George's cries rescued her.

'I'll go,' Barry said, withdrawing, wiping himself with a tissue, and handing one to her.

She laid staring upwards and listening to the exchange in the next room.

'Now, what's the matter?'

'I want Mummy.'

'Mummy's asleep.'

'I don't feel very well.'

'Ursy? His forehead's a bit hot.'

Wearily, Ursula climbed out of bed, felt a trickle of her husband's semen on her thigh, sighed, and walked into the children's bathroom. She rifled about in the cupboard for the thermometer.

'37.5. Just on the high edge of normal,' she said, taking it from under the child's arm after a minute. 'Would you like a drink?'

'Yes, please. An orange juice,' George said.

'I'll get it,' she told her husband. Barry slumped back to bed.

'I think actually I would like an apple juice,' George announced.

'OK,' Ursula replied.

'And a biscuit.'

'Don't push your luck,' she told him.

When she returned from the kitchen he was fast asleep again. She stood in the doorframe looking at him for a couple of moments, thinking how utterly innocent he was in repose with his arms stretched up above his head on the pillow and the slight gleam of sweat accentuating each of his perfect little features like a Della Robbia angel.

When he was awake, demanding attention, wanting to help with the cooking and generally getting in her way, it was easy to forget how young he was. His language was advanced and he parroted phrases they both used with astonishing accuracy. On occasion she would look at him when he was telling her something he had done that day and see a miniature Barry, and she was entirely capable of being cross with him when he reneged on his part of a negotiation whose terms were far too adult for him to understand. In sleep, he looked just as vulnerable as he had done when he was a baby. He was just three years old, her last child, and as she watched him sleeping, she loved him so much it frightened her.

Chapter 8

The smell of his in-laws' house was the same as it had been on the first occasion he had slept there. Geraldine made her own pot-pourri. A Chinese bowl of shrivelled petals stood on the walnut chest of drawers on the landing just outside the guest room. The sweet-stale perfume of old roses permeated every timber of the Cotswold vicarage. He had known whenever Penny had been to see her parents for the afternoon because he could smell it in her hair. It was as much of a giveaway as the scent of another man's aftershave on an adulterous wife's skin. Not that Penny had ever made any attempt to disguise her frequent visits home.

If he had been asked to choose one word to describe the family he had married into it would have been 'polite'. If he had been allowed a list, then the top five would have included middle-class, Christian, honest and kind, all of which would have sounded like put-downs when he was younger, but which were qualities he had come to value. He had never been one of them, and never would be, but they had welcomed him, and their sense of doing the right thing was practised as well as preached.

Roy lay in bed, watching the colour of the plaster walls turn from grey to pale blue to bright white, as the rays of early morning sun seeping through the floral curtains intensified.

The first time he had slept in the guest room the paint and matching soft furnishings had been new and he suspected that the refurbishment had been partly in his honour. Penny was their only daughter and it had been hard for them to give her away, but their genuine good manners made them want him to feel completely at home. Turning Penny's old bedroom into a guest room where they could spend their first Christmas as husband and wife was the sort of project Geraldine took on with gusto. He could imagine her talking to Penny about it.

'We do want Roy to feel comfortable. You're not just *our* little girl any more darling. Anyway, if we're buying a double bed for the room, we might as well do the whole thing...'

And Penny protesting, knowing that he probably wouldn't even notice, but secretly rather enjoying the idea of choosing new fabrics and colours, of having her new status given the full stamp of parental approval.

He had been, and to some extent still was, an unknown quantity to them: left wing, an atheist, and not perhaps the husband they would have expected her to choose, even though he had agreed to a blessing of their marriage in Trevor's church.

The vicarage was less than an hour's drive from Oxford, but it was the sort of home where you stayed over if you went for Christmas. You did not drive back across the deserted frosty landscape in the early hours of the morning laughing about all the inadvertent *double entendres* in the conversation. There were rituals that had to be observed, like the men chopping up vegetables for coleslaw on Boxing Day morning to go with the cold turkey, just as cream sherry had to be consumed after the morning service with nibbles. One year, Penny had contributed a packet of Japanese rice crackers and their unusual flavour ('seaweed', you say? well I never!) had become an important theme of the conversation for that season and for several thereafter.

He didn't know why he was thinking about Christmas, since it was mid-July, and the quality of the sunny air streaming into the room filled him with optimism that it was going to be a beautiful day.

Perhaps because he had only ever slept there at Christmas. Even the last two Christmases without Penny.

If Penny could have lasted another couple of weeks she might even have slept her last sleep there at Christmas, but Death was not sentimental and did not wait around to give people picturesque endings. She had died in the third week of December just eighteen months before, and they had buried her in the churchyard on Christmas Eve. He didn't know whether it seemed like a long time or a short time ago. He had no sense of her sleeping underground as the girls seemed to have, but there were reference points in the fabric of the house that sometimes made it seem as if she were startlingly still there. Even the most banal objects like the Staffordshire china dogs on the mantelpiece downstairs could evoke a remembered phrase.

'Roy can't stand them,' she had announced one day quite early on, when her mother tried to interest him in her latest find from an antique shop in Woodstock, adding, daringly, 'and I must say I agree with him!'

It had not been appropriate to say goodbye to Penny's sunny personality on one of the shortest days of the year. It had not even been a pretty Christmas. There had been no snow, not even the icing-sugar rime of frost. After the committal, it had begun to rain so heavily it seemed as though the very earth and sky, even God himself, were weeping at her passing.

Few people had been able to come to the funeral because of the time of year. Ursula had urged him to postpone it, but Roy hadn't wanted the girls to spend that Christmas, and every Christmas afterwards, waiting for a kind of closure, suspended in a state of unresolved grief. So it was just the two families who had stood at the graveside, and Manon. Afterwards Manon had walked away, to be by herself for a moment, he had assumed. Later Ursula told him that she had said she was going to hitchhike back to London.

Today Penny's friends would say goodbye to her properly. He had always known that something must be done, but by the time he came round to thinking about it seriously, too much time had drifted by for there to be a memorial service. Then Leonora had suggested asking Penny's college to dedicate the twenty-year reunion to Penny. Roy had agreed, partly because he thought that Penny would have approved, partly because it meant that he could turn the organization of the event over to someone else.

Leonora had thrown herself into the task, sending out invitations to everyone whose address the college retained, renaming the reunion 'A Celebration of Penny's Life', which made Roy uneasy. He wasn't inclined to celebrate something taken so prematurely. Time had only slightly blunted the peculiar sequence of surprise, disbelief and agony when the reality of her absence occurred to him each new day. But he hadn't been able to think of a better word. The invitations had gone out and lots of people had said yes, and the ones who hadn't sent donations saying how grateful they were for the chance to do something. Leonora had wheedled an amazing deal from the caterers and assured Roy it would still be top-class nosh, as if he cared about such things. The sum collected for Penny's charity was now in excess of four thousand pounds, which fact alone made it worthwhile, he kept telling himself.

The only thing he had declined was Leonora's suggestion that the college principal present Saskia with the cheque. The idea of parading the girls around in ballerina frocks was abhorrent to him, however much they themselves might enjoy it. He didn't want them to become little angels with identities wrapped in tragedy. It would make a travesty of their bravery, and the fact that most of the time they wore brightly coloured shorts and T-shirts, and shouted and laughed with surprising, sometimes almost chilling, equanimity.

At the same time as the arrangements for the reunion were falling into place the rest of his life seemed to follow suit. The housing market had picked up and a newly married couple made an offer on the house in Joshua Street. A suitable cottage in Geraldine and Trevor's village had come onto the market. It was almost as if a guiding force had decided to take charge of their day-to-day existence. At times, it had felt so much like Penny that he had given serious thought to the possibility of an afterlife. Sometimes he even found himself feeling angry with her, because it felt as though she were still directing events without being there to share the burden of responsibility. It had made him wonder if she had ever felt angry with him. Before her illness, he had had little idea of the work involved in running a household. He realized he had been lazy and it felt terrible to think that she might have entertained secret resentments towards him. He had not imagined that her death would change their past as well as their future.

Saskia had a place in the village school for September. Lily was on the waiting list for the playgroup. Geraldine's trundle sewing-machine had been brought out and dusted down like a steam engine restored by enthusiasts and put to a useful purpose. A heap of new curtains now lay in the living room of the vicarage ready to be hung when the purchase of the cottage finally went through. In the meantime, they were all staying in the vicarage.

Tonight we would go into Oxford for dinner. He just had to get through today, he kept telling himself, and after all that, things would settle down and they could start their new life in the country.

He was sure that it was sensible to be near Penny's parents even though it meant that his daughters would inevitably end up doing things he would have questioned, even objected to, when their mother was alive. Sunday school,

Brownies, handing round bridge rolls at the annual garden party, all the things that Penny had done when she was a child.

'When did you rebel?' he had asked her, that first Christmas after they married, lying together where he was lying now, their arms around each other under a duvet that rustled with newness.

'I never did,' she replied with surprise in her voice, 'why should I? I was never made to do anything I didn't want to...'

He looked at her face to see if she was joking, but she wasn't.

'How could I have fallen for someone with not an ounce of subversion in her?' he asked himself out loud.

'I've never understood it,' she said, matter-of-factly.

And then they both started giggling.

Love made conspirators out of ideological opponents, Roy thought. And if having children didn't drive out ideology, then death put an end to it. Since Penny had gone the only thing that had felt significant to him was survival. His mind was fully occupied trying to achieve the purely practical tasks of getting the children up each morning into clean clothes, having food on the table, entertaining them and still finding space for them to talk if they needed to.

He swung his legs out of the bed. The carpet beneath his feet was warm from the sun. On his way to the bathroom, he looked in on the girls. Lily was covered, only a brightly coloured arm of her outgrown Teletubbies pyjamas showing. Her left hand was tightly clasped around a hard plastic Barbie doll also dressed for bed in pink baby doll pyjamas. Saskia was lying on top of the bedclothes. Her floral sprig nightie had ridden up and her legs were flung wide, in a position of exhausted abandon. In her fist was a little stoppered bottle filled with layers of coloured sand. Gently he unfurled her fingers and re-placed the bottle on the bedside table where it would be the first thing she saw when she woke up.

Chapter 9

'My cab's here,' Ursula whispered into her sleeping husband's ear.

'Uh? Do you want us to meet you at the station?' he asked, sitting up rubbing his eyes.

It was endearing when he woke up saying something that didn't quite make sense, as if he was trying to show that she had not caught him napping in the middle of a conversation.

'I'm not sure what time I'll be back tomorrow. I'll call you. I've felt George's forehead. I think he's a bit hot, but he's sleeping very peacefully.'

'George?'

'He woke up in the night.'

'Yes, yes, of course.'

She watched the memory of their nocturnal exchange filter back into his consciousness.

'I've got my mobile on if you need to call,' she said.

'Right. Good. Isn't it a bit early? The do's not until this evening, is it?'

The train journey from Nottingham to Oxford took about three hours if you made a good connection at Birmingham.

'But I'm having lunch with Annie...'

She was slightly exasperated at having to explain something she had told him days before. She couldn't stand it when he forgot things. She never forgot things. Forgetting was a luxury she could not afford in her busy schedule.

'Of course you are. Send her my ... whatever.'

Barry considered Annie overbearing, which also irritated Ursula, although she supposed it was partly her fault for always complaining about her. She had known Annie so long she was almost like family, which meant that she was allowed to criticize her, but no-one else was.

'I'll see you tomorrow then,' she said crisply.

'Yes. Have a good time,' he said, automatically, 'I mean ... well, you know what I mean.'

He turned over, eager to get a little more sleep.

As the minicab accelerated away from the house, she felt a momentary sense of dread, and at the lights at the end of the street she turned in her seat and looked back. For a moment she wanted to stop the cab, run back down the street to say goodbye to each of her children properly, but she knew that if she did that she would miss her train. She told herself that it was natural that she should be thinking morbid thoughts when she was going to the memorial of her best friend. She still thought of Penny as her best friend, even

58

though she had subsequently become her sister-in-law too.

As soon as the lights changed and she could no longer see the house through the back window she turned to face the front again. The sense of dread disappeared and a less familiar feeling of freedom, elation almost, took its place. She was going away for two whole days by herself! If she had been walking she would have done a little skip. She was going away. Away from work; away from the weekly shop at the supermarket; away from wondering how to fill that hour before Saturday tea when all the boys and their father sat staring at the football results on the television screen. Away from the sense of responsibility that seemed to weigh so heavily on her these days.

The station concourse was almost deserted. The peculiar uninhabited coldness of it, and the smells, a not unpleasant mingling of disinfectant and baking croissants, reminded her of arriving in the early morning in a foreign city after spending the night on an Inter-Rail train.

During the first summer vac, she and Penny had spent a month Inter-Railing. They had intended to do two months, but after a week or so they'd both got a bit drunk on sweet wine in some German city and admitted that they couldn't see the point of it. Their exhaustive tour of Europe was proving simply exhausting (they had consumed so much Riesling, she remembered laughing quite a lot at that pun). The next day they set off for Florence and spent the rest of the time there, throwing student convention to the wind by taking a room in a *pensione* rather than squeeze into the youth hostel. It had used up all their money, but they had decided that two comfortable weeks would be preferable to six poring over timetables and traipsing round unfamiliar streets in search of a launderette.

Whenever Ursula thought of Penny, the image that sprang to mind first was of her hanging up underwear on a piece of string she had tied from her bedpost to the window catch, then turning round and smiling triumphantly at Ursula, happy in the tiny home they had made together. Their room was at the back of the *pensione* and it didn't get any sun, but the heat was scorching and knickers dried in an hour.

It was strange how a memory like that could sneak up on you, just when you thought you were beginning to come to terms with it, Ursula thought, wiping her eyes as she bought a ticket.

'Return to Oxford, please. Coming back tomorrow.'

'Hay fever? My daughter gets it,' the woman replied, as the little rectangular cards flew through the printer.

The weekend ahead was bound to be full of moments like this, Ursula thought, wondering why that had not occurred to her before. The word celebration on the invitation had cajoled her into a false sense of jollity and she had envisaged only the pleasure of spending uninterrupted time with friends whose lives she had followed in the pages of the college magazine without the worry of having to get back for a babysitter. She had always enjoyed the conviviality of college dinners and the great swell of chatter which embraced you as you walked in.

Ursula sat down at an empty table in a non-smoking compartment and put her small week-end bag on the seat next to her. She was looking forward to making an entrance in her cream linen dress and navy blazer and seeing their amazement at how slim she was. They would all be taking stock, comparing their achievements and she knew it was ridiculous when she was a partner in a respectable firm of lawyers, and married with three intelligent children, to take most pride in the fact that she was slim. But it was not simply vanity, she told herself, more something to do with feeling in control.

Everything was so much easier for a slim person. You didn't have to make so much effort to be taken seriously. At lunch, people looked at you and not at your plate. (How on earth did she get like that eating so little? She must binge at home.) Your clients thought of you as a person, not just a sounding board. Strangers suddenly started making passes.

Liam.

The train slid slowly out of the station.

Liam.

It was as if Liam had triggered another self inside her that had lain dormant, an attractive woman with a slim body hiding beneath an eiderdown of fat. After she had met Liam she lost a stone in a month, then another and another, even though her intake of food remained virtually the same. She could only surmise that the mix of attraction and guilt that fizzed in her

61

brain must make calories simply evaporate, like bubbles escaping a champagne cocktail.

It was all the fault of *Hill Street Blues*. She liked *ER* as well, but *Hill Street Blues* was her all-time favourite television series. She had become hooked one evening late in the 1980s when, elated after winning a protracted case, she had come home to find Barry already in bed and snoring. Unable to fall asleep beside him, she had gone downstairs, poured herself a glass of wine and turned on Channel 4 in the hope of catching some late night political discussion, but found instead gorgeous Frank Furillo and his beautiful long-haired girlfriend in a bath, talking about the law at the end of an episode. People said the series was like real life, but Ursula knew that police stations were not buzzy places filled with high drama and intrigue, they were slow and depressingly predictable. Petty criminals offended again and again and eventually, these days, went to prison. They rarely made inadvertently profound remarks or taught you anything about social deprivation that you didn't already know. Their plotlines never tied up neatly.

But something in her must have longed for a world where these things did happen, and in particular where female lawyers were tough, but beautiful and slim, and had intensely attractive, but troubled, lovers to give them back-rubs at the end of a hard day.

A lad wearing an ill-fitting uniform was pushing a trolley down the aisle towards her. She asked for coffee.

'Anything to eat?'

A perfectly simple question now, but when she had been fat it would have been said with a smirk, and she would have refused for reasons of dignity, leaving herself hungry and vulnerable to the sweet buttery smell of *pain au chocolat* in the pâtisserie of the destination station.

She took the polystyrene cup of hot, bitter black liquid and watched the boy trundle on awkwardly, his trouser legs somehow managing to be both too big and too short. She looked at her watch, alarmed to see that a whole hour had passed in which she had not thought of Barry or the children. With a flicker of guilt, she checked the screen of her mobile phone for missed messages. Sometimes, when the phone was in her bag, it would ring and she would not hear it. George usually woke at around this time. She imagined him walking in half-asleep to their room, finding her gone, but hoisting himself into the big double bed anyway, to finish off his sleep in the warmth of his father.

A couple of tables down there was a lone man also sipping coffee. She caught his eye and half smiled as travellers do, acknowledging a shared environment. She wondered for a moment whether he was someone she had encountered at work. Not a barrister, nor a criminal, she thought, but perhaps a plainclothes policeman wearing the sort of middle-of-the-range, off-the-peg suit in beige that they always wore. Perhaps he knew Liam.

Liam was a psychologist the police sometimes

used as an expert witness. She had first encountered him outside the courtroom where the case against a client of hers had just been dismissed by the judge. In a flush of triumph from arguing the case well, she had not been able to resist remarking, as she brushed past him,

'Evidence. You can have all the theories in the world about his relationship with his mother, but evidence is what you need to deny him his freedom.'

And Liam had replied, with complete equanimity, 'That remark tells me a great deal about you.'

'Oh?' She had stopped walking, turned to face him, seen the laughing eyes in the otherwise serious face, thought Frank Furillo, and felt the first spur of attraction snagging her gut.

'Not that I could ever prove it, of course.'

He began to walk away down the corridor towards the exit.

'What do you mean?' She found herself chasing after him. He stopped abruptly in front of her, so that she stepped into the two feet of personal space strangers keep around them. She took a step back, literally wrong-footed by him.

'Shall we discuss it over a drink?' he had asked as they stepped outside into a misty autumnal afternoon.

Flustered, she had already forgotten what it was they were supposed to be discussing.

'Sorry,' she had said, gathering herself together, 'I really don't have the time.'

'Oh, but you should make time for yourself.'

His tone had been a mixture of teasing and

64

concern. It was as if he had taken one look at her and understood her whole life. Women's magazines called it juggling, a jokey happy word for the relentless struggle to keep a career, a marriage, a house and three boys going at the same time.

She hadn't known whether to smile at him, or look offended. In the end she had walked away purposefully, feeling his eyes on her back and wondering how far she would go in the wrong direction before being sure that when she turned round he would not still be looking at her.

For the next few days, she had thought of almost nothing except him. After a week, she looked him up in the telephone directory.

'Ursula,' he had repeated, as she announced herself.

It was as if he had been expecting her call.

'I'm interested in what you do ... like to have that drink ... hear more about it.'

'When?' he had interrupted, making it easy for her.

She thought that brief concession of power was when she had fallen in love with him. That, and his voice, and the way he seemed to see depths to her, depths that she was never really sure existed.

The train picked up speed as it charged through the Midlands on its way south. Ursula stared out of the window. Each time the door to the compartment opened with a whoosh and clunk, she half expected to see Liam approach sit down opposite her, his face dangerous with possibility. And each time it was not him, she fought with disappointment, although realistically she knew that he was not on the train.

Ursula's coffee was cold. She glanced towards the man in the beige suit but his seat was empty. Is slightly unnerved her that he had disappeared without her noticing him leave. Her thoughts of Liam had put her into a kind of trance. She did not know whether she had been asleep or simply staring into space, or even talking out loud.

Chapter 10

If you woke up at the right moment, four hours' sleep could be better than seven. Annie felt miraculously un-hungover. If the birds had started singing even five minutes later, then they might have interrupted a phase of rapid eye movement, or deep sleep or whatever it was, and she would have woken up with a brain feeling as if it had expanded in her head like a balloon that was just about to pop. She had once read about sleep cycles in a book called *Successful on Six* or something, and she had impressed people at dinner parties for weeks afterwards with the depth of her pseudo-scientific knowledge.

Cautiously, she inclined her cheek one way, then the other, testing whether her early morning lucidity was just a momentary feeling that would disappear as soon as she made a sudden movement of her head. There was no rush of nausea. Still slightly drunk, but refreshed, she thought.

Sunlight streamed in through the floor-to-ceiling window of the airy room she used as her office. She opened and closed her eyes a couple of times. The colour of the walls was the outcome of a conversation with the interior designer who bought his cigarettes in the same corner shop as she did. It surprised her every time she caught sight of it, jolting her with its unexpectedness, rather than creating the light carefree atmosphere he had promised. Try one room first, he had said, which had been his only piece of good advice. Her living room was still unfashionably white, but she thought that she would go mad in an environment entirely painted in lurid Miami pastels. Lilac was simply not restful, and the lime green window frame, door and skirting boards did not make her feel as if she'd just taken an early morning dip in the Atlantic Ocean, as the designer had claimed.

Annie frowned at the office chair that was standing on its own in the middle of the room. The memory of moving it back filtered to the front of her consciousness and provided an explanation as to why she appeared to be lying half inside a grubby, white, easy-assembly tent.

The bones in the bodice of the dress left red marks on her ribcage, but the relief at stepping out of it and seeing it drop to the floor like a collapsing pavlova made the pain almost worthwhile. She'd once read a book about quitting smoking which said that the only reason people smoked was to relieve the craving for nicotine. Apparently, it was like taking off a shoe that pinched. Why put the shoe on in the first place when there wasn't such a thing as an active desire to smoke, just a desire to end the pain, the book had asked. Why indeed? Annie had thought, turning the page, kicking off her Manolos and lighting up, but how does that help me?

Annie stepped under a scorching shower and stood for several minutes letting the water stream over her head and flatten the pile of curls that had taken so long to construct the previous afternoon. Before the party, the hairstyle had looked rather magical; this morning Maurice's dusting of silver powder simply made it look grey. Annie picked off her beauty spot. A fat lot of good that had done her. The only available men at the party had been wimps, embarrassed to speak to a woman in a bodice, let alone to rip it off her.

If she thought about the men at the party (which she didn't intend to, for long), they constituted a pretty comprehensive cross-section of London's thirty-something intelligentsia. Why was it, she wondered, lining them up in her imagination, that none of them got anywhere near the person she imagined herself marrying. And yet, if she was being really honest, she knew that if one of them had shown the slightest interest in her, her mind would almost instantaneously have found a dozen good reasons why he would actually be most suitable.

Not particularly witty or good-looking? Obviously an ideal partner for life. Better to keep your own circle of friends, but nice to have someone who was just there when you fancied going out to a local movie and couldn't face walking back in the dark alone. The great thing about marrying a nobody was that he would look after their children while she continued to work. If she decided she wanted children...

Within seconds her mind would have sketched out the plot and, after a minute or two, a whole television series of their future life together would be in production in her brain. Often it made it quite difficult to concentrate on what her future husband was saying. On one occasion, after being introduced to a mildly attractive man who was a concert pianist, she had spent the entire conversation with half of her mind trying to work out how on earth they would get a Steinway up the stairs to her flat.

Arriving at a party, Annie would scour the room for men above a certain height she did not already know. If there weren't any of those, her eyes would drop a few inches, and she would take the first excuse she could find (dancing, just-bought-them-today, trying to give up smoking) to remove her shoes. She was good at opening conversations, and it was best to take control, try to establish immediately that they weren't married, Tories, or having a mid-life crisis (although in truly desperate moments she had even been able to persuade herself that a more mature man with different politics might broaden her outlook in a positive kind of way). Usually it needed no more than a reference to the progress of the Euro, and a passing remark about Woody Allen. Two strikes and you're out, was her motto. Life was too short to waste chatting up someone who thought that Woody had been un-fairly treated by the press.

Her fame didn't make the whole process any easier. After the first flattering five minutes, would-be starfuckers became embarrassing. Yet she didn't really like it if someone had no idea who she was (after all, there had been a cover feature in the *Guardian* tabloid section, as well as all of her appearances in the red tops). She hadn't quite got past the point of thinking that if someone didn't mention the show it meant they hated it, although she had trained herself to resist asking, because they always said yes, they loved it, and then she just thought they were being two-faced.

Sometimes in the cold light of a hangover, she wondered whether she really wanted to get married at all, but it didn't matter how feminist, rich or successful you were, if you weren't married, or at least living with someone, or divorced by your mid-thirties, there was no getting away from the fact that everyone thought you were a failure.

Annie took two large white towels from the airing cupboard, wound one round her head and wrapped the other round her body. At a time like this she wished she had one of those white cotton robes you got in expensive hotels. She had owned several but had found that they were never quite as luxurious when you were the person responsible for getting them clean and dry. One had broken the spin mechanism in her washing machine, another had gone mouldy in the corner of her bedroom where she had casually flung it on the last occasion she had had sex on the floor.

It was light outside, but the sun was not yet warm. Annie sat down at her desk and opened her laptop computer. First she checked her e-mail box, which was empty, and then she opened the file named ILOVEANNIEXMAS, which was also empty, apart from the header, which she had spent some hours customizing with holly and snowflakes. With a sudden flash of inspiration, she typed a title in capital letters.

FRANKLY, MY DEAR ...

In her most detailed fantasies, Annie never imagined that she would become the eponymous star of a sitcom that she also wrote. She had wanted to act ever since going to her first panto-mime at the age of five and volunteering herself from the cheap seats at the back for the role of a helpful elf. At school she was always a man because of her height, and at Oxford she was always one of the chorus whether the production was *Cabaret* or the *Lysistrata*, except for the time when she had gone for the role of Juliet in a garden production, and been cast as the nurse.

After Oxford, she had spent several years appearing in meaningful fringe productions financed by meagre Arts Council grants to audiences of five or six, but her nearest brush with earning any money from her craft was getting into the last three for the girls in the Philadelphia advert. She made her living as a serving wench in one of London's theme restaurants which catered solely to Japanese and American tourists, where she handed out whole spit-roasted chickens on wooden platters and

71

poured ale from earthernware jugs. The hours enabled her to go for auditions during the day. One morning a week, she went into the BBC to write gags for radio shows.

By the time she was thirty, she had just enough income to rent a dark little ground-floor flat in Shepherd's Bush, on her own instead of sharing co-ops with other struggling actors. Seeing some of her peers making millions in the City, she was not entirely ecstatic about the hand life had dealt her, but was satisfied at least that she had not sold out as so many people seemed to have done in the Eighties. She would probably have continued like that if she hadn't one Saturday night, in the days when comedy was still called alternative, agreed to stand in for a gag-writing friend of hers who had flu and didn't want to lose his regular stand-up spot in a pub in Islington.

Annie was neither booed off the stage, nor greeted with any reaction other than a couple of misogynistic comments about her bra size which she thought she handled quite well. Afterwards, in the loo, she bumped into a fretful woman who had lost three consecutive pound coins in the tampon machine. Annie offered her a new-shaped Lil-let from the box, like a fellow smoker offering a clandestine cigarette in a smoke-free office. The woman had nipped gratefully into a cubicle and started talking to her from behind the door as if the gift of sanitary protection had made them instant friends.

'Do you think comedy is the new rock 'n' roll?' the woman had called.

'Err...'

'Not on tonight's showing,' the woman continued.

'Umm...'

'I thought most of it was *so* bad,' the woman said, making it sound as if so had at least three syllables. 'Jesus, it's depressing out there...'

Annie didn't know whether she ought to leave. The woman seemed to be taking a long time. But she decided it might be rude just to slump off. There was something curiously intimate about talking to someone on the other side of a toilet door.

'...the only one I liked was the one with the observational monologue. That I could relate to. I'm just so sick of women telling jokes about periods and how men don't understand, aren't you?'

'Hmm...'

'Angie McSomething...'

'Annie McClintock?'

Annie's stage name, which was very close to her real name, had been an instant decision before she went on, chosen because the publican had a photo of the winning Arsenal double team from 1971 behind the bar.

'That's it.'

'That was me.'

'Oh bugger,' said the woman in the toilet, 'well, I blew that, didn't I? Buy you a drink?'

With the door separating them, Annie had not known whether the offer was made in earnest. Then the woman flushed and reappeared.

'I'm blind without my glasses,' she explained. 'I forget to bring them unless it's work, although

73

this is work too, bloody hard work sometimes.'

For a comedy producer, Annie thought later, Tessa was an incredibly disconsolate person.

She had never known whether it was her act or the tampon which had given her her lucky break, but after a couple of pints Tessa had informed her that she was looking to commission comedy from women. They got talking about their favourite sitcoms of all time, and Annie had sensed that she was on to something when her passionate championing of *The Lucy Show* brought the first smile of the evening to Tessa's face. By the end of the night, she had improvised an idea for exactly the sort of American-style observational sitcom that Tessa said she was looking for, which was based on a would-be actress who earned her living as a serving wench in a theme restaurant.

'Yes, yes, yes!' Tessa said, getting out her Psion organizer to fix a date for Annie to come into the office, 'it's sort of twenty-something *Cybil* but set in London. When can you do a treatment?'

The friend who usually did the stand-up routine never spoke to her again, although Annie still sometimes saw his name in the listings for the Edinburgh Fringe.

The only minor hitch in Annie's meteoric rise had been what to call the show. In the end they had settled on *I Love Annie.*

After spending years dreaming of being Rosalind, Lady Macbeth or anything whatsoever to do with Théâtre de Complicité, fame and fortune had come to Annie when she was herself. She was sure that there was a lesson in there somewhere.

74

Annie wrote non-stop until she ran out of ideas. By the time she looked up from her screen, she had mapped out the shape of the *I Love Annie* Christmas special, which involved Annie going to a party where the invitation said 'Dress: Something you've always dreamed of wearing'. Annie McClintock was wearing a dress with a hooped petticoat and the only other person who had noted the dress code was a skinny prat in a Tarzan outfit. She had three storylines going but she could only think of jokes to make two of them pay off, and she couldn't think of a satisfactory ending. She saved the file and switched off the computer, so pleased with her morning's work that for a moment she was tempted to flop into bed and sleep for an hour or two, but when she looked at her watch she remembered that she was supposed to be meeting Ursula in Brown's in Oxford at noon.

Panic.

Ursula was bound to have some sarcastic comment about how she had come halfway across the country and managed to be there on time, whereas Annie just lived down the road.

Annie tried to think of a valid excuse not to go, but the writing had exhausted her creativity. She thought about ringing Brown's and saying she had broken her leg, but annoyingly Ursula watched her programme religiously and would be able to work out when it was screened that that wasn't true, unless she pretended she had broken her leg for the programme too, but Annie McClintock had broken her leg two series back and it might seem a bit repetitive. Anyway, a broken leg would not be a serious enough malady as an excuse to miss the whole day. She had been bullied by Leonora into agreeing to read something at the dinner. If she was going to get out of it altogether, rather than just reading from a wheelchair, she would have to invent a much more critical illness, which would be in pretty poor taste. It was bad enough to have missed Penny's funeral because she was on holiday in the Caribbean, but if she missed this, Ursula would never forgive her, nor would Leonora and more importantly, nor would Roy.

The prospect of seeing Roy again made Annie shiver with excitement.

A couple of nights after the invitation to the reunion arrived, she had woken herself up with an orgasm in the midst of an incredibly erotic dream in which Roy had been fucking her on a tennis court. What was so weird was that she had never been aware of fancying him, yet what they had been doing together in the dream was unbelievably sexy. In fact it was so intimate and wonderful, she somehow felt that Roy's subconscious must, in a curious telepathic way, have been involved too. It was the first really randy dream she could remember having since her early teens, when, still a virgin, she used to get up to all sorts of things with Ilie Nastase in her sleep. She imagined that the connection between sex and tennis stemmed from the fact that when she was a teenager, the sports pavilion in the recreation ground near her mum's council house had sometimes been the venue for discos, and she had experienced her first snogs against the wire netting surrounding the courts.

The wall of wardrobes in Annie's bedroom was one of the interior designer's better ideas. He had designed them as a row of beach huts at some unfashionable English seaside resort. The first hut was a washed-out chalky pink colour and contained her underwear. The second had weatherbeaten white paint and was full of dresses and suits. She took a long time making up her mind before choosing her new Gucci dress and a Donna Karan little black dress as a stand-by. The third hut was painted with vertical red and white stripes and held her casual separates. She took out a pair of cargo pants, a pair of jeans, and a couple of white T-shirts for the next day. The fourth, for shoes, was white again. She selected a pair of red sandals to go with the dress, some Nike trainers and her ponyskin mules. The final hut, in bright yellow gloss with ice-cream company logos stuck onto it and half a stable door, was filled with shelves for her collection of bags.

Annie had handbags in every shape and colour. There were hard plastic 1950s bags, and soft leather drawstrings, there were briefcases and vanity cases, suitbags and, on the floor, a complete set of Louis Vuitton cases including a small shipping trunk. There was almost the entire range of the Gucci Jackie bag which everyone had been photographed with that season. She had one in yellow and black, one in white and black, and one which was black and the same fabric as the dress she was going to wear. Her only regret was that she had stopped herself buying the black on black on the basis that she had at least ten plain black handbags already.

On the upper shelves of the cupboard there were several dozen of the free make-up bags that department stores give away with two purchases, all complete with miniature sets of face cream, doll's size lipstick and mascara and tiny bottles of cologne. The yellow hut was taller than she was and several feet deep, but when she opened the door, bags tumbled out of it.

With the right bag, Annie felt she could face the world. She'd once read that your handbag was a symbol of your vagina, which had worried her for a while, especially since she preferred a bag with a zip, but even with her scant knowledge of popular psychology she knew that her collection (fetish, Maurice had called it) was more to do with her childhood, which had mostly been spent living out of bags.

One of her earliest memories was her mother picking up their tatty old grey cardboard suitcase with a bright, determined smile, and saying,

'Have bag, will travel, hey, Annie?'

Chapter 11

All the garments Manon owned were black. She chose the sleeveless black jersey dress Rodolfo had bought her many years before in a tiny boutique in Milan. The price label had contained

78

so many zeros, Manon had not even attempted to work out what the cost might be. She had never really got the hang of lire. It was the dress she had worn when she left him, the only remnant of his wealth that she retained. She hung a soft black cardigan around her shoulders and went to look at herself in the bathroom mirror. With her hair loose the overall impression was dowdy, but when she gathered the hair back into a severe ponytail she became elegant but sombre, like a strict ballet teacher, she thought.

Manon began to rifle through her belongings for some sort of appropriate adornment, knowing that she would find nothing but still hoping to surprise herself. Her mother's string of pearls was too formal and the ruby earrings Frank had given her were flashy and would invite comment. There were a couple of scarves, but they made her look like an Italian countess and she did not want that. Then she remembered the Lulu Guinness bag Frank had bought her on Valentine's Day. A tiny black silk flower basket with red silk roses on the lid.

When every shop window had been filled with red roses and red helium hearts, she had thought the bag a cliché, but now, still in its tissue paper, it was like a piece of art. Carefully, she took it from its box and held it in her right hand slightly awkwardly, like a woman from the 15th *arrondissement* holding the jewel-encrusted lead of a pet poodle. She went into the bathroom and looked at herself in the mirror, amused by the way the bag changed her posture, turning her outline into a drawing from a Fifties fashion

79

magazine. Back in the bedroom she opened the bag to throw in her keys. Nestling inside was a roll of banknotes tied with narrow red ribbon. She stared at it, not understanding. Then the *frisson* of excitement brought about by owning something so beautiful froze to numbness. She flung the bag across the room as if it were contagious and she wanted to be as far from it as possible. It sailed towards the open window, a disappearing fluttering of scarlet and black, like a bird of augury. Then it caught the window frame and dropped unceremoniously to the floor.

She went to pick it up and count the money. There were twenty fifty pound notes. A thousand pounds. Her brain replayed the last few times she had been with Frank and saw how those notes, which he assumed mutely accepted, changed the entire complexion of their relationship. As she tried to recall each detail and every word they had exchanged, she found the irony too fascinating to be painful. A thousand pounds. She had no idea how much abortions cost, but she was sure a thousand pounds would cover it. It was as if he had donated the means to destroy his baby. It was a sign.

The man in the greengrocer's shop downstairs took the new note and held it up to the light.

'There's a lot of fakes around,' he said, 'but seeing as it's you, seeing as I went to the bank yesterday and got myself a load of change...'

She was only buying an apple for her breakfast.

'Sorry,' Manon said, 'if it's not OK, let me know?'

'I know where to find you,' he told her with a friendly wink.

Manon took a bite of the apple and walked up the street towards the main road. She liked living in this place. She liked the fact that the shop-keepers recognized her but were too busy, too urban, to pry further into her life. It was not a residential neighbourhood and most of the buildings nearby were offices or hospitals. She liked the blend of anonymity and acceptance you found in the heart of a city.

You couldn't bring a baby up in a city, she told herself, as she waited at the bus stop, watching a young mother on the other side of the road who was bent with the effort of pushing a toddler and a baby along in a double buggy.

Stop it. Stop thinking about it.

When the bus came, Manon went upstairs. There was no-one else on the top deck. She allowed her vision to become blurred with welling tears, then she wiped her eyes with her forearm, wishing she had thought to put some tissues in the flowerbasket bag that sat on the seat next to her like a toy.

It was the kind of glorious summer day that makes people walk along the street with their faces tilted upwards to the sun. Even the ugly grey buildings along the Euston Road exuded a kind of grandeur in the sunshine. She got off at Baker Street. The forecourt of Pizza Express was busy with people eating lunch al fresco. As she walked past, the yeast and oregano wafts from the pizza oven brought back the balminess of summer evenings in the Piazza Navona.

She waited for the Citylink coach at the stop in Gloucester Place. A dad with two boys, all of them in orange baseball caps, jogged past her bound for Regent's Park. When the coach came, she sat halfway down. The airbrakes sighed with relief as the traffic began to move and they soared up onto the Westway, over the tops of the buildings, away from the city streets that today seemed to be taunting her with happy family life.

The tinted windows made the clear blue sky outside almost violet. Manon wondered if people on buses looked at her when she was with Saskia and Lily and smiled. Did they watch the little girls in their Laura Ashley pinafores bouncing down the street beside her and assume she was their mother? Did they think that the three of them were as happy as they looked?

How easy it was to imagine uncomplicated lives for strangers.

The coach charged along the outside lane of the flyover. Manon closed her eyes. She was quite used to the road from London to Oxford now, because she went up most Wednesday afternoons to see Penny's daughters, but as she passed the familiar landmarks of the journey, Trellick Tower, the traffic lights near Acton, the huge advert for a car dealer at Park Royal, she was reminded of the day almost two years before, when she had gone back to Oxford for the first time since leaving college, for Penny's thirty-eighth birthday party.

That day had been almost mockingly sunny too.

Penny's letter, which had been tucked inside the party invitation, had explained that she was ill again, and Manon had been alarmed by the PS at the bottom.

'I must see you!'

Penny had the neatest handwriting in the world, but this was a giant scrawl.

Nothing had prepared her for what she was to see, and the shock made the very air that she breathed taste different. There was an unmistakable gauntness about the dying. Penny had always been slim, but now she was almost ethereal. Her hair was cut short as a precaution against the chemotherapy. She looked very young and very old at the same time. She was too frail to stand for very long, but when Manon embraced her, her clutch was desperately strong, as if to graft herself onto something living.

Manon's first reaction had been pure white anger.

'It's all happened a bit quickly,' Penny said understanding, as Manon held her, unable to stop herself shaking with fury. 'They said I was free of it, but I wasn't.'

They had looked at each other for a long time, seeing each other's thoughts, and then Penny had said, 'When are you going back to Italy?'

And Manon had replied, 'I'm not going back.'

And it had been as simple as that.

'I'm so glad because that means that we don't have to do the christening today as well as the party...' Penny said, ever practical.

'The christening?'

'We never got around to christening Lily

because of all this...' she waved her hands vaguely up and down her body, 'and anyway you've never been here.'

A letter asking Manon to be Lily's godmother had arrived long before with a picture of Lily a day old. Manon had been flattered, but had not taken the request seriously. She had sent two tiny Lacoste polo shirts in white and pink. Now it would not just be about birthday presents and saints' days, she realized, wondering whether she could rise to the challenge of being a proper god-mother.

The coach sped under the tunnel at Hangar Lane and out through the greener suburbs. Manon tried to imagine what Penny would say to her now. Theirs had been the sort of friendship where they could go for years without seeing each other, but still find themselves communicating when they met as if they had parted only the day before. She sometimes thought that if she tried hard enough she would be able to conjure up a kind of virtual Penny in her mind, who would talk to her in the same calm, non-judgmental way. But it didn't work like that. Penny was gone, and although her looks and spirit seemed to continue almost uncannily in Saskia, there was no phantom Penny wafting around to connect with. Penny had always been straightforward. She had died and was gone. Manon missed her terribly.

The evening after Penny's birthday party they had sat together on the swing chair in the back garden of the rectory, talking rapidly and quietly as they had always done since the friendship was forged on the cold stone steps of the Examination Schools in their first Hilary term.

All the guests had left tactfully early, some, like Annie, unable to stop themselves crying, still demanding that Penny comfort them, as she always had, instead of offering her comfort. Even though she had so much to say herself, and so little time, Penny had listened without interrupting as Manon explained what her life had been like in Italy. They rocked backwards and forwards on the yellow-and-white striped cushions as the heat grew more intense and the shadows longer. And after Manon had finished speaking, a silence had fallen, punctuated only by the creaking of the swing's hooks on the frame.

Then, as it grew quite dark, Penny asked her,

'What are you going to do now?'

'I'm going to be around to help you,' Manon replied.

'But what are you going to do about you?'

'I don't know. Begin again?'

She remembered feeling guilty for having the chance to say that when she had made such a mess of her life and Penny had made such a success of hers. She didn't want to tell Penny that she had only finally made the decision to leave Rodolfo that afternoon. She had not even considered what she would do.

'I've written some stories and I might send them to a publisher,' she said, grabbing at the first idea that appeared in her head.

'Annie knows everyone. Why don't you ask her?'

'I may do. She told me I could have her spare room if I needed it.'

'Oh, but you can stay with us in Joshua Street. You could have your old room!' Penny offered. 'It's kind of Roy's office, but he never uses it. There's a futon.'

'Maybe, for a couple of days. You need time on you own, and so do I.'

Penny had not pressed her further, and when she left to go to London a couple of days later, she had asked, concerned, 'Do you have any money?'

'Not really. I was wondering whether you could lend me some. Just a couple of hundred to get me going...'

Penny started writing a cheque, and then they both realized that Manon didn't have a bank account in England, and so without even thinking about it, Penny handed over her cashcard and made her memorize the PIN number testing her several times so she wouldn't have to write it down.

'Why don't you just take it until you get yourself sorted out. There's a couple of thousand in there, just bits and pieces I've saved, sort of sinking fund really.' She gave a short, ironic laugh.

Manon had memorized the number until the coach journey back to London when she had written it on her wrist. She had used all the money, and returned the card and half the cash to Penny when she had received her first advance from the publisher for her collection of short stories. Penny had not lived long enough for her to pay back the other half.

Now, as the coach raced through the rich arable landscape of the Thames Valley, she found herself looking at her arm, as if the mark of the biro might still be there like one of her tattoos, but the skin on the inside of her wrist was pale and white.

Chapter 12

'If we're not going to Oxford with you, how will Manon be able to take us punting?' Saskia interrupted, as Roy discussed the timetable for the day with Geraldine, who had insisted on cooking him a proper breakfast.

'Are you sure she said she would?' Roy asked, 'this weekend?'

'Of course I'm sure,' Saskia said, as if she could only barely tolerate his stupidity.

'Of course she's sure,' Lily echoed.

For a moment he found himself feeling cross with Manon, until Geraldine spoke his own thoughts out loud:

'I do think she should have told you, really.'

And Roy felt obliged to rise to Manon's defence.

'She often rings the girls when they're at Nancy's house. I think she works in the evenings, so it's difficult to talk directly to me.'

Geraldine looked at him sceptically.

'Is she still working in that nightclub in Soho?'

The disapproval in her voice made it sound as

if Manon was a stripper at the very least.

'It's just called a club, not a nightclub. Soho isn't like it was.'

'I should hope not,' Geraldine said, whacking an egg on the edge of the frying pan and dropping it into the pan with a determined sizzle.

He hadn't seen much of Manon since Penny's death. She made most of her arrangements to see the children through Nancy the childminder, except for the unexpected call to his office a month or so ago:

'Roy, it's Manon. Look, I'm coming to this thing, all right?'

'Of course,' he had replied, delighted. 'I always seem to miss you when you come to see the kids. They're always talking about the things they do with you. I asked Saskia who her best friend was the other day and she said you...' then he realized that he was talking to an empty line. Manon had said what she wanted to say and then hung up on him.

'I have to say,' Geraldine was saying, as if somebody had asked her for a balanced assessment of Manon's character, 'she has been wonderful with the children. Better than some people I won't mention right now...'

'If you mean Ursula, she is a long way away,' Roy said, wondering why it had fallen to him to defend women who were perfectly able to stand up for themselves, but Geraldine had an uncanny knack of saying things out loud that he had secretly thought himself. He couldn't deny that he had expected Ursula, who was his sister as well as Penny's friend, to do more.

'Cracking toast, Gromit,' Lily suddenly said. Her face was covered in marmalade and crumbs.

Saskia laughed.

'What did she say?' Geraldine asked.

'Cracking toast, Gromit!' Lily and Saskia chorused.

'It's from one of their videos,' Roy explained. 'You know, *Wallace and Gromit,* the ones that won Oscars?'

'They watch so many videos,' Geraldine sighed.

'Are we going punting or not?' Saskia enquired, sensing that a change of subject was required.

'Of course you are, if Manon's promised,' Roy said, and was rewarded by both little faces breaking into smiles full of innocent joy.

'Manon, Manon, Manon,' Lily chanted, like a miniature football hooligan.

'Manon is our favourite auntie,' Saskia explained, as if Geraldine did not know who they were talking about, 'except, she's not really an auntie. She's more of a godmother without the god bit,' she went on.

Roy couldn't help laughing, glad that his mother-in-law's face was looking the other way. He noticed that she was scraping at the crispy bits stuck to the bottom of the blackened frying pan with a little more agitation than usual.

'Did she tell you that?'

'Yes,' said Saskia earnestly.

'Why do you like her so much?' Roy asked, curious to know what she would say.

'She makes up the best games.'

'What sort of games?' Geraldine asked suspiciously.

'Well, there's the waitress game,' Saskia began.

'We are pretending to be waitresses and Manon is the cuttomer,' Lily explained, 'and she say, "a cup of coffee and the bill, please" and we bring it to her ... and then she gives us some money, and we give her some change ... in fact it's only pretending...'

So much for the expensive plastic kitchen that had been Lily's Christmas present, Roy thought. Manon could create a whole restaurant just by sitting down at a table and asking them to use their imaginations.

'What other games?' he asked.

'Hatchet girl, Hatchet girl, Hatchet girl!' Lily screamed, getting slightly overexcited.

'Hatchet girl?' Geraldine repeated, making it sound like a violent computer game for adolescent boys.

'Yes,' Lily said, impatiently, 'I have to sit behind the counter...'

'...or I do,' Saskia interrupted. 'We take it in turns, don't we Lily?'

'...and then Manon and Sas give me coats and bags to look after, and you have to stick one ticket on the coat and give the other to the cuttomer,' Lily said breathlessly.

'Manon stole the tickets from her work,' Saskia said, 'but we're not allowed to tell anyone.' She put her finger against her lips and made an exaggerated shush noise.

Roy chuckled and as he looked up he saw that

even Geraldine was smiling. 'That sounds a lovely game,' she said.

'May we be excused from the table?' Saskia asked.

Roy shot a glance at his mother-in-law. It was starting already. The formal manners, the strait-jacket of rural conservatism.

'Of course you may,' Geraldine replied, clearly pleased with her granddaughter's polite request.

The two girls slid off the ladderback chairs and ran into the garden.

'It's a wonderful garden for children,' Geraldine remarked as she slid two fried eggs onto Roy's plate, along with some triangles of fried bread, 'because you can see them wherever they are.'

She stood staring through the window above the sink, her eyes glazed with tears. He knew that she was remembering watching her own daughter turning cartwheels on the lawn, and he suddenly felt too sad to be irritated with her any more.

'Well, it looks like a change of plan. I'll take the girls in with me, then I'll bring them back again and change for dinner. It's probably more sensible. I didn't want to wear a suit all day anyway.'

'I thought that Leonora was going to take care of everything.'

'She said she'd appreciate a hand with the placement,' he said. 'I don't know what use I'll be. I don't even know half the people coming, but I thought I ought to show willing.' He wiped the plate clean with a piece of toast from the rack in the middle of the table. 'By the way, can I borrow your iron?'

'Don't be silly. I can iron a shirt for you.'

'No, really...'

'No, really,' she repeated firmly, smiling at him.

She was trying so hard, he thought. It was churlish of him to mind.

'Cracking breakfast, Gromit,' he said, putting down his knife and fork and smiling at her.

Chapter 13

Annie was fond of saying,

'I have no idea why I bought this Ferrari...' because she thought it made her sound endearingly scatty as well as impressively rich, but in fact she knew exactly why she had bought it. On the evening she had signed her first syndication deal, she corralled all the people on the show that she liked for drinks at the Crompton Club. Max, the cameraman who was also the current unattainable man she had a crush on, had been in a flirtatious mood and she had asked him, casually, what he would do if he suddenly found himself £100,000 richer than he had been when he got up in the morning.

'Buy a Ferrari,' he had immediately replied.

'Funnily enough,' Annie had heard herself saying, 'that was my thought too, but I don't really know how to go about it...'

Two bottles of Rioja later, he had taken the bait and arranged to come round on Saturday morning with an armful of specialist magazines. You needed to know something about it if you were going to venture into the second-hand market, he had told her.

The first time they'd gone Ferrari hunting, to an address in deepest Essex, they'd had a ball, and Annie had been delighted when the newly redundant foreign exchange dealer who was selling the ridiculous car was unable to produce the relevant documentation about its history, because that meant there was another date with Max on the cards. They'd had a test drive, just the two of them, with Max driving, and it had felt almost as exciting as sex.

I've found the ultimate chat-up line, Annie thought, as she wrote up the day when she got back home, and saved it for a future episode.

The second time, Max's wife had come along too, and the two women had talked about girls' things while the men walked slowly around the car. Then they had gone for a test drive together.

'It's a lot of money, but the poor guy's got to educate his children,' Max said loudly, then lowered his voice to urge her, 'Snap it up. We've found you a bargain.'

'Can't he send them to state schools?' Annie asked, grasping at the first excuse that came into her head to get out of it.

'Don't you like it?'

'It seems a bit low.'

'Low?'

'Near the ground, I mean...'

'That's what they're like.'

'And I'm not sure about red.'

'But Ferraris should be red. Ferrari Red. It's a colour in its own right.'

Gloomily, Annie had handed over her banker's draft for the best part of £30,000 terrified at the thought of having to drive the thing home. She'd only passed her test a couple of years and never felt completely comfortable behind a wheel.

'You go on,' she urged Max and Mrs Max, not wanting them to watch her try to reverse down the drive, then added brightly, 'I think I'll just go for a spin to the coast.'

Max looked at her enviously at that point, which made her think she was still in with a chance. Since then she had offered several times to give him a lift home from the studios because she just happened to have the car with her, but on the last occasion he had shouted, 'God, you really know how to rub it in, don't you?'

And they had never reached the kind of *rapprochement* which would allow her to ask his advice about selling it.

Annie was the only person she knew who looked with envy at Nissan Micras as they drove past on the motorway. Generally, she liked to be in the slow lane behind a big lorry where she felt protected. She was nervous about overtaking because she always felt that the draught from the lorry might blow her into the path of another car speeding up the fast lane. The only trouble was that in the slow lane people would draw alongside to have a good look at the car and she would have to lift one hand from the steering wheel to point at a non-existent problem with a front tyre, pretending that it was responsible for her remarkably sedate progress.

Annie felt a twinge of guilt as she passed the exit to Northolt, the undistinguished suburb where her mother lived in the little council house that she refused to move from, but had at least allowed Annie to buy after Annie had produced proof of her bank balance.

What the hell was she going to do with her mum? The question had floated unanswered in her brain since Christmas when she had stayed there. It wasn't until she had spent consecutive days with her mother that she had realized there was a problem. She knew that people got a bit repetitive as they got older, but Marjorie wasn't even sixty and she repeated herself all the time.

At first Annie had thought her mum might be going deaf when on Christmas morning she asked three times what Annie wanted for breakfast.

'Cornflakes, please,' Annie said, sitting down in her mother's pink chenille dressing gown, staring at the service on the screen.

'Rice Krispies or cornflakes?'

'Cornflakes,' Annie replied a little louder, over the strains of 'Ding Dong Merrily on High.'

'I was wondering what you fancy for breakfast.'

'Have you got any cornflakes?'

'Of course I have. Now what are you going to have for breakfast?'

'Oh, for God's sake, Mum!' Annie had

shouted at her.

The visit had been punctuated by similar exchanges, but she hadn't been unduly worried, and when she had asked her mother, 'Do you know you're repeating yourself a lot, Mum?' her question had met with the defiant riposte:

'You should hear yourself after a few Bristol Creams.'

At Easter, Annie had driven up to take Marjorie out for lunch and found her completely unprepared, even though they had rehearsed the arrangements many times on the phone. Marjorie had been delighted by the nice surprise and had dressed herself up in the pale blue suit from British Home Stores that she used to wear for work. Annie had taken her to a pub in Ruislip, and Marjorie had sat eating her roast dinner, recalling in vivid detail the few meals out they had been able to afford when Annie was a child. Her memory of those times seemed stronger and brighter than it had ever been, and Annie had driven back to Notting Hill telling herself that maybe there wasn't anything wrong after all. Her mother was getting a bit forgetful, which was what happened when people had been forced into early retirement and hadn't replaced work with anything to keep their mind busy. She would enrol her in U3A, she told herself, and pay for her to go on a Saga holiday.

Her optimism evaporated when her mother rang her that very evening and asked, 'When am I going to see you? You never seem to come here these days.'

Recently, she had taken her mother to her GP and told him that she wanted a private referral to a consultant.

'What do you want that for?' her mother had asked.

'Because you're getting a bit forgetful,' Annie had explained.

'Rubbish,' her mother said, but the next day, when they went to collect the typed-up letter from the surgery, she had asked, 'What's this about, then?'

The neurologist had been pleasant enough, but confirmed Annie's worst-case amateur diagnosis of the possible onset of Alzheimer's.

Annie put her foot down tentatively as she passed RAF Northolt. The street lamps in this particular section of road were truncated to half their normal size. She presumed it was because of low-flying aircraft coming in to land, but the idea of aeroplanes flying lower than the height of normal street lamps alarmed her. A couple of years before a plane had crashed on the motorway, narrowly avoiding fatalities. The passenger, a minor television personality, she seemed to remember, had been treated for shock. She slowed down again as the road widened out and the street lamps grew tall again.

Sometimes, in the early hours of the morning when she was alone and suffering a bout of existential despair after an evening of fighting talk and alcohol with girlfriends, she would decide to buy the flat downstairs and move her mother in. Her mother had sacrificed everything to look after her when she was little, she would tell herself, weepily, and now she would do the same. It would be a different life, but a moral one.

In fact she had become rather keen on the image of herself as a carer with a life of self-sacrifice instead of indulgence. She knew that some of her friends would think her mad, but anyone with any decency would admire her, seeing strengths they had not seen in her before and that they could not find in themselves. Marjorie might be going barmy, but at least she was pleasantly and politely barmy. As long as she didn't become incontinent...

Doomed to be an old maid, Annie's reasoning went, she might as well do it bravely, proudly, giving herself up to duty as a daughter from a less selfish age might have done. It wasn't as if any men were interested in marrying her any-way, so caring for her prematurely senile mother was hardly likely to put them off. In a funny kind of way, it might even make her more attractive. At least to the sort of kind and decent man that must exist out there somewhere.

Sometimes, at two or three in the morning, the prospect of her meaningful and self-sacrificing future life with Marjorie was so attractive, she thought she might find the bones of a screenplay in it. Or at least a new angle for the sixth series of I Love Annie, which was becoming a little tired.

But as yet the flat downstairs had not come on to the market.

Once she had passed the M25 exit, the traffic thinned out and the road was empty enough for her to feel confident at seventy. Annie surprised herself by overtaking the Oxford Tube just past Thame, but then she had to slow down again in front of it as the turn-off to Oxford loomed much sooner than she had expected. The coach's horn sounded angrily behind her.

Oxford. The very sight of the word on the motorway signpost filled her with apprehension. She couldn't work out whether she was looking forward to the reunion or not. Her hangover had caught up with her and was now making everything feel slightly hazy, as if she were out of sync with real time.

It would be nice to see Ursula again. Even though she was a bit of a boring housewife these days, her transparent envy of Annie's life always made Annie feel better about things. Every couple of years or so, Ursula escaped down to London for a weekend, and they spent Saturday trawling up and down the Portobello Road. Lucky you to have all this on your doorstep, Ursula would say, wide-eyed as they sat at a pavement table eating brunch and watching the world go by, and Annie would see her life through a tourist's eyes and feel rather pleased with it.

As she stopped at the traffic lights just outside Headington, Annie tried to remember the names of Ursula's boys, but could only get Luke, whose godmother she was supposed to be. With a panicky intake of breath she realized she had forgotten his birthday again this year and glanced at her giant plastic watch, deliberating whether it would be better to make herself later for the lunch date but arrive with a present, or whether she would be able to get away with nonchalantly handing Ursula a cheque at the end of the weekend, saying that she hadn't wanted to put it in the post. Then she remembered that it wasn't until September anyway.

Then there was Roy. She didn't know whether she was going to be able to look Roy in the face without blushing. On nights when she couldn't fall straight to sleep, she had found herself deliberately thinking about Roy in the hope of getting a repeat of the dream. It hadn't happened but the fantasy had escalated a bit, and it was starting to look blindingly obvious that there was a solution to all her problems and his. Annie and Roy. It even sounded right.

Fresh-faced blonds had never been her type, but Roy was undeniably attractive if you liked that sort of thing. He was also intelligent and left wing (a bit unfashionably old Trot, but that was better than a Tory). Like her, he was working class made good. A Nottinghamshire miner's son who had become a don at Oxford. He would understand how difficult it was to feel secure when you'd jumped out of your socio-economic band. And he needed her. She would be a friend to his girls, not a horrid stepmother, and they'd do fun things together like visit Disneyworld, which they would never be able to afford without her money.

They'd have to move, of course. The little house in Joshua Street was too full of Penny, and

Annie's flat in London would hardly be suitable. She'd keep it for when she had meetings in London, and the rest of the time they'd live in a rambling manor house near one of the honey-coloured stone villages round Oxford, near enough for Roy to travel into college each day. Annie would have an office in one wing, as far away from the nursery as possible, and Roy was such a kind person he would welcome her converting one of the stables in the courtyard into a granny flat for her mother.

Annie slammed on the brakes at red lights, so deep in her fantasy she had hardly noticed driving over Magdalen Bridge, and now she was in the wrong lane for cutting up by the University Parks. The traffic inched up the High and then forced her to loop right round the back of the town, to places she'd never ventured when she was a student. Had there been an ice rink then, she wondered. She only reorientated herself as she passed the back of the bus station and narrowly missed hitting a reed-thin stick of a woman crossing the road who looked a lot like Manon.

Perhaps it was Manon, Annie thought, her heart pumping adrenalin. It would be typical of her to not notice she was about to be knocked over by a Ferrari, but she didn't dare look round to confirm her hunch because the Randolph Hotel was coming up and she didn't want to miss the sign for the car park and end up whirling round the other half of the Oxford one-way system.

Chapter 14

Manon's very first view of Oxford was the bus station. Even then she had been a misfit, leaving her boarding school in the morning wearing the navy and white uniform, but arriving at Oxford bus station in a black skirt and a black V-neck sweater. Her mother had sent her a genuine Hermès scarf which Manon tied round her neck at the last minute for luck. She assumed it was stolen. She did not like to think about what her mother might have done to earn it.

In her memory, the other girls waiting in the common room to be interviewed had all been wearing the same Laura Ashley dress in sludge green with a pattern of tiny cream flowers. They had divided themselves into two groups. The talkers and the loners, Penny was later to call them. Penny and Ursula must have been among the big group of girls where the volume of chatter rose almost to screeching point when one of their names was called. They had made instant friends with each other and exchanged letters all the way through their gap year. Manon could remember neither of them from that day.

The loners had dotted themselves around the room in mathematical formation, like passengers in a half-empty London tube carriage, each sitting as far from the others as possible, each pretending to be deeply immersed in a book. Manon could remember only Annie because her hair was peroxide white and her book was *Kinflicks* rather than the dusty volumes of Milton or Livy the others seemed to be studying. At one point in the interminable wait, Annie had caught Manon's eye as she glanced furtively round the room and attempted to engage her in a complicit smile of exasperation, but Manon had looked away, too shy to respond. That initial failure to communicate had set the pattern of their relationship ever after. Twenty years later both of them had changed beyond recognition, but Annie still made showy attempts to be friendly, and still Manon inadvertently rebuffed her.

Annie was uncertain how to speak to her now that she was a hat check girl at the Compton Club, even though she had been instrumental in getting her the job.

'Manon and I shared a house when we were at Oxford,' she would announce to whoever was accompanying her when she came in.

'You will come up and have a drink with us later, won't you?'

She always made the offer with such enthusiasm, it would have been rude for Manon to decline, so she usually replied, 'I'd like that' or 'Yes, perhaps later,'

And Annie would smile over-eagerly for just a moment too long before turning, flustered, and hurrying up the stairs talking in an even louder voice than usual.

Twenty years earlier, Annie had arrived for her

Oxford interview by bus too. Both of them assumed that all the other prospective students had a parent waiting outside the college in a smart Volvo, or anxiously drinking tea in the Randolph lounge, but somehow even that shared experience had not created a bond between them.

Manon headed for the exit that led out almost opposite Worcester College. She had to dodge out of the way of a red sports car as she crossed over to Walton Street.

She had always loved the area known as Jericho. It was tatty and human, and so different from the forbidding stone colleges on St Giles just a couple of hundred yards away.

For Manon who had spent all of her education imprisoned in unforgiving institutions, Oxford had been an unfortunate choice of university, but the house in Jericho, which she had shared with Penny, Ursula and Annie for their second and final years, was one of the places that she had been happiest in her life.

The house belonged to Penny's parents, who lived in a village about an hour away from Oxford. Penny's mother often popped in on one of her shopping trips to the city, but Penny was deemed sensible enough to be left in charge of the tenants and rent arrangements. Manon was the last of Penny's friends to be invited to share and so had the smallest room, above the front door. It was the first time in her life she had charge of a little piece of space that was her own.

When her own parents had been together they

lived in barracks, and after the divorce she and her mother had moved to a cramped rented apartment in Paris with a shared toilet two floors down. The rest of her life she had spent in a dormitory at school.

Manon's father was in the army. During her youth he had been posted in Hong Kong which she could not remember, and Germany which she could, because her mother had been so wretched there. They had not seen him since she was twelve years old when he had thrown her mother out, blaming her drinking for ruining his promotion prospects, and giving himself the perfect excuse to move in his brassy girlfriend. Her mother had used the meagre divorce settlement to keep Manon at her boarding school, mistakenly believing that a proper English education was the best thing she could give her. She herself had returned to Paris, depressed and unable to quit the bottle that had become her consolation as a lonely army wife.

Manon strolled along Walton Street. Everything was uncannily as it had been. On her left, the Phoenix cinema where she had sometimes gone to movies that started at midnight, returning home refreshed to write an essay for the next morning's tutorial. On her right, the best cheap Indian restaurant in town, still there, still serving callow youths their first really hot vindaloo. It was all so remarkably the same that when she turned into Joshua Street, she noticed immediately that something was different. She told herself that the estate agent's sign was outside another house, but she knew it was not, just as she knew, even though she could not at first read it at distance that the sign had only one word in bold black lettering. SOLD. She began to run the length of the street, stopping outside number 3 breathless, unable to believe that Penny's house had been sold and she did not know. The house was a boxful of memories. It was impossible to imagine anyone else living there. In the sunshine, the curtainless front windows reflected her bewilderment back at her.

She remembered lying on Penny's bed the day after the thirty-eighth birthday party, with Penny under the covers and Manon next to her on top.

Manon had brought sandwiches upstairs for their lunch and after they had eaten she had put the tray down on the floor and asked,

'Do you want me to take the children out this afternoon so that you can get some rest, or shall I stay here?'

'No, Roy will take them out later,' Penny had replied, too exhausted in her body to pull herself up to sitting, but still clear and businesslike in her voice. 'If you wouldn't mind, I want to make memory boxes for the girls. What I want you to do is take my purse and buy two of the prettiest boxes you can find. Little Clarendon Street, I should think.'

'Little Trendy Street?' Manon had asked, trying to remember the layout of the town.

'Yes!' Penny smiled.

'How big?'

'Hmm. What do you think? I don't even know what I'm going to put in them.'

When Manon returned with two gift boxes the size of shoe boxes, Penny was asleep. She sat on the end of the bed and watched her friend's frail chest moving up and down.

Then Penny had stirred and woken up.

'Perfect,' Penny said, seeing the boxes, 'but which one should get which, do you think?'

'Should I have bought both the same?' Manon asked, perfectly willing to go back and change them.

'No, I don't think so. I want them to be individual, but I just don't want one of them thinking that the other's is prettier and that I loved her more...'

'Stripes for Lily and flowers for Saskia?' Manon suggested.

'Then Lily might think that I thought she was a tomboy. Oh, it's so difficult!' She giggled like a teenager on a shopping trip weighing up which shade of eye shadow to spend her pocket money on, and then suddenly the smiling mask dropped from her face.

'How can I possibly encapsulate what I feel about them in a box?'

'You could write to them,' Manon suggested, frightened by the sudden emotion.

'I'm not much good at letters.'

'Of course you are,' Manon lied, thinking of the long, chatty screeds she had received in Rome, which had told her nothing. They were all about things the children had done with long descriptions of the weather and holidays, but there had been no hint of what Penny had been going through.

Together they rummaged through photos of Penny to find a special one for each of the boxes. There was a particularly beautiful one of her breastfeeding Saskia.

'There's none like that of Lily, though,' Penny said, 'because you just don't bother to take all those reels of film with your second.'

They deliberated whether to include Saskia's anyway and finally Manon found a photo of Penny throwing Lily in the air, which they deemed a satisfactory alternative for her.

The pair of gold hoop earrings Penny had worn when she was confirmed, and the pair of pearl studs she had been married in were divided one in each box.

'What else? Toenails?' Penny laughed.

'Hair?' Manon said.

'Nail scissors on the dressing table,' Penny pointed.

Manon snipped a lock for each box. It was like down.

'I know, get a couple of plastic sandwich bags to put it in. There's some in the kitchen drawer,' Penny had instructed, ever practical.

But when Manon returned, Penny's tears were dripping onto the cotton sheets.

'I should have done this before the chemo,' she said in a strangled, desperate voice. 'They won't even know what my hair was like.'

After staring at the house for a few seconds, minutes, she did not know how long, Manon heard a voice behind her. The old lady who had always lived opposite and had observed their comings and goings, was calling from her tiny square of front garden. Manon took a deep breath, wiped her eyes with her forearm and walked across the quiet road.

'They've moved to be nearer her parents,' the old woman told her knowledgeably. 'Did you know about...' she nodded woefully at the house.

'Yes.'

'Tragedy, it was. I'd known her since she was a girl. Wait a minute!' Her watery eyes narrowed as she focused on Manon. 'You're the French one, aren't you?'

'Yes.'

'You haven't changed.'

Her tone made what most people would have taken as a compliment into a criticism.

Manon couldn't stop a tiny nervous laugh escaping.

The woman turned her sights back on the empty house opposite.

'Tragedy for the little daughters, and hubby.'

'Yes.'

'Do you have children?' the woman wanted to know.

Her name was Mrs Harris, Manon remembered suddenly, but Annie had given her a nickname. She racked her brain to remember what it was.

'No ... no, I don't...' she replied.

'Well.'

'Well,' Manon repeated, suddenly feeling the need to justify herself, but not knowing how to.

'I've come to take the girls punting,' she faltered. 'I've been to see them quite a lot since Penny died.'

The woman peered at her again.

'You think they'd have told you they were moving, then,' she said, as if she did not believe her.

Mata Harris, Manon suddenly thought, as a bright image of the four of them sitting round the remains of a pasta dish popped into her mind. Mata Harris was the wildly inappropriate nickname Annie had given the old woman.

'Why Mata Harris?' Ursula had asked.

'Because she's a spy,' Annie had replied.

'And it sounds a bit like Mata Hari, I suppose,' Ursula had added.

Annie looked at her pityingly.

'And she's obsessed with our sex lives,' Annie had concluded.

'Those of us who have sex lives,' Ursula had said, giving Annie a critical glare, 'If some of us didn't forget our keys all the time and wake the whole street up at midnight.'

'Oh, you're as bad as the witch across the road,' Annie had retaliated.

'She's just lonely,' Penny had said, always the conciliator, 'poor old thing.'

She's just lonely, Manon thought as she walked away, not quite knowing which direction to go in, but wanting to look as if she knew. She could feel the old woman's malevolent eyes following her all the way back along Joshua Street.

Chapter 15

Ursula looked at the clock. It was typical of Annie to be late, even though she lived just an hour's drive away, but she might have known. She fished about in her handbag. Her hand touched the little package Liam had dropped in. She hesitated, then let it go and pulled out an envelope containing a photograph.

It was the four of them in the yard at Joshua Street during their first summer there. She was taking a strawberry from a bowl that Penny had just put on the table. Annie was pulling a ridiculous face at the camera. Manon was barely visible, reading a book in the criss-crossed shadow of the trellis that Vin had nailed to the back fence for Penny's clematis.

For a moment she wondered how it could have been that Penny had gathered together such different people in the house in Joshua Street. They had had nothing in common then, and even less now. Perhaps it had been the fact that they were all poor. Penny was a vicar's daughter and even though she had been as agnostic as the rest of them in those days, the duty of charity had been drummed in since childhood.

They were all her friends, but almost everyone in college had been a friend of Penny's. People liked her because she was fun and because she seemed so grown up. While the rest of them lurched from one crisis of self-esteem to another, Penny was the person everyone wanted to be. She knew how to do things like remove limescale from a bath and cook a proper omelette. She had a steady boyfriend with whom she had had sex before she even arrived at the University. She advised on the advantages of getting the pill from the Family Planning Clinic rather than the college doctor. Her naturally blond hair was cut in a square bob with all the ends exactly the same length. When she smiled, dimples appeared that made her straightforwardly pretty face look winningly naughty.

Ursula asked for a cappuccino, telling the waitress, 'I'll be ordering my food when my friend arrives.'

They had chosen Brown's because it had been the height of trendiness when they were students.

'How about Brown's?' Annie had suggested on the phone when they were arranging to meet up before the do, and Ursula had felt a slight thrill, replying without hesitation, 'Good idea!'

Twenty years before, neither of them would have been able to afford lunch at Brown's, but now both of them could casually eat there every day if they wanted to without even considering the expense.

The waitresses were still sexily sulky. When she was a student they had made her feel huge with their white tea-towels tucked over their mini-skirted bottoms like upmarket bunny girls. Now that their skinniness could no longer mock her, they just made her feel old instead.

The restaurant had expanded but it still had wall mirrors, brown wooden furniture and palms that made it feel like a colonial veranda. Thousands of cheap eateries had imitated the style, but she had never been in one that had quite succeeded. The hands on the old-fashioned station clock seemed to be moving incredibly slowly. For something to do, she looked in her handbag again. Liam's little package was like a guilt grenade.

'Not to be opened until tomorrow evening...'

His admonition had made her frightened of what might happen if she opened it.

She took out her mobile phone and dialled home. Barry answered.

'I've arrived. Is everything OK?'

'It's fine. Good journey?'

'Fine. How's George?'

'He's fine. A bit grizzly.'

'I expect he'll cheer up when you go off to football.'

'We were just on our way out.'

'Oh. Won't keep you then. Bye.'

'Bye.'

'You will phone if you need me?' she said as an afterthought, but the line had already gone dead.

She pushed down the aerial and shut the phone, feeling slightly self-conscious. The waitress brought her coffee. Speaking to Barry had made her feel superfluous, his barely concealed impatience implying that she was being a bit of a nuisance delaying their departure to the training session.

Shifting around on the unforgiving wooden seat, she wished that Annie would just turn up. She read the menu several times even though she knew most of it by heart. Apart from the salmon fishcakes most of the dishes were the same things she remembered wanting to eat twenty years before.

Finally she picked up the mobile again and dialled Liam's number, picking out each digit tentatively and waiting several seconds before pressing the button that would make the connection. He answered immediately, as if he had been waiting for her to call.

'Hello?' the muzziness of his voice made him sound as if he were lying in bed with a duvet pulled right up to his chin.

'Did I wake you?'

'No, not really. I was just having one of those waking dreams.'

'Ahh,' she giggled, relaxing against the bent-wood back of her seat.

'Ahh, indeed,' he replied.

'I've arrived,' she said, not really knowing why she had called him but feeling better just to hear his voice.

'The dreaming spires,' he said with a yawn. 'Is it a fine day?'

'Yes,' she said, giggling.

They had discovered over their first drink that they had both been students at Oxford at the same time. She had found herself speculating even then what would have happened if their eyes had met across one of the T-shaped tables in the Radcliffe Camera. Except that he had read PPP so he wouldn't have been using the Radcliffe Camera, and she had been so fat then that whenever a man she fancied looked up, he usually looked away.

Not now, she thought, looking at herself in the huge mirror on the wall next to her table.

'I'm in Brown's,' she told him.

'Near Little Trendy Street,' he said.

'Yes!' she giggled again.

'You know, if I left now, I could be with you in time for tea.'

It was the first time he had pinned down in words the floating possibility of meeting her there. She couldn't help smiling ridiculously at herself in the wall mirror, flirting like a school-girl with the voice in her ear. Then suddenly Annie was standing right beside her in the reflection saying,

'Sorry, sorry, sorry, I am so sorry...'

Beneath the spicy perfume, Ursula could smell the clinging sour odour of a recently extinguished cigarette. For a moment, she felt the pure white heat of anger that Annie could still be stupid enough to be smoking when they had a friend who had died of cancer.

'I've got to go,' Ursula said into the phone, 'love,' she added, trying to make the farewell sound more normal for Annie's benefit. Then, flustered, she switched off the phone.

'Don't tell me, I'm late and I only live down the motorway. Sorry, sorry, sorry. I've had the most horrendous twenty-four hours, and I've been driving round for an age trying to find a parking place. God, I'm so hungover! You know when you wake up you sometimes feel really bright and buzzy? I think it's probably still being a bit drunk or something, and then you kind of slip into collapse? Ugh! I need about a gallon of fizzy mineral water and a strong cappuccino. Caffeinated, of course.' Annie grabbed a passing waitress.

The waitress looked at her, wrote down the order, then looked again.

'Yes, I am,' Annie told her briskly, sitting down and turning her full attention to Ursula, 'You look incredibly slim and very cross,' she said.

Ursula couldn't help smiling back. Annie was completely unreliable but there was something so direct and unstoppable about her personality that made it very difficult to be angry with her for more than a minute.

'So who were you talking to? A secret lover?' Annie asked, pointing at the phone that was lying between them on the table.

The way she said it made it sound as if Ursula had about as much chance of having a secret lover as she herself had of being punctual.

Ursula put the phone back into her bag.

'Just Barry,' she said, picking up her coffee cup and tipping it up too hastily so that a blob of cappuccino froth attached itself to her nose. She wiped it away. Then she picked up the menu again for camouflage, stealing a surreptitious glance at Annie across the table. She was wearing a bright silk chiffon dress in a kind of Seventies print in red, black and pink. It clung

to all her curves, making her look more voluptuous and overblown than ever. Her hair had
been expensively highlighted so that if you
hadn't known you would think her a natural
blonde. She was not wearing make-up except
for a slick of letterbox red lipstick which was
exactly the same as the red of her dress and her
smooth leather handbag. She looked like a cross
between Kate Winslet and a barmaid. She made
Ursula feel anaemic.

Annie fished around in her handbag and
pulled out a packet of cigarettes. Ursula glared
at the slim red and white packet.

'Oh don't be cross with me,' Annie said.

'I'm not cross, I was just thinking about Penny.
She didn't smoke, or drink or anything. It's so
unfair.'

'Unfair that it was her that died and not
somebody unworthy like me?' Annie asked,
putting a cigarette into her mouth.

'No, of course not,' Ursula said, now unable to
ask Annie not to smoke. How did Annie always
manage to make everything something to do
with her?

'Look at this,' Ursula said, pulling the photo
out of its envelope again. 'I was thinking what an
odd combination of people we were in Joshua
Street. The only thing we had in common was
Penny.'

'We were her waifs and strays,' Annie said,
lighting up and blowing a cloud of smoke
straight up into the air.

'That makes it sound like Battersea Dogs'
Home.'

117

'I was little orphan Annie and you were the poor Northerner with the posh name because your downtrodden mother had a secret passion for D. H. Lawrence.'

'Don't...'

'Who took the photo?'

'Must have been Vin.'

'I suppose it must. Actually we had other things in common,' Annie said.

'Like?'

'We were all only children.'

'I'm not,' said Ursula.

'Oh, you're right,' Annie acknowledged. 'Well, bang goes the surrogate sibling theory then, although of course she did marry your brother.'

'None of us were what you'd call Oxford types, were we?' said Ursula. 'We were educated at comprehensives.'

'Penny wasn't, nor was Manon...'

'But Manon wasn't a typical boarding-school girl, was she? All of us were the first in our family to go to university. We were all misfits here.'

'Penny wasn't,' said Annie, drawing impatiently on a cigarette, 'but perhaps that's it. You make friends to fill the deficiencies in your own life. Penny liked being with unconventional people because she was so ordinary. It was her way of being unconventional, if you like, except that it just made her appear more normal than ever in comparison. I don't mean that in a nasty way,' she added hastily, seeing Ursula's shocked face, 'and anyway, we're not going to spend the whole day talking about then, are we? I mean, we haven't seen each other for ages. I loved

Penny and all that, but I just can't spend every minute of today reminiscing. D'you know what I mean?'

'Yes,' Ursula said; 'anyway she wouldn't have wanted it.'

'Do you think she would have wanted a Celebration of her Life?' Annie put heavily ironic emphasis on the words.

'If it raised money for her charity, yes, I do,' Ursula said.

'But don't you think we're all here because secretly we're trying to ward off the demon cancer with a donation and a bit of piety?' Annie waved her cigarette around like a wand.

'You may be,' Ursula said.

'So, if she had died in a car crash, would we still be doing this?'

'Oh come on!' said Ursula.

Annie had broken a taboo but it felt uncomfortably as though she might have a point.

'Maybe we would,' she offered weakly. 'I mean, Penny loved college life. I think that's why Leonora thought of it.'

'Lea-bloody-nora!' Annie said, as if she had forgotten her involvement in the project. 'It's probably just an excuse for her to sing to a captive audience.'

'That's so unfair,' Ursula said, barely able to suppress a giggle.

'I bet you ten pounds she sings tonight. See, not even willing to bet a tenth of your per-hour fees!' Annie said.

'I charge two hundred an hour these days,' Ursula corrected.

'...still I suppose what you're saying is that if Penny had still been around, she'd have come to this twenty-year gaudy. You're right. I certainly wouldn't, but Penny would and you would,' she said almost accusingly, 'but Manon definitely wouldn't. Actually I was surprised when she said she was coming to this.'

'How is Manon?' Ursula asked politely.

'Elusive as ever. She works in my club so I see her quite a lot, and you know, even though she's a hat check girl and I'm a famous television personality,' she put a self-mocking emphasis on the words, 'I'm still as jealous as I ever was.'

'Were you jealous?'

'Of course I was. So were you.'

'I was not!'

'Liar! We used to spend half our time bitching about her. I remember you saying that she was so slim you could see the bones in her hands.'

'What's wrong with that?' Ursula asked.

'It was the way that you said it,' Annie replied. 'Anyway, it's not just that she's the sort of person who's effortlessly slim and doesn't fall down stairs when she's wearing Moroccan slippers, it's everything. I mean, did you read her collection of short stories?'

'I don't get time to read.'

'Oh for heaven's sake! Why do people with children always say that?'

'Because it's true,' Ursula offered.

'Well, make time. You'll be shocked.'

'Why?'

'You'll have to read and see,' Annie teased. 'Needless to say, as soon as you write about bizarre sex, all the critics rave about a "rare new voice in fiction", whereas everyone simply assumes that every word I write is sheer autobiography.'

'Well, isn't it?' Ursula said sharply.

'Not entirely,' Annie said, blushing. 'What I mean is Manon does serious readings in Waterstone's, and I have a photographer from the Mirror watching my house.' Annie turned her attention back to the menu. 'Do you want wine, because I know I bloody do.'

'What about your car?' Ursula asked.

'Oh, I left it at the hotel car park, eventually,' Annie confessed with a sheepish look of admission that her initial excuse for lateness had been weak.

'Where are you staying?' Ursula demanded.

'The Randolph. Thought I might as well. What about you?'

'I'm staying in college.'

'In college?'

'I was going to stay with Roy and the girls, but he's sold the house.'

'Sold the house?' Annie repeated, shocked. 'Why?'

'Well, he says it's because it's sensible to be nearer Penny's parents. He's buying a cottage in their village. It will make things easier for him, I think, when he has college dinners and that sort of thing. And I think Joshua Street reminded them all too much of Penny.'

'So they're going to live near where she's buried, that's logical,' Annie said.

'Now you're the one that's looking cross.'

121

'Sorry. It's none of my business. I just feel a bit odd about him selling the house.'

'I did too.'

'I mean, it was our house, wasn't it?' Annie said, picking up the menu.

How come Ursula has got so slim? Annie thought, stealing a glance at her round the side of the menu.

She felt somehow betrayed. Ursula had always been larger than her. Ursula being fatter than you was something you could rely on. How dare she lose weight without even telling her?

She let Ursula order first. A salad, as she suspected.

'So have you been eating nothing but salad?' she asked, trying to think of all the wonderful meals she had eaten recently, but unable to convince herself that they had been worth the fact that the dress she was wearing was actually the largest size and still creased up across her thighs. Gucci was generally quite skimpy and the Italian sizes didn't translate exactly, she told herself. What anyone else would call a 12 they called a 14.

'Not really,' Ursula replied.

There was one thing that Annie hated more than an effortlessly slim person, and that was an obsessive salad eater who pretended that she ate a wide and varied diet.

'Fettucine carbonara and a bottle of the house champagne,' she told the waitress, and was pleased to see Ursula's frown. On Monday she would start a diet in earnest, she promised herself. At the moment she needed a carbo-hydrate fix.

'Champagne?' Ursula repeated.

'It's all I seem to drink these days,' Annie said, airily. 'Oh come on, Ursy, you look like one of those awful people who thinks that champagne is only for weddings and christenings.'

'Don't be ridiculous,' Ursula replied sharply.

'So how is Barry?' Annie asked, feeling slightly more in control.

Their relationship had always been a bit of a power struggle. It was very childish because underneath it all they both knew they liked each other a lot, although they would have been reluctant to admit that to one another.

The waitress brought an ice bucket and twisted the cork out of the bottle with a satisfying pop. Annie tasted the champagne.

'Cheap and cheerful,' she told the waitress; 'a bit like me, really.'

The waitress laughed, hesitated, looked for a moment as if she were about to ask for an autograph, then poured.

They both watched the pale gold liquid foam up to the top of the narrow flutes and settle, then Annie clunked her glass against Ursula's, took a mouthful and said 'Cheers!' all in one go.

'What are we drinking to?' Ursula asked.

'Oh hell, I don't know. To us.' Then, noticing the crestfallen look on Ursula's face, she added, 'well, to Penny if you like.' Annie emptied the rest of the glass into her mouth and poured another.

'Barry's fine,' Ursula said, which reminded

Annie that she had just enquired, although she couldn't have been less interested in the answer. She thought it incredibly boring of Ursula to have married a barrister, especially one called Barry. Barry the barrister. It sounded like one of the characters in a game of Happy Families.

'And the boys?'

'They're fine. George is not too pleased with me leaving him for a whole weekend...'

Drone, drone, drone. Annie pretended to listen, but the champagne had bypassed her stomach and gone straight to her ears. It sounded as if Ursula was talking under water. She could see her lips moving and hear a sort of murmur, but she just couldn't seem to take in any of the words. Ursula was smiling, with that God-they're-hard-work-but-they're-so-fucking-interesting look that mothers always adopted when they were relating their child's latest naively profound utterance.

Did having babies remove certain layers of sensibility from your brain? Annie wondered. Was it actually a chemical reaction born of the massive hormonal change that made mothers fail to notice non-mothers' eyes glazing over as they described the cute phrases their offspring had just coined?

'...and then he said, if Jesus has got the whole world in his hands, what's he standing on?' Ursula finished her anecdote triumphantly.

'Oh, how sweet!' Annie tried to smile sincerely.

'Anyway, how's Max?' Ursula suddenly asked.

'Max? Oh, him. How is he? I don't know, really. Married...'

Annie wished that she had never mentioned her pursuit of Max to Ursula. She tended to divulge confidences to Ursula, partly to shock her and partly because Ursula lived so far away and didn't know anyone, so couldn't possibly tell. She always forgot that Ursula not only remembered everything, but had the annoying habit of correcting Annie on the details of a story she told months before but amended with the passage of time. Ursula's enquiries were sometimes as agonizingly embarrassing as re-reading a teenage diary.

'Anyone else around?' Ursula wanted to know, although she looked about as interested in the answer as Annie had been in George's thoughts about Jesus.

'No. Well, not exactly, unless you count...' for a moment Annie wavered on the edge of telling her about Roy. She took another glug of champagne. Of course she couldn't. You couldn't tell a sister that you had been having wet dreams about her brother. She was quite sure Ursula wouldn't approve of the liaison at all. Ursula was very big on disapproval.

'Actually, I am thinking of having my mother come to live with me,' she announced.

It was the first time she had said it out loud and it sounded rather moral and martyrish. Ursula looked suitably chastened.

That'll teach you to think of me as a selfish bitch who isn't good enough for your brother, Annie thought.

'She's getting rather forgetful,' she elaborated.

'But she's not old,' Ursula said.

Ursula's parents were so ancient, Annie couldn't remember whether they were alive or not. She thought she'd better find out before getting too involved with Roy. Her own mother was one thing, but she didn't want the stable block at the side of their manor house turning into a geriatric nursing home.

'I got her referred. The consultant thought it was probably the onset of Alzheimer's...'

An image of her mother sitting in the huge posh waiting room of the Harley Street neurologist sprang unwanted into Annie's head.

'Well, this is nice,' she had said, leafing through the pages of *House Beautiful,* as if they were about to pick out a whole new look for her dining room.

'... you don't have to be old, apparently.'

Annie tried to fight back the involuntary tears that had suddenly appeared just behind her eyes. If you kept it to yourself it didn't seem as bad as this. She wished she hadn't let Ursula draw her out.

Looking up, she saw the genuine concern on Ursula's face, then remembered exactly why they were friends and why she had told her something that she hadn't told anyone else. Ursula was a kind person and they had known each other all their adult lives.

'I'm so sorry.' Ursula stretched her hand across the table.

'Yeah, thanks,' Annie said, pushing her hair back from her face and looking towards the window desperate for something to distract her attention.

'It *was* Manon,' she suddenly said.

'Manon?'

'I nearly knocked someone over outside Worcester who looked like Manon. Look!'

Manon was standing outside on the pavement facing them, but she hadn't seen them because she was reading the menu. They both started waving at her. Still she didn't notice.

'Wait a minute.' Annie's napkin dropped from her lap to the floor as she stood up and raced towards the door.

Manon took a moment to translate the bright flurry of colour jumping up and down on the other side of the glass into the recognizable figure of Annie.

'You're on another planet,' Annie told her as she pushed open the door: 'we've been shouting and waving for about half an hour.'

It was the first time they had not been separated by the cloakroom counter for quite some time. They were both tall, but Annie's personality and vivid choice of colour made her seem much more corporeal than Manon. Annie was not the sort of person who exchanged air kisses; she hugged with enthusiasm. Manon hugged her back, oddly comforted by her presence. With the house in Joshua Street deserted, and no idea how to get in touch with the children, she had not known what she was going to do with the afternoon.

'You look wonderful,' said Manon.

'So do you,' Annie said, giving her a once-over, 'you've got the body to get away with a cardigan.

They're no good if you've got tits. Like those flat bags you're meant to wear around your waist this season. I mean, great for a credit card, but hopeless if you're carrying round a hairbrush and a couple of tampons.'

Manon stared.

'Joshua Street has been sold,' she said, as if to explain her presence.

'Yes, Ursula's just told me. She's over there.'

'Oh.' Manon hesitated in the entrance.

'What?'

'I didn't expect to see her until tonight.'

'She's not that bad,' Annie said, bringing her voice down to a whisper. 'We've been through all the children bit already.'

For a moment Manon didn't know what she was talking about. Then she smiled. 'I'm starving,' she said.

'So, what else is new?' Annie asked despondently.

Manon knew that her fast metabolism, which allowed her to eat enormous quantities of food and never put on any weight, was one of the many things that stood between them ever becoming very close friends.

'Come and make me feel less guilty about ordering pasta,' Annie said magnanimously, grabbing Manon's arm and guiding her to the table.

'Hello, Ursula,' Manon said.

'Hello, Manon.'

Using each other's name made the exchange seem formal. Manon did not know whether to kiss her. They had shared the house in Joshua

Street for two whole years, but she had known that Ursula tolerated rather than liked her. The only occasions on which they had met since university were at Penny's party and Penny's funeral. The unexpectedness of a chance pre-reunion in Brown's seemed to throw them both back to that awful rainy winter's day when they had stood at the graveside next to one another.

'Is that a Lulu Guinness bag?' Annie enquired, never able to let a silence last for very long.

'Yes,' Manon replied, grateful for the intervention.

'It's gorgeous. I've got one with pink roses on top, but I didn't know she'd done one with red.'

'I think it was a sort of Valentine special,' Manon said.

'Oh ... lucky you.' Annie's face fell dramatically.

'I love your dress,' Manon said quickly.

'Thanks. It's Gucci. Cost a fortune, but when I got it home I suddenly thought, oh God, it looks just like every dress I had in the Seventies and gave away to Oxfam.'

'No!' protested Ursula and Manon simultaneously.

Manon picked up the menu and told the waitress she wanted fishcakes.

'Bloody fishcakes,' said Annie, 'the obligatory fare of the Nineties. I mean what's so great about a bit of mashed potato and a teaspoon of salmon, unless you own the restaurant of course, when you're laughing all the way to the bank. It's like pizza. Whoever thought up pizza was a bloody genius. Make some dough, get some wanker to spin it around a bit, then smear on a teaspoon of genetically modified tomato purée, about a tenth of the salami you'd get in a sandwich, and charge ten quid.'

'Would you rather I chose something else?' Manon asked.

That made Ursula laugh and the tension around the small table suddenly evaporated.

'Well,' said Annie, 'so here we all are...'

'When was the last time we were all together?' Ursula asked, rather pointedly, Annie thought, as if to underline the fact that she had missed Penny's funeral.

'Penny's thirty-eighth birthday party,' Manon said.

'Yes, of course,' said Ursula.

'The last time before that must have been after finals,' Annie said. 'We were all sitting in the Parks wondering where we'd be in twenty years' time. God, the year 2000 seemed unimaginably far away, didn't it?'

'I remember,' Ursula said.

'Do you remember, Manon?' Annie demanded.

'Yes, I do,' Manon responded, but she had a sense of foreboding about the conversation they were about to get into. She did not want to revisit that day with them.

'Have some champagne,' Annie offered, picking the bottle out of the ice bucket. 'Oh, it's empty, how did that happen? Let's get another!'

'I'm not drinking,' Manon said.

'Never?' Annie asked.

'Just not today.'

'Whyever not?'

'Some people don't drink all the time,' Ursula snapped at Annie, intervening on Manon's behalf. 'I don't usually,' she said feebly, looking guiltily at her glass.

'We had a picnic in a hamper,' Annie continued her reminiscences where she had broken off. 'Trust Penny to have a bloody picnic hamper when the rest of the world had plastic carrier bags from Safeway...'

She called the waitress over and ordered more champagne, then she turned to Ursula, and said, slightly accusingly, 'You were the one most likely to be Prime Minister.'

'I don't think so.'

'Yes, you were,' Annie insisted. 'Mrs Thatcher was Prime Minister, and suddenly it was something a woman could be...'

'I certainly didn't think of Mrs Thatcher as a role model,' Ursula said sharply; 'it was only just after the Falklands.' She turned to Manon, making an effort to include her.

'I think you were the one most likely to be rich because you always made more money in the vac than we did,' she said.

'Well, that's a joke,' Manon said, 'I haven't got any money at all!'

She thought briefly of the notes that she had stuffed under her mattress before leaving her flat in Bloomsbury.

'But you could have,' Annie persevered, 'if you wanted to...'

'I suppose if I'd married Rodolfo,' Manon said.

131

'You must be mad,' Annie repeated. 'I'd give anything to be married, let alone rich too.'

'I lived for a long time with a very rich Italian,' Manon explained for Ursula's benefit.

'So he wasn't Mr Right, then?' Ursula asked, feeling stupid as soon as she said it.

'I'm not sure I believe in Mr Right,' Manon said cautiously.

'No, nor am I,' Ursula agreed. 'Do you, Annie?'

'What? Do you think we all have One Great Love? Trouble is, I do. And I mistake him every time.'

The waitress brought their food.

Annie peered into Ursula's salad bowl.

'I always think that rocket tastes like dope smells,' she said, 'but sadly it doesn't make you giggle or say "wow, this green salad is fantastic!"'

Ursula frowned at her, and turned to Manon.

'So what do you do?' she asked.

'Nothing much. I've never had a proper job,' Manon admitted. 'I've travelled a lot. I'm not sure I ever understood the concept of a career...'

'You came from an army family, didn't you?'

Bits of long-forgotten information were filtering back through Ursula's brain. Manon had always moved swiftly from talking about herself to talking about concepts, she remembered. At the time, it had made everyone else's conversation seem rather base and unintelligent. She wondered now whether it hadn't been Manon's way of protecting herself against spilling her soul as the rest of them were always doing.

'What were you going to be then, Annie?' Ursula asked.

'I was going to be a famous actress,' Annie said.

'Well, we got you right, then.'

'I'm not really an actress, not like Judi Dench or something,' Annie protested, looking as if she hoped someone would correct her.

'How is work, by the way?' Ursula asked.

'Fine. The American show is just about to start filming in Toronto. Apparently Canadian crews are cheaper or something and they make it look like New York.'

'I can't believe there's an American version when you stole the whole idea from American shows,' Ursula said.

'I did not steal it.'

'Well, you know what I mean.'

'Who's going to play Annie?'

'Me, of course, and before you tell me that everyone except Tracey Ullman flops when they go to the States, let me tell you that I don't intend to. Penny was the one most likely to be happily married with a family,' Annie suddenly remembered, 'except we all assumed she'd be with Vin.'

'Nobody even knew Roy then, except me, of course,' Ursula said.

'He was there,' said Manon, 'after finals.'

Both women were startled by her contribution to the conversation.

'You're right, I'd forgotten that. He'd come to meet me out of my last exam. It was his first time in Oxford,' said Ursula.

'He was taking the Oxbridge exams in the autumn,' Manon added.

'Yes, he was,' Ursula looked at her oddly.

'We didn't think of who would be most likely to be dead,' said Annie breezily. 'Do you think statistics work like that?' she asked. 'I mean, if one in four women is going to get breast cancer, does that mean that the rest of us are in the clear?'

'Honestly,' Ursula said, 'do you have to be so flip about it?'

'Don't tell me you haven't had the same thought,' Annie said.

Ursula's face, which was slightly pink already, flushed a deeper shade.

'Well, I'm not Prime Minister,' she said, trying to change the subject.

'Would you want to be?' Manon was interested to know. People in England these days didn't seem very interested in politics. She thought perhaps it had gone out of fashion.

'Well, I suppose I would like to have done more. I mean I've been a councillor and a school governor and I'm active in my local party. If I hadn't got pregnant with George, I might have put myself up for selection.'

'I forgot you were chair of Soc Soc,' Annie interrupted.

'I was the one most likely to be Prime Minister because I was the only one of you who ever did anything political,' Ursula said righteously.

'I thought it was because you were so bossy,' Annie teased.

'Do you think all students think that they're

going to do something special, or is it just Oxford?' Ursula wondered. 'I mean, the one most likely to, for God's sake, who did we think we were?'

'The only reason I wanted to be something was to prove to everyone that I could do it despite Oxford, not because of it,' said Annie with feeling.

'And it's our generation of women,' said Ursula, thoughtfully. 'We're the first ones to have the real benefit of the Pill. We were ones our mothers invested all their hopes in. We were the ones who could have it all, you see. Careers, independence, men and children on our terms. The world looked so full of opportunity then.'

'It still does, doesn't it?' said Annie.

'So, have we got it all?' Ursula asked so seriously that Annie and Manon couldn't help giggling. Ursula had always tried to turn an informal conversation over a meal into a properly structured debate.

'You have,' Annie said. 'I mean, a career, a husband, children and, more importantly, you're relatively rich and positively thin.'

'Am I?' Ursula's stern face softened.

'Svelte,' Annie snapped. 'Hey,' she picked a dripping champagne bottle out of the melting ice, squinted at it, saw that it was empty, looked at it crossly, then shoved it top first back into the bucket, 'more?'

'God, no,' said Ursula, 'I'm drunk already.'

'You Manon?' Annie asked.

Manon shook her head.

'Well, what are we going to do?' Annie asked,

135

pushing her chair back onto its two back legs and only just righting herself before she toppled over.

'I think I'll check into my room and have a little nap,' Ursula said. 'I was up early.'

'Oh, for heaven's sake, don't be so bloody middle-aged! It's still early because you would insist on lunch at twelve and now we've got hours to kill. I know, let's have a game of croquet. Are you up for that, Manon?'

'OK,' Manon agreed.

'We'll get the bill,' said Annie, miming writing a cheque at the waitress. 'I'll get it, I've had most of the champagne.'

'No,' both the others protested.

'Of course I will, since I'm the one who did actually get to be rich and famous,' Annie said, unable to resist pointing this out, since no-one else had.

Manon and Ursula exchanged sympathetic looks.

'I need to go to the toilet,' Manon said.

'Me too,' said Ursula.

'Well, I'll go on ahead and see if I can't charm some croquet mallets out of the porter,' Annie said.

'In this mood, we'd better make sure she wins,' Ursula said to Manon's reflection in the mirror as they washed their hands at adjacent sinks.

Manon smiled.

Ursula dusted her nose with powder and reapplied her lipstick.

There was something different about Ursula's

136

face, Manon thought.

Ursula noticed her puzzling.

'Coloured contact lenses,' she said.

'Oh.'

'They are blue, but for some reason they make my eyes look green.'

'Yes. You do look different, and you've lost so much weight... You look lovely.'

It sounded even better with Manon's slight French accent. Ursula felt her face suffusing with a satisfied glow of affection towards her. She tried to think of something nice to say back, but Manon's beauty was so obvious, it seemed silly to point it out.

They walked up Banbury Road side by side. The sun was blindingly bright and hot after the cool gloom of the restaurant.

'Who organized this event?' Manon asked, not really knowing where to re-start the conversation.

'Leonora,' Ursula replied.

'Leonora?'

'You know, JCR president, music scholarship. She used to sing...'

Manon still looked blank.

'You'd be up all night having an essay crisis in the library and you'd come down blearily to get a cup of coffee and check if you'd got any post, and there she'd be, mid-aria by the pigeonholes.'

'Oh, her! And what does she do now?' Manon asked.

'Teaches a bit, I think, sings in a choir, the one Penny sang in, so they remained friends. She's divorced. Two kids.'

Manon detected a certain sourness creeping into Ursula's voice then Ursula stopped walking and looked sideways at Manon as if sizing up whether to go further.

'Actually, I think she's got her sights on Roy – both of them single parents now and both with two, although hers are a bit older,' she said, then sighed. 'It's very well, this reunion, but I can't help thinking it has given her a marvellous excuse to be in touch with him all the time.'

'Oh!' Manon's first thought was of the little girls, and then of Leonora trilling by the pigeon-holes all that time ago. She couldn't imagine now how she had forgotten her.

'And what does Roy think about that?' she asked.

'Oh, I haven't told Roy. It's just not the sort of thing a man would notice, is it? I don't suppose he has any idea that he's quite an attractive proposition for all these single thirty-somethings that seem to be around.'

'And the girls?'

'You'd probably know better than me,' Ursula said, giving her a long look. 'I gather that you see quite a lot of them.' She stopped walking suddenly and turned to face Manon. 'I want to say how grateful I am...'

Manon didn't know what to say. It hadn't occurred to her that Ursula knew anything about her life now, and there was no reason for her to be grateful. She wasn't doing it for her.

'...you see, it is difficult for me because it is a long way and with the best will in the world, I've got three of my own,' Ursula continued.

'Yes, of course,' Manon interrupted. She didn't have the kind of friendship with Ursula that merited excuses and explanations. She did not know what to say to her. 'I enjoy seeing them,' she faltered.

They began to walk again in silence.

'You haven't ever wanted some yourself?' Ursula asked, pushing further at the boundaries of their relationship.

'No,' Manon said quickly. Too quickly.

'I'm sorry,' Ursula said, 'I shouldn't be so nosy...'

Manon said nothing.

Annie appeared at the entrance to the college lodge holding three croquet mallets over her shoulder like muskets.

'Bagsy the red ball,' she said, 'because it matches my outfit.'

Ursula stopped in the lodge to get the key for her room from the porter while Manon and Annie wandered into the quad.

'The smell by the pigeonholes is exactly the same as it was,' Ursula shouted, running to catch up with them. 'I've just had a Proustian memory of college life.'

'What smell?' Annie asked.

'Oh, it's a sort of combination of dust and slightly unwashed femininity.' Ursula said.

'Ugh!' said Annie, 'I thought Proustian memories were meant to be of biscuits or something nice.'

The croquet hoops were already laid out.

'I'm going to dump my bag in my room,'

Ursula told them. 'I'm in the new building,' she said, excitedly.

'Bully for you,' Annie said, 'but we're not going to wait here while you recapture your lost youth. You'll just have to catch up with us when you come down. Be quick!'

Annie looked at Manon. 'You go first,' she commanded.

Manon hit the yellow ball. It reached the first rung but did not go through.

'Shot!' called Annie. 'God, I can't remember the rules. If I hit you through, can I roquet you or not?'

'I've no idea,' said Manon.

'Well, shall we say I can, if I do?'

'OK.' Manon smiled.

It was typical of Annie to want to make the rules to her advantage, but she was so brazen about it, you couldn't help going along with her. The champagne seemed to have made her more competitive than ever. In the sun, her face was almost as red as her dress.

Annie swung wildly at her ball. It veered off the lawn into a border of flowers. 'It's no fun with just two, is it?' she said, quixotically. Then suddenly sitting down on the grass, 'Let's wait for Ursula.'

Manon sat down next to her.

The college quad was exactly as she remembered it, except that the building Ursula had disappeared into had been part of the garden then. She watched a tortoiseshell butterfly flit from a rose bush to a yellow dahlia.

'Shall I tell you a secret,' Annie said suddenly.

'If you want to.' Manon wondered uncomfortably whether Annie would have wanted to reveal what she was about to if she hadn't drunk so much.

'I've decided to have a go at Roy. Do you think that's terrible?'

'No,' said Manon, cautiously.

'For God's sake, don't tell Ursula,' Annie hissed, looking behind her to see that no-one was in earshot. The quad was empty and silent.

'I won't.'

'It would be so perfect, don't you think? I mean, without being too crass about it, I've got money, he's got a ready-made family...'

What would count as too crass? Manon wondered.

'...we're both old enough and wise enough not to fuck each other up. I thought I'd buy a manor house. There's loads round here, aren't there?'

'Oh, you mean, permanently,' Manon said.

'Well, I'm not thinking of a one-night stand, am I?'

Suddenly Manon couldn't help laughing.

'What?' Annie asked, ready to take offence.

'All these women after the attractive widower,' she said.

'All what women?'

'Well, Leonora, you...'

'Leonora?'

'Ursula just said. Oh sorry, I assumed you knew.'

'Bloody Leonora. I might have known. God, that's pretty low, isn't it, to organize a bloody dinner in Penny's memory just to get off with

141

her husband?'

'Well ...' Manon said, unwilling to point out the obvious hypocrisy.

'But Penny was like a sister to me,' Annie said, trying to defend herself.

'Have you seen a lot of Roy, then?' Manon asked.

'Not since ... well, I didn't really know what to say, when Penny died, I was so upset myself and well, I'm not very good at saying the right thing and I didn't want to put my foot in it.' She sighed. 'Actually, I was hopeless when Penny was ill as well. I think I was so nervous about trying to be cheerful all the time, I just couldn't seem to stop using illness metaphors.'

Manon raised an eyebrow.

'...like I'd be telling her about a film I'd seen and I'd find myself saying "I nearly died laughing", and, God,' Annie winced at the memory, 'you remember that hot spell? We were sitting in the yard and she offered me some of the sun cream she was plastering on the babies, which was factor 50 or something ridiculous, and I said, "Oh fuck skin cancer as long as I get a tan!" I can't believe I said that!'

Manon smiled. It was always difficult to know with Annie where fact ended and her imagination began.

'So, anyway,' Annie continued without pausing for breath, 'I sent Roy a card after the funeral, and said if he ever wanted lunch, you know, to cheer him up.'

'And he replied?'

'He sent a nice card saying thanks, and

perhaps when he had got himself sorted out.'

With such scant encouragement, Manon couldn't believe that Annie was entirely serious about taking up with Roy.

'If you really want to know,' Annie went on, oblivious to the fact that Manon didn't, 'I had this dream ... tell you later...' She stopped as Ursula appeared again. Her cream dress had dark spots from where she had splashed water on her face. She sat down beside them on the grass.

The sound of children's voices reverberated suddenly through the stillness of the quad. Simultaneously all three women's heads turned in the direction the noise was coming from.

Chapter 16

'Just one more time!' Lily squealed.

'All right, but this is the last time,' Roy agreed, taking her by both hands and spinning at speed so that she flew round and round horizontal to the lawn, her laughter bubbling through the air.

'Just one more!'

'No,' Roy said, out of breath, 'that was the last time, remember?'

'Oh no!' Lily's expression crumpled from joy to abject despair. 'I want to go home now,' she said.

'You can't go home because we haven't got a home any more,' Saskia told her.

143

'Of course we've got a home,' Roy began, feeling control slipping from his grasp. Sometimes he was so concerned to say nothing that would affect the girls adversely he dithered and he knew that vacillation made them less secure and more frightened than any small untruth he might tell them. Some parents seemed to have complete confidence in their own authority, but he was not one of them.

'Where?' Saskia stood with straight legs, elbows bent, palms upwards looking around the garden as if to say, I can't see it. Is it hiding in the bushes?

'Home is a term we use to mean where our family is,' Roy began.

Both girls stared at him as if he were crazy.

'You've got a new home, but it just isn't ready yet, so you're staying with me and Grandpa until it is,' Geraldine said.

He hadn't been aware that his mother-in-law was observing him. Sometimes he felt as if he was being given marks out of ten.

'I've ironed your shirt, Roy,' she told him.

'Thanks,' he said.

'In fact, I don't want a new home,' Lily announced.

He wondered why she kept saying 'in fact'. Was it something he inadvertently said all the time? It was only when Saskia began to speak that he had been made aware how much he swore.

'And I don't want to stay here either,' Lily added. 'I want to be with Mummy.'

He didn't know in what sense his younger

daughter could remember Penny. She had only been two when she died. He thought that what she missed was the total security of Penny's mothering that nothing he could offer would ever approach. He wondered whether she could see Penny's living face when she closed her eyes, or whether her recollection was a static image from a photograph.

'If we're going punting, you'd better get shorts and T-shirts on,' he told them.

Geraldine had dressed them in pretty pastel dresses with matching cotton hats. He didn't like them being dressed in the same clothes, but he didn't think it was the time to say it. Their looks and characters were so different. Saskia like a tiny diffident model of her mother, and Lily so much darker and braver with brown eyes and curly hair that had to be cut short to keep it tame.

'But they look so pretty,' Geraldine said.

'They're not starring in a Merchant Ivory film, Geraldine, they're going on the river, which is muddy and full of weed.'

'You're quite right,' she told him, tacitly admitting her mistake. 'Come on, girls!'

'Punting, punting!' Lily galloped after her.

It was a beautiful summer day. The verges were lush with grasses and clouds of cow parsley. The air was sweet with pollen. It was the sort of day when whatever your anxieties, you couldn't help feel glad to be alive.

It was right for children to grow up in the country, Roy thought, watching their faces in the rearview mirror as the car wound up out of the village towards the main road. They were pink from a morning playing outside and Saskia's nose had a spattering of freckles.

The house he and Ursula had lived in as children had no garden, only a yard outside. Their mother, who was a nursery school teacher, had read to them of children who spent holidays with distant aunts who lived on farms. He realized now that the books had been anachronistic even then, with their nostalgic descriptions of hand-churning butter and running barefoot to watch steam trains. They had made him yearn for a life that had already disappeared.

Even with crop-spraying and organophosphates, country life must still be healthier for children, mustn't it? There was a stream in the village with fish in it. His children would grow up with the sound of the wind around the rafters as they fell asleep breathing clean air, far away from the drone of traffic and the invisible threat of exhaust.

'Where did Manon say she'd meet you?' Roy asked as they approached North Oxford.

'She didn't say,' Saskia replied.

'Well, where do you usually go, Cherwell boathouse or Magdalen Bridge?'

He looked in the rearview mirror and saw that Saskia was mystified by his question.

'Normally, she meets us at Nancy's...'

He didn't want to get into the debate about home again.

'Well, I think we'll just pop into Mummy's

146

college and see how Leonora's getting on, and then we'll see if Manon's at Cherwell boathouse, shall we?'

'OK, Daddy,' Saskia said.

'I don't like Leonora,' Lily announced.

'Why? She's always very nice to you,' Roy said.

'She sings,' Lily said.

Roy wondered at what age his younger daughter's honesty would be suppressed by a developing sensitivity to other people's feelings. At the moment she was hoovering up vocabulary and testing it out with no idea at all of the effect she was having. On being introduced to the Master of his college she had announced in a voice like a bell, 'You are quite bald, aren't you?'

'But you like singing,' Roy told her.

'Not all the time,' Lily replied, sulkily.

His three-year-old had pinpointed exactly what it was about Leonora's company that made him feel agitated. She was one of those people who could not let silence reign for more than a few seconds. Even if there was a natural pause in the conversation, she felt obliged to fill it with a hum or a short blast of a scale, like a professional soprano warming up. He knew she had quite a good voice and sang in several choirs. Leonora was an operatic name. He wondered suddenly whether her parents had had ambitions for her when they named her, and for a moment he felt himself feeling a little sorry for her.

'I want you to be on your best behaviour because Leonora has put such a lot of work into

147

this evening,' he said.

'Why?' asked Lily.

'For Mummy's charity,' Saskia told her solemnly.

'Mummy's charity,' Lily echoed as Roy pulled into the college car park.

'Ah, here you all are!' said Leonora, greeting them in the lodge, which threw Roy off balance because he was about to explain why he had brought the girls along when he had expressly stated that he would not.

'Yes.'

'Take a look. I think it's come out very well, don't you?' Leonora handed him a printed menu.

The food was described in French. He looked at Leonora's expectant face, thought how he and Penny would have laughed about it and said, 'Yes, fine, Lovely.'

'We've had a couple of cancellations, which brings us down to forty-two, so I thought four tables of eight and ten on top table. There'll be enough room to serve drinks in the hall beforehand too.'

'Whatever...'

She smiled indulgently at him, then bent to talk to the children.

'Have you come to help Daddy?' she asked them in an over-loud voice, as if someone listening in was about to award points for her ability to get on with children.

'No,' said Lily, 'we're going punting with Manon.'

'Manon?'

'Where is she?' Lily demanded.

'I'm afraid I don't know,' Leonora replied.

'Why are you afraid?'

'Come on, Lily,' Roy said, taking her hand, 'lets have a look around. If you can spare us?' he added, remembering his manners.

'You'll be taking the girls home and changing later, will you?' Leonora said.

Roy looked down at his jeans.

'That's the general idea, yes,' he said.

They turned the corner into the quad and there, sitting on the grass, were three familiar figures. For a moment, the arrangement of their bodies was so familiar it made him reel with déjà vu and a terrible sudden feeling of loss. There should be four, he thought, struggling against displaying anger or grief.

Then his two children let go of his hands and started running across the lawn.

'There she is, there she is!'

Only one of the women moved. In a split second she was on her feet, crouching at their height, with both arms outstretched to catch them as they hurtled towards her. He watched her face at the moment of impact, the broad abandoned smile and her eyes closed with the sheer pleasure of two small bodies pounding against her chest.

As he drew nearer, her countenance changed, almost like a cartoon transmogrification, to the reserved, withdrawn, mourning figure he had stood opposite at the graveside. Her eyes would not meet his.

'Hello, Manon,' he said.

'Hello, Roy.'

Conveniently, the girls tugged her away.

'Manon, do you know we haven't got a home now?' Lily announced.

'Manon, are we punting from a boathouse or a bridge?' Saskia asked.

Slowly the other two women stood up, Annie brushing grass clippings from her bottom and smoothing the figure-hugging garish dress over her thighs.

'Hi, Roy,' she said.

'Annie. Good of you to come.' He held out his hand. She had always made him feel awkward and unsophisticated as the teenager he was when they first met.

'Hello, sis,' he greeted Ursula, kissing her on the cheek. She looked different, he thought. There was something very different about her features, but he couldn't work out what it was. It was as if he only vaguely recognized her. She looked almost beautiful.

'We're going punting,' he said. 'Would any of you like to join us?'

'I think I can just about resist,' Annie replied. 'People always think that punting is about reclining in a white muslin dress and trying to look like Helena Bonham Carter, but all I remember is pulling a great heavy boat over runners and getting covered in mud.'

'Have you bought us anything nice?' Lily wanted to know.

'Lily!' Ursula scolded.

'Are you coming, sis?'

Ursula looked nervously at her own cream dress.

'I don't think so,' she said.

Manon was already walking in the direction of the back gate with a small child attached to each hand. Roy shrugged his shoulders apologetically at the rest of them and ran after her.

Chapter 17

'Manon,' said Leonora as she, Ursula and Annie watched the chain of people making their way across the lawn towards the back gate of the college. 'Wasn't she the one with the boyfriend who hung himself?'

'Hanged,' Annie corrected automatically. She'd been hauled over the coals by the headmistress of her secondary school for making the same error in an essay about capital punishment: 'the word is hanged'.

'Was that her?' Leonora asked.

Roy and Saskia reached the gate first. They held it open for Manon and Lily. Then the little group disappeared.

'Yes, she was, but it really wasn't anything to do with her,' Annie said.

'It was in the paper. Wasn't she the daughter of someone famous?'

'No, he was,' Ursula began, then stopped herself, wondering whether Manon was still as sensitive about people knowing that.

'She's awfully pretty,' Leonora remarked. 'What's she done with her life?'

'Her mother was French, so she lived in Paris, modelled a bit, and then she was a croupier I think, and then she met this incredibly rich Italian count and lived in a palace in the middle of Rome.'

You make friends to fill in the deficiencies in your own life, Annie thought, and Manon provided her with exoticism. She liked the fact that she knew her better than Leonora did.

'Goodness! Sounds like a fairy story,' said Leonora. 'And what does she do now?'

'Haven't you read the stories?' Annie asked her.

'Yours?'

'No,' Annie struggled to suppress her irritation. 'Manon's. You must have seen the wonderful reviews,' she forced herself to say. It was the first time she had admitted the brilliance of Manon's work, even to herself.

'She's a writer!' Leonora's face lit up. 'Perhaps I should have asked her to read something tonight?'

Annie thought of one of the most memorable stories, which was entitled 'A Leopardskin Bedspread'. She didn't think that it would have quite fitted Leonora's programme for the evening.

'She's a bit shy.'

'Yes, she seemed a bit quiet,' Leonora said, adding, 'almost sullen.'

Whenever she was with Manon, Annie was

152

eaten up with envy. Manon was not just beautiful, she had the sort of beauty that men died for. She was not just slim, she had the body of a catwalk model. There were umpteen perfect reasons to hate her, but as Annie looked at Leonora and recognized the *schadenfreude* in her face, and the eagerness to embark on a major bitching session, she suddenly felt enormously protective of Manon.

'So what have *you* done with your life, Leonora?' she asked.

'You mean apart from running a home, raising two children by myself, cooking three healthy meals every day and singing in a local choir?' Leonora asked.

'Yes, apart from that,' Annie said, cruelly.

'During term time, I run a music class for the under-fives,' Leonora replied huffily. 'It's not exactly a brilliant career like yours, but it fits in with my children.'

Annie pictured her singing in front of a row of astonished toddlers.

'Anyway, la, la, la, la, la, la, la,' Leonora trilled bravely, 'I'm glad I caught you, because I'm dying to know what you're going to read? And will you go last?'

'What am I going to read?' Annie repeated. 'Well, you tell me!'

Leonora looked bewildered.

'You said you wanted me to read something,' Annie continued, 'so what is it?'

'Oh, I thought you'd have something you'd written.'

'I write about sex and the single girl. I don't

153

think it would be very appropriate.'

'Oh, I see what you mean.'

'Who else is doing something?' Annie asked.

'I've got Jennifer doing Elgar on the cello, then there's Mel, she's the woman who runs the Oxford branch of Penny's charity. She's got cancer too and she's going to read Letter to the Corinthians.'

'Letter to the Corinthians?' Annie asked.

'You know that Faith Hope and Charity one, the one Tony Blair did at Diana's funeral except that he said "Love" instead of "Charity". I think Mel's sticking to the traditional version. What else? La la la. I'm going to sing some *Lieder*, but I was hoping you'd finish us off with something a little more cheerful, so to speak.'

It was going to be worse than Annie had imagined.

'Is this before or after dinner?' she asked.

'After.'

'Wouldn't it be better before? Everyone will be so nervous they won't enjoy their food,' Ursula intervened in Annie's support.

'Mm, you may be right. But I've printed the programme on the back of the menu, you see.'

'I think I'll have to go and work on something in my hotel,' Annie said.

'I'm off for a nap,' said Ursula quickly.

'Fine, fine ... la, la, la ... see you later.'

'How much organization can a dinner for forty take?' Annie whispered, as they watched Leonora marching purposefully towards the dining hall with her clipboard and mobile phone.

'She keeps checking her watch. It's as if she's

154

masterminding a military campaign,' Ursula giggled.

'I mean, what can possibly go wrong?' Annie asked.

She and Ursula exchanged looks.

'You're right, I'd better have a think about what I'm going to say,' she admitted. 'You don't fancy having a wander round, to give me inspiration?'

'I need to sober up,' Ursula said, yawning.

Ursula watched Annie walking towards the back gate slightly unsteadily in her red strappy sandals, then she made her way up to her room.

It was far better equipped than the one she had been allocated in college in her first year, but the bed was just as narrow and hard. Sex had been discouraged then, and obviously still was. She prodded the bed, sat down, bounced, then lay down on her back, looking at the ceiling.

During their first year at Oxford, the college had still been all female. After midnight, men had only been able to enter or leave the college by climbing over the back fence. She had always envied those women who emerged from their rooms with dark shadows under their eyes and the blotchiness of sex around their mouths.

Along with many of the other colleges, St Gertrude's had changed from all-female to mixed in their second year. She supposed that meant the rules had been relaxed on the subject of 'overnight guests', as the college authorities had quaintly called them. By then she had been living out in Joshua Street with Penny and the others. It wouldn't have made any difference to her, anyway, because she had come up to Oxford a virgin, and gone down in the same intact state.

Like everyone else, she had fallen in love, but the man she had chosen was so far out of her league she had been doomed to worship from afar, apart from the one time he had taken her for a drink.

In those days, the number of male students had far exceeded the number of women, but it had never felt to her as if there was a surplus around.

'There are meant to be five of them for each one of us...'

She remembered Annie sounding off about it at the kitchen table in Joshua Street.

'...the trouble is, one has a girlfriend at home, one plays rugby with the boys, at least two are poofs, and the other one wears an anorak and a college scarf.'

Ursula had never understood how someone's choice of clothing could affect their suitability as a boyfriend, but these things had always mattered to Annie.

Annie had been quick to fall in and out of love and bed with men, which must be why she had never married, Ursula thought. In recent years, the more desperate her search for a man, the more picky she seemed to have become. The last time Ursula had visited her in London, there were endless nice men popping round to her flat, or bumping into her in the street, but Annie dismissed all of them in the same peremptory way that she had dismissed the men at Oxford.

'Yes, he's very nice, but you couldn't marry a man who wore a brown leather jacket,' or 'Yeah, he's OK, apart from his shoes.'

The only men she ever went for seemed to be impossible, or married, or both.

Ursula wondered what they would have predicted then if they had tried to foresee their love lives in twenty years' time.

Penny was always going to get married, but they would all have assumed that she would marry Vin, who had been her boyfriend since before Oxford. He had been the head boy of the boys' school when Penny was the head girl of the neighbouring girls' school. They had spent their sixth form together and come up to Oxford together. He rowed for Keble. Penny was a tennis blue. After Oxford they were going to do teaching diplomas, then VSO, then, everyone assumed, return to England to marry, teach and raise a family.

Manon was the most beautiful of them, but eschewed the company of men, or women. Manon was a loner. Men adored her. She could have slept with any man in Oxford, but she was so private a person that Ursula had no idea whether she had been with anyone apart from the boy who had killed himself.

As for herself, well, everyone would have expected her to become a spinster don. She wondered if that expectation had been the reason she had fallen for the first man who ever really paid any attention to her.

Barry's so nice, Annie had said, but Ursula knew that what she meant was Barry's so boring.

I was the one most likely to be Prime Minister, Ursula thought, turning on to her side and staring out of the window as the sudden rainstorm spattered against the glass. When Annie said that, she had felt a *frisson* of pride that people had once thought of her as a person who was going to be someone.

Ursula followed the rivers of rain sliding down the glass. What had she done? Nothing. She wasn't Prime Minister, she wasn't even an MP. It was easier now than it had ever been to be a female MP and yet she wasn't one. If she had been, she would be a bit less docile than the rest of them, but it was too late for hypotheticals. At forty, you either had or hadn't, time had run out for should'ves and could'ves. She had done what she had done, and that was that. Life did not begin at forty any more. She doubted that it ever had.

She was a successful lawyer, she told herself, trying to stave off the sudden gloom that had descended in the room. But not as successful as she would have liked. She had not brought about the release of the Guildford Four or uncovered any major miscarriages of justice. She was married to a barrister who would never take silk, and she was not even a good wife to him.

She was the mother of three healthy, intelligent boys. But she was not a very good mother. She had handed them over to au pairs at quite an early age, and although her children respected her, feared her even, they were not affectionate as some sons were to their mothers. She had never felt comfortable doing the things that mothers were supposed to do with their boys, like taking them to theme parks or buying them baseball hats and hamburgers in loud American restaurants.

She could not call herself a good aunt to her nieces, nor sister to her brother. She was not even sure that she had been a good daughter to her mother since the death of her father. Her insistence that she move to a bungalow near to where they lived meant that her mother was spending her last few years friendless and lonely in a city she did not know and was too old to find out about.

Suddenly, Ursula found herself weeping for the mess she had made of her life.

If Penny were here, she thought, sniffing, trying to conjure up her friend's good sense, she would find a success to balance every failure. But Penny was not there. Her death, which should have made everyone who knew her value their lives more, seemed to have had the opposite effect on Ursula, making her more dissatisfied.

She was painfully aware that she had not even been a good friend to Penny. She had failed to get to grips with Penny's illness because she had been so sure that Penny's strength of character would conquer it. Now she realized that she had only made it more difficult for Penny.

'You have to keep fighting,' she had urged her on the last occasion she had seen her conscious, and Penny had looked cross for the first time in their friendship, and spoken sharply to her.

'The cancer is killing me, Ursy. Don't make it my fault.'

Even right at the end, when Penny sank into madness as the cancer spread to her brain, even in those last days, Ursula had still kept on insisting that there was hope. She had simply refused to believe that Penny could die.

And that had not helped anyone.

Her entire life had been a failure, Ursula thought, staring across the room at the two blobs of Blu-Tack on the wall which were the only sign that this room had ever been occupied, and tears flooded down her cheeks.

Just before the rain stopped, the sun began to shine making the room seem light and dark at the same time.

Somewhere there would be a rainbow, Ursula thought, wanting to run downstairs and out into the quad to catch it, but almost immediately the room was filled with a bright, almost magical, silvery light, and she knew that the rainbow would be gone.

She and Liam had seen a rainbow once, a clear arc of pure colour over the muted grey, yellow and purple of the hills. They sat in the car staring at it through the windscreen, and then it faded so quickly that she wasn't sure that it had ever existed. Neither of them had mentioned it, as if the magic would be broken in the telling.

Liam. Twenty years ago, they had walked the cobbled streets of Oxford unaware of each other's presence. It seemed almost inevitable that they had been unwittingly together in this beautiful city whose every stone seemed to confirm her failure.

Were you talking to a secret lover? Annie's patronizing question rang in her head.

Yes! Yes! Yes! she wanted to scream.

'I could be with you in time for tea...'

If Annie had not arrived at that moment, what would she have replied?

For a second, she envisaged him climbing in over the back gate of the college and stealing up to her room like the man from the Milk Tray adverts.

No. It was a fantasy. The sort of fantasy that the city of dreaming spires conjured up. The sort of fantasy that could only lead to disappointment.

Chapter 18

Annie was on a nostalgic walking tour of the city centre. She passed the St Giles Café which looked exactly as it always had, with green vinyl banquettes and wood-effect Formica tables. Egg and chips was £3.20, which seemed a reasonable increase in the light of inflation. They were still serving transport café fare to students who thought it cool to pack away as much cholesterol as the average HGV driver. She noticed that there were no baguettes or ciabattas here, although she couldn't be sure that there had been a Gaggia machine in her day.

She crossed the tree-lined boulevard to St John's College and ducked her head through the ancient wood door of the lodge. She couldn't remember whether she had ever slept with anyone at St John's, but she did have a vague memory of eating dinner there once. Potato croquettes, she thought, as she walked once around the first quad wondering what it said about her that she could remember the choice of vegetables but not the name of the bloke who had invited her, nor what he looked like, nor whether she had fucked him afterwards. Probably not, she decided. Dinner at St John's had not been worth a fuck. Dinner at Merton, on the other hand...

The food at Balliol had been plentiful but not subtle, she recalled, as she walked past the back entrance before turning into the Broad. Lasagne and chips, cheese and crisp butties in the JCR which opened after the pubs closed for the massive carbohydrate binge they used to call Midnight Raiding. For a while she went out with a guy who lived on Staircase 6. His neighbour, who back then had been a bit of an anorak, the sort of guy who wore bicycle clips on his trousers whether he was cycling or not, was now a successful publisher. She had recently bumped into him and his surprisingly elegant wife at a party.

'Do you still snore?' she had asked him, playfully.

'I don't know,' he replied.

162

'My boyfriend and I used to lie there placing bets on when the next snore would be,' Annie whispered conspiratorially to his wife.

'Sound travels both ways, of course,' the publisher retaliated sharply, and Annie blushed as she thought of all the things she and her boyfriend got up to in those wonderful experimental days of sex, when you didn't yet know what you liked, but were prepared to try anything.

At Trinity, she met her first gay couple, who modelled themselves on characters from *Brideshead Revisited* and owned an *Encyclopaedia of Cocktails*. While everyone else made tea in horrid stained mugs with the teabag still in, they had served Brandy Alexanders in clean martini glasses.

The centre of Oxford was making her feel peculiar. Everything looked the same as it had then. It wasn't really surprising that buildings which had been around for centuries had not altered, but it wasn't just the buildings, it was the shop fronts and the banks, even her favourite pub, the King's Arms. The fruit machine was in the same place, and the noticeboard, which was covered with out-of-date posters advertising garden productions. The walls were the same dark green, the hand-pumps at the bar still dispensed Wadworth's 6X. The same big bowl of coleslaw stood in the chiller cabinet next to what looked like the same greying-pink slabs of veal and ham pie. In London this sort of pub would have become an Irish bar, or a café with minimalist décor, bottled beer and char-grilled vegetables.

There was something distinctly unsettling about the familiarity of it all. Annie walked along the corridor beside the snug bar and down the steps to the loos. The same pink tiles, the same slightly wet floor. It even smelt the same. She was amazed that her own graffiti was not still etched on the wooden door. She sat on the loo craning her head to read the messages.

The graffiti was the only thing to indicate that a new generation inhabited this medieval city. Today's young women had given up lusting after the public school boys and appeared to be lusting after each other instead. Probably very sensible. She remembered all the angst she had been caused by those haughty rich boys who had been denied female company until they came to Oxford. Life would have been so much easier as a lesbian. Trouble was, she had never fancied women. If she was honest, she thought, she didn't even like women very much, except for her mum, and Penny, and Ursula, although she had preferred her before she lost all that weight.

How come Ursula had got so thin? She always had been a bit of a traitor. During the second year when everyone was competing to do the least work, Ursula had snuck off to the college library in the middle of the night. Annie had once caught her returning with a guilty look on her face pretending she'd just gone to the shop to get milk for breakfast. And now she'd gone on a secret diet, so that all the time they'd been sympathizing with each other on the phone

164

about how many clothes seemed to be cut more skimpily these days, Ursula had been chewing on closet celery.

Manon was just as bad. Sitting there laughing about all the women who were after Roy, and then going off with him as soon as he turned up.

Roy had hardly even noticed that Annie was there. But she had to acknowledge that she had felt nothing whatsoever for him either. The moment she saw him coming round the corner of the quad, she had realized that she simply did not fancy him. Never had. Never would. Even making a huge effort to remember exactly how it had felt when he was licking her in the dream didn't do it. So that was that.

Oh well.

In any case manor houses in the Cotswolds were full of mice and stank of manure. Roy was welcome to it, but she wouldn't have been able to stand it for more than an afternoon.

Nevertheless, it was a bit much to see Manon sauntering off with him and the children just like that.

Every man at Oxford had fancied Manon.

'Tell me the truth, is it just her looks? Is she so much more beautiful than everyone else?' Annie had asked the Balliol boyfriend (what was his name?) one afternoon in bed after a marathon session.

'It's not just her looks,' he had said, failing to understand that Annie did not require an honest reply, 'It's that she has mystique.'

'And I don't, I suppose?' Annie had asked, hotly.

'No, but you've got great tits,' he had replied.

The relationship had petered out soon after that.

Annie never had a boyfriend who lasted more than a term. She was fine for a laugh and a fuck, but when reality loomed and the question of introducing her to Mummy and Daddy arose, she never made the grade. Not all the men there were public school boys, but the ones who weren't generally didn't have the confidence to go out with her in the first place. When she arrived she was loud and brash to overcome her nervousness, and the more insecure the experience of Oxford made her, the louder and brasher she became.

She accepted the public school boys' reluctance to take her home with a certain equanimity, because she would never have dreamed of taking one of them home to her own council house in Northolt. During term time, Marjorie kept in touch with her by writing letters on Basildon Bond lined paper that appeared in her pigeonhole once a week, sometimes more often, but Annie could never bring herself to invite her up even for a day.

Annie looked at herself in the mirror above the sink in the King's Arms' ladies' loos and she washed her hands, and felt a terrible sense of regret that there was nothing she could now do to make up for that.

Slowly, she began to walk back along the Broad in the direction of the Randolph, stopping to buy what was left of the daily papers and a copy of

OK! magazine. There was a copy reserved for her at her local newsagent's in London, but she hadn't had time that morning to pick it up and she was dying to see what Posh Spice's wedding dress was like.

It had clouded over, and rain looked imminent. She was passing the Martyr's Memorial when the skies opened and rain poured down in great arcs as if someone were emptying buckets from on high. It was not sensible to run across wet cobblestones in Roberto Vianni sandals. Annie chose to get drenched rather than to break an ankle.

Under the canopy of the hotel entrance, a man still holding a newspaper over his head pushed open the door for her.

'Thanks,' she said, shivering.

'You'd win any wet dress competition...'

The remark cheered her up even though she knew she ought to be offended.

She looked down at her dripping dress – eight hundred pounds-worth of couture clinging to her curves like a bathing costume – then looked up and smiled at him, trying to look disapproving and indulgent at the same time.

He smiled back, then suddenly she was aware of his eyes doing that focusing thing that happened when people recognized her.

'Hang on a minute, you're Annie McClintock, aren't you?' he said.

A fan, she thought, or worse, one of the barmy misogynists who rang the duty log to complain every time her character said something mildly true about men. She took a quick look at his grinning face. Prematurely greying hair, a touch of the Desmond Lynams. He looked harmless enough, if a little eager. They were often the worst.

'No,' she said.

'Oh!'

'But we're often mistaken,' she conceded.

'I'm sorry...'

He looked so embarrassed, she almost felt inclined to tell him the truth. He was wearing a tweed sports jacket, white polo shirt and jeans, and he had the build of someone who played too much golf and not enough tennis. He was the sort of person, she thought, that you might strike up conversation with in the cosy bar just inside the hotel lobby, then go on to tea, or a drink, even a pleasant dinner together. He would be charming enough at making small talk, as long as you kept well away from politics, but he was definitely married. If you went to bed with him it would be a grown-up thing. Ships that pass in the night. He looked as if he would be competent with a condom, but not much more than that.

'Bye then,' she said, walking over to the reception desk.

'Cheers!' he said.

He was the sort of man who said Cheers.

When she was a student, Annie had often wondered what it must be like to stay at the Randolph. It was the place where famous people stayed when they came up to see productions at the Playhouse. Richard Burton, Elizabeth Taylor,

168

people like that. She remembered the time that Ian McKellen, long before he was a Sir and everyone knew he was gay, had come up to see a production of *Dr Faustus*. OUDS had put on a little backstage party for him. When she finally pushed her way into Mr McKellen's orbit, he was so handsome and slight and looked at her so superciliously, she forgot all the intelligent questions she had prepared about his own recent interpretation of the role at a RSC season at the Aldwych, and ended up saying 'I think you're gorgeous' before stumbling backwards and wishing that she could instantly disappear like one of the visions in the play.

The memory of her embarrassment was still so acute that her heart rate quickened at the thought of it. How come memories of shame remained so much longer than memories of praise? she wondered, as she walked up the grand staircase and along the carpeted corridor to her room.

It was decorated rather over-abundantly with heavy curtains and pelmets in the same slightly too dark velvet. The bathroom was equally luxurious. There was a basket containing little bottles of shampoo, conditioner, body lotion and an individually wrapped soap as well as a sewing kit, vanity kit and shoe polisher. Annie had only recently trained herself not to empty these instantly into her spongebag. As a poorly paid actress she had never been able to resist a freebie in case it might come in useful later, even if it was only a showercap that looked like a plastic bag.

'Nice touch,' she said out loud, fingering the complimentary bottle of mineral water standing beside the basket.

In the bedroom she discovered the sachets of instant hot chocolate beside the tea- and coffee-making facilities (or kettle, as Annie preferred to call it). She was disappointed to find no little tartan package of shortbread. The only time she ever ate shortbread was when she was staying in this type of over-fussy hotel room, lying on the bed, watching satellite television, and spooning out globs she had dunked too long in her cup of complimentary hot chocolate. Then, with delight, her eyes fell on the Heritage Hamper which contained four whole packets of organic biscuits, and three full-size pots of conserve. This was really living, she thought, and was weighing up whether to open the lemon curd or the strawberry jam first when she caught sight of a little price card. She put the jars back. There was nothing in the least exciting about the prospect of munching biscuits and jam that you had to pay for.

Annie took off her dress and hung it on a hanger in the wardrobe. It was one of those detachable hangers that wouldn't hang anywhere except in its casing on the rail and it annoyed her. Did hotels really think that people were going to steal their poxy coat hangers. Well, how much did a coat hanger cost, anyway, for God's sake? If you were charging over a hundred pounds per night, surely a stolen coat hanger or two would not eat too voraciously into your profit? She threw open a window. The rain had stopped and the air was cool on her damp skin, like witch hazel.

She looked out of the window at the world going by below. When she was a student the idea of having enough money to check into a hotel like this would have been unimaginable. It was a mark of her achievement, she thought, to have become so blasé that these small pleasures no longer held any excitement for her. She wondered if this had been Liz Taylor's room and whether she had felt the same way. Then she spied the room service menu and ordered a cafetière of freshly ground Colombian coffee and a cream tea. She would run a bath and while she soaked she would think about what she would say about Penny at the dinner. She caught sight of herself in the mirror above the sink and rang down to cancel the tea.

Annie stepped into the bath and sank down through the cool caress of bubbles into the deep, fragrant warm water. The hangover and lunchtime champagne had depressed her spirits, she reasoned, but really there was nothing to be depressed about. She was certainly the most successful and famous woman of her year in college and she was damned if she was going to let anyone ruin her triumphant return. And yet however logical she tried to be, Oxford still made her feel inferior, as it always had.

Since leaving, she had tried therapy (individual, group and aroma), reflexology, detox diets, vitamin supplements, pop psychology, serious psychology, crystals, and even a couple of quasi-cults, but still deep down, or sometimes

171

quite near the surface, she was a trembling mass of insecurity. Particularly the mass bit, Annie thought, sinking further into the water to submerge the folds of her tummy. Maybe she had a chemical imbalance, she thought. Maybe her serotonin-inhibitor levels were too high or low or whatever it was, and she would be better off with Prozac, but having read *Brave New World* at the age of fourteen, she was suspicious of it. Maybe she should stop eating sugar. Or maybe the simple explanation was that she really was inferior.

'Girls like you do not go to Oxford,' her headmistress, Miss Greer, had told her on the occasion she had been caught in the cloakroom selling lipstick samples she had nicked from her mother's demonstration kit.

Annie had never been sure whether it was the lipstick itself (shade: Purple Grape) that had offended the headmistress, or the fact that she was asking money for something that had NOT FOR RESALE stamped all over the box, or whether it was simply that she was the daughter of an Avon lady, when most of her peers had nice families with fathers who were surveyors or solicitors.

Girls like her did win places at Oxford, it turned out, especially when they had something to prove, but Miss Greer had been right in another way because when they got there they were even more out of place than they had been as scholarship girls in posh schools.

The first evening at college made Annie cringe now as it had then. There had been a sherry party to welcome the freshers. Annie had no idea how to hold a glass of sherry and a cigarette and shake hands with her tutors all at the same time. Several times her shoulderbag clonked down her arm to her elbow, jolting the half-schooner of Tio Pepe, and splashing its contents onto her new clompy-heeled suede shoes.

If you didn't have class, you were no-one at Oxford. The strange thing was that until she changed schools after O levels, she and her mum had always thought that being an Avon lady was class. Her mother always made her talk nicely and the television in their home was rationed to costume dramas and *University Challenge,* which was where Annie had heard about Oxford in the first place.

'You can do anything you want to,' Marjorie had always told her. 'Look at me!'

Annie's childhood had been spent in and out of hostels and bedsits while Marjorie struggled to find a job that would provide the income and flexibility to look after them both. But they had learned to cope, the two of them. Every time there was a setback Marjorie would put a bright face on it and call it a character-forming experience. Annie had had enough experiences to form fifty characters by the time she went up to Oxford, and yet silly things like sherry parties and the casual cruelty of emotionally retarded rich boys had undermined her self-confidence more than anything life had previously thrown at her.

Annie stepped out of the bath and put on the towelling robe that was hanging from a hook at the back of the door. It was luxuriously capacious with over-long sleeves and enough material to go round her twice. Inside it, Annie felt almost elfin. With perfect timing, her cafetière arrived and she sat down at the little desk, took some of the notepaper headed Randolph Hotel from the writing folder, and her Mont Blanc biro from her red leather Furla handbag and sat poised for a moment or two. Then she put the pen down and picked up *OK!* to have a quick look at Posh's dress before she started on her speech.

Chapter 19

They reached the river just as it began to rain.

'What are we going to do now?' Roy asked, still holding his jacket over his head, though they were sheltering in the shed where the punts were kept. It smelt of creosote.

Manon shrugged.

'I'm hungry,' Lily said.

'I'm not,' Saskia added, 'I'm starving!'

Roy groaned.

'I've forgotten all about lunch. I never eat during the day, you see, and ... and there's no excuse, is there?'

'It's not such a big deal,' Manon said, alarmed to see him floundering: 'we'll get something here. It's on me,' she added.

She pushed open the door to the Cherwell

Boat House restaurant. The last two diners were paying their bill.

'Last bookings were at two,' the waitress told her.

'Oh.'

The proprietor came out from the kitchen, saw Manon, the children and the rain bucketing down outside.

'It's OK, come and sit down, but you'll have to have the salad and pasta.'

'Thank you!'

Roy watched the man's face change from slightly cross to blushingly privileged as Manon smiled her gratitude at him.

'Haven't you already had lunch?' Roy said to her as they sat down at a wooden table.

'Only fishcakes,' Manon said.

She was sitting opposite him with Saskia, and Lily was beside him. Lily's chin only just reached above the top of the table. Manon picked up a menu and Saskia imitated her, looking at it ever so seriously as if she could read what it said.

'Ricotta and mushroom tortellini in a creamy cheese sauce,' Manon read from the menu. 'Sounds delicious, doesn't it?'

'No,' said Lily.

'Oh Lily!' Manon scolded lightly. Her slight French accent put the emphasis on the second syllable of the name.

Lily frowned.

'I think it sounds delicious, Manon,' Saskia said, looking up at her devotedly.

There was something about the child's

expression and the way that Manon smiled back at her that made it look as if the two of them shared a secret. It was exactly the way Penny and Manon had been together. Penny's natural grace had shone a flattering light on almost anyone in her company, but when she was with Manon, the pair of them seemed almost a greater entity than the sum of both their characters. If it hadn't been so joyous to see their pleasure in each other's company, he would have felt excluded.

'In fact, it is delicious!' Lily said with surprise as the food arrived and she set about manoeuvring the adult-sized fork towards her mouth, dripping sauce on the slats of the table.

'I'm glad we found you,' Roy spoke across the table to Manon.

'You sold the house,' she said. When she spoke to him her words were clipped.

'You went there?'

She nodded.

'It happened quickly. I didn't want to let the sale fall through. I'm in a better position to call the shots on the purchase now.' He stopped talking suddenly as if he had just heard himself. 'I think, I've been spending too much time with estate agents lately. I should have let you know. I thought the girls would tell you. Sometimes they're so grown up I forget that they're only five and three. I probably should have let you all know.'

'It's OK,' Manon interrupted his meandering self-incrimination, 'it's really nothing to do with anyone else.'

She picked up the menu again.

'Let's all have home-made ice cream,' she said.

'Now I know why they enjoy seeing you so much,' Roy remarked. 'I mean, I didn't mean...'

'It's OK,' she said, more softly, 'I know what you meant.'

The rain stopped almost as suddenly as it started. When they emerged from the restaurant the air had cooled.

'Are you still up for this?' Roy asked her.

'Of course.'

'You're hardly dressed for it.' His eyes ran up and down the black dress.

'Well, now you're here, you can punt and I can sit with the girls,' she suggested.

'I want a paddle,' Lily interrupted.

'You'll still get wet. You always get wet on the river,' Roy persisted.

'I don't care,' Manon insisted.

He shrugged his shoulders. The he pushed the punt out from the bank and jumped in. 'We're off!' he said, suddenly sounding excited, like a little boy. 'I'm always in *Swallows and Amazons* when I'm in a boat,' he explained.

'What's Swallows and Amazons?' Saskia asked him.

'It's a book. I'll read it to you.'

'And me?'

'And you, Lily.'

Manon relaxed back against the plastic-covered cushion. She had not really seen Roy with his children since they were much smaller and she

177

sensed that he wasn't entirely comfortable with his role as father and didn't know whether he ought to be strict or relaxed.

He still looked not much older than a boy himself with his longish mop of straw-coloured hair, but he punted downriver with a confident firm technique that showed that he had lived in Oxford for some time. Manon was sitting at the front of the boat, facing him. The little girls were opposite her looking in the direction the punt was travelling. Punting was a wonderfully peaceful and gentle way to spend a summer's afternoon when you were the one being punted. Otherwise, it was a lot of hard work. She looked at her flat black leather-soled ballet shoes and wondered how she had ever imagined that she would be able to punt and look after two small children dressed as she was.

The sun was out again and the air was slightly steamy, as the heat boiled away the clouds. The sudden downpour had driven everyone else off the river. Apart from the sluice and plop of the punting pole, the only sound was of birdsong after rain. The tranquillity silenced even Lily.

Under the deep shade of overhanging trees it was sometimes impossible to see the sky. The surface of the water changed from deep reddy-brown to evanescent turquoise, pale and shimmery as polished silver, as the punt slid into the sunshine.

'Did you see the Monet exhibition?' Manon asked.

'No, I meant to, and the next time I thought about it, it was over. Did you?' Roy crouched down as he pushed the pole into the water, then stood up again.

'He said that he wanted to paint the air around things and the beauty of the air, and just then, I suddenly knew what he meant...' she said.

Roy smiled, not at her particularly, but at the loveliness of the thought. She sighed and let herself relax to a deeper level of peace. Her body was wound up and each breath released another cog on the wheel of tension inside her. Here, now, she could not remember how it had felt to dread seeing Roy again. It was fine. They were grown-ups sharing an afternoon with children. The grass on the riverbanks was long and wavy, the sun-baked pavements of London were far away, and her anxiety too.

'It's heaven, isn't it?' she spoke upwards in Roy's direction.

The sun was shining directly into her eyes now. She shaded her face with her arm, but she couldn't see his expression.

'Mummy is in heaven,' Lily announced.

'Yes,' Manon swallowed, regretting the use of the word.

There was a long silence.

Sluice, plop, sluice, plop. The punting pole marked out time passing like a very slow clock.

'Why isn't she here, then?' Lily asked.

'Come here, my darling...'

Manon leaned forward and put her hands on Lily's waist then jumped her into her lap. She kissed her on the nose, then turned her round so that she was facing Saskia and Roy.

'Heaven is what people call somewhere really

179

beautiful,' she began to improvise, folding her arms over Lily's chest, trying to press love and security into the tiny heart that beat so fast inside the little ribcage, 'and sometimes we find a place in our world that we think is so lovely that we call it heaven, but sometimes we have to go to another world to find it.'

'Do we go on British Airways?' Lily asked.

The sudden shade of a tree brought Roy's face into focus. It was caught in a grimace halfway between laughter and pain. His eyebrows shot up questioningly. You started this, he seemed to be saying, you get out of it yourself. It was a quintessentially adult exchange.

'Of course you don't,' Saskia said, 'it's just your spirit that goes...'

'It's quite difficult to explain,' Manon said. 'Even adults don't really understand all about heaven.'

'Grandpa does,' Saskia corrected her.

'Yes, you're right, he probably does,' Manon acknowledged, grateful for a way out. Sometimes religion made things so much easier.

'Are there any fish in this river?' Lily asked, with no sense of a change in subject.

'I expect so,' Manon said.

'And dolphins?'

'Not dolphins, no.'

'Why?'

'Well, because dolphins live in the sea.'

'Are there dolphins in heaven?'

'There may be. I really don't know.'

Roy was smiling now.

'Lily, don't ask so many questions,' Saskia

scolded her little sister in a tone she must have learned from an adult.

'No, Sas, don't say that,' Roy said gently. 'It's good to ask questions,' he added.

'Manon, did you know there was a whale and he jumped right over a wall!' Lily said.

'Did he really?' Manon giggled.

She loved it when Lily's imagination took flight, or she recounted her impression of something she had seen on a video.

'Yes! In fact, he swam right out to sea, like this...' Lily stood up and jumped. Manon caught her.

'It's very important to sit down when you're in a boat,' she said.

'It's not a boat, it's a punt,' Lily squealed.

'I think we'll stop in a minute and let them have a run around,' Roy said.

They were approaching the Parks. Roy steered the punt towards a spot where it would be easy for the girls to clamber out. As the end of the boat clunked against the riverbank, Manon felt the thud of *déjà vu*. It was the very spot that Annie and Ursula had been talking about at lunch. The one tree of all the hundreds of trees along the river that he could have picked. It was where they had come for a picnic on the day they all finished finals. Had he chosen it, or was his decision to stop there entirely unconscious? He was concentrating on pulling the end of the boat out of the water and she could not see his face, nor find the words to ask him.

The girls leapt out of the punt with the casual

dexterity that children have before they become aware of danger. They ran into the sunlight. Manon stood up and picked her way unsteadily along the boat. Roy offered his arm to help her on to the bank. She looked at it, nervous about taking his hand, not wanting to feel his skin against hers, and then she stumbled and he caught her wrist, taking her choice in the matter away. She regained her balance. He held out his hand again, in an exact repeat of the gesture he had made seconds earlier. This time she accepted it gratefully. His palm was dry and slightly rough. His fingers closed firmly around hers and she felt his strength as he pulled her onto dry land. As he let go, she looked into his eyes, but he was deliberately staring over her shoulder. Then he said, gruffly,

'Where have the girls got to?' and ran after them.

She sat down under the tree, in the place she had sat that time, and kicked off her shoes, wriggling her toes in the air. She watched Roy chasing the girls and listened to their innocent laughter, thinking that uninhibited gurgle of enjoyment was her favourite sound in the world.

'Don't chase me, don't chase me!' Lily shouted, meaning just the opposite, and then they all fell down on the grass.

'Come over here, I've got something to show you,' Manon called, picking up her flowerbasket bag.

'What?'

'Look inside.'

Tiny grass-stained fingers opened the lid.

Inside there was a piece of bread that Manon had filched from the Cherwell Boat House.

'It's bread,' said Saskia matter-of-factly, giving Manon a suspicious look.

'I thought the ducks might be hungry,' Manon said.

'Daddy, Daddy! Come! We're going to feed the ducks!' Lily snatched the bread and began to run along the riverbank toward some ducks she had spotted further down the river.

'Lily, stop!' Roy shouted, suddenly conscious of the danger.

'Wait!' Manon got up and began to run after her. Twigs and hazelnut shells bit into the tender soles of her shoeless feet. She knew immediately that Lily was going to fall in and that she was too far away to do anything about it.

It happened very quickly. Lily stopped running, threw her arm back and hurled the bread with all her body's strength, but failed to let go of it. Then there was a splash and she was in the river, and even though Manon was only running for seconds, her mind raced through all the headlines in the *Oxford Mail* about students drowning, pulled under by mysterious currents, intercut with the opening scene from *Don't Look Now*, which she had seen at a midnight show at the Phoenix, and whose images had haunted her as she walked back home through the darkened streets of Jericho. Lily was going to drown and it would be her fault.

The child was under the water, then Manon was in with her, waist deep, pulling her up and holding her against her chest, not knowing

183

whether it was her own heart or Lily's that she could feel racing against the limply wet cotton of their clothes.

Then Lily began to cry, and Manon's heart filled with gratitude for that frightened wailing sound, loving it even more than the gurgling laughter she had heard only seconds, a lifetime, before.

'Hand her up to me!' Roy was standing on the bank, arms outstretched.

'Mummy! Mummy!' Lily pleaded, clinging on to her. 'Mummy, please, I want my mummy!'

'Give her to me,' Roy ordered.

Manon watched his face as he lifted Lily from her arms and held her to his chest. His eyes were closed as if in silent prayer as he smoothed the wet hair gently away from Lily's brow. The little girl stopped crying almost immediately.

'Are you OK, my darling child?'

She sniffed and looked right into his face.

'In fact, I'm fine.'

'Brave girl,' he said, then he knelt down with her still in his arms and began to peel off her wet clothes. She ran naked into the sunshine.

Manon became aware of the slime of mud and something sharp under her feet, and the chill of the water around her. For a moment, she felt desperately alone. Then she saw Saskia watching her, her face white with shock, and she began to wade towards a shallower place where she could get out.

'You're bleeding,' Roy said.

Manon looked down at her foot. It was covered in brown fronds of weed and a trickle of

184

bright red blood snaked its way down towards her heel.

'Walt a second.'

There was a group of picnickers fifteen yards away. She saw Roy point at a large bottle of Evian on their checkered tablecloth. He returned with it. He picked her foot up by the ankle and poured the water over it. It was lukewarm from the sun.

'It's only a small cut. Does it hurt?' he said gently.

'No,' she replied.

'Are you up to date with your tetanus jabs?' he asked.

She looked at his head, bent solicitously over her foot in the pose of a kindly nurse, but not really knowing what to do. He became aware that she was looking at him. He looked up. Their eyes met.

'It's exactly what Penny would have asked, isn't it?' he asked.

'Yes,' she said.

'Perhaps I'm getting better at this,' he said.

'Yes.'

'Shall we take you to Accident and Emergency?'

'I'm more concerned about Lily,' Manon said. 'Look at her!'

The little girl was prancing around naked in the sunshine, aware that she was the centre of attention, and playing to the gallery.

'I've got the car at St Gertrude's,' he said, looking in the direction of the college.

'But the punt...'

'We'll leave it here and ring them up to explain. They'll send someone to collect it.'

'How practical you are. I never would have thought of that,' Manon told him.

'You'd have punted all the way back upstream with an injured foot and a naked child. Really?' he beamed, then, as if remembering that he was not supposed to look happy, ever, his face fell back into seriousness. 'Well, I suppose having children does make you understand priorities better. Look, I'll take Lily on my shoulders, if you think you can hobble back?'

'Yes, I'm fine.'

'Where are you staying?' he asked.

She looked at him as if she had not understood the question.

'I'm not staying.'

'Well, I've got to take the girls back, so come with us. Maybe Geraldine can find you something to wear tonight. You are coming to the dinner, aren't you?'

He looked at her so pleadingly, she realized that he was dreading it as much as she was.

'I don't know if Geraldine would want me to wear one of her dresses,' she said.

'Well, I've got some jeans and a shirt.'

He was as boyishly callow and sweet as he ever had been. She imagined Ursula's expression if she turned up wearing baggy Levis and a shirt.

'Are you coming?' he asked again, sensing her resistance ebbing away.

'OK, why not?' she said, smiling at him.

Chapter 20

The dress was more elegant than she had expected, but didn't look like the £60,000 Posh had allegedly paid for it. Annie flipped through *OK!* again. The bridesmaids were sweet. She threw the magazine down and looked at her watch. Only three hours to go before the dinner. She had to find something to say. She picked up a newspaper, trying to find a human interest story that might give her a starting point for her speech, but there was nothing appropriate. There was an article which said that most families would soon include a step-parent, another about Mick Jagger and Jerry Hall haggling over the division of their property. If it wasn't marriage, it was divorce. Apparently they had sacrificed a chicken at their Balinese wedding ceremony, but it still wasn't deemed legal.

'The bird died for nothing,' Annie wrote. Then balled up the piece of paper and threw it in the direction of the bin.

It was a matter of finding the voice, but every word on every sheet of Randolph Hotel paper Annie had started had so far failed to achieve the right tone. Why had she ever agreed to say anything? The only reason she had been asked was that she was famous, but she was famous for being the flawed, scatty protagonist of a sitcom and she didn't think that was the right voice for when you were talking about the death of a dear friend.

On the other hand, there was no point in her standing there like an unlikely vicar reading something dignified and uplifting about death. The charity woman would do that and anyway there had been nothing particularly dignified or uplifting about Penny's death. According to Ursula, in the last few weeks she had gone horribly mad, refusing to see Roy or the girls.

'There's nothing particularly dignified or uplifting about death, but...'

Annie crumpled up another piece of paper.

Why could Leonora not just have asked someone to read out the Auden poem from *Four Weddings and a Funeral*, and be done with it?

How about a shared cultural reference point? Shakespeare? A Motown song? The Who? Of course, that was it.

'We all hope that we'll die before we get old...' Annie wrote at the top of a new page. Then under it she scribbled in capital letters:

NO WE DON'T.

What was it that had made Penny mad? she wondered. The physical cause of it was the secondary tumour on her brain, but all that anger that Ursula talked about, had it always been there, hidden beneath layer upon layer of good breeding and good manners? Had the tumour merely eaten away inhibition, or had it actually changed the make-up of the brain? Had there always been a dark side to Penny? Was there a dark side to every human being, that only revealed itself when defences were stripped away by cancer, or age, or Alzheimer's? Was that what people meant by original sin?

If it was, she herself was going to be a vile old woman, because her dark side was so very near to the surface it would only take the most minor illness to strip away the semblance of decent human behaviour. She suddenly realized that she was actually feeling jealous of Penny for her death. Not the madness, of course, but to die so young that everyone remembered you as a saint, and you never had to worry about broken veins on your thighs (or, horror, the side of your nose), or what to do about a pension, or what you were going to wear when black became impossible.

Annie threw down her pen again. The fact was that she was not worthy to make this speech. She had not even been a good friend to Penny when she most needed friends, because selfishly, she could not bear to see Penny deteriorating.

Had she ever been a good friend to her? She was the only one Penny had not made a godmother to her children. Ursula was Saskia's godmother, which was understandable, since she was Roy's sister, but Manon? Who could have chosen Manon over Annie? Penny could. And actually she had been right, because Manon really did take the time to see the little girls every week or so. It was easy to tell herself that Manon *had* the time. But that was rubbish because if Annie had spent half the time seeing the girls that she spent making up excuses not to see them she would see them at least once a month. Perhaps she could still take them to Disneyworld, she thought, even though she wasn't going to marry their father after all.

She stared out of the window, chewing the end of her pen and wondering who was going to be there apart from Ursula, Manon and Leonora. Probably some of the same crowd who always turned up at rites of passage like weddings and fortieth birthday parties. People you thought you were pleased to see and rushed across the room to hug, shouting 'How *are* you???!!!' But after less than half an hour in their company, you understood why you never saw them, even though you only lived half an hour away from each other. It wasn't because you didn't like them exactly, just that time was limited and you simply didn't like them enough to spend an evening of it with them.

Leonora said that there were people who had written to say that they hadn't known Penny well, but had nevertheless been devastated by her death and would like to come. Probably the same people who had written to her, Annie thought uncharitably, the first time her series got a BAFTA nomination. Sad people who didn't have enough drama in their own lives and wanted to have yours by association.

She wrote down RITES OF PASSAGE, then 40TH BIRTHDAY.

In a way it was Penny's fortieth birthday party. It was even close to the date. The only difference was that Penny wouldn't be there herself. Penny had had her big birthday party two years earlier and that was the last time that Annie had seen her.

It had looked much the same as Penny's

wedding. The same yellow and white marquee in the garden of her parents' Cotswold stone vicarage, the same garden-fête smell of recently cut lawn and prize-winning Victoria sponges, and Penny smiling her wonderfully dimpled smile as all the guests filed past her. But at her wedding Penny had not been in a wheelchair, and this time she was not welcoming the guests but saying goodbye to them.

At the time, Annie had thought that if she were having a last birthday party, it would be an evening affair with very loud Seventies music, cigarette girls offering free Marlboro, lines of coke, and cocktails so lethal that the morning after you would be happy to die. But that was because she was single, she realized. When you had children, you had to make the party a nice memory for them of you being alive. You had to be selfless for them even when it was your last chance to be selfish.

It had been a perfect day, if any day like that could be perfect. Penny's daughters, dressed in pinafores and sunhats had waddled around the skirts of the guests. Penny's parents, Geraldine and Trevor, put on a remarkable show of courage under pressure, managing to remember little details about every one of Penny's friends as if they had memorized a list of three facts per person for weeks before.

'Annie, of course. We sometimes watch your programme when we're in. We do enjoy it. And you've just sold your first film script to Hollywood, how exciting ... and Penny said you've just moved to Notting Hill Gate from Shepherd's

Bush. I'm sure that your mother is proud of you. Penny certainly is ... and here's Ursula, well, George is big for his age, it's hard to believe he's only a month or two older than Lily ... Penny says you've been busy at work. We don't know how you manage with three boys and a demanding career ... Manon, you've come a long way from Rome and Penny is so pleased to see you...'

Penny had even made the perfect fortieth birthday party speech.

'I must be the only woman in the world who pretends she's forty, two years early, but I didn't want to miss my own party. Most people die with things left unsaid, but the one good thing about cancer is that you don't, because you have a little notice, and I think I've said everything that I want to say. I've been so lucky in my life. I've had wonderful parents, friends who made me laugh in good times and supported me in difficult times, a dreamboat of a husband and two beautiful children. I am so sorry that I'm not going to see Saskia and Lily grow up, but I know that you will all look after them, and talk to them about me sometimes, and tell them how much I wanted to be with them and how happy they made me. Thank you.'

If Annie had made a speech like that, people would have laughed nervously and waited for the neurotic sting that was bound to be following, but when Penny said it, it was a statement of fact and there was not a dry eye in the marquee.

How could you die at thirty-eight unneurotically?

Chapter 21

'I think it'll get dry if I wash it through by hand and hang it out straight away,' Geraldine said, looking at Manon's dress. 'Come on, let's have it off you.'

'I'll get you a T-shirt,' Roy said, hastily leaving the kitchen as if Manon was about to strip in front of him.

'Run the girl a bath, Roy!' Geraldine called up the stairs after him, then she pointed at a kitchen chair. 'Now let's have a look at this foot.'

Manon sat down. Geraldine inspected her foot seriously and silently, then took a clean plastic bowl from under the sink, filled it with hot water and decanted some salt into it.

'Stick it in there!'

Manon obeyed. The salt stung the cut.

'It was brave of you to jump straight in,' Geraldine said.

'I didn't think about it,' Manon replied.

She knew Geraldine had never liked her, and conversation had always been a strain.

'Mummy is jealous of my friendship with you,' Penny said once, 'because she knows that I tell you things that I don't tell anyone else.'

'Would you like a cup of tea?' Geraldine was asking.

The good old English stand-by.

'Yes, thank you, that would be very nice,'

Manon replied.

Geraldine turned her back to her to fill the kettle and gazed out over the kitchen sink into the garden.

'I don't think we've seen you since the funeral,' she said.

'No.'

'But I know that you see my granddaughters. They talk about you all the time.'

She was trying hard to be friendly, Manon thought.

'I come up for an afternoon every couple of weeks.'

'Is it easy to get time off from your job?'

'I work in the evenings. In the day I try to write.'

'Yes, I bought your collection of stories.'

The unexpectedness of the statement took Manon aback. The whole process of being published and letting other people read her work had been difficult, as well as strangely cathartic, but she had not for a moment considered that someone like Geraldine would get hold of a copy. She waited nervously as Geraldine weighed up what she was going to say.

'Some of them were interesting. I found others a little...' there was a long pause before she said, 'adult.'

'Yes.'

Manon rarely blushed but she could feel her face burning.

'Well written, though. In other circumstances I would recommend them to my book group.'

194

Manon didn't think she could ask what those other circumstances might be. If she had left out 'The Leopardskin Bedspread', the story about two Parisian prostitutes, or 'Purple Sunset', the woman studying the bruises from her first beating, would the volume then have been deemed acceptable?

Or was the problem that the author was someone she knew, so that the work would somehow reflect on her? She hoped that Geraldine wasn't going to ask whether the stories were autobiographical, as one member of the audience always did whenever she read her work in bookshops, as if it were the most original question in the world.

'Are you going to write anything else?' Geraldine wanted to know.

'The publisher wants me to write a novel, but I'm not sure that I have anything to say.'

Manon pictured the table in her anonymous Bloomsbury flat and the yellow notepad lying there with nothing written on it.

'Writers' block?'

'I suppose so.'

The conversation was weird. She had never mentioned her novel to anyone and it was most peculiar that the first person should be Geraldine.

Cautiously, she smiled as Geraldine placed a cup and saucer in front of her, and Geraldine smiled back. Penny's death had softened them both, Manon thought. The same sorrow occupied a huge space in both their lives, and beside it the differences in age, class, morality did not seem so huge.

Roy came back into the kitchen carrying a pair of clean Levis and a handful of T-shirts. She selected a crumpled white one.

'Let me iron it for you,' Geraldine said.

'But I'm only going to be wearing it for an hour or so,' Manon protested.

'Nevertheless...'

She saw that it would please Geraldine to iron the T-shirt.

'Well, thank you,' she said.

'Come on, then.' Geraldine shooed her up to the bathroom and waited outside the door as Manon stripped and handed out her damp dress and knickers.

'No bra?' she said.

'I don't wear one,' Manon replied.

'Nearly forty and not wearing a bra yet,' Geraldine said, and Manon could not tell whether her tone was disapproving or envious. 'I'll send Roy up with the T-shirt and a plaster for that foot.'

Their relationship seemed to be wavering somewhere between mothering and girls' changing-room talk, Manon thought, surprised to find Geraldine's presence warm and comforting, like the big warm apricot towel she had handed her from the airing cupboard.

She turned and caught the reflection of her naked breasts in the mirror above the sink. Was it the light, or just a different mirror that made them look rounder and more pronounced than usual, or could pregnancy already be changing her body? Very tentatively, she cupped her breasts, then dropped her hands suddenly. She could not have a baby, she told herself, crashing back to reality. She was not a fit person to have a baby.

In the bath she washed herself briskly, efficiently, scrubbing away at her skin as if to slough off the patina of sentimentality, then she stood up and hosed herself down with the feeble shower attachment.

There was a knock at the door. She wrapped herself in the soft apricot towel and opened it. The white T-shirt and jeans were lying on the landing outside, pressed and folded with a pair of cotton knickers and box of Elastoplast on top. She picked them up and closed the door again, wondering whether the knickers belonged to Geraldine and whether she had brought them to the door, or whether it had been Roy. She could not imagine Geraldine handing a pair of her knickers to Roy.

She pulled on the jeans and they fell down. Improvising, she pulled a silken rope from the paisley dressing gown that hung on a hook on the back of the door, and tied the jeans up around her waist. She slipped the T-shirt over her head and tucked it in. Then she sat on the bathroom stool and applied a plaster to her foot and towel-dried her hair as much as she could. She stood up, throwing her hair back from her face, and washed out the bath, put the plug in again and began to run another bath for the girls. There was something so homely about the bathroom that she did not want to leave it. She looked out of the window, guessing from the shadows in the garden that it must be at least six o'clock.

On the washing line, her black dress flapped in the mild breeze. Beyond the end of the garden was a small meadow and beyond that the old graveyard of the church.

When she opened the bathroom door, Roy was leaning against the banister of the landing, and his presence made her jump. She had imagined herself all alone upstairs.

'I've come to do the girls' bath,' he said, slightly bashfully, as if he needed to explain his presence.

'It's running.'

'Thank you.'

They both took a step forward at the same time, almost collided, then took a step back.

'Sorry, after you,' he said, then as she did not move, he took a step forward again and so did she, and the same thing happened, like an awkward country dance.

They both laughed nervously.

'You first.'

This time she stepped quickly past him.

Chapter 22

The light was different when Ursula opened her eyes. It was not yet dusk but the sun's rays were soft and golden. Her mouth tasted sour and furry and there was sweat on her forehead, as if she had been startled mid-dream, although she could not remember what she had been dreaming about. She turned over, lazily, willing herself back to sleep, knowing that the headache that was prickling behind her eyes would disappear with just an hour's more rest. Then she sat up, suddenly aware of where she was and why she was there. The noise she had tried to blot out by closing her eyes was not the children playing on the stairs at home, but the sound of women's heels walking along the corridor outside and down the stairs to dinner.

Dinner in Hall. She jumped out of bed and stood in the middle of the room, wondering what to do first. Dinner in Hall had always been ridiculously early and she could remember panicking in exactly the same way now as she had almost every evening of her first year. The food then had been awful, but it was included in the fees. In those days, she had no money apart from her grant. Everything was deep fried, even the most sophisticated dish which they called Chicken Maryland and which consisted of a piece of deep-fried chicken with half a deep-fried banana. It was such a nondescript pile of fat and carbohydrate, it did not deserve a name. The only advantage of the food was that you could always strike up conversation when you sat down to eat. Even if you were in a different year doing a different subject from the other people at your table, you had the pallid, fatty offerings on your plate in common.

There wasn't time to find the bathroom, so Ursula washed her face and under her arms at the hand-basin in the room. Then she slipped on the stone-coloured dress again. The bottom had bagged out slightly, but that only made her look more slim, she decided, as she reapplied her make-up and brushed her hair. It was after 7.30, but she thought she would call home quickly just to check that everything was OK.

As she tipped the contents of her shoulderbag onto the unmade bed, the small department store carrier bag that Liam had slipped into it fell out.

Not to be opened until tomorrow evening, when you're wearing the dress.

There was a little box inside the bag. She toyed with the lid, challenging herself, and then she opened it quickly. Inside was his business card. She smiled and turned it over. There were just three words written on the back:

'You look beautiful'

A current of pleasure ran from the nape of her neck, where he had once kissed her, down to her ankles and back up her legs.

Beneath the card was a necklace in silver and turquoise. It looked vaguely South American, slightly hippyish, and not something that she would have glanced twice at in the shop, but when she put it on, it transformed the simple elegance of her dress into something subtly exotic. The polished silver beamed light onto her face. She looked into the mirror above the sink and saw that her sharp features had softened with desire.

It was the first love token she had ever received from a man. Barry dutifully bought her a mixed bunch of flowers from himself on Valentine's Day, and one from the boys on Mother's Day, but ever since she had rejected the first engagement ring he had bought because she didn't like clusters, he had given up the task of choosing gifts for her and instead bought vouchers. He was not an ungenerous man, but he had no sense of taste.

Liam on the other hand was so stylish and charismatic that she often wondered why he chose to lavish attention on her. She had no idea what it was that he saw in her, especially since when she was with him she always seemed to say stupid things and found herself behaving like a silly girl rather than a mature woman with a good brain.

When she and Barry had been going out for about six months or so she had asked him what it was he liked about her, and he had replied, 'Everything', which had made her feel nice and contented, but she had yearned for specifics. Was she just a nice, plump, clever girl who was up for sex two or three times a week, or did he feel something in his very core when he kissed her? she had demanded to know. Well, both really, came the reply, which she had found frustrating, even though she was grateful.

She could not imagine daring to ask Liam such a question, but looking at her reflection she thought she saw the possible answer in her face. Thinking about Liam made her eyes languid and wicked at the same time. Normally, when she paused to look in the mirror, she saw someone preoccupied, rushing from one commitment to another with no sense of self. Now, she saw a woman contemplating a completely selfish act, a woman inhabiting her body for the first time and liking it enough to indulge it, a woman on the verge of an affair.

She walked across the quad to the dining hall feeling light-headed, then remembered that she had not called home. There was no need, she told herself. If something was wrong they would have rung her. Relax. Enjoy your night of freedom.

As she approached the entrance to the hall she recognized several faces.

'Ursula, is that you? You look wonderful!'

'Ursula, I love your dress.'

'Ursula, you're the only one of us who has improved with age!'

The turquoise and silver necklace at her throat was a talisman.

'You look beautiful, you look beautiful...' Liam's voice was in her head, as she greeted women that she had not seen for many years.

Gillian, the Christian with whom she had enjoyed heated intellectual discussions on the question of faith, and who had always had a supply of biscuits in her room, was now a teacher in a big comprehensive school. Gemma was a freelance editor of women's fiction and had two small children. Lorna, who had been her tutorial partner for Middle English, announced herself as a full-time mother and part-time NCT teacher. They were all juggling their lives between career and family much as she was doing, with the same limited successes and probably the same failures. It occurred to her, as she sipped a glass of sherry, that the main reason she felt such a failure in life might be that the only person she saw these days from Oxford was Annie. Annie was so incredibly successful and her contempt for family life so palpable that whenever Ursula went to visit her in London, she had the definite feeling that Annie was giving up some of her precious time to do a bit of charity work, a bit like a star taking an underprivileged child on a Variety coach to the seaside.

Ursula glanced round the room. Annie had not yet arrived and she couldn't see either Manon or Roy. There was a tall, well-built man standing by the serving hatch chatting to a couple of women she didn't recognize who were giggling over-loudly.

Pinned to an easel near the entrance to the hall was a seating plan with placements.

Leonora came hurrying over. She was wearing a dark green silk dress, clearly home made, that made her look like one of those awkward maids of honour you sometimes see trying to hide from the photographer as you pass a country church wedding on a Saturday afternoon.

'Where are they all, Ursula?' she asked, as if Ursula had hidden her brother and her friends.

'I've no idea,' Ursula replied, 'but it's not late, is it?'

'Seven-thirty for eight and it's now seven forty-five...'

'I'm sure they'll be here,' said Ursula.

'A man has turned up,' Leonora whispered,

taking her to one side and pointing at waist height towards him.

'Yes, I noticed. Who is he?'

'He's the husband of Chloe Brown, née Colefax.'

'What's he doing here, then?'

'Well, he's an alumnus too, one of the first St Gertrude's men. Says he knew Penny a little. Apparently Chloe had to go on a field trip, so he showed up instead. What shall I do with him?' Leonora asked in an urgent whisper.

Ursula shrugged her shoulders.

'I mean, should I put him on the top table? Would that be sensible?'

'Eminently,' Ursula replied. 'With you and Roy?'

She gave Leonora a look that said she knew what she was up to.

'Yes. He'll be more comfortable with another man.'

Leonora turned and hurried away to fuss over something else.

Ursula looked at the seating plan again. She noticed that Manon had been put on the same table as she had, the one furthest away from Roy. Inside the hall, she could see Leonora rearranging the placement cards on the top table. But as she hurried off to check the kitchen staff, the man detached himself from the group of women he was with, sidled over to the top table, and swapped the cards around again.

Chapter 23

Manon was wearing the black dress again.

Geraldine looked at her critically for a moment.

'It looks so plain,' she said. 'Would you like to see if I have any jewellery to cheer it up a bit?'

'No, thank you,' said Manon.

In the almost tangible flatness following her refusal. Manon seemed to sense she might have given offence.

'Perhaps I might borrow this?' she asked, pulling the gold dressing-gown cord she had used to keep up the jeans she had been wearing. She wound it twice round her waist and the result was so effortlessly stylish that even Geraldine's bemused, sceptical face broke into a involuntary smile.

'I'll send it back with Roy,' Manon offered.

Roy felt a slight thrill hearing her voice speak his name. The trace of a French accent that she had brought to the R made the prosaic syllable sound different. When she said it he felt as if he had the potential to be someone else.

'You're very welcome to stay, you know,' Geraldine offered.

'Thank you, but I'm going back to London tonight,' Manon said carefully.

'Well, some other time perhaps, while the girls are with us?'

'Thank you.'

Much to his surprise, Manon approached Geraldine and gave her a kiss on each cheek which Geraldine was clearly not expecting, but accepted with obvious pleasure. He had been nervous of bringing Manon wet and smelling of river to the rectory that afternoon, but perhaps her vulnerability had brought out Geraldine's profound sense of charity, and Manon seemed to have blossomed in the bosom of the older woman's mothering.

'We must be getting a move on,' he said, looking at his watch, 'we're going to be late.'

He and Manon walked down the garden path to the car then turned and waved. Geraldine stood in the doorway waving back. Two little faces blew kisses from the window halfway up the stairs.

'Thank you for rescuing Lily,' Roy said, as they pulled away.

'I was the one who let her fall in,' Manon replied immediately.

She was sitting in the passenger seat next to him as he drove up to the main road away from the village for the second time that day. He took his eyes off the road for a moment to look at her. Her back was stiff and she was staring ahead as if determined not to look at him.

The evening was drawing in and the quality of the light on the fields had changed from glaring to soft, from Brilliant White to Golden Amber, he thought thinking of the myriad colours of paint in the interior decoration magazines that

Geraldine had started buying recently.

He wanted to say something that would make Manon smile at him as she had this afternoon when, thrown together by the spontaneous closeness of near disaster, she had let the invisible barrier between them drop for a few moments.

'Penny once said that you always jumped at the chance to take responsibility for things that went wrong, but you would never jump at the chance to be kind to yourself,' he ventured, and saw immediately that his words infuriated her. Nobody knew better than Manon what Penny had said.

'Anyone would have done what I did,' Manon retorted, opening a window as if she could not breathe in the car. If she could have climbed out and sat on the roof for the rest of the journey to avoid talking to him, he knew that she would have done that.

'Anyone?' he tried to inject a little lightness into the conversation, which seemed to have become much more portentous than he had imagined it could only seconds before. 'You've got to be kidding. Annie would have spent thirty seconds weighing up whether to take off her designer dress, and Ursula would have had to calculate whether the potential danger to her was worth the risk, given that she has three children of her own.'

'That's so unfair!' Manon said, but he could detect the slightest warble of laughter in her voice that acknowledged the accuracy of his sketches.

'And Leonora?' she asked.

'Oh God, Leonora! You don't think she's after me, do you?' he asked.

Manon's sudden peal of laughter turned the inside of the car momentarily into a bubble of happiness, but he didn't know whether she was laughing because the suggestion was so preposterous, or because it was true.

'Are you looking forward to this evening?' he asked.

'Not really.'

'Me neither,' But he found he was smiling at the road. 'I think it was a good thing to do though, don't you?' he asked.

'Penny would have liked it,' Manon said.

She knew the subtext of his question without him having to bring up Penny's name again.

'Yes.'

'She was someone who joined in,' Manon said.

They were not, she was saying. It was something they had in common.

The silence that followed was easier, as if they were both comfortably lost in their thoughts. Several miles passed without him even being aware that he was driving. He was getting to know the route so well.

'When you think about her, do you remember her before she was ill?' he suddenly asked Manon and then wished he had resisted. The barrier between them came down again.

'Of course,' she said, in a clipped voice.

He gripped the steering wheel.

Then, suddenly, as if regretting her bluntness, she turned her head and looked at the side of his face. He could almost feel the thoughts rolling through her head as she understood what he had been asking.

'I think about her in the last few weeks too,' she said, kindly, 'but I don't think that was really her.'

'Don't you?' It was a plea more than a question.

In the month before she died, the secondary tumour that had grown in Penny's brain changed her personality completely. She became angry and towards the end almost violent, lashing out at him and her children whose futures had been denied her. The only person she had been able to tolerate in her presence was Manon.

Roy had been torn between Penny's unspoken wish to die in Joshua Street, and her spoken wish, her first and immediate reaction to being told of the brain tumour, not to let her children see her go mad. He wanted no part of the responsibility for choosing, but everyone seemed to expect it of him. Finally, he had taken the agonizing decision to move her into a hospice. Geraldine and Trevor had supported his decision, but he had never been able to see moving Penny as anything but a failure of care on his part.

The silence in the car was full of unspoken thoughts and questions. He glanced again to his left. Manon's eyes were on the road. Her arm was casually draped along the bottom of the open window, her hair blowing back from her face.

He found himself thinking of a passage in one of her stories where she described the sound of a trickling fountain in the Tivoli gardens and then the sound of a bath running in a flat in the city. Both sounds were of running water, but the first image was filled with calmness and tranquility and the second was alive with threat and fear. He understood suddenly why she had called the book *The Quality of Silence*. He was trying to think how to tell her that when she said, very quietly,

'She loved you very much.'

It was simple, and yet it meant so much because nobody else had bothered to say it to him, and even if they had, it would have meant nothing.

He gulped back the swell of emotion beginning to engulf his throat and eyes and ears.

'I know she did,' he said, finally.

He indicated and stopped the car outside the college.

'And I loved her. Do you think she knew that?'

Manon looked at him.

'Yes, she did.'

He pulled the handbrake up with a loud crack. It felt like the end of a long journey.

Manon turned to him and smiled the same sweet smile he had seen this afternoon, and suddenly he found himself thinking that life could be liveable again.

Chapter 24

The Gucci dress was almost dry, but it had shrivelled in the rain and Annie hadn't the first idea of how to make it go back to its original shape. There wasn't time to request an iron and she would be nervous about applying one to such delicate material. She glanced at the trouser press. Trouser presses had always held a certain fascination for her because every hotel room she had ever been into had one, but she had never met anyone who had used one.

Have you ever used a trouser press? wasn't the first question she asked men she didn't know, but it was fairly high on the list. You could tell quite a lot about a man from the way he reacted.

Trouser press? What do you mean? Wicked smile. Usually meant you were in with a chance.

I've always wondered who does, myself! Inviting laugh. Meant that you were going to be friends.

What's a trouser press? Meant he wasn't really in the right income bracket.

She'd never met one who said: 'Trouser press, yes, I find them very useful when I'm away on business.'

Around the time of the last election a journalist had asked her for a soundbite for a piece he was doing about the sex appeal of the political leaders. John Major was a trouser press man, she had told him. Tony Blair was not. You had to point out these nuances because their political views were virtually indistinguishable.

It was not going to be the Gucci dress, which was just as well, because it was a bit frivolous, she decided, relieved that she had packed an alternative.

Annie pulled it over her head and smoothed it down her body. The trouble with little black dresses were that they were never as little as she would have liked. Also Manon, the thinnest person on earth, was wearing one, which would make her look bigger by comparison. On the other hand, everyone knew that black looked better on blondes. And it was Donna Karan. She looked at the label with satisfaction. The wonderful thing about Donna Karan was the American sizes, which meant she could wear a 10. She knew it was daft and irrational to feel better about wearing a dress with a smaller tiny number sewn into the label that nobody else was likely to see. So, she was daft and irrational.

Annie brushed her hair, reapplied her lipstick, then remembered with dismay that even though she had brought a choice of handbags, she had only packed Nike trainers or ponyskin mules as alternatives to her red sandals. There was a whole cupboard full of black shoes in her flat. The unfairness of it made her want to cry.

She tottered to the taxi rank in the middle of St Giles and instructed the driver to take her to St Gertrude's College. Grumbling, he started the engine, and Annie slumped back into her seat, feeling rather proud of the fact that she was the sort of person who could afford to take a taxi a distance of half a mile if it suited her, as well as having a car that most men would kill for standing idly by in the Randolph garage. Then she wondered whether it wouldn't have been a better idea to drive up to the college gates in her Ferrari so that the others would see her arriving. It would make the red shoes and handbag look more like a stylistic decision than a packing oversight. She would casually drop the keys to her red sports car into her colour-coordinated handbag ... but knowing that lot, she thought, remembering a mass of pasty-faced girls troughing at plates of uniformly brown, fried food, they would all be sitting down to dinner unfashionably early, and wouldn't even notice her accessories.

In the end, it was a good thing that no-one was looking because she always found it impossible to extract herself from a taxi with any dignity, especially in a short dress.

She psyched herself up for an entrance, then took a deep breath and pushed open the door to the hall. There was a split-second drop in the volume of chatter, and then the noise resumed. Annie strode past the easel with the table plan on it, feeling both relieved and slightly irked. Nearly everyone was wearing black. The New Black, she thought, the only colour to wear at the memorial of your first friend to die.

For a second she could not see anyone she recognized, then she spotted Ursula and walked over to the group of people she was talking to.

They were looking at the official photograph of the year's intake at matriculation the week after they came up. They were all wearing subfusc: black skirt, white shirt, black tie, four-cornered hat and gown.

'Now, where are you?' Ursula said, looking up and smiling at Annie.

Annie had been one of the few who refused to buy a copy of the photo at the time. She had been appalled by the degree to which this great University she had dreamed about resembled the school she had hated. But she knew exactly where she was on the photo. Right in the middle wearing an expression she had intended to be ironic, but came out looking fat and smirky.

'Oh, there you are!' said one of the other women, picking her out: 'just the same!'

'Annie, do you remember Gillian?'

'Of course I bloody do,' Annie said, unable to stop herself swearing, as she always had in Gillian's very Christian presence. She did not know whether to shake the woman's hand or kiss her, and ended up doing both,

'You had a never-ending supply of Hob-nobs,' she said.

'You were one of the only people who ever replaced the packets they ate,' Gillian replied.

'Was I?' Annie asked, peculiarly pleased with this recollection of decent behaviour.

'You said that you ate fewer if you kept them in someone else's room.'

Everyone laughed.

'So what are you doing now?' Annie asked her.

'Still doling out biscuits. I've got three kids

and I teach. And you're still eating them,' she added.

'How do you know that?' Surely the black dress wasn't that tight?

'Because I always watch *I Love Annie*.'

Annie found herself blushing.

'So you didn't have kids?' Gillian went on.

Didn't made it sound so final.

If Annie was grateful for one thing in her life it was that she had never heard the ticking of her biological clock, but she thought that might be because she had never met the right man. She didn't want to think that doors were closing around her.

'Not yet,' Annie said, and was grateful to feel a tap on her shoulder.

'Excuse me,' she said to Gillian, then turned round.

The man looked slightly familiar though she could not think where from.

'Hello, Annie,' he said.

The bloke from the Randolph. What on earth was he doing here?

'Ian, Ian Brown,' he said, as if that would jog her memory. 'Do you know, the weirdest coincidence is that there's someone staying in my hotel who looks exactly like you.'

'What are you doing here?' Annie asked him abruptly as if he were at best a nuisance, at worst a stalker.

'I'm a guest.' His eager smile faded slightly.

'But...' she looked around. Everyone else was female. Roy wasn't even there.

'Do you remember Chloe Colefax?' he asked.

Annie searched her memory. What a peculiar question.

'Oh, yes, wait a minute, the one who turned St Gert's boys into St Gert's men,' she said, remembering a rather voluptuous contemporary of theirs with a voracious sexual appetite who had worked her way through the entire intake of spotty youths who had littered the college corridors in their second year.

Ian laughed raucously.

'Whatever happened to her?' Annie wondered out loud, thinking how strange it was not to think of someone for half a lifetime and then suddenly be able to remember everything about them right down to their perfume (Opium). Chloe Colefax.

'I married her,' Ian said.

'Oh...'

'I was a St Gert's boy. You probably don't remember...'

'Sorry. I lived out after my first year.'

'We once had a snog at a party in Exeter,' he continued.

'You and Chloe?'

'You and me.'

She thought it impertinent of him to remember that when she clearly hadn't the slightest idea who he was. She glanced around the room hoping to catch someone's eye, but everyone seemed to be deep in conversation. Nobody had overheard her companion's remark. She looked back at his face, wondering what it was going to take to shrug him off. He smiled again. He was both over-familiar and discreet. It was a peculiar combination, a bit like being in a dirty joke, but not as funny.

'Can't have been very memorable,' she said, sharply, and was delighted to see that she had wounded him.

'The fuck afterwards wasn't,' he countered, 'but the snog, well...'

'We didn't...' suddenly coy, '...make love ... did we?' Annie asked, horrified, although nothing much would have surprised her after one of those Exeter parties. She'd been able to match pints with almost any man in the University, but not joints.

He held her eyes for a good ten seconds. Then his expression changed from teasing to regretful.

'No,' he said, 'sadly we didn't.'

Well that was quite charming anyway.

'So you married Chloe?' Annie said, warming to him a little more. 'Well I never!'

Then suddenly Leonora was tinkling a fork against a glass and everyone began to wander towards their places.

'Have you looked at the table plan?' Ian asked her.

'No, I was late.'

'Well, as chance would have it, you're sitting opposite me,' he said.

'Really?' said Annie. This piece of information came as a relief: she was generally more at home in the company of men. She didn't know why it was exactly, but she often felt a bit of a fraud when she was surrounded by a lot of women and she wasn't feeling very comfortable in this gathering. They were the sort of women who would all start menstruating together, given half a chance.

When they lived in Joshua Street, Ursula and Penny had always had their periods at the same time of the month, she remembered. She didn't know about Manon. It wasn't the sort of thing that Manon would talk about. Annie had been proud that her own cycle resolutely refused to fall into line.

They sat down. There was one empty space at the top table. She wondered whose it was, and then she remembered Roy.

The crockery and cutlery were the same as she remembered. White plates whose glaze had deteriorated to cracked and slightly brown; very large forks and knives. In the middle of each table for eight was one opened bottle of college white and one of college red.

'Penny for them?' Ian said across the table.

'Penny?' she repeated, not understanding, 'Penny for what?'

'Your thoughts.' He looked a little ashamed at his inadvertent *double entendre*.

She hated people who used that expression, especially now that a penny seemed such an insulting amount of money for somebody to offer to see inside your soul. Why had it not gone up with inflation? She looked at him, thinking how much she would charge him for one of her real thoughts and whether he would have the credit to pay it, then she replied.

'I was thinking about menstruation, if you must know. I mean what is the evolutionary point of a group of women menstruating together? It means that they can all only get pregnant at the same time of the month, which is ridiculous if your concern is the perpetuation of the species, isn't it?'

He wasn't as taken aback as she expected him to be.

'That's more Chloe's field than mine,' he said; 'she's a zoologist.'

'Oh, yes, we always did say that she was interested in the lower forms of life,' Annie remarked tartly.

He laughed good-naturedly.

'And where is Chloe today?' she enquired.

'The Galapagos Islands,' he said. 'She wouldn't have missed this for anything else, but the funding came through for the trip and...'

'Oh, everyone's going to the Galapagos Islands these days,' said Annie, impatiently. 'If it's not Tuscany, it's the bloody Galapagos Islands. Why is everyone going to the Galapagos Islands?'

'Turtles,' Ian replied.

'Exactly. What's suddenly so great about turtles?'

'My thoughts entirely.'

'Which is why you're here.'

'Seemed a pity to waste it.'

'Right. And did you know Penny at all?'

'Of course I did. Everyone knew Penny, didn't they? She was the woman every woman wanted to be, and every man wanted to marry.'

'To marry?'

'Well, maybe not then, but ten years later, when they thought about the opportunities they'd missed.'

'I didn't realize that men thought like that.'

'I don't know whether they do. It's what Chloe said.'

'Women think like that all the time,' said Annie. 'We used to sit around the table in Joshua Street doing all those daft games, you know, Tinker, Tailor and all that. What do you do, by the way?'

'I'm a GP,' he said.

'Oh...'

'Something wrong?'

'I just didn't have you down as someone with a responsible kind of job. You look more like a rogue.'

'I think I'll take that as a compliment.'

'Don't, because it means you've ruined this evening for me already. I'm going to spend the rest of dinner feeling guilty that I haven't done something proper with my life,' she complained.

'Tell you what,' he said, 'why don't you pretend I'm a derivatives trader, just for tonight?'

She gave him a long look.

'That's very nice of you. I think I will, if you don't mind.'

He threw back his head and laughed so loudly that the rest of their table stopped talking and looked at Annie in the expectation of her repeating the extremely witty thing she had said. When she didn't, they went back to their *Avocat aux crevettes Marie Rose* starters.

Annie exchanged looks with Ian.

'Have a glass of wine?' he said, picking up the bottle of white wine that everyone else had been too polite, or too abstemious to touch.

'Just a little,' Annie said. 'I've got to say something later.'

Her stomach was full of butterflies and she thought a little alcohol might settle it.

'So who were you going to marry,' Ian said, adding swiftly, 'in the Tinker, Tailor game?'

'Rich man, of course,' Annie said, 'or possibly thief, depending on how broadly you're meant to interpret these things. Actually, I'm surprised each generation doesn't update it. I mean how many tinkers and tailors are there nowadays?'

'Quite a few tailors...'

'You mean designers.' Annie thought for a second. 'Today it would go something like plumber, designer, Gulf War veteran, round the world yachtsman, celebrity chef, novelist, teacher, literary agent ... and instead of silk, satin, cotton, rags, you'd have Vera Wang, Berketex, Monsoon, British Home Stores.'

She seemed to remember Ursula taking great offence at rags being her designated choice of wedding attire. But she needn't have worried because things hadn't worked out as predicted in the fruit stones. Penny (cotton) and Ursula (rags) had been the only two to get married, and, as far as she could remember, both of them had worn silk.

'What's the other one?'

'Coach, carriage, wheelbarrow, dungcart,' Annie replied automatically. 'I always rather liked the idea of being pushed to my nuptials in a wheelbarrow. One of the only romantic things that happened to me here was when some bloke pushed me home from a ball in a shopping

221

trolley. I remember lying there in this bloody great borrowed Anna Belinda dress, gazing at the stars as I trundled along and thinking that this was how Oxford was supposed to be...'

'This place made you think you could do anything.' Ian smiled nostalgically.

'Oh, don't go all *Glittering Prizes* on me,' Annie said sharply. 'It was freezing cold most of the year, and full of public school twits.'

'I know what you mean,' he said.

'Do you?'

'I was a grammar school boy and they never let you forget it.'

She was beginning to like him.

'So when did you and Chloe tie the knot?' she asked.

'Straight after I graduated. A bit young, really, but Chloe wanted kids fast so that she could get on with her career after.'

'I thought we were the generation that did it the other way round?'

'Not Chloe. Human biology A level, you see. She thought her body would be more likely to conceive, bear and recover if she had them early.'

'So did you?'

'One of each, before I was even a houseman. Zoe's applying to St Gert's next year, Michael has just done GCSE's.'

'How very organized,' Annie said.

The waitress removed their small white plates and placed a larger white plate with a slab of very pink salmon, a pool of yellow sauce and a sprig of lamb's lettuce in front of them. At the other end of the table there was a bowl of new potatoes.

They appeared to have come to the end of what they had to say to each other. Annie turned to the person sitting next to her, but she was deep in conversation about nannies and professional distance. At the far end of the hall, Annie saw, Roy had just arrived, with Manon. Roy made his way to the top table, while Manon looked around for a place and eventually caught sight of Ursula waving at her.

Annie turned back to Ian who had just put a forkful of salmon into his mouth. 'Have you ever used a trouser press?' she asked him.

A flake of fish flew across the table, as he coughed with surprise, then he swallowed the rest and replied with quite a naughty smile:

'What for?'

Chapter 25

'Where have you been?' Ursula whispered to Manon, as she sat down next to her.

'Lily fell in the river.' Manon saw the alarm on Ursula's face and added, 'She's fine, but we all got a bit wet and went back to Penny's parents to clean up...'

'I saved a starter for you,' said Ursula.

Everyone else was on to their second course. Manon began to wolf down the fan of avocado decorated with pink sauce and a prawn on the small white plate in front of her.

It was difficult to unstick the labels that attached themselves to you, particularly in somewhere as claustrophobic as Oxford, she thought, glancing around the room.

Ursula was the organizer. As an undergraduate she was always collecting money for causes or putting up posters about demos. Now she was marshalling the circulation of the bowls of vegetables on their table, counting the new potatoes and declaring that there were three each.

On the far side of the hall, Annie, the flirt, had landed herself the only other man in the room while she was waiting for Roy to arrive. Manon could tell from Annie's body language that he was getting the full Annie, the smiling, self-mocking, slightly risqué performance that she did when men were around.

The woman opposite her leaned across the table.

'You're Manon, aren't you?'

'Yes.'

'I'm Gillian.' She smiled in a friendly way. 'You were the one who ... got a double first.'

Was there a slight pause, or was she just imagining it, Manon wondered, knowing her own label was the one with the boyfriend who killed himself. It had haunted her time at Oxford, and it haunted her still. Leonora had not been able to wait until she was out of earshot before repeating it this afternoon.

Just before Mods, the exams at the end of the

first year, her first boyfriend had been found dead in his room. His suicide note was addressed to Manon. It was that piece of information, rather than the fact that he had a history of depression, that had made the local paper, and because he was the son of a newspaper magnate, the story had added *frisson* for the tabloids and spawned a rash of fatuous articles about the pressures on the children of famous parents, posing the usual questions about sex and drugs.

In the days following Carl's death, just as she was beginning Mods, Manon's life had been invaded by reporters. They had stationed themselves outside the back and front gates of the college, and followed her in cars as she cycled to her exams. Her stricken face had appeared in several national newspapers, which had only added to the unreality of the knowledge that Carl was no longer alive. Ironically, the one place she had been able to find any kind of peace was sitting in the huge halls of the Examination Schools answering questions on Tennyson.

Manon had been an outsider in the college from the day she arrived. She knew that she had been labelled stand-offish because people did not understand that you could be shy at the same time as being beautiful. The appearance of an association with Carl's death singled her out as truly peculiar. Girls who had grudgingly said hello to her by the pigeonholes now hurried away when they saw her coming. She felt as if she had been tried and found guilty of Carl's murder.

If it hadn't been for Penny, she didn't know whether she would have survived. Penny was the only one who tried to understand what she was going through. Before Mods, Manon had only ever spoken to Penny in the Anglo-Saxon tutorials they had shared during the first term. The pressure of work at Oxford made it frighteningly easy not to speak to a soul for weeks on end.

After their first exam, Penny approached her.

'I'm going to go and get us both some lunch, then you won't have to run the gauntlet outside,' she announced.

And before Manon could say anything, she disappeared, reappearing five minutes later with cream cheese sandwiches from the café across the road from Schools.

'I forgot to ask you what you wanted,' she said, 'but cream cheese is easy to eat when your tummy's full of nerves, isn't it?'

And to Manon, who didn't know when she had last eaten, the soft white bread and soft white filling of the sandwiches had tasted ambrosial.

'We're not supposed to be here between exams,' Penny said, sitting down on the cold stone staircase, 'but I had a word, and they're going to make an exception.'

The Examination Schools had emptied for lunch and her voice echoed around the cool stone chambers. Manon sat down on a lower step. stunned that Penny had managed to charm the brutish university officials who wore bowler hats and were known as bulldogs.

'Don't you have to...?' she had faltered,

suddenly so tired from the effort of holding herself together, she could not even finish her thought.

'What I don't know now, I'm not going to find out in the next hour, am I?' Penny interrupted the rest of the sentence.

For a while they said nothing, then Penny seemed to sense that the weight of the silence between them was becoming difficult to bear and said, 'Please say if you don't want to talk about it, but if you do, I'll be glad to listen.'

And Manon had known that the offer was genuinely altruistic and not in the least prurient. She had felt Penny's sympathy right in the core of her, and she had begun to tell her how terribly lonely she was.

After Mods, Manon had returned to Paris for the summer. It had been easier there, speaking a different language, anonymous in a great city where nobody looked at her twice in the street trying to figure out where they had seen her face. She had almost decided not to return to Oxford, when her results arrived. She had a first. And then Penny had called on her way home from an Inter-Rail trip around Europe. They had coffee together between trains on the concourse of the Gare du Nord, and Penny had offered her a room in the house on Joshua Street. She thought she would be safe there, and so she had returned.

Nobody mentioned Carl again during her time in Oxford, until almost the end, just before finals, when the university paper ran an article about contemporary Oxford characters which compared Manon to Zuleika Dobson, Max Beerbohm's fictional beauty who had cost a whole college of Oxford undergraduates their lives. The day after exams finished, Manon left Oxford vowing never to return. It was a promise she had kept until Penny's thirty-eighth birthday party.

'I lived upstairs from you in the first year,' Gillian was saying.

Manon only vaguely remembered her. She racked her brain for something sensible to say.

'I thought your book was absolutely brilliant,' Gillian went on. 'We all read it at our book group and I'm afraid I was a bit of a show-off, because I knew you.'

'Oh. Thank you,' Manon said, bewildered by the fact that another unlikely person had read her stories.

'Do you live in London now?' the woman continued.

'Yes.'

'Perhaps you'd come to one of our evenings and talk to us about your writing?'

I haven't got anything to say about it, Manon thought.

'Well, if you...' she nodded.

'Oh good! Shall we swap numbers now? We'll only forget later.'

'I don't have a number,' Manon said, 'but you can always leave a message at the Compton Club in Soho.'

When she had first moved into her flat, the phone had been disconnected and she hadn't been able to afford the reconnection charge. She knew very few people in London, and anyone could find her at the club if they wanted to. She had grown to like the fact that no-one, not even a voice, could enter her home without her permission.

Gillian stared at her.

'Well, I'll give you mine.' She burrowed around in her capacious handbag and pulled out a reel of gold sticky labels on which her name, address and telephone numbers were printed.

'Have you got anything to stick this to?' she asked, looking at Manon's tiny flowerbasket bag.

'Not really,' Manon said.

Gillian delved again and came up with a till receipt from Asda to which she stuck the label and handed it over.

'My business card,' she said, which made them both laugh.

Manon handed the waitress her empty plate and received her pink slab and yellow pool.

'It looks like custard,' she whispered to Ursula.

'Tastes rather like it too,' Ursula said, emptying the wine bottle in front of her in her glass, then holding it up in the air. Another waitress came and replaced it with a full one. A moment later there was a hand at every table holding an empty bottle in the air, and the noise level seemed to increase a decibel or two.

Manon sat and listened to the conversations going on around the table. Gillian was explaining how her book group worked to a woman called Gemma who had some connection with publishing. Ursula, who was looking rather flushed, had aggressively taken on the woman opposite her who turned out to be a New Labour MP.

'You weren't in the Labour Party when you were here, were you?' Ursula demanded.

'Not really,' said the MP. 'Thatcherism seemed so insurmountable, then, didn't it? There didn't seem much point after the Falklands.'

'There was for some of us,' Ursula replied.

'Are the women making a difference to Parliament?' Manon asked, neutrally.

'Oh yes,' the MP said, 'It's a quiet revolution, but it is happening.'

'Revolution? Really? That's not a word you expect to hear from the mouth of a Blairite!' Ursula said tartly.

The woman smiled at her fixedly.

'I always wanted to be in politics myself,' Ursula went on, 'but I don't think I could have kept my mouth shut long enough for the Labour Party nowadays.'

'Perhaps not,' the woman said.

Ursula downed another glass of wine and looked the other way. Manon noticed that the fingers of her left hand kept creeping to her throat and twiddling with the beads of a silver and turquoise necklace that she had not been wearing earlier.

Raucous laughter pealed across the room from where Annie was sitting.

'Are you married?'

As the dinner plates were swept away from the table, Gillian leaned across the table and attempted to engage Manon in conversation again.

'No,' Manon said, then realized that it would sound rude not to elaborate further, 'I was...' *fidanzata,* she thought, unable to remember for a moment the English word: pledged? no 'engaged', she said, finally, 'I was engaged for a long time, but, in the end, I, I just left.'

She didn't often think about Rodolfo these days, which was odd considering the number of years they had been together, but she had never felt deeply about him, and she did not think that he was capable of feeling deeply about anyone. Some people were born so rich and privileged that they did not understand need. The capacity to feel someone else's pain depended on having experienced pain yourself, and Rodolfo had not. That was one of his attractions.

They had met in the casino in Estoril. He was there for the Grand Prix, following the Ferrari team. She was working as a croupier. One of the drivers had wanted to take her out, but she had chosen to accept Rodolfo's invitation instead. They had dinner together. His eyes were like a bird's. You could not see a soul in them.

A few days later, when he asked her to go back to Italy with him, he described the garden of his palace in Rome, and she pictured herself sitting in the sun, breathing air scented with orange blossom, and the sound of fountains playing around her. She decided she had spent long enough listening to the clatter of the roulette ball, the plastic clack clack of stacking chips, long enough breathing refrigerated air in rooms with no windows or clocks while the rest of the world slept.

'What about you? Are you married?' Manon asked, suddenly remembering the rules of normal conversation.

'I married Mark,' Gillian responded. 'He was at New College,' she elaborated, as Manon's face showed no sign of recognition, 'he knew Carl. We all went to a garden production of *Songs of Innocence and Experience* together.'

A misty image of wet seats in New College garden after a shower filtered to the front of Manon's mind.

'I don't remember much about that time,' she said.

Gillian's face had lost its bright smile.

'It took us a long time to come to terms with Carl's death, and it must have been so much worse for you,' she said.

Manon stared at her in confusion. She had always thought of Carl's death as her own burden. She had never really considered the other lives it had affected.

'I haven't talked about Carl for a long time. Never, really...' she stuttered.

Gillian smiled at her encouragingly.

'Perhaps you should,' she said, and then when Manon did not reply, she added, 'I'm sorry, I'm training to be a bereavement counsellor at the moment, so I'm more interested than I should be.'

'No, you're probably right,' Manon said, trying to show her that she wasn't offended.

'You see I understand more about it now than I did then,' Gillian continued. 'There are certain distinct stages of bereavement and each one takes its time, but it is important to go through them all...'

Manon began to feel oddly as if Penny's spirit was taking over their conversation, just as it had taken over her life during her first-year exams all those years ago.

'...first denial and shock, of course. Some people will experience this as numbness, or a sense that it isn't really happening, then loss, then often anger and nearly always guilt, you know, "if I'd just been there", that kind of thing?'

'Yes, I know about that,' Manon said.

'Depression often, and loneliness,' Gillian rattled on, 'they don't have to be in that order, and finally, acceptance which is the beginning of the healing process...'

'I think I got stuck ... somewhere between guilt and loneliness,' Manon said, with a glimmer of a self-mocking smile.

'Then perhaps you *should* talk to someone. It's never too late.'

'Perhaps,' Manon agreed.

'I'm glad we've spoken. Your stories brought it all back, you see,' Gillian said.

'My stories?'

'They are resonant with loss.'

Manon fell silent again. Resonant with loss was a good enough phrase, the sort of phrase that would have impressed their modern literature don who had been a published poet himself. Gillian was not wrong, exactly, but Manon suddenly felt uncomfortable being the subject of literary analysis. Writing was a strange process of sifting experience and thought to form a different reality that had its own logic and language. It was not the simple cut and paste of autobiography. She did not think that she would go to talk to Gillian's book group.

'What do you think of the food?' Ursula said, as an individual raspberry pavlova was placed in front of each of them.

Manon looked at it, and then at Ursula's face which was distinctly flushed.

'Pink,' she said, 'it's all very pink...'

'Which is more than you can say for the politics,' Ursula said with a significant look at the MP, who was now chatting to Gillian about failing schools. 'She won't get away with it with Gillian,' Ursula whispered, 'she's better at proselytizing than I am. You two seem to be having a very animated conversation about death,' she added.

Then, realizing the absurdity of what she had just said, Ursula began to giggle and Manon couldn't seem to stop herself giggling too.

Chapter 26

'I think Penny would have liked this' – Leonora blew a puff of meringue crumbs towards Roy as she spoke – 'don't you?'

He nodded, but could not bring himself to agree with her. He couldn't stand the banality surrounding death. He hated the smugness of mourners and the way they congratulated themselves at every opportunity for knowing what the dead person would have wanted. He hated the way that intelligent people were suddenly unable to say anything controversial about the person who had died. There is no doubt that Penny would have enjoyed a reunion of her friends had she been alive. The point was that she wasn't alive.

Penny had not been sentimental about death. He remembered very clearly a conversation he had had with her early in their relationship, shortly after his father had died. They were eating an Indian meal after seeing a movie. He recalled particularly the sound of her crunching poppadoms as he recounted some of the family canon of stories about Roy Senior: his adventures as a young communist, his bravery during the war, his disillusion with his colleagues during the miners' strike, which seemed to have led directly to his decline. It was the first death of a close relative that Roy had experienced, and as he struggled to make sense of his loss, he found himself saying,

'People live on, don't they, in all the stories others tell about them. It's a kind of existence, isn't it?'

And Penny had replied with glorious bluntness:

'It is for the people left behind.'

He had watched her scraping the last of the mango chutney from the little stainless steel dish between them and seen her suddenly as someone different from the pretty friend of his sister who was fun to go out with every so often. He realized that he had expected her simply to agree with him, not to point out the uncomfortable emptiness of his proposition. Her clarity that day had come as a delightful surprise to him and significantly altered the way he felt about her. It wasn't that she was unsympathetic. Penny was the most sympathetic person in the world. But she was also the most rigorously honest.

Penny had not even allowed herself many moments of sentimentality about her own death. The first punch of fear had sent her reeling, but she had steadied herself, and set about sorting out the practicalities. Penny was a great believer in practice over theory. She had made him repeat endlessly the different rituals that Saskia and Lily liked to observe, the names of their teddies and dolls, the books they most enjoyed at bedtime.

'Just because they're losing their mother doesn't mean they have to lose the whole structure of their world. You must not go to pieces, Roy. That wouldn't be fair.'

He looked around the hall at the women exchanging stories about his wife. He knew that all of them were sharing memories of Penny's kindness and goodness. He knew that was as it should be, but sometimes he yearned for someone to remember how sharp she was capable of being, or some distasteful habit she had. Even something as petty as the fact that on occasion she peed in the bath, because she couldn't be bothered to get out.

'Oh, I've weed in here,' she had told him, laughing, the first time he had climbed in with her. 'I'm afraid it's the lazy habit of an only child.'

Penny was a gorgeous human being, but she was no saint, and remembering her with no edges diminished her and seemed to make the loss of her even more intense than the plain, terrible fact that she was dead.

These are not thoughts he had yet dared to voice to anyone else for fear of expressing himself badly, or them taking it the wrong way. But now, as he looked across the hall to where Manon was sitting, he thought that she would probably understand.

Or perhaps he was just trying to find excuses for the inexorable disorientating sensation of being drawn towards her.

'The girls seem very happy and confident.' Leonora tried to engage him again.

'Yes,' he said, defensively.

Confident was usually a euphemism for rude. He knew she was referring to Lily.

'It's quite a job doing it all on your own, isn't it?' Leonora persisted.

'I have a lot of help. Especially now, my mother-in-law...'

He didn't want to be pitied, but he saw that his rejection of her sympathy wounded her. He remembered urging his daughters to be nice to Leonora earlier in the day and felt bad that he wasn't capable of making the effort. She was irritating him more than usual tonight because his mind was already struggling to pay attention to what was going on around him, and every interruption made him lose his concentration.

He smiled apologetically at her, but she turned towards Jennifer, the cellist, and began to discuss the moral outcry over a recent film about Jacqueline du Pré.

He looked at Manon again. She was nodding at something the earnest woman opposite her was saying. He wanted to know what it was that she was agreeing with.

It occurred to him that he would never have an answer to the question that was preoccupying him. He had no way of judging whether Penny would have approved or disapproved of the way he was feeling about Manon. He could sometimes almost hear what Penny would say about the children's education, or moving house, but it was beyond the power of his imagination to summon up her opinion about whether this attraction to her best friend was shameful or perfectly natural.

It was a question he would never have asked her, he suddenly realized with a ripple of relief, because when she was alive he had not felt this way.

The earnest woman had turned to talk to her neighbour. Manon's expression was bewildered, like a shy little girl at a children's party where she did not know anyone. He wanted to go and rescue her. He wished that the two of them could just slip out of the hall together unnoticed and go for dinner in some quiet restaurant. His need to talk to her was almost physical.

'...you'll find it easier when they go to school. At least they come home totally exhausted...' Leonora was speaking to him again.

'Do they?' he smiled inanely.

The idea of having a relationship with another woman had not even crossed his mind until this afternoon on the river (or was it earlier, in the Cherwell Boat House, or even before that, on the lawn of St Gert's quad the moment he caught sight of Manon's face animated by love for his children?). Now he wondered whether it would ever be possible, or whether it would always be a betrayal. He knew without asking that Ursula, and Penny's other friends, would see it that way. It felt almost sacrilegious to be having such thoughts at this gathering, and so lonely to have the responsibility of deciding.

He poured himself another glass of college red, and pushed his pudding to the side of his plate.

'Full up?' Leonora asked.

'Yes.'

239

'If you'll excuse me, I have some breathing exercises to do,' Leonora told him, paying him back, he thought, for his reluctance to talk.

He didn't know whether he was meant to watch or not as Leonora warmed up, but he thought it politer to look away. He could feel the exaggerated rise and fall of her chest next to him. He thought how he and Penny would have howled about it in bed, and couldn't stop himself smiling.

He looked over to Manon and Ursula's table again. Now they were both laughing together. Penny would have been pleased to see that, he thought, wryly acknowledging his own slide into cliché.

Then Leonora tinkled her fork against her glass and stood up.

'Jennifer is going to play Elgar's cello concerto while coffee and *petits fours* are served,' she announced.

Chapter 27

The noise level in the hall dropped to near silence apart from a few coughs and some throat-clearing.

'Why does that always happen?' Annie whispered.

'What?' asked Ian.

'Why do people clear their throats before someone plays?'

'I suppose because they know that they won't be able to during the performance,' he suggested.

'But, I mean, who does need to? Nobody clears their throat normally, do they? I've been talking to you for the best part of an hour and I haven't cleared my throat once.'

'Perhaps it's nervousness...'

'But what have they all got to be nervous about? They're not playing, are they? I'm nervous because I'm giving the keynote bloody speech, but I'm not clearing my throat...'

'That's because you're talking.'

'Sssh,' hissed Leonora from the other end of the table.

Jennifer was a rather plain and serious girl who read classics. Her shoulder-length mousy hair which she had always worn in a longish bob was now streaked with grey and her fringe had been cut too short, which made her look permanently surprised. She was wearing a gathered calf-length skirt of Indian cotton with a batik-type pattern in purples and greens. It was the sort of fabric that had been fashionable in the Seventies and had tried to make a comeback in recent years, but never really succeeded unless it was by Gucci and cost several hundred pounds. Jennifer's skirt had not cost several hundred pounds. You could tell from the unflattering gathered waistband and the way the hem dipped at the back. She sat down on the solitary chair that had been provided for her beside the top table, and as she struggled to get her instrument in tune, Annie wondered idly whether she had bought the skirt from a market stall or whether it was one she had kept since she was an undergraduate. It didn't look faded enough to be an original, and yet she could not see Jennifer having the fashion sense to buy a new one.

Then Jennifer looked up, as if taking a cue from an invisible conductor, and began to play. The low, rich notes from the instrument slid through the hall like syrup, settling the twittering gathering, and reaching depths in Annie's consciousness where considerations about fashion became suddenly shameful. Jennifer could really play, she realized, shocked, and grudgingly admiring.

There was no coughing now. Annie glanced around. Everyone was staring at the stage. Some had tears in their eyes. The music had taken over the room, joining every one of them there together. In twenty years' time, if they were all to meet again, she thought, they would look back and remember not Penny, but the way Jennifer had played that time. The music was moving them on. Not towards forgetting grief, because grief was in the music too, but towards celebrating grief as part of their humanity.

Annie found herself looking at Roy's distant gaze as he stared out from the platform. His hair was still thick and fair and he still had the sort of fresh, classically handsome face that was every mother's dream date for her daughter. Over the last few years his features had changed somehow from a boy to a man. From Brad Pitt to Robert Redford, she thought. Robert

Redford as he was in *All the President's Men,* not ancient and lined like he was in *The Horse Whisperer.* But she had never fancied him even when he was the Sundance Kid.

Roy's gaze travelled past Jennifer's bow, through the huge darkened glass windows of the hall, and beyond, to some faraway time when he had heard this music with Penny, or perhaps to some even more distant place, some point in his life where he had found his identity.

Everyone had a point in their life like that, where great music, or art, took them, or where they imagined themselves for a split second when they were called upon to say who they were, Annie thought.

For her, it was standing in the empty front room of the little house in Northolt with its gas fire and onyx-coloured carpet, just before they moved in, long before they had any furniture, and her mother saying,

'Well, Annie, I think we've arrived!'

She had experienced a similar moment when she had looked out of the tall front windows of the flat in Notting Hill for the first time. There was a huge pink cherry tree in full blossom just below the window and expensive cars parked in the street. The airy room had thirteen-foot ceilings, cornicing and stripped floorboards.

'What do you think?' the estate agent had said behind her.

I think I'm the type of person who could buy a place like this, she had told herself excitedly.

Then the music stopped.

243

There was a hush, and then, next to her, Ian started clapping and everyone else followed him, and all the faces in the room changed from serious contemplation to laughter and congratulation. Jennifer took a modest bow and looked towards Leonora, not sure what to do next. Leonora stood up and the clapping gradually died down. Annie felt a peculiar combination of elation and sadness that the moment was over. Reality filtered once more into the room and there was a chorus of coughing. Jennifer had upped the ante. Annie reached for her handbag to extract a packet of cigarettes. There were no ashtrays, but surely no-one was going to object when she had a speech to deliver?

'Give us one of those,' Ian said, as she lit up a Marlboro.

'But you're a doctor!' she whispered, shocked.

'Oh, we're the worst. But I don't often.'

'I'm going to take it up again at sixty,' she told him, taking her first drag.

'But you haven't given up.'

'No, but I'm going to when I'm forty.'

'It's very bad for you,' he said, inhaling.

'Don't start. I know all the health risks and they make me feel so terrible I need to smoke even more.'

The woman from Penny's charity was talking about the support group she and Penny had set up in Oxford for young women with breast cancer. Annie noticed Ursula glaring up at her from the other side of the hall. Guiltily she

244

extinguished the cigarette in her untouched meringue nest.

Then Leonora stood up and handed the woman an envelope which she said contained a cheque for £4,823, the money raised from tickets to the dinner and donations. Annie wondered who could possibly have given three pounds, until she remembered that Leonora had had to fund the food and wine from the contributions too and that was bound to make it an uneven number. She kicked herself for not asking Leonora how much had been raised, because she would happily have made it up to £5,000. It seemed so cheap of Leonora to have been so precise about it. Even £4,800 would have sounded better than £4,823.

Then suddenly, Leonora was singing, and Annie noticed a couple of women turning over their menus to check the running order because in her haste and determination, Leonora had actually jumped the queue, before the cancer woman had had a chance to do her reading.

Leonora's performance took on a slightly comic edge. The atmosphere in the room changed from concert to music hall. From the strange contortions her face managed to achieve, the songs she had chosen were clearly meaningful, but the lyrics were all in German. Annie's emotions balanced briefly between pity and hysteria, and ended up bubbling out of her mouth in a cough of barely disguised giggling. Ian looked at her with feigned sternness.

Leonora sang three songs when two would have been more than enough. By the end of the third, Annie was making exaggerated faces towards Ursula and Manon's table, trying to get them to laugh too. All at once, Leonora sat down. There was a burst of feeble clapping, then the cancer woman read from the Bible, which calmed everyone down. Just as Annie decided she ought to pop to the loo before her turn, Leonora tapped her fork so forcefully against her glass that it shattered.

There was a moment of stunned silence. Then Leonora was pointing at Annie with the fork as if accusing her, and Annie realized that her time had come. As she pushed back her chair, it grated on the floor.

'You're probably wondering why Leonora asked me to speak. I certainly am...'

Small rumble of laughter, a bit like the first joke in her show when the people in the live audience were still a bit nervous about laughing and the crew hadn't quite got themselves organized.

'...I was a friend of Penny's. I'd like to say her best friend, but there are several others in the room who have a better claim than I do, and it was indicative of Penny's character that if I asked these forty people gathered here who was Penny's best friend then at least three of you would stand up and probably the other forty-seven would wish they could...'

There was a murmur of agreement.

'Penny was simply a fabulous person. She had everything. She was intelligent, kind and pretty and she could do things like make a soufflé. I mean, do you remember how we were then? I had trouble working out how to cook a Pot Noodle...'

Slight laugh.

'Penny was a great listener...'

Lots of nods.

'And a great giver... As a matter of fact, she gave me my big break. I rang her up to tell her how nervous I was about doing a stand-up routine, and I went on for hours about how I didn't have anything to say ... and Penny said to me, just be yourself, which was a really in-sightful piece of advice ... or maybe she just wanted to get me off the phone...'

Polite laughter.

'It was typically unselfish of Penny to start with Mel–' Annie waved in the direction of the cancer woman – 'a branch of a charity to help others when there was no time for it to help her... I would have spent my last few weeks choosing the flowers for my funeral and buying the perfect dress to be buried in ... but then Penny was a proper person, she knew who she was and if she hadn't been so incredibly nice we all would have hated her...'

Silence.

'...or at least I would, because I'm a very jealous person...'

A glimmer of redemptive laughter.

'I was thinking on my way here tonight...'

This was getting a bit too much like a variety act, thought Annie: wrong tone.

'...that it would have been Penny's fortieth birthday in a couple of weeks' time. Some of you are probably already forty, and some of you, like me, coming up to it any moment now, and you have that really big decision to make, don't you? Should I have a fortieth birthday party? The dilemma is basically this: would it be more depressing to see the whole of my life in one room, or to stay at home, watch television and pretend it isn't happening?'

Uncomfortable shifting around as people wondered where the speech was going.

'...and I was thinking that we are a uniquely disadvantaged generation of women, because we're the ones who hit our mid-life crisis exactly as the millenium draws to a close, so not only do we have this huge weight of expectation that we should have done something significant before we're forty, it's multiplied a thousand times by the fact that we definitely should have done something significant before the dawn of the new century...'

One or two smiles as she touched a nerve.

'I call it Pre-Millenial Tension.'

A belly laugh from Ian's direction.

'But we're uniquely lucky too. We're the have-it-all generation. We're the first real products of the pill because as soon as we were sixteen doctors were handing us little green packets of Microgynon even if we'd come about an ingrowing toenail...'

Laughter.

'...and we had several years to have tons of sex before AIDS arrived.'

A few sniffs of disapproval.

'We're the ones who looked at our mothers

and thought, I don't have to be like that...'

Awkward shifting of bums.

'...we were even the last generation to leave this town with no real fear of unemployment. It was possible then to be a real student, have a good time, do very little work and still expect to rule the world in twenty years' time. We had free education and equal opportunities without ever having to fight for it. We had ambition. We had the two most powerful forces guiding us – our mothers' expectations, and women's magazines. Education, liberation, ambition, advertising ... it's a pretty potent cocktail...'

Annie took a sip from her wine glass.

'D'you remember cocktails? Do you remember how cool you thought you looked with a paper umbrella and a wedge of pineapple stuck up your nose as you tried to sip lurid green froth?'

Laugh.

'...of course, our generation's chunk of metaphorical pineapple was choice. That great Thatcherite buzz word that falls out of the lips of Blairites just as easily as the novelty straw in your first Pina Colada did.'

Smiles of recognition.

'You know what happens when you drink cocktails too enthusiastically? Well, we drank our cocktail of ambition, education, freedom and choice just a bit too recklessly, and what did we get?'

Pause, while people wonder what the answer will be.

'...I'll tell you what we got. We got a massive

hangover called angst. How much of your day do you spend worrying? I don't just mean about whether the world's going to end tonight – I think it's tonight, isn't it, according to Nostradamus? – I mean every day. Let's start in the morning. If you're single, it's trying to remember how many alcohol units you consumed the night before, and if you're married with kids it's how much fibre there is in your breakfast. You go to work, or you stay at home, and if you're not worrying about whether you've come as far as you wanted to, you're worrying about where you're going. If you've got a family, you worry about whether you're a good mother to your children, you try to remember all the hamburgers they've eaten and whether they were before or after the new food regulations were brought in, and whether gelatin in fruit pastilles counts, and even if you convince yourself that they've never eaten a BSE prion in their lives, you've got genetically modified food to contend with which you may have been inadvertently consuming for several years. If you're single, you just worry about whether you're fat. You worry about getting a suntan, and then you worry that you'll get osteoporosis if you don't, and then actually you begin to worry about worrying. You wonder whether you should get yourself analysed, or whether you should be on Prozac. You buy a crystal, you join a yoga class, you splash out on a facial, and that leads to more worry about whether you're following a skincare routine properly or flossing your teeth often enough...'

Laughter. Got you, thought Annie.

'...and whatever your circumstances your biggest worry is getting old. Be honest, isn't it? Even if you couch your own worries in terms of how long you're going to be around to look after your children, your primary fear is your own mortality, which you didn't even think about until somebody called you an elderly primi-gravida, or you had that awful realization that you could no longer get away with Top Shop clothes, or your best friend died...'

No coughs now.

'...you see lines on your face and you try Vitamin E and when that makes no difference, it's on to AHAs, and then you worry that if you start plastering on the retinol, you'll have to do it every day for the rest of your life. You suddenly understand why film stars inject their lips with collagen – you never knew that you were going to get lines round your mouth too. And whenever you see your friends you end up discussing the politics of plastic surgery, and whether any of you would be daft enough to have injections of botulism to freeze your muscles in your forehead to make it just the way it was before you noticed the frown lines...'

More laughter. Thank God, I'm not the only one, Annie thought.

'...and isn't it true that once you've seen those lines, they seem to get worse in certain lights, and you wonder how long they've been there without you even noticing? Then people stop saying "you don't look thirty-six" when you scrape two years off your age. Weird, isn't it, that

251

when you were fifteen you'd have given anything to look twenty-one, and now you wonder why you didn't start shedding years before it looked so obvious. Then you start getting invited to fortieth birthday parties, and because yours is still a way off, you feel a little bit smug and you think, "is so-and-so really forty already?" but then you're choosing the gift and you're wondering why you're spending so much money and then you realize it's because it's your turn next. If you're still single, friends of your parents have got beyond asking, partly because several of them have recently died, and the ones who are alive now assume that you're old enough to be called an old maid, or you're a lesbian...'

Annie caught a whiff of smugness from several tables.

'...and if you're married, your husband is very likely to have had one affair already, I'm talking statistics, and there are friends of your teenage daughter getting pregnant, so you don't even have the dignity of being the age that mothers are any more...'

That wiped the self-satisfaction off their faces.

'Doesn't it feel weird that our generation is in power now? We are the grown-ups. It is our time. What does that mean? It means that the Prime Minister is someone whose years at Oxford must almost have coincided with ours, and if things had been just a little different any one of us could have married him, that is if you can forget that he used to be a guitar-playing Christian in those days...'

Annie looked round the room, seeing several

people who might well have fancied Tony Blair with long hair strumming 'Lord of the Dance'. She decided to change tack.

'You worry about whether it would have been better to do something selfless like being a nurse, or sell out completely and go into the City (how could you have missed all that cash in the Eighties?). You worry about things you don't understand and it's got a bit late to ask, like how do personal pension plans actually work, and where exactly is the Internet? You worry publicly about whether it is more responsible to send your children to state or private schools, and you worry secretly whether all those weirdo cults might be right about the world ending in the year 2000. You worry about whether you'll actually get to see the Millennium Dome if you've been able to decide whether it's right to go or not ... the money would have been better spent on hospitals and what is holding up all that tenting anyway?'

Another laugh from Ian.

'...you go to a Meat Loaf concert at Wembley expecting to see loads of long-haired blokes on motorbikes and a lot of leather, and you wonder why there's a great long queue of middle-aged accountants waiting to go in, and then you realize that nobody is looking at you, because you fit in ... and Meat Loaf has to sit down for half his concert because he's out of breath ... and you can remember singing "You Took the Words Right Out of my Mouth" along with the jukebox when you were playing bar footy with a bloke you fancied from St Peter's and it seems like a bloody lifetime ago...'

For a moment, Annie was lost in her own nostalgia. She decided to wind up.

'...And you know something? When someone dies, people sometimes say that they're at peace, because they don't have to worry any more. But you know what? I'd rather be alive. There is one alternative to getting old, and it's not plastic surgery...'

Complete silence.

'...The Who got it wrong with the anthem of our generation. We don't hope we die before we get old. It was indulgent to think it then, and it's getting a bit late now...'

Annie had the strange sensation that she was holding an audience as she had never done before.

'...And people think that death is so horrible that something good must come of it, but I don't believe that. There is nothing good about Penny being dead. It leaves Roy without a partner, and the little girls without a mother and all of us without our best friend ... but maybe, just maybe, if when we think about her, we stop worrying for a second and realize what a luxury it is to be able to worry, and how we should ration it, just like we ration the Godiva chocolates we got for Christmas, then maybe we'd have more time to do some of the things we meant to do, to be the person we hoped we'd be, and, you know, I think Penny would approve of that.'

PART TWO

White Lies

Chapter 28

It was a warm, almost muggy, night. Clusters of friends had taken their coffee outside and were sitting chatting and laughing in the arc of light cast on the lawn by the hall lights. Jennifer was replacing her cello in its case, and Leonora was talking to Roy. One waitress was sweeping up the shattered glass around the top table, others cleared dessert plates away from the women who had decided to remain at the tables inside.

'That was a super speech, Annie,' Ursula said, reclining on the grass. Her body went down with a thump as she misjudged the space between her back and the ground. She lay perfectly flat, staring up at the dome of night sky.

'I feel as if I'm an undergraduate again,' Ursula said, 'except that I never was the sort of undergraduate who got drunk. I'm not that drunk, am I?'

'Not at all,' both the others lied simultaneously.

She was bursting to tell them about Liam. She knew she shouldn't, but she couldn't for the moment put her finger on why it was so important to keep it a secret. She prided herself on her ability to keep confidences, her very livelihood depended on it, she told herself, but still the urge to talk about him became more and more pressing as each minute passed. Her hand went to her throat to touch the necklace.

'I must go to the loo,' she said, taking rather a long time to stand up and then heading very purposefully towards one of the halls of residence and stumbling over a croquet hoop on the way.

'Annie, you're meant to strike the equipment after you've played,' she called crossly.

'Oh fuck off!' Annie said.

'Annie? Is that you? Come and join us? Leonora called, emerging from the hall and peering into the darkness.

Annie and Manon held their breath until they heard the sound of court shoes on concrete receding into the distance.

Ursula found a toilet at the bottom of the staircase, just where she had expected it to be, which made her think that she couldn't be that drunk after all if she could still remember the geography of the college.

The interior of the toilet was utilitarian and there was a small square of polished steel instead of a mirror. Ursula stood on tiptoe so that she could see all of her necklace in it.

'You look beautiful.'

'Don't tell them,' she spoke sternly to her reflection: 'do not tell them. You will only regret it.'

Then she bent her head over the basin and splashed water on her face and the back of her neck.

'It was a good speech,' Manon volunteered.

258

'Really?'

'I thought it was quite profound,' Manon said.

Something had happened to her this evening. It was as if she had been carrying the entire weight of her life in her head, and she could feel it was now dispersing throughout her body, making her feel strangely light. Enlightened, she thought, I feel enlightened.

'Profound, really?' Annie said.

'Sometimes we think too much about things that are very simple. This place taught us to intellectualize about truth and to question the value of emotion but sometimes the truth just is very stark. An idiot can see it, but an Oxford graduate cannot. That's what you were saying, isn't it?'

'I suppose so,' Annie said, wondering if there was a subtle put-down in there somewhere. Was Manon suggesting that she was an idiot?

The quad fell dark as the last guests left the hall and Leonora switched off the lights. The other groups gradually picked themselves up and headed off to cars, or rooms, depending on whether they were spending the night in Oxford.

In the dull glow of the lamp by the lodge, Annie caught sight of Ian's silhouette. She wondered whether to call him over, but it was nice, just the two of them sitting in the dark and she suspected that Manon would clam up again if a man were to join them.

'There's one thing that's been puzzling me all evening,' Annie said, needing somehow to get back at her for the remark about idiots, 'and that's why you've got a dressing-gown cord

259

round your waist.'

'Oh no!' Manon said, 'is it so obvious?'

She explained again about the incident on the river.

'...and you see, Geraldine wanted to lend me some jewellery...'

'That I can understand,' Annie interrupted, 'but why didn't you just take it off in the car?'

'I don't know!' Manon laughed.

'I'll tell you why, because you're the least vain person I have ever met, and it is so bloody unfair, because you're beautiful too! You don't worry about how you look, do you?' Annie said, adding bitterly, 'you don't bloody need to.'

'No, but,' Manon searched for something to restore the equilibrium she had been enjoying between them, 'no, but that part of your speech was just a metaphor, surely?'

'It bloody wasn't,' Annie said petulantly.

Manon laughed.

'What's so funny?'

'Because you're so honest. You're so honest that you do yourself down all the time. It must be so hard to be that honest about yourself,' Manon said.

'Do you really think that?' Annie asked.

'Yes, of course.'

She had an impatient French way of saying of course.

'Don't you think that I might be as dishonest as everyone else. Perhaps I just pretend to reveal my innermost failings, but there's much worse underneath?'

'I can't know the answer to that, can I?'

Manon said, 'but I suspect not.'

Annie fell silent for a moment or two.

'Why have you always snubbed me then?' she asked.

'I haven't!' Manon protested automatically.

'You have.'

Yes, it was true, thought Manon.

'You're right,' she admitted finally. More light-ness.

Although she could not see her very well in the darkness, she knew that the frown on Annie's face was smoothing itself out.

'Why?' Annie asked, more gently. Now that she had her on the hook, she was suddenly afraid of what Manon might have against her.

'I suppose because you wrote that piece about me being Zuleika Dobson,' Manon said.

'I did not!'

The denial was immediate.

'But you were the one who coined the nick-name that evening we were all talking in Joshua Street.'

'I know I called you Zuleika once or twice, and it was tasteless, but I was only joking. I admit I've always been eaten up with jealousy of you, but I would never do you harm,' Annie said, outraged.

The axis of Manon's world shifted again.

'Well, who did?' she asked. 'It must have been one of us and it certainly wasn't Penny.'

Her eyes were getting used to the dark: she could see Ursula wandering back in their direc-tion.

'Leonora is holding Roy hostage in the JCR,'

261

she announced. 'There are a few others still there, but I think we ought to go and get him.'

'Oh fuck that,' Annie said, 'we're having confession time. Manon wants to know who wrote that piece about Zuleika Dobson.'

There was an awkward silence, then Ursula said, 'I didn't know that he was going to write it down. I was flirting. Showing off ... oh Christ!'

The student journalist responsible for the anonymous article had been called Oliver. Ursula had spent three years loving him from afar. One evening in the last term they were leaving Radcliffe Camera together at closing time when he asked her if she would like to go for a drink. The dream-come-true excitement she had experienced then was exactly the same shivery state that took her over now whenever she saw Liam. It made her unable to control the volume at which her voice left her mouth.

Oliver had sauntered towards the Turf Tavern. She had picked her way along beside him, terrified of tripping on the cobblestones, wanting to stretch the moment for as long as possible, praying that somebody she knew would walk past and be able to confirm the next day that she had been with him.

One glass of mulled wine had made her ridiculously garrulous. In ten minutes she had gone through every funny story about herself, and was struggling to come up with something interesting that would keep him sitting opposite her, his right knee brushing her left whenever he laughed. And so she had told him Manon's story. She hadn't known that he wrote most of the university paper. Later that week she had been aghast when he asked her to get him a photo of Manon, but it hadn't stopped her doing it.

It was only when she had seen the utterly defeated look on Manon's face when Annie had waved the paper around the kitchen at Joshua Street, that she had known that she had done something terribly wrong. But she had never admitted it. Not, if she were honest, because of any lasting feeling for Manon, but because Penny would have stopped being her friend. Even this evening, when she had overheard Manon talking to Gillian, Ursula had not thought about what she had done to Manon, but about how Penny was no longer there to find out. It had been a peculiar mingling of shame and relief.

'I was an ugly duckling and he was the first good-looking man who had ever shown any interest in me.' Ursula tried to excuse herself.

'You see,' Annie said, triumphantly to Manon.

Manon said nothing.

Say something horrible to me, Ursula thought. Anything would be better than silence.

'Say you're sorry,' Annie demanded of Ursula.

'I am, very sorry.'

'No, it's OK, actually,' Manon said at last. 'It was only what people would call a youthful in-discretion, after all. I think it is one of the things that I have given far too much space in my life.'

'She thought it was me, so she's been horrible

263

to me ever since,' Annie told Ursula.

'I haven't,' Manon said.

'Why didn't you suspect me?' Ursula asked, suddenly feeling desperately wretched. 'But of course, I know the answer to that one. I wasn't the sort of girl who knew the journalist set, was I? I was the boring, bossy old bluestocking.'

'No!' Manon and Annie said together.

'It's true,' Ursula said.

'Labels,' Manon said suddenly, 'don't you think we've all spent our lives just confirming the labels that we got here?'

'I was the tasteless tart, you mean,' Annie said, 'and you were the *femme fatale*, Ursula was the sexless swot, and Penny was perfect.'

'Well...' It was what Manon had meant but she wasn't willing to be so blunt about it.

Ursula fiddled with her necklace. Her face and body were no longer sexless, she knew that, but inside she felt just the same, and Annie's way of putting it was like a knife in her gut.

'I'm not going to have that label any more,' she blurted out.

'Really?' Annie asked, always attuned to the slightest nuance. 'OK. So tell me, on the eve of the millennium, how are you going to change your life?'

'None of your business. If you must know, I'm going to have an affair,' Ursula said.

There was a short silence as the tumble of words arranged themselves in the warm night air, and then both Annie and Manon screamed together:

'What?'

In the darkness, Ursula felt herself glowing with ridiculous pride.

'Tell us,' ordered Annie.

'My lover is a psychologist,' Ursula said, as nonchalantly as she could, 'he looks like Frank Furillo and I have just decided to have sex with him.'

'Who is Frank Furillo?' Manon asked, but Annie drowned her out.

'Hold on a minute, how can he be a lover if you haven't had sex, or are we talking the Clintonian definition here?'

Ursula blushed. Annie had an uncanny knack of catching her out.

They had kissed, and they had touched each other down to the waist. And once, up in the hills, the day of the rainbow, he had unzipped the straight black skirt of her best work suit and pulled it down to her knees, then buried his face in her lap while she sat perfectly still stranded halfway between total abandon and the horror of him seeing her stretch marks. When everyone else had held Clinton's legalistic definition of sexual relations up to ridicule, she had been the only person in the world who could see the distinction between what Monica had done and proper sex. She had found herself sympathizing with the President as he wriggled and squirmed his way out of a perjury charge. Yes, she had had sexual relations with Liam, but she did not yet feel she had betrayed her husband.

'Well?' Annie asked.

'Some people spend time getting to know someone before they jump into bed with them,'

Ursula snapped.

'Ow, that really hurt,' Annie said with deep sarcasm.

'And I'm married,' Ursula added, as an after-thought.

'So when are you going to?' Annie demanded.

'Soon.'

'You wouldn't dare!'

'I would too! He wanted to come with me this weekend,' Ursula said, pulling a blade of grass out of the lawn and twirling it between her forefinger and thumb.

'Where does he live?' Annie demanded.

'In Nottingham.'

'Oh, that's too far to get him to come over right now.' Annie sounded disappointed.

'Not really. He said he could be here in less than three hours,' Ursula argued, then clammed up, as if she was being talked into something.

'Three hours, really?'

'The North isn't nearly as far away as you seem to think,' Ursula said, sarcastically.

'Then call him now, go on!' Annie said.

'No.'

'It's only half-past ten,' Annie said, pressing a button on her gigantic watch and reading the fluorescent display.

'Is it? I thought it was much later.'

'Well, then ...'

'What do you think, Manon?' Ursula asked.

'I think that this is like a scene in a film,' Manon did not want to be involved: 'three friends meet after twenty years and discover things that they never knew about each other and that they never knew about themselves.'

'It's been done,' Annie said. *The Big Chill.*'

'And what happens in *The Big Chill?*' Manon asked, innocently.

'They all have loads of sex,' Annie said, bringing them neatly back to the subject after discussion. 'Here, use my mobile and call him.' She took her Nokia out of her red Furla handbag.

Ursula looked at it.

'No, I'll call him from my room.'

'You won't. You'll bottle. Call him right now!'

'Why are you so keen?'

'Well, if I'm not going to get a fuck tonight, at least I can have the vicarious pleasure of knowing you are.'

'Oh, honestly,' said Ursula, 'Manon, what do you think?'

'It's really nothing to do with me,' Manon said.

'You only live once,' Annie said.

'Oh God!'

'Go out of earshot, if you like,' Annie conceded. 'Do you know his number?'

'Yes.'

'She knows his number,' Annie said.

'Oh, just...' Ursula got to her feet, and walked towards the back gate, trying to force herself to think of Barry and the children, but it was as if they were in another world that had nothing to do with the one she was in now. Her fingers pressed the numbers on the handset slowly and deliberately. The phone rang, and rang, and suddenly she was gripped by the panicky anticipation of failure. Was this love to be unrequited too? Was Oxford going to play a cruel trick on her?

Then he answered.

'You've called,' he said.

'How did you know it was me?'

'I was dreaming about you. I dreamt that I was going to wake up with you in the morning.'

He was making it easy for her. She did not know what words she would have used.

'You are,' she said. The words were soft, like a breath.

'Shall I climb over the back fence?'

She laughed.

'No, I'll meet you outside the lodge.'

'I'll be there by one o'clock.'

And before she had a chance to think again, he had switched off his phone and she stared at the tiny slab of chrome technology in her hand wondering whether the conversation had really taken place. They were going to wake up together tomorrow.

'He knew it was me!' she said, as she returned, doing a little skip in the air.

'He probably has caller display,' Annie remarked.

'What's that?'

'Your phone has a display of the number calling you. Don't you have it on your mobile?'

'No.'

Ursula's spirits suddenly fell flat. Why had he never mentioned caller display? He must have assumed she knew, assumed that whenever they said telepathy to one another, they really meant technology. She felt a fool.

'But it's your phone,' Manon said.

'So?' Annie asked.

'So, he wouldn't have known if it was Ursula even if he did have caller display.'

Ursula smiled.

'Thank you,' she said to Manon, then stuck her tongue out at Annie.

'I'll tell you what we can do until one o'clock,' Annie said, standing up and brushing bits of grass from her dress, 'Manon and I can get very drunk, and you,' she pointed at Ursula, 'can get very sober.'

'I'm going back to London,' Manon said quickly.

'Just one drink. Come on, back at the Randolph. Might as well make use of the room. It's on your way to the bus station.'

'All right then,' Manon agreed, 'but I must have a wee first. I'll catch you up,' she called, running across the grass.

'You don't think Manon's pregnant, do you?' Ursula said. 'She keeps going to the toilet and she's not drinking.'

'She doesn't look pregnant, does she? Anyway Manon never really drinks. Her mother was an alcoholic, remember? And she doesn't have sex either. She's an ice maiden. I know several very attractive men who've tried for months to get off with her. Manon doesn't do sex.'

'But we do,' Ursula giggled.

'Speak for yourself.'

'Oh, Annie, you're always having sex.'

269

'You're thinking of Annie McClintock. It's not all straight autobiography, you know. Some of it is wishful thinking.'

'Well, you seemed to be getting on very well with the only man in the room tonight,' Ursula said, waspishly.

They walked through the lodge.

'Moustache,' said Annie.

After a moment's thought, Ursula said,

'He didn't have a moustache.'

'Didn't he?' Annie asked. 'Well, the point is that he looks the type who might. Probably wears Y fronts.'

'What's wrong with Y fronts?' Ursula asked, picturing a washing line of Barry and the boys' underwear.

'Oh, get real,' said Annie. 'Anyway, he's married.'

'He didn't look very married.' Ursula tried to be encouraging.

'Married men never do. Married women, on the other hand ...' Annie rounded on her.

'Don't.'

'Oh, for God's sake, you're allowed a fling occasionally, aren't you? A reward for long service.'

Ursula dissolved into uncharacteristic giggles.

'Do you think that all-night hamburger van is still around?' she asked as they approached the beginning of St Giles. 'I'm starving.'

'Probably. Probably serving the same hamburgers. Do you know, whenever somebody mentions BSE, my first thought is that van.'

'But, God, they tasted good, didn't they?'

Ursula said.

'You're not going too?'

'I bloody am!' Ursula said defiantly running ahead.

'Well, you are living dangerously. I don't know which is the riskiest – the burger or the bonk,' said Annie behind her.

Chapter 29

'Manon?'

The voice made her jump.

Roy's fair hair caught the light like an angel as he emerged out of the darkness.

'How did you know it was me?'

'Your footsteps fall in a certain rhythm.'

'You haven't been hiding?' she asked, amused.

'Not exactly, well, yes, I had to get away from Leonora, and I think I've drunk too much to drive just yet. I was just lying on the lawn looking at the stars.'

There were blades of grass in his hair to prove it.

'Would you like to come for a walk with me?' He shifted from one foot to the other, his head slightly inclined, like a teenage boy asking a girl on their first date at the school bus stop. Here in the deserted quad there was no compressed-air hiss from the doors of the departing bus to drown out difficult words.

'I'm supposed to be going back to Annie's

room at the Randolph,' she replied.

'Walk you there, then?'

She hesitated.

'OK.'

The silence between them was tense as they started to walk down the Woodstock Road trying to adjust to each other's pace and to maintain a distance that was neither too close nor too distant.

'It wasn't too bad, was it?' Roy finally asked, as they passed the Radcliffe Infirmary.

'No,' said Manon. 'For me, it was better than I expected. Quite interesting.'

She wondered if he had any idea about his sister's surprising secret life, but decided he did not. She did not think that Ursula had told anyone before tonight.

'What did you make of Annie's speech?' he asked.

'I thought it was wonderful,' she said immediately.

'Did you?'

'Didn't you?'

'It was more about Annie than Penny.'

'Of course!' she laughed, as if to say, what did you expect?

'I suppose so.' He laughed too. 'Do women really spend all their time worrying about their bodies?' he asked. 'It seems such a waste.'

'That wasn't really what she was talking about. Women use their bodies as a gauge of their success...'

None of the worries that Annie had talked about had ever actually bothered her specifically, and yet the speech had touched a chord in her.

'So what do slim women do?' he asked, half jokingly.

'What she was saying was that we dwell on things that are fundamentally immutable,' Manon went on, 'and that is a waste when you might only have a short time. I do think she's right about our generation of women feeling this enormous pressure to be everything, but perhaps every generation feels that way.'

'So Annie's Pre-Millenial Tension is just another name for a mid-life crisis?'

She laughed nervously.

'I suppose so.'

'Do you feel like that?' he demanded.

He sounded aggressive because he was nervous being alone with her, she realized.

'Not so much, because I've completely failed to do everything I was supposed to do. I have no career, and no home, and no family.' Her tone was self-mocking.

'Is that what you wanted?' he asked.

'I don't know.'

His gentle questions were beginning to feel like an interrogation. It would only take five minutes to a walk to the bus station, she told herself, and then she could escape back to the anonymity of London where nobody knew or cared about her.

'You've published a book, and you're a wonderful godmother to Saskia and Lily...' He began to list her achievements.

She looked at him and smiled.

Everyone spoke about her visits to the children as if they were a duty, not a pleasure.

'I think they do more for me than I do for them,' she said.

He stopped walking suddenly.

'Are you with someone at the moment?'

His voice croaked as the words left his mouth.

'At the moment, I'm with you,' she teased him.

'I meant...'

'I know what you meant. No, no, I'm not.' She thought of the cluster of cells in her womb, the grain of rice, and felt a shiver of betrayal.

There was a long silence. A pregnant silence, she thought. Then they started walking again.

'Are you?' she finally asked, for politeness' sake.

'No,' he said, abruptly. 'It's difficult enough looking after the children.'

Part of her felt very sorry for him. Penny had been the practical one who managed everything. Penny had wanted children so they had had children. It wasn't that Roy didn't want them or didn't love them when they arrived, but he probably would never have made such a decision himself. He was still so much a boy, perhaps because he had grown up with such a domineering big sister. Patterns of behaviour laid down in childhood were difficult to change. Often you did not realize that you were conforming to their shape.

The pavement on St Giles was dark and narrow. The effort of negotiating it side by side without becoming closer to one another and risking the possibility of contact made them silent again.

The smell of the burger van was the same as it had always been. Onions and cheap meat frying. As they reached the intersection of St Giles and Beaumont Street they slowed down and both exhaled, as if they had been holding their breath the entire distance.

'This is where I leave you,' Manon said. 'Are you sober now?'

Her voice was a little French, a little scolding.

'Maybe.' He did not want her to go, but could think of nothing to say to make her stay.

'Send my love to the girls.'

'Yes. Look next time you come, I could join you. We could go punting again,' he offered, 'or maybe, maybe something less watery?' he added seeing surprise pass across Manon's face and remembering Lily's accident.

'Maybe,' she said.

'Well ...' He felt utterly defeated. Her refusal to be drawn exhausted him.

'Farewell!'

She smiled and began to cross the road, then she seemed to change her mind and walked back to him. She grasped his upper arm with surprising force and kissed him on both cheeks. It was like a greeting between two Soviet generals, he thought, and contained as little affection. Then she stood back one pace and looked at him, that same bewildered child's look.

In desperation, he dipped his head and touched her lips with his.

Manon froze. Not this, please, she pleaded to some higher presence she did not really believe in. Please not this. She had got away, and then she had let herself come back for this. But his kiss was like the stroke of a magic wand, and she could feel her defences dropping away like the creepers round the palace of Sleeping Beauty.

It was as gentle and tentative a kiss as anyone had ever received, and it was achingly familiar.

Just the same as the first time.

She closed her eyes and let herself relax for one blissful moment, and then she tensed and drew away.

'Why are you so angry with me?' he asked.

'I'm not,' she said in a clipped voice. She was not ready for this conversation.

'You are,' he persisted.

'You know why,' she insisted.

'Tell me,' he said more softly.

'Not here,' she said, glancing around as if an oasis of calm where they could talk privately would suddenly reveal itself in the traffic.

'Where then?' he asked.

'I'm going home now,' she said, trying to convince herself as she walked away from him.

'We could go to Joshua Street,' he called after her.

Chapter 30

'Well, well, well,' said Annie, swishing the curtain in front of her face.

Manon and Roy. Whoever would have thought it? From her window, she had seen them emerge from the darkness of St Giles and observed them kiss in the shadow of the monumental Ashmolean. Where were they off to now, strolling down Beaumont Street, side by side? If they didn't cross the road soon, they would miss the bus station. But she did not think that they were going to the bus station.

'What?' asked Ursula from Annie's bed. She had made herself very comfortable on the counterpane, her shoes flipped onto the floor and her toes wriggling in the air. The room stank of hamburger.

'Nothing,' Annie said, with uncharacteristic continence. 'Coffee or tea?'

As she filled the kettle from the mixer tap over the bath, she began to calculate how long the thing with Manon and Roy might have been going on. The kiss she had witnessed was hardly the passionate clinch of the first intensely sexual moments of a relationship, so it could not have started this afternoon. There had been something natural about it, something almost inevitable as Roy's blond head was drawn magnetically towards Manon's dark one, both their faces white under the street lamp, eyes closed.

With a ghastly pang of embarrassment, she remembered telling Manon of her own proposed seduction of Roy. Manon had laughed. All these women after Roy. Well, she should know.

'So how long has this affair of yours been going on?' she asked Ursula.

'I met him soon after I went back to work after Georgie.'

'Is he married?'

'No.'

'Why?'

'Divorced.'

'Children?'

'No.'

'Why?'

'Never asked him.'

'Is he the reason you've lost so much weight?' Annie demanded.

'No.' Ursula looked up, 'I just don't seem to be so hungry any more.'

'Perhaps you were eating to replace love?'

'Barry loves me,' Ursula said defensively.

'But do you love him?'

Ursula felt herself redden.

'He's the father of my children, and he's a good man,' she said.

'So that's a no, then,' Annie said. 'What if he finds out?'

'He won't.'

Stop asking all these questions. It's too late now, Ursula wanted to say.

'Do you think you're just bored, or wasn't Barry ever the love of your life?' Annie asked.

'I don't really want to talk about Barry, if you don't mind,' Ursula said.

Reality was beginning to creep back into the conversation. She took the cup of tea that Annie handed her, but what she most wanted was another drink.

She sipped the tea. Tea tasted of home. What she really wanted were the bubbles of sinful champagne pricking her tongue. She put the cup and saucer down on the bedside table.

'Let's have another drink.'

'Ursula, you can't. You're pissed enough already.'

'So?'

'Well, you're not a very good drunk, actually. You're a bit aggressive and you laugh too loudly. Not very sexy.'

'Oh.'

'However, if you insist...' Annie dialled room service and was ordering a bottle of champagne to be sent up.

'No, you're right.' Ursula's confidence suddenly drained away. Was she really a loud shouting drunk?

'...sorry, forget it?' Annie dropped the phone back into its cradle and looked at her watch.

'It's nearly an hour since you called. He'll be well on his way.'

Ursula thought about it. Liam had been patient so far, but he was not the sort of man you could muck around. This was her opportunity. If she did not snatch it, it would be gone.

The choice was simple.

'Just one night,' she said.

'What?' Annie asked. She was trying to give her full attention to Ursula, but she could not help twitching back the curtain to see if anything was happening on Beaumont Street. There was no one about.

'Do you think that Roy was the love of Penny's life?' she asked, hoping the roundabout question would elicit a revealing answer.

'Penny and Roy?' Ursula asked, 'I've never really thought about it. I suppose I was a bit surprised when they got together, but they always seemed very happy.'

'Did Roy have other girlfriends?'

'Girls were always after him at school. Our phone at home never stopped ringing. But he was incredibly shy.'

'But when he was away at Oxford?' Annie pressed.

'Well, I don't know, do I? He came up after we'd already gone down, didn't he. We were quite good friends when we were children, but since we left home we've hardly seen each other. The first I heard of him and Penny was the Christmas she came back from Africa. She was teaching and I suppose Roy must have been postgrad by then. She said on her Christmas card that they'd seen each other a few times. I thought nothing of it. She was still getting over Vin.'

'Whatever happened to Vin?' Annie asked.

She tried to picture Penny's former boyfriend

but found she could not remember any details, just a general impression of a hulking great brute who occasionally stayed the night at Joshua Street and emptied all their packets of breakfast cereal into his bowl in the morning. Apart from vapid sporty kind of good looks, he had no discernible attractions and wasn't at all good enough for Penny, so it had come as a shock to hear that he was the one to have left her. He had gone off with a woman who was working on the irrigation project he had set up in Africa, sending Penny back to England with a broken heart. Privately, Annie always had thought it a very lucky escape for Penny.

Roy could not have been more different from Vin. Roy was blond, gentle and sensitive almost to a fault, and behind his even-toothed smile there was a brain that had achieved a double first and a PhD. Vin never seemed to possess much in the way of a brain.

'I think somebody said that he had gone to Australia.'

'Good riddance,' said Annie. 'With the female irrigator.'

'No, she dumped him for an English teacher, I believe.'

'Serves him right. Poor Penny. She loved Africa so much.'

'She didn't. She hated it,' said Ursula. 'She found it totally frustrating because it was just so desperate where they were.'

'Really, I never knew that,' Annie said.

That's because you never listen, Ursula wanted to say.

'They've asked me to do something for Comic Relief next year. Do you think I should?' Annie said vaguely.

Ursula sighed. However far-ranging the conversation, Annie had the ability to make it return to her in one sentence. And just when you thought she was the most selfish person in the world she would start talking about what she was about to do for charity.

'Of course you should.'

'I don't know. I was wondering whether I might do something for Penny's charity. I mean I could really help them, whereas anything I do for Africa is a drop in the ocean, a grain of sand in the Sahara.'

'Sounds a good idea.'

Ursula looked at her watch. It was after midnight. She couldn't concentrate any longer on what Annie was saying.

'Could I have a bath here?' she asked, 'it's so much more luxurious than trailing down the corridor at college and then finding out you've forgotten your towel.'

'Be my guest,' said Annie, lying down on the bed and listening as Ursula ran the taps, stepped in and let out a great wallowy sigh, like a satisfied hippo.

Annie felt restless. The air outside was warm and the steam from Ursula's bath was turning the room into a sauna. She flicked through the channels on the television. It was all tennis and films she had already seen.

'You're not going to put that old sack on again, are you?' she said, wandering into the bathroom as Ursula stepped out and began to dry herself.

A look of sheer mortification flew across Ursula's pink face, as she tried to reapply lipstick in the misted-up mirror. She wished she had made the bath a little cooler. The night air would whiten her out, she thought, frowning at the pink blotches around her neck.

'I mean it's a lovely dress, but it's got grass stains on it and, well...'

'Well what?' Ursula interrupted.

'Well, sometimes people who have been fat still dress fat, you know what I mean? It's the sort of dress you wear to hide that fleshy bit above your pelvic bones. But you don't need to do that any more. You've got a great figure, really you have, I'm spitting with envy, but you have to learn to dress thin.'

Ursula wasn't sure what to make of this advice from someone who always seemed to be bursting out of her clothes.

'But I don't have anything else,' she said.

Unless he had been stopped for speeding, Liam would be waiting at the lodge by the time she walked back. His first sight of her would be a pink-faced, aggressive drunk staggering out of the shadows in a soiled sack.

Annie held out the dress between her thumb and forefinger as if handling a piece of evidence. She hadn't been exaggerating about the grass stains.

'Didn't you bring a change of clothes?'

'Yes, but for tomorrow. Casual. Anyway I probably won't be able to get back to my room without seeing him now.'

'True. Well, I don't suppose it matters. You're not likely to have the dress on for long anyway, are you?' Annie said.

Now that she had entertained the doubt, Ursula didn't think she would ever wear the dress again.

'Tell you what. Borrow mine,' said Annie. Standing up, she pulled her little black dress over her head. Then she turned it inside out and sniffed at the armpits.

'It's fine. Stinks a bit of Obsession, but that's probably not such a bad thing.'

Ursula didn't know what to say.

'It's Donna Karan,' Annie insisted.

When it wasn't stretched round Annie's curves, Ursula recognized the dress as the very same one Liam had urged her to try on the evening before. It seemed like weeks ago. How peculiar, she thought, taking it from her friend's hand and gingerly stepping into it. Perhaps she was fated to wear it.

It was a little loose on, but the overall effect was far more appealing than her linen dress.

'Are you sure?' she asked.

'Positive. You look great,' Annie said, delighted that although the dress didn't exactly cling to Ursula, the looseness wasn't as dramatic as she had feared.

'Go on, then,' she said.

Ursula stood immobilized by the sense that it was a significant moment in their relationship and that something profound should probably be said, but she couldn't think of anything.

'Go on!' Annie began to nudge her towards

the door, like an older sister pushing a shy younger one up to receive a prize.

'I don't know what I'll say to you tomorrow,' Ursula said, as if she were going off to lose her virginity.

'I hope you'll be too busy humping to see anyone tomorrow.'

'But what about Roy's barbecue?'

'I'll say you've been unavoidably detained.' Annie winked.

'No, please don't say anything. I'll deal with him. You promise you won't say anything.'

She could imagine Annie concocting a ridiculous excuse on her behalf.

'Oh, for heaven's sake! Just piss off, will you?' said Annie.

Ursula opened the door, then closed it again.

'Annie,' she said, seriously, 'will you promise not to put any of this in one of your programmes?'

'Jesus H. Christ, what do you take me for? I never use anything...'

'What about the time I got locked in the loo at the vodka bar?' Ursula managed to get her counter-claim in before Annie could finish her protestations of innocence.

At closing time the manager of the restaurant had heard Ursula's desperate wails, and, assuming someone was overdosing, called the police to kick down the door.

'Well, that *was* funny.' Annie tried to justify herself.

'Not for me, it wasn't.'

'It was more a joke against me, for being so

285

drunk that I forgot all about you and went home.' Annie couldn't suppress her laughter as she remembered the incident.

'Don't laugh,' Ursula said, crossly, then found herself unable to stop giggling too.

'Was that the same weekend as the fake tan?' Annie asked, getting unwisely carried away.

'No,' said Ursula, suddenly serious, 'that was a different weekend, conveniently. You made a whole episode out of that as well.'

'Well, you were much fatter then. If you'd been as thin as you are now, the tube wouldn't have run out halfway through.' Annie tried to turn the débâcle into a compliment.

'You said it wouldn't show.'

'Oh well, no lasting harm done,' Annie said breezily.

'Only the minor humiliation of going to one of your media parties and having one arm and one leg turn orange while the other side of me remained white and pasty...'

'Your face was quite even,' Annie protested.

'...and then the major humiliation of seeing the whole thing acted out on television six months later with an actress playing me who was virtually obese.'

'People say that if you made it up, no-one would believe it,' Annie said, trying to draw the conversation to a close. She didn't think she could bear another argument about the episode in which Annie McClintock was maid of honour at her fat friend's interminably boring wedding. She had accepted long ago that she had been wrong to heckle the groom's speech, but Ursula would never let it rest.

'Your secret is safe with me,' she said, giving Ursula a push out of the door.

'Well, that'll be a first,' said Ursula.

'Off you go,' Annie said, 'and wipe that expression off your face in case the wind changes. That's better. And give him one from me.'

Annie closed the door. Almost immediately there was a knock.

'Oh for fuck's sake, what now?' she asked, opening it.

'Room service,' said Ian. 'I couldn't help over-hearing you order some bubbly.'

He was holding an ice bucket with a bottle of champagne in it. His eyes ran appreciatively up and down her body, which made her realize that she had just given her dress to Ursula and was wearing nothing but a black bra, black panties and high-heeled red sandals.

She closed the door again in his face.

'Have you had a glass to the wall?' she asked from inside the door.

'No, but the window is open,' he tried to explain himself.

'You've got a bloody nerve,' Annie said, racing back through her brain to try to remember if she had mentioned him. Not since they left college, and he couldn't have been eavesdropping then, could he?

He did have a nice smile, and a bottle of champagne, and she was feeling a bit tired to put on a great performance of being cross.

'It's stifling in here,' she shouted, rifling through her small weekend bag, pulling on a white T-shirt, jeans and a pair of ponyskin mules with thick rubber soles; then opening the door again transformed. 'Let's get some air.'

His contrite face brightened.

'And let's take that with us,' she said, pointing at the bottle and marching towards the stairs.

Chapter 31

'Do buses go back to London all night?' Roy finally dared to say something as they approached Joshua Street.

'I think so,' Manon replied. 'Doesn't it say twenty-four hours on the side of the coach? Later than the train, anyway.'

She sounded slightly anxious, as if he was implying that she should be going back to London now after all. He had meant only to ask a question of fact. Something safe. But there was no safe ground. Which was why they had both walked in silence the entire length of Walton Street.

He was nervous now. What were they doing? Why had he been so insistent that they talk? Nothing they could say to each other would change anything. Perhaps it would be better to say nothing. There was nothing in number 3 Joshua Street to help them with the rest of their lives. Nothing there at all except dust and a fitted carpet. Their footsteps echoed along the deserted pavement as they walked towards the empty house.

'The train station's so inconvenient,' he said neutrally, trying to say something that could have no meaning except that which was contained in the words.

'Yes. And the train's more expensive.'

He saw her shoot a furtive glance towards the house where Mrs Harris lived, but the windows were dark and there was no twitching of the front curtain.

'Why do you still have the keys?' Manon asked.

'Completion is on Monday,' he said, pausing as if unsure what day it was, 'the day after tomorrow. But I decided to move us on Friday, yesterday, so that it would be done before the dinner, before tonight.' He paused, thinking what a long time it had been since he had driven away the day before with Saskia and Lily in their car seats behind him.

'I saw it as an ending, you see, after which we could have a new start,' he tried to elaborate.

'A rite of passage?' Manon said.

'Yes, a rite of passage,' he sighed and looked up at the stars. 'Of course life has this funny habit of refusing to fall into neat parcels.'

'Doesn't it just?'

He smiled at her as they walked up the short path to the front door. Two minutes before he had yearned to be inside, so that they could talk without fear of her running away. But now that they had fallen into a certain rhythm of conversation, he hesitated before opening the door, not wanting the whole business of undoing locks, opening doors, deciding who would go in first, to staunch the flow of words between them.

It was colder inside than out and she pulled the edges of her cardigan together.

'I switched the boiler off, but there's automatic ignition on the pilot, I could light it,' he offered.

'No, it's OK,' she said.

'It's not really cold.'

'No.'

'But you're shivering.'

'I always do. I think it's something to do with my metabolism,' she told him.

In the darkness she could not see his face, but she imagined that he was having the same memory as she was, of another warm sunny night, long, long ago, when she had taken him upstairs and showed him how to cheat the meter on the ugly gas fire that had taken up so much space in her little room.

They both walked determinedly past the foot of the staircase and he showed her into the long-knocked-through room which had been two rooms when they were students. Ursula's at the front, and the communal sitting room at the back.

When Penny had returned from Africa, she had thrown herself into renovating and re-decorating the house, spending all her spare time and money undoing the 'improvements' that had been made to the house before she had owned it. She had been particularly proud of the cast iron Victorian fireplace with patterned tile surround which she had rescued in pieces from a builder's skip all on her own in the middle of the night.

They sat down on the carpeted floor in front of it, a yard or so away from each other, their eyes gradually adjusting to the darkness.

'We were going to strip the floor once the girls were a little older,' Roy said.

'Yes, said Manon, then taking courage, she asked, 'What are we doing here?'

He thought for a long time, then he said, carefully, 'I was her husband and you were her best friend, and we should be able to talk to each other.'

'But it's not as simple as that, is it?' She sat up straight, immediately on the defensive.

'I know that you suffer. And I do too...' his voice trailed away.

Manon remembered one of her last sensible conversations with Penny.

'List...' she had said, blinking agitatedly with her eyes until Manon understood and took the notepad and biro that were permanently on her bedside table. Then as she fell in and out of consciousness, Manon had obediently written down what she said.

'The girls, the girls, and ... I do want you to be a friend to the girls.'

It was as if she feared saying anything else in case anyone should mistake her. It was almost as if she dared not name either one in case her

291

strength would fail before she could name the other. And so the litany went on, the girls, the girls, the girls, and just once she had said, in a barely audible whisper, Roy.

Manon had not known whether she was supposed to get him from downstairs or to be a friend to him too.

'I'm sorry,' Manon said softly.

'No, don't be sorry,' he said.

They were talking at cross purposes even though they were not really speaking.

'I'm not sorry in the way that you think.' She tried to keep her voice level.

'How then?' he asked.

He was so gentle, so much more gentle than any man she had ever known and it frightened her.

'Somebody told me this evening that there are certain distinct stages of grief,' she began to explain, 'and one of them is anger, and I think I am still very angry with you for letting Penny be ill. I know, I know that it wasn't your fault, but I suppose I think that you should have known, you should have noticed the lump in her breast before, or you should have made them do a biopsy straight away. You should have questioned the GP who said it was a cyst, and if you couldn't find the courage to do that, then at least you could have asked someone else. You could have rung me...'

She realized the futility of her words as they hurried out of her mouth. Locked away in the mind, the arguments seemed completely coherent, but spoken she knew they were un-reasonable.

'And what would you have done?' he asked.

'I would have come back,' she insisted.

'Would you? And would that have saved her?' he asked.

The calm equilibrium of his tone seemed to accuse her.

'But I didn't know it was so serious.' She began to defend herself.

'And you think that we did? You only saw her towards the end, but she didn't look like that all the time, you know...'

She could see his eyes quite clearly now.

'...and all they talk to you about is success rates. They want to keep your spirits up, so they give you statistics about survival rates, and they never bother to update you with new statistics, say, when they find that it's in the lymphatic system too. You kind of know inside, but you put your trust in them and you don't want to ask – well, Penny never did – because you don't want to hear that you might die, because once the words are out, then it's like you're admitting that it's a possibility...'

'OK, OK...' Manon interrupted, unable to bear any more.

'No, not OK. Tell me, should I have written to you and said that Penny is probably worse than she is letting on? I didn't know what she was writing to you, did I?'

The letters Penny had sent her had barely mentioned her illness. Perhaps he was right about her being unwilling to embrace the possibility of dying, Manon thought.

'And you and I have never been good correspondents, have we?' he continued.

She looked at him, her eyes pleading with him to stop now.

'Do you think you're the only one who thinks they could have saved her?' he pressed on with controlled fury. 'Don't you think I've spent every waking minute thinking that? That's a stage of grief too, you know. It's called guilt. It doesn't help anyone, but it seems you have to go through it...' His voice suddenly lost its volume. 'Though it implies that you come out the other side. To me it seems never-ending...'

'Have you had bereavement counselling?' she asked him.

'I read a book,' he said, more calmly.

Then, for some reason they both laughed. He was a literature don. Books were where he sought comfort.

'I'm sorry,' she said, embarrassed by the laughter and feeling claustrophobic in the empty room.

'But it's not just that is it?'

'No,' she said, reluctantly, knowing that the inevitable was approaching, 'it is not just that.'

'Say it...'

In the cool still darkness, her whole life pivoted.

'You should never have married her when you loved me,' Manon said.

The words which she had held back for so long now, finally, when given their freedom, simply hung in the air.

It seemed like an hour before Roy replied, an hour in which she felt that all the regrets and guilt in her life had been pushed into a syringe and injected into her bloodstream until the pain of the needle feeding the solution through her became almost unbearable.

'I loved Penny,' he said finally, 'and I married her because I wanted to live with her for ever. But I can't deny that once I loved you too. But my decision to marry Penny had nothing to do with you. That's the truth ... I think that's the truth.'

It was so very honest of him to qualify his statement, she thought she could not bear him to continue.

'The love I felt for you tore me to pieces and when I was young, I thought that was how love was meant to be "Nescio, sed id sentio, et excrucior", he quoted Catullus. 'I am, literally, crucified. That's how I felt about you.'

He let out a short ironic laugh.

'Probably because I'd just done A level Latin, and there is a bit of a self-dramatizing streak in our family.'

He took a deep breath.

'The love I felt for Penny was a healing love. And the love I felt for you destroyed me. Penny made me feel whole again.'

Tears began to run silently down Manon's face, but she knew that he was not trying to be cruel.

'Don't,' he said, 'please don't...'

He went to touch her arm, but she shrank away from him.

'I wasn't conscious of wanting to hurt you back,' he said, 'when I married Penny, but maybe...'

Manon suddenly found a voice.

'But I didn't mean that you shouldn't have married her because of *me*,' she insisted. 'I meant, you shouldn't have because of *her*, because it wasn't fair to her. She deserved better.'

'But she wanted to marry me. And I loved her. She didn't even know about us.'

'She didn't because I stayed away,' Manon said, 'and that's what I hate you most for...'

'Hate me?' He sounded surprised and wounded.

'I don't hate you,' Manon corrected herself. 'What I'm most angry about is that you stopped Penny and me having a friendship. I couldn't see her with you. And she was my only friend. You took away my only friend. It was too great a punishment for what I did to you.'

'It wasn't a punishment,' he protested, then corrected himself, 'I don't think it was a punishment. I admit it took me a long time to get over you. But you were never part of my relationship with Penny. And you never saw each other anyway,' he added.

'Because I stayed away,' she insisted.

'Is that really true?' he asked, 'or is it a convenient excuse because now you wish you'd spent more time with her?'

'God, you really hate me,' she said.

'I don't.'

Now that it was spoken, the complex structure

of the relationship between the three of them that she had built in her mind didn't seem as obvious as it had when stowed away, un-examined. Had she really convinced herself of something that was not true in order to excuse her own weakness or laziness? Tears were rolling down her cheeks. She did not bother to wipe them away.

'When you came to Rome that time...' she began again, trying now to convince herself as much as him.

'Our honeymoon,' he said.

Yes, honeymoon. Why had she avoided saying the word?

'Yes. Your honeymoon!' she said, exasperated. 'Why did you have to come to Rome for your honeymoon, for God's sake?'

'Because we wanted to see Italy. And Penny wanted to see you, she was really upset that you didn't come to the wedding,' he said.

'There was one moment in the Piazza Navona when Rodolfo and Penny went to buy ice cream,' Manon pressed on, 'one moment when you I were alone, and you looked at me, and I knew that you still loved me.'

'That's not true,' he protested, 'it's just not true. I didn't even want to come to Rome. I thought it might be awkward...'

'There!' she said, as if that proved her argument.

'It wasn't like that,' he said defeatedly, 'it just wasn't like that.'

He remembered the moment. Everything about

297

that evening had been shrouded in softness: the warm damp air, the golden lamplight in the square, a group of Scandinavian teenagers strumming guitars quietly. The scream of brakes and the drone of mopeds seemed to have faded to somewhere in the distance. The air was scented with pizza ovens and rosemary.

Penny had formed a friendship with the saturnine Rodolfo solely on the basis that they both liked ice cream, he remembered with a sudden feeling of enormous affection for her. She had been brilliant at finding trivial threads of connection on which to hang a relationship. It was her great gift to make every individual think that they were special to her. It was what had made her such a good teacher, and it was why Saskia and Lily were so free from jealousy of one another.

It had been their last evening in Rome. The next day they were off to Venice. Rodolfo suddenly remembered that they had not yet tried the *gelati* at Gioliti, and had wanted to drive all of them across town, but the Piazzo Navona had been so idyllic that evening, both Roy and Manon had resisted moving from the pavement table where they were drinking tiny china cups of espresso.

'Oh, never mind,' Penny had said, 'let's just have one here.'

But Rodolfo wouldn't hear of it.

'What?' Manon's question interrupted his thoughts, and he realized he was smiling.

'What differentiates the English from other

Europeans is that they are so proud of their cuisine,' he said, as if that explained everything.

'What?' she asked again, amused because his mind seemed to have strayed so very far from what they had been talking about, she couldn't imagine how it had got there.

'I was just thinking of Rodolfo's insistence that Penny sample ice cream from a particular place. Can you imagine an Englishman caring one way or the other?'

'He probably just wanted to fuck her,' Manon said.

'Oh?' Roy was embarrassed by her sudden crudeness. He stumbled for words. 'I thought you were happy together?'

'Did you really?' She inclined her head in the knowing Gallic way she had, immediately seeing through his attempt to lie.

In the golden softness of the Piazzo Navona that balmy evening so many summers ago, Manon's misery had been starkly apparent. And the look that they had exchanged, which she had mistaken for his love, had not been that. Or perhaps it had. He remembered only feeling desperately sorry for her, and wanting to ask why, why she lived in the thrall of this shallow rich man, this playboy, when she could do anything, be with anyone, she wanted.

The next day, sitting on the train, waiting for it to leave Termini station, Penny had sighed.

'Poor Manon!'

And her sympathy had ignited irrational fury in him.

299

'Why poor?' he remembered shouting. 'I'd have thought poor is the one thing she isn't. She doesn't have to live with some fabulously rich count, or whatever he is, does she?'

Penny looked momentarily shocked by his outburst.

'She feels safe with him,' she said.

Then the train jolted, hissed, and began to pull out of the station. Penny had given him a little excited smile, and it was only then, several days after their wedding, that he had felt that they were starting their married life together.

In a way, Manon was right, he realized. If she had not been so conscientious about staying away from them, she might have become a raw nerve in their marriage, sensitive to the touch. And the business of sharing your life with another person was complicated enough.

In the silence, he wondered now what was going through Manon's mind as his sifted through the years that had passed since their encounter in the Piazza Navona. There had been four people then, and now there were just the two of them. It was a terrible truth that the reasons for their anger with one another no longer existed.

Finally, he asked her.

'So where do we go from here?'

Chapter 32

Ursula hurried past the burger van, sober enough now to regret her earlier binge. She cupped her hand over her mouth and breathed, unable to work out whether she had bad breath or whether it was simply the pervasive smell of. burger vans that permeated the fabric of this part of the city. They used to call them squirrel burgers, she remembered. She had read recently in one of the lifestyle supplements that came with the Sunday papers that there was a restaurant in London actually serving squirrel. Perhaps it had been an April Fool. She was always the one in the office who read out the spoof article with earnest outrage before looking up and realizing that everyone else was laughing.

Was the same thing about to happen? Was it all a joke, designed to make her look a fool, or to test her qualities as a human being? Would Liam be there? If not, how long was she supposed to wait? Ten minutes? An hour? What if he had drastically underestimated the driving time, or got lost, or run out of petrol, or crashed? For a moment she let herself imagine his body being collected by ambulance and rushed to the hospital in *Casualty*. Holby City. It even sounded like the sort of town you would find halfway between Nottingham and Oxford. She envisaged Charlie the male nurse pulling a sheet up over Liam's handsome face and shaking his head mournfully.

'Rushing to his lover in the middle of the night, apparently,' he might explain to appease the curiosity of the funny little dark-haired one with the nose ring.

Ursula shuddered as she walked past the gates of the Radcliffe Infirmary. North Oxford was uncannily still. It was summer vacation and this part of the city was sleeping. The click of her footsteps was as loud as a hammer on an anvil. What on earth was she doing strutting along like a trollop in a borrowed dress, on her way to begin an affair? The questions beat in her brain as fast as her racing pulse. Excitement in her stomach turned to nausea. There was no way out now.

But of course there was a way out. She could tell Liam immediately that it had all been a mistake. Apologize, shake hands. Offer to put him up in a hotel if he didn't want to drive all the way back straight away. She would deny herself her one great love and never see him again. And she would bear it, just as Meryl Streep had in *Bridges of Madison County* which had been on telly a couple of months back.

Then she saw him standing beside his metallic grey sports car outside the college. She began to run towards him. And as she launched herself into his arms and felt the insistence of his mouth on hers, she told herself that even the virtuous Meryl had allowed herself one weekend. Just one weekend away from real life.

'You got here, then,' she said, suddenly shy when their kiss ended, not knowing how to do the small talk.

'I got here.'

'Good drive down?'

He looked amused.

'Reasonably good, thank you.'

'Err ... would you like to go for a walk or something? There might be somewhere open we could get a coffee or a drink?' she asked.

'Why don't you show me your room?'

She giggled nervously.

'All right. I'll show you my room. It's not much of a room.'

They had to wake the porter to get through the lodge. It reminded her of visiting one of her clients in prison. The porter had the same mix of servility and suspicion that all guards and janitors seemed to have. She felt she ought to offer some explanation as to why this dashing man who had not been with her before was now accompanying her, but the only acceptable word she could think of was husband, and she could not say that.

As they walked across the quad she was suddenly terrified that one of the other women who were staying in college would see her. Was Leonora still hanging about? Was she still chatting to Roy up in the JCR? What on earth would she say to Roy if she saw him? All the questions she had been too drunk to consider earlier flooded soberly through her brain. But the quad was completely quiet.

'Was it a good evening?' Liam asked.

'Sssh,' she hissed as they picked their way through the darkness.

As soon as she opened the door to her room she saw that she had left the bed unmade and thrown her damp towel on top of it.

In the harsh light of the 60 watt bulb the curtains at the window looked thin and shabby. There was a cigarette burn she hadn't noticed before on the utilitarian carpet, and miscellaneous dried spillages. It was as if the soft-focus fantasy she had dared to dream was turning tawdry before her eyes.

Then Liam said, 'Turn off the light.'

Her hand, still on the switch, obeyed instantly and she felt a flood of sheer gratitude that he was taking over. She wanted to relinquish responsibility. In the darkness she closed her eyes, not wanting them to become adjusted and bear witness to what was going to happen.

Liam ripped the fastening of Annie's precious designer dress apart. It dropped to the floor and as Ursula stepped forward, he pushed his body against her back, felling them both. He twisted both her hands up behind her back and she lay with her nose pressed hard into the carpet breathing the odour of stale wine and dust and feeling his hands exploring her body like a brutal body search. Then his hands left her body and she could feel that his attention was on something else but she did not know what. She did not know the rules.

She heard the plastic snap of a condom packet being torn open.

The question of contraception had not even

occurred to her, she realized with shame, because she had never really dared to think that this would happen. Barry had had a vasectomy after George was born. Their GP had said it would make his penis look like an aubergine for a while. 'In shape or colour?' he had asked, turning white. She must not think of Barry.

She tried to flip over to look at Liam, but he placed his knee on the small of her back to keep her down while he put the condom on. She could sense his impatient concentration in the air, then suddenly the heat of his body close above her. He put a hand between her legs, and hoiked her to semi kneeling. In the moment before he entered her she was frightened that he was about to bugger her. She said,

'No...'

and then he plunged his penis into her vagina and began to shunt backwards and forwards in the slick of her juices. Her elbows and knees chafed against the carpet, which smelt like the inside of a vacuum cleaner bag. She tried to push herself up to kneeling, but Liam pushed her head down. She tried to give herself over to the sheer physicality of the way he was taking her, but all she could think was that it was like a punishment for wanting him so much.

He leaned forward, arching his back to achieve a new angle. It made him feel bigger inside her. His face was next to her ear.

'You're so fucking wet,' he was saying, 'you've been thinking about this all afternoon, haven't you? You're gagging for it. Come on,' he urged.

She began to move as she thought he wanted

her to, mirroring his movements, backwards and forwards, but his penis slipped out of her.

'It's not like this in the movies,' she whispered with a little giggle.

It was what Barry always said to her when something funny happened during sex, like her vagina farting as he went in, or his bad back twinging when they tried to do it in the bath.

Liam did not laugh. He shoved himself into her again, raising her bottom further. For a moment she thought he was going to touch her clitoris and she yelped with expectation, but both his hands came back to the cheeks of her bottom and he squeezed there hard, as if he was trying to press out his own orgasm. She felt the hot shudder of his ejaculation, then the wilting and withdrawal.

He stood up and dealt with the condom. She turned onto her side and watched him giving his penis a quick sluice in the handbasin. He seemed very used to the routine, she thought suddenly. Then he knelt on the floor beside her and kissed her on the nose. It was the first moment of affection since they entered the room.

'It's been a long time,' he said, smiling at her.

Since what? she wanted to ask. Since you last had sex, or since we met, or what?

He pulled her to her feet and led her to the bed, throwing the damp towel to the floor. He lay down first, then pulled her down beside him. He was still fully clothed. She put her head in his T-shirt smelling him, trying to recapture all the fantasies she had ever entertained about being alone in a bedroom with him. Her fingers worked their way under the soft cotton to his flesh, but she was nervous when he did not respond.

She had only ever slept with one man in her life. She wondered suddenly whether she had been doing everything wrong for the last fifteen years. The movements that made Barry's penis stand proud, seemed to have no effect whatsoever on Liam's. It nestled like a sleeping mouse. He took her hand and pushed it away gently.

'It was a long drive,' he said, with a yawn.

Then she understood. How selfish of her to demand he satisfy her when he had driven all the way through the night. He was tired. They would sleep and in the morning they would do it all properly.

A moment later, he was breathing regular damp blasts of air into her ear.

I am in bed with my lover, she thought. She shifted her head to look at his face, trying to relive the feeling she had had outside the lodge when she saw him waiting there.

In the space of less than an hour she had gone from feeling like an attractive woman in her prime embarking on a grown-up affair, to feeling like the sort of stupid teenage girl she often defended on minor drugs or prostitution charges. The sort of girl she asked, exasperated, 'But why did you let him do that to you?'

She watched Liam's sleeping face, but the magnetic field of desire around him that had drawn her whole mind and body in, had gone, as if the current had been switched off.

The bed was too narrow for two adults to share. The comforting intimacy of lying so close to him turned rapidly to frustration that she could not move. She wanted to get up and shake the fidgetyness out of her limbs but she was on the wall side of the bed and she would have to roll over him or wriggle down to the bottom of the bed, neither of which she could see herself doing without waking him.

No wonder girls whose boyfriends regularly climbed over the back gates had always looked so exhausted at breakfast.

His body looked unnaturally hot and the places where her skin touched his were wet with sweat. She found it impossible to get into a position where there was no point of contact. Her head ached, and her thirst was so profound she imagined herself drinking the entire contents of the huge upturned bottles in the mineral water dispenser at work and still having a dry throat.

It's not like this in the movies.

Her inappropriate remark kept repeating in her brain and she winced at the dismissive response he had given it, and then, even though she was trying really hard not to, she thought of Barry. She thought of him lying alone in their big double bed with its fresh-smelling cotton pillowcases and the summer-weight duvet and she felt safe for a moment. Then the full horror of the situation she was in shuddered through her body, and she began to cry.

Inching her way down to the bottom of the

bed, she stood up, stretched her arms and shook them vigorously. At the sink, she splashed her face with water and then cupped her hands and drank some, but it tasted of chlorine and the moment it reached her stomach she felt sick. She couldn't decide whether it would be better to make herself throw up or just lie down on the floor and try to sleep. The toilet was several doors down the corridor. She could not bear the thought of sticking a finger down her throat and choking her guts up in some chilly, unfamiliar loo.

She tried to make a pillow of the hard foam cushion from the armchair. The fabric was rough on her face, and the dust in it made her want to sneeze. She bit her tongue to stop herself. The floor was cold. Suddenly, from being overheated, she was shivering. She stood up and tried to push Liam gently towards the wall, but he flopped over, taking up even more room. She lay down on the floor again, using his leather jacket as a blanket.

The last time she had been really drunk was after the office party the previous Christmas. When she got home, she only just made it to the bathroom and Barry stood outside the door as she retched in case she choked. Afterwards he had sponged her forehead with cool water and ferried her mugs of hot sweet tea in bed before cleaning up the mess.

She had been terrified that she'd made a fool of herself at the Christmas party, but he had reassured her: 'They were probably all as drunk as you.' And even though she had known that was not true, it had eased the guilt enough to allow her to sleep, and by the next morning it didn't seem to matter nearly so much.

Now she needed him there to tell her that everything was going to be all right. She looked at her watch. Not yet two o'clock. Time seemed to have slowed down to prolong her agony, and sleep would not come to help her.

Chapter 33

'The trouble with having dreams come true is that even when you get everything you thought you wanted, you're still you, and you still have the same history and nothing really has changed,' Annie observed.

They had climbed over the railings and were sitting a yard or so apart on the curved steps of the Radcliffe Camera. The surfaces of the ancient stone buildings in the deserted square were ghostly white in the floodlights. The buildings looked flat, as if there were nothing behind the frontages. It was so much like a picture postcard of Oxford by Night that it felt like sitting in a film set replica of the square rather than the square itself.

Halfway between them on the step was the half-drunk bottle of champagne. She stretched out her hand and took a swig of it.

'That sounds a bit profound,' Ian said after a few moments.

'Not really. What I'm saying is that fantasies are two-dimensional. You fit yourself into an image of what it would be like to do something and you forget that you would still be the same person doing it with all the baggage that you already have. You know when people say approvingly, "all that money hasn't changed her..."'

'Yes.'

'Well, I would like to be the first person where they said "she's a completely different person now that she's rich!"'

A short loud burst of laughter emerged from his mouth and bounced around the square. She liked his laugh. One minute it was not there at all, and the next it was really loud and you never quite knew when it was going to surface. She thought she should get him to come along when they were shooting the next series. They recorded the programmes in front of a live audience, but they took a kind of average of the best laughs and added it on in the appropriate places afterwards. It was good to have someone with a really different laugh each week to make it sound more authentically live.

'What were your dreams when you were here?' she asked him.

'I'm not sure I really had any. I just remember it being bloody hard work. You arty farty types could skip tutorials and miss lectures, but you couldn't do that as a medic if you wanted to qualify. I was the first one in my family to come up and I felt enormous pressure to show that I deserved it. If I dreamed of anything I suppose it was having more sex,' he added.

He was a flirt, and she had to admit that she liked it. It was fun to flirt when you both knew it was going nowhere. It was the first time in ages she had talked to a man without reading something into everything he said.

'Really? I was just the opposite,' she responded, 'I was the first one too, and my mum hadn't the slightest idea what it involved, so there was no pressure whatsoever. I just wanted to have a good time. Loads of sex.'

'So if you had such a good time why so wistful now?' he asked.

'I don't know. Missed opportunities, wrong directions. Now I feel I should have done something proper, you know, and, well...'

'What's proper?'

'Something that I could rely on. Like, I have no qualifications at all apart from a poor degree. You have a profession. Ursula has a profession. Something you can take anywhere. Something that would make my mum less worried,' she admitted.

'I'm sure your mother isn't worried about your career!' he said.

'Why are you so sure? You don't know anything about it.' She suddenly felt enormously protective of her background, which a minute before she had been wanting to dream out of existence.

'Sorry,' he said.

'No,' she said, feeling instantly more reasonable since he hadn't taken the opportunity to argue with her, 'I'm sorry. You were only trying to be nice.'

'What do you mean, you don't have a proper job?' he asked, steering the conversation back.

'What I do you could write on the back of a postage stamp.'

'But making people laugh is a great gift.'

'That's my whole point,' she interrupted: 'if it's a gift then whoever gave it could take it back. It's not the same as a qualification.'

'This is all getting a bit semantic for me,' he said, taking the bottle from the mid-point where she had replaced it and having a swig. 'You have to remember that I'm a derivatives trader this evening and I don't understand about existential dilemmas.'

'Do you think what I've got is an existential dilemma?' Annie asked enthusiastically. It was always a relief to put a name to these vague insecurities. It made you feel less neurotic.

'Would you like my diagnosis?'

'Yes,' she said.

'I think you're a bit pissed off with life at the moment. Not surprising after what happened to Penny.'

She waited expectantly.

'That's it?' she said after a second or two.

'That's it.'

'I show you my soul, and you tell me I'm pissed off?'

'Yup. I could give you the Latin, of course.'

'Which is?'

'Pissedofficus minor.' Another short burst of laughter.

Even though it was a dreadful joke, she found herself joining in, then she leaned over and punched him hard on the arm.

'Ow!'

'You do know that I'm going to have to use that in the show. You won't mind, will you?' she asked.

'Delighted,' he said.

'Was that an example of your bedside manner, then?' she asked him.

'Now, that would be telling,' he said.

The floodlights suddenly went out.

Neither of them said anything for a few moments as their eyes adjusted to the darkness. The surfaces of the buildings began to look softer and more like stone than cardboard.

'Do you remember how if you weren't invited to anything on Saturday night, you'd wander round the streets listening, and soon enough you'd hear strains of "Suffragette City" or "Brown Sugar", and then all you'd have to do was follow your ears and crash the party?' Annie asked, wishing that she could hear some music now.

The city was very quiet tonight. She didn't want to go back to the hotel, but without flood-lights on it was as if they no longer had an excuse to sit and natter into the night.

'So that's why you were at every party I ever went to, even though you didn't know any of my friends?' Ian said.

'Was I? Saturday night wasn't all right unless you had at least three parties to go to,' Annie said, then suddenly jumped up. 'Hey, didn't there used to be a disco in the back of the shopping centre?'

'Did there?'

'It was a townie kind of place. More disco than pogo. Students weren't very welcome. I seem to remember twirling manically to "I Will Survive". Do you remember the *Top of the Pops* video of it? That girl on roller skates twirling and twirling. It was the anthem for my generation of women. In fact, we should have had it tonight after the Elgar...' she stopped for a moment, suddenly aware of how incredibly inappropriate that would have been.

'God, the number of times I've twirled alone at the end of parties,' she continued sadly.

'Come on, let's see if Tramps or Scamps or whatever it was called is still there.'

She jumped up, grabbed his arm and attempted to drag him down the steps.

'I never went there,' he said, refusing to budge.

'No, you wouldn't have done,' she replied, tugging at him, insistently.

'Why not?' he enquired, still sitting firm.

'It was only gay men, really, who thought they were being ironic and could dance.'

'I'm not a bad dancer,' he defended himself.

'Really?' Her tone said: tell me another.

'I go to Latin American classes with Zoe.'

'Zoe?'

'My daughter.'

'You go to dance classes with your teenage daughter?'

For a moment she couldn't work out whether that was pathetic or admirable. She hadn't had a father when she was a teenager, but if she had, she was almost certain that she would not have

315

wanted to go to dance classes with him.

She gave up trying to pull Ian off the steps and sat down again.

'Her idea,' he said. 'We didn't seem to be seeing much of each other. We both like dancing. Just seemed like a sensible plan,' he said.

'You don't have to explain it,' Annie told him grumpily.

The moment she thought she had a take on him, he would say something that made her think that she had got him all wrong.

'Can you dance?' he asked gently.

'Not really,' she admitted: 'to be honest I'd love to be able to dance properly, but it's like careers, I never put my mind to it. And I know it sounds really poncey, but I'm a bit too famous now to go for lessons. What I mean is that someone would recognize me and take a photo when I got my legs tangled up.'

'It's never too late to learn something new.'

'You're beginning to sound like a brochure for an active over-sixties holiday. I think I'd rather not learn at all than end up an old biddy waltzing the afternoon away with another old biddy in Blackpool. Sadly, I haven't got a pubescent partner of the opposite sex to call upon.'

'Come on!' He got up. 'I'll teach you.'

Now he was trying to pull her off the stone steps.

'I can't,' she protested.

'Why not?'

'Wrong shoes and look, there are cobble-stones, I'll break my ankle.'

'Kick your shoes off. I'll try not to tread on your toes. We'll dance on the grass.'

Having exhausted all the sensible excuses, she was obliged to follow him down the steps.

'Now,' he began to hum, then took both her hands and pulled her this way and that, 'very good,' he said, 'one two three four five six seven eight, that's it? Terrific!'

She felt herself relaxing with his encouragement.

'Wonderful,' he said, 'now, one two three four five six de dum de dadada two three four five six de dum de dadada... Oom, cha cha cha!' he tried a spin and almost dislocated her arm. 'Other way! Good. Try again. Oom, cha cha cha! Great! You're not at all bad at being led!'

'Don't sound so surprised!' she cried, exhilarated by the achievement of following his steps.

'Much better than Zoe, as a matter of fact. Now, let's try another spin. There! Magnificent! What a shame you changed out of that red dress.'

'I'll wear it next time there's a Latin American ball in Radcliffe Square!' she joked, touched that the dress had made such an impression on him. She began to sway her hips exaggeratedly and clap her hands at her shoulders.

'It's even better with music,' Ian said, breathlessly, as he twirled her one final time and they both fell down on the grass laughing.

'That was fun,' she said. 'If Zoe ever decides you're too old for her, you know who to call,' she said, adding quickly, 'If Chloe wouldn't mind.'

'I'm sure Chloe wouldn't mind,' he said.

'Good, well,' she sat up rather primly with her

back to him.

'You have a great body for dancing,' he remarked.

'Thank you.'

'A great body for anything, actually,' he said, leaning across and letting his forefinger run down her spine.

'You'd be surprised,' she said, shifting out of his reach. 'It's a hopeless body for getting into a size 10 dress, for instance, and hopeless for wearing cardigans.'

'Well, you can probably live without cardigans,' he said.

'Maybe next winter. It was pretty tricky last season,' she said. 'Tell you what, that dance has woken me up. Shall we go for a walk?'

'Why not?'

'Perhaps we could even see the dawn come up over Magdalen Bridge?'

'I thought you were supposed to do that on May the 1st?' he said.

'Well, better a couple of months late than never.'

'Didn't you ever do it while you were here? Maidens were meant to look in the mirror on May morning and see a vision of the man they were going to marry.'

'Well, (a) I hadn't been able to call myself a maiden for quite some time when I arrived in this city, and (b) if I had looked in the mirror on May morning I would have seen double vision of a man leaving my room saying, "That was great, I'll be in touch." I always ended up drinking too much or getting too stoned to go down to Magdalen Bridge. How about you?'

'In the third year I managed, but only because we had an early night beforehand, and Chloe set her alarm clock!'

'That's cheating!' Annie protested.

'OK, so it'll be the first time for both of us tonight,' he said, suggestively.

'How long have we got till dawn?' Annie asked him quickly.

'About three hours, do you think we'll manage?'

'Of course we will!'

She thought for a minute and then announced: 'I know, we'll take it in turns to choose a typically Oxford thing to do.'

'You first,' he said.

'OK,' Annie pondered for a moment, 'got it. We'll get into Christ Church and put ourselves in Mercury.'

'Mercury?' he asked warily.

'It's a pond with a statue of the winged Mercury in it. Oh, for heaven's sake, you philistine, *Brideshead Revisited*. It's what they do to Anthony Blanche. If you haven't read the book, you might at least have watched it on television.'

'All right then, you're on. How do we get in?'

'Just follow me,' Annie said, jumping up.

She threw her shoes over the waist-high railings.

'Would you give me a leg up?'

He put his hands on her waist and hoisted her over, then jumped over himself as they strode past Brasenose College towards the High Street.

'I remember Christ Church as being a bit like

319

a fortress. We'll never get over the wall.' Ian hurried along behind her.

'Who said anything about scaling walls?'

When they reached the lodge it looked forbiddingly closed. Undaunted, Annie rang the bell. A sleepy-looking porter eventually opened the door.

'A very good evening to you, Jim,' Annie leaned forward and kissed the surprised old man enthusiastically on both cheeks. 'Don't say you don't remember me!'

'Well,' the man stood back to get a better look, and Annie stepped through the door, pulling Ian in behind her.

'I was one of the first Christ Church girls. I can't believe you've forgotten me!' She stood under the dim light so that he could get a good look at her face. Because she was on television, people often mistook her for someone they knew. 'I haven't forgotten all the tellings-off I got from you, but listen, I know it's naughty and I'm old enough to know better, and all those other things you used to say, but I've just got married and we're spending the first night of our honeymoon in Oxford, you know, for old times' sake. Did you know my husband Ian, by the way? He was here too. Not at this college, of course. St Gertrude's! Who'd have thought I'd end up with a St Gert's man? But there we go. Anyway, he's never been in Mercury and you don't mind, do you? We'll just be a minute or two ... yes, I am on the telly now...'

And with that she made a dash towards the

fountain in the centre of the huge quad, still pulling Ian along behind her.

'He's just beginning to wonder why I'm wearing jeans and you're in a dinner jacket,' she said, looking back as they reached the pond. 'We haven't got much time, so you first!'

Ian jumped in enthusiastically, losing his footing as he did and belly-flopping. Annie gingerly extracted her right foot from her mule and put a toe in. 'A bit cold for me,' she announced, laughing and taking her toe out again.

'Oh no, you're not getting away with that,' Ian said, standing up and pulling her in with surprising strength.

'Ooh, you m ... m ... m ... meaty boy!' Annie said, doing an Anthony Blanche impersonation while trying to hold her hair up and out as he ducked her in the water. 'Enough!' she shrieked, seeing that the porter was beginning to walk towards them.

'He's just woken up enough to remember that he's not called Jim,' she said into Ian's ear. 'Time for us to go.'

They got out and walked dripping towards the lodge, picking up speed as they passed the porter who looked as if he still wasn't quite sure what was happening.

'I thought it was amazing that you could remember his name after all this time!'

'They were mostly called Jim,' Annie told him authoritatively.

'So which charm school taught you how to do that?' Ian panted, as they ran all the way back up to Cornmarket.

'My mother was an Avon lady,' Annie told him, 'we were very good at getting ourselves into people's houses. You just have to keep talking and keep moving forwards.'

'So now that we're wet and cold, and we've probably got incipient Weil's disease, what's next?' Ian asked her.

'Your turn, remember?' she said, like a challenge.

He seemed to be looking into the distance, ignoring her when suddenly he said, 'Follow me!' and started walking quickly down Cornmarket in the direction of McDonald's.

'Was this your first McDonald's?' Annie asked, as they found themselves under the yellow arches sign. 'It was mine. Can you imagine what life before McDonald's was like?'

'Ssssh,' he said.

Inside there was only one till open and an attendant was sweeping up around the tables. Two lanky men were the only customers. They seemed to be getting in a large order. Their server looked distinctly bored as she ferried shakes and polystyrene boxes in various pastel colours to the counter.

'I bet they've got the munchies,' Annie said. 'Once I had the munchies so badly I had three Big Macs and I didn't remember the last two until I discovered that all my money for the week had mysteriously disappeared from my purse. I still have to have one sometimes. It's the sauce.'

'Will you be quiet?' Ian hissed.

'Why?'

'Come on.' He turned suddenly.

'What?'

Leaning against a lamppost in front of the shop were two unlocked bikes.

'Orange or purple?' Ian asked her.

'We're not going to...?'

'Borrow them,' he said. 'I've been observing the owners closely and quite honestly I don't think they'll even notice.'

But before he could finish his sentence. Annie had grabbed the orange bike and was pedalling fast down Cornmarket towards St Giles. The bike rocked from side to side as the skill not used for twenty years returned to her.

'It's like riding a bicycle!' she shouted breathless with excitement as he caught up with her at the traffic lights. 'Where to?'

'There used to be an all-night café at the Woodstock roundabout,' he suggested.

'No hills on the way?'

'I don't think so.'

'Lead on!' she shrieked, as the lights turned green and she dared to look back to see the stoned men standing under the lamppost unable to work out what had happened.

Chapter 34

There was a hazy mist on the water. The punt slid through clusters of lily pads. The pond was so vast she could not see the banks, nor the horizon, only the silver surface and the chalky air above it. She let her hand drop into the water and drag along beside the boat. The water was ice-cold. Her fingers became numb almost immediately. She looked at Roy. He smiled at her, then he brought the punt pole out of the water and rested it along the length of the boat so that they were drifting. He sat down opposite her, shifting along the cushions to make room for her beside him. She stood up, wobbling slightly, and took a tentative step towards him. Then she was falling out of the punt, arms flailing, but instead of sinking into the cold water, the lily pads held her up like a lifebelt, oddly warm around her body, and she realized she had fallen into a giant nest. She could see Roy's stricken face drifting away from her, but she felt safe there, surrounded by soft downy warmth.

Manon woke up. The wonderfully calm feeling remained for a few seconds as her mind tried to establish where she was. She closed her eyes again, willing herself back to the nest, but one of her arms had pins and needles.

They were in the living room in Joshua Street, she remembered. Roy was sitting cross-legged on the floor behind her, cradling the upper part of her body in his arms. Most of her weight was resting on her left arm, which was why it had gone numb. She tried to extract it, alerting him to the fact that she had woken up.

'Are you OK?' he asked gently, as she wriggled out from his embrace and shook both arms.

'How long have I been asleep?' she asked.

'I don't know. You were lying on my watch. Not too long. It's not even light yet. Sleep overcame you. I thought that only happened in novels but one moment you were talking, and the next, you just lay down on the floor. I was trying to keep you warm,' he said, as if he needed to explain why he was holding her.

'It's all right,' she said, yawning and stretching again, 'I had a wonderful dream.' But as soon as she said it, the dream seemed to shimmer out of reach and she could not remember it properly.

As her eyes became accustomed to the darkness, she could see that his were sparkling with concern. He was such a serious boy. Still only half awake, she allowed her mind to drift back to the day she had met him.

Finals were over, the last paper written, champagne popped in the street outside Schools, hugs delivered to people she did not really know, goodbyes said. The celebration picnic that Penny had prepared had been eaten, more champagne drunk.

Roy had arrived just as she was leaving the others to while away the afternoon at the river.

She had ambled back to Joshua Street in the hot sun, feeling the tension of the exams unravelling in her shoulders.

The house was cool inside. She tore off the ridiculous gown they made you wear to sit exams. In the back yard, she struck a match. The black fabric took a moment to catch, then it burned so hungrily that she had to drop it and stamp on it for fear of setting Penny's hanging baskets on fire. Then she went inside again.

She sat in the kitchen at the back, enjoying the stillness of the empty house and trying to think, at this significant watershed in her life, something profound about Oxford. She had little idea what lay ahead. She had not bothered to make the trip to the Careers Advisory Service in the large yellow brick house in North Oxford where they told you to sit the Civil Service exams and apply for advertising agencies. If she had learned only one thing, it was that she would not be shoe-horned again into some English institution. In Paris, she had always found ways of making enough money to support herself through the long vacations. She knew enough about the world to know that for a woman a word-processed CV was not as valuable a resource as a slim body and a pretty face.

Then the doorbell rang and Roy was standing there, pink-faced from the exertion of carrying the heavy wicker hamper all the way back from the Parks.

'Penny's gone to see her boyfriend, Ursula and Annie got picked up by a party in a punt. There wasn't enough room for me,' he explained, in his soft Northern accent, lugging the basket over the threshold. 'Something burning?'

His hot presence intruding on her moment of contemplation, his casual reference to her friends' names and their assumption that she would be in to open the door for him, all irritated her. Indicating the location of the kitchen with a contemptuous Gallic wave of her hand, she escaped upstairs to her room, closing the door with a bang behind her. She took off the white polo shirt and black skirt and gathered them with the rest of her possessions into a rucksack. Then she lay down on the bed in her knickers. The sun on the front of the building made the small space stiflingly hot, and as she lay there trying to regain the sense of peace she had attained in the kitchen, she couldn't help picturing the boy sitting alone down there, wondering what he was going to do for the rest of the day. He had hitch-hiked all the way down into unfamiliar territory and then been abandoned. She could quite imagine how it had happened. Penny looking at her watch and making excuses to go off to Keble in time for tea, a boatload of inebriated finalists splashing past on the river, waving at Annie to join them, and Ursula having to decide between looking after her kid brother or her last chance to score.

In the hot stuffy room Manon fidgeted and frowned, pulled cutoff jeans and a black vest from the top of her rucksack, put them on and went downstairs again. The others would not return until much later and there was no particular point in she and Roy sitting in different parts of the house doing nothing. She knew that it was his first time in Oxford and that he was preparing to sit the entrance exams in the autumn. Perhaps a tour of the sights would be a good thing for both of them, an introduction to the city of dreaming spires for him, for her a farewell. But as she stood in the doorframe to the kitchen, she found she was not altruistic enough to offer him a guided tour after all.

'I'm going to go for a country walk,' she told him, 'do you want to come?'

He looked up, his face such an innocent picture of gratitude that she had felt strangely moved. And it was only then that she had seen just how young he was. Eighteen, he told her later that evening as they sat drinking in the garden of the Trout, with exaggerated certainty and a look over his shoulder which made her suspect that he was younger.

'When is your birthday, Roy?' she asked suddenly. It seemed a very odd question to be asking him now, so many years later, without explaining why.

'January,' he replied.

'I was trying to work out whether you were old enough to go into a pub that time we...' she hesitated, realizing that she had just revealed where her thoughts were.

'I was just thinking about that too,' he said.

'Whether you were old enough?' she asked, prepared to be amazed at their empathy.

'No!' he laughed, 'about our country walk. I always remember that you said that. A country walk. The words stuck out, you see.'

'Why?' she asked.

'Because a truly English person would just have said, let's go for a walk. It gave me a thrill,' he admitted.

'You were easily thrilled,' she remarked tartly.

'We ended up at the Trout,' he said.

'Yes,' she spoke cautiously.

'You drank bottles of Pils. I drank pints of ale. I couldn't believe I was there with you, drinking pints in a perfect country pub, with you.'

'We talked about D. H. Lawrence,' she said.

She had felt rather superior to him because she had passed the adolescent stage of thinking that Lawrence was the God of All Things Sensual, and begun to see him as a bit of a misogynist unjustly fêted for his understanding of women's sexuality. But Roy was very intelligent, and his sheer passion for literature was exhilarating to hear after three years of dry academic study. She remembered thinking that all his enthusiasm would be drained away just as hers had been, and she had fought back the urge to tell him not to come to this place. He quoted long passages that she had forgotten, until she was almost convinced that Lawrence was, after all, the greatest writer in the English language.

At some point, as darkness began to fall, one or other of them banged the wooden table to make a point with such force that pale brown liquid slopped over the top of Roy's glass, spreading in an inexorable puddle and dripping between the wooden slats onto their legs. It was the surprise with which her knees registered the splatters of beer like unexpected rain that had first alerted her to the fact that she was drunk. But by then it had been too late to do anything about it.

'I was seventeen,' Roy suddenly admitted.

'I was twenty-two,' she said.

Curiously, five years seemed a significant difference now, with him in his mid-thirties, and her approaching forty, but then it had not seemed so great.

'You don't really look any different,' he said.

'That's because it's dark in here.' She tried to deflect his compliment, but she could feel their bodies inching together, just as they had been drawn together that evening when they got back to Joshua Street and found everyone still out.

She had been filling the kettle to make coffee when suddenly he was right behind her and she turned into his arms. Mid-kiss they heard the sound of a key in the door, and sprang apart as Annie marched into the house.

'I can't understand whether your objection is on grounds of morals or taste,' she was saying loudly.

'Both!' Ursula said, letting herself into her room at the front downstairs, and closing the door with a loud bang.

'I got laid, she didn't,' Annie said in explanation as she looked into the kitchen. 'Is there any alcohol in the house?'

'No,' Manon replied.

'Shit, I'm going to bed then,' Annie said, turning round to reveal that her back was covered in bits of grass.

It was easy to guess what had happened, and both girls were clearly too drunk to show any concern for Roy's sleeping arrangements.

Manon made strong black coffee. They sat at the kitchen table, awkward now in each other's company but unwilling to be the first to say goodnight. She could remember staring at the brown foam that clung to the inside of the

330

empty mugs as she asked him politely what college he was applying to. Balliol, he said, because of its left-wing tradition. She thought it would be too unkind to disillusion him about student politics.

'What about you? What are you going to do now?' he had asked her, equally blandly, and she had given him a meaningless answer, knowing that they weren't really having a conversation, only marking time before one of them dared to move a fraction towards the other again.

'Travel the world. Leave all this behind.' She waved vaguely, so that she might have meant the kitchen, or the University, or life itself.

He was young enough not to have learned that his face was a barometer of his emotions. She thought that when he came to understand it he would break many hearts. He was very attractive, poised at the perfect moment in his life where his beauty was exactly balanced by his naivety. It was a combination that had made her feel both vulnerable and powerful in his presence.

Then they were kissing again. She did not want to want him, but she could not help herself. She unwound his hand from the back of her neck and pulled him to his feet, putting a finger to her lips to show that he must not make a sound. Then she led him upstairs to her tiny dark room.

In the darkness they discovered each other's bodies. The silence was a pact between them and their exploration of each other a ritual enacted with the utmost tenderness and reverence. He was on her, under her, beside her, beneath her, part of her, pressing all of his skin against hers. And then he was inside her and they were both gasping with the glory of what they were doing together. She put her hand over his mouth to quieten him as she moved on top, staring into his eyes, and as they came together, she fell down onto his chest shuddering. It was the only time in her life that she had felt as if her body and soul were the same entity.

They lay together on the floor as the air in the room grew chilly and grey.

'Have you got any 50 ps?' she whispered, breaking the uncanny silence.

He had used all his money buying rounds the previous evening.

'Oh well, it is my last day,' she said, showing him how she had learned to open the padlock on the meter. Then she struck a match and lit the hideous gas fire. 'Don't tell the others!' she told him, blowing out the match, then looking over her bare shoulder with a little wicked smile as the blue flames whooshed in the dawn light in the tiny room.

It was that sentence and that image of her perfect back in the flickering blue light that had stayed with him for many years after.

He had fallen asleep, and when he awoke she was no longer in the room. The fire was off. At first he assumed that she was in the bathroom, then he imagined her in the kitchen making coffee. As he dozed, he even convinced himself that he could smell the coffee. Every creak of the house was the sound of her footfall tiptoeing up the stairs. He moved from the floor onto the narrow single bed, shifting as far as he could to one side to leave room for her, kicking the counterpane off, then pulling it back up as he remembered that she liked to be warm. He lay there, with the cover pulled right up to his chin, smiling at the door, expecting it to open any second. But she had not come back.

After a while, he had begun to invent new reasons for her absence. The revised scenario was that she had gone for an early morning walk. He was crestfallen that she had not asked him to go with her, then suddenly scared as he heard the sound of movement coming from the other rooms. He realized that if he didn't want to be caught in her room, he would have to make his way downstairs very rapidly. As he pulled on his clothes, he noticed that her black vest and frayed cutoff Levis were no longer on the floor, but thought it only logical that she would have dressed before going out.

In the darkness of the night before, he hadn't seen that there had been a rucksack packed and standing by the door which had now disappeared too.

As he closed the door carefully, it occurred to him that the room looked very clear and very empty. Then he heard Annie getting up and was only saved from being discovered because she had found a cigarette in her room and had collapsed back on her bed to smoke it. The acrid fumes wafted onto the landing as he tiptoed past her door.

He remembered the joy in his step as he went

downstairs, the blue sky visible through the pane of glass above the front door, the sensation of being in love. He was longing to be outside with Manon, in the open where when he told her that he loved her, no-one would be able to hear. He wanted to shout 'I love you' so much that it was almost physically painful to keep the words in. He had murmured it silently again and again into her hair and her skin during the night, but he had not yet said it out loud. But she knew. And she loved him. He knew it. He sat down at the kitchen table to hide his growing erection. And only then had he seen the note.

Enjoy your lives! love Manon.

He was still staring at it when his sister emerged bleary-eyed from her bedroom.

'Oh hi! Where did you sleep?'

'In there.' Thinking quickly, he pointed at the small back room that had a battered old sofa and a television in it.

She did not notice his lie because she was peering at the piece of paper in his hand.

'What's that?'

He handed it over.

'Oh, she's gone then. Typical of her not to say goodbye, but I suppose we weren't really in a fit state...'

'Gone?'

'She couldn't wait to get out of here,' Ursula said with a sniff.

He noticed for the first time that whenever his sister talked about Manon she adopted a disparaging tone.

'You don't like her much, do you?' he asked.

334

'Not really,' she replied. 'You never know what she's thinking.'

It had felt as if a piece of his soul had been amputated.

After a couple more days in Oxford he eventually accepted that she was not going to come back and he returned to Nottingham where he re-read *Lady Chatterley's Lover* in the light of sexual experience. When Ursula returned home a few days later he asked for Manon's address, pretending that they had discussed a book that he had promised to send her. His sister had not suspected. Ursula was the sort of person who was always surprised by other people's deviousness. Privately he had wondered whether the law was really the best career choice for her.

His first letters to Manon were cautious, then when she did not reply, more passionate, until the letters became a kind of secret refuge from the constant agony of his infatuation.

Finally, she wrote back. His mother handed him the pale blue envelope with a quizzical look on her face. Seeing the French stamp and the scrawl that he recognized from the note on the kitchen table at Joshua Street, he rushed out of the house and ran all the way to the park to read it. There was just one small piece of paper

Dear Roy,
Please do not write to me any more. I cannot love you and if you knew anything about me, you would not love me.

335

Congratulations on getting a scholarship to Oxford. I hope all your dreams come true there.
Manon

He had tortured all sorts of meanings from those few simple words, but he had never understood.

Now his lips were kissing the top of her head distractedly and repeatedly, like an adult comforting a child.

'Hold me,' she said, turning to face him.

He held her quite still. She could feel his heartbeat against her cheek. She pulled her face away from his shirt. They looked at each other. Then their heads tilted slightly to one side as if asking a silent question, and then his moved towards her and he kissed her lips and she kissed him back. She shifted to kneeling. Then they were both kneeling, holding each other's faces. Then his hands were in her hair, and her palms were cupping the fine sandpaper of his chin, and then simultaneously they stood up, and she stepped towards him so that the length of her body was pressed against his. They kissed, stopped kissing, kissed again, then stepped apart and looked at each other, and the exchange of souls in that look was more intimate than any kiss could be. Fully clothed, she felt naked.

She took his hand, as she had taken it many years before, and led them upstairs, to the tiny room above the front door.

The street light outside cast a dull shadow of the cross of the window onto one of the walls. Roy hung his jacket on the empty curtain rail. He came to her, wrapping his arms around her shivering shoulders, transmitting his warmth to her. She wanted nothing except to be held like that.

Then again, smelling him, the wonderful mixture of spray starch and masculinity, she unbuckled the belt of his formal trousers, unzipped him, and let the smooth wool fabric drop to the floor, feeling herself flood with longing as she saw his erection trying to force its way out of his innocent white cotton pants.

He stepped out of his trousers. Then stepped backwards and took off his shirt. She slipped her feet out of her shoes. The carpet felt very dry against the soles of her feet. He was standing, waiting, in black socks and white cotton pants, and she still had her dress on but she felt completely vulnerable. In the dull light seeping into the room, she saw that there were a few tufts of wiry hair on his chest. He was a man now. Suddenly, she could no longer bear not touching him. In one swift movement, she bent, grabbed the hem of her dress in both hands and unfurled it all the way up her body and over her head. She could feel her skin contracting into goosebumps. Then she stepped towards him.

He grasped her hair in both hands twisting it high up on her crown and then letting it tumble again to her waist. He drew her to him, enveloping her skinny form in his body, his head dipping towards hers to kiss her. She put her hands on his shoulders and climbed his body like a tree until she was sitting above the branch

337

of his erection, her legs wrapped tightly round his waist, and kissed him back as she had never kissed anyone else.

Cradling her bottom in one hand, he hooked his finger round the edge of her black cotton panties, pulling the fabric just enough to allow his penis to slip straight into her. She shrieked with unexpected pleasure and they both collapsed laughing to the floor, still joined together, with her on top of him, her insides liquefying around him until the moment when they both became liquid together.

'Don't say it,' she put a finger to his mouth as he opened his eyes and looked up at her face.

'How did you know?'

'It was the quality of the silence,' she told him.

'Don't you think we have been silent for too long?' he asked, suddenly impatient with her silences.

'Yes. Probably.'

'Why don't you want me to say I love you?' he asked, breaking the taboo she had silently imposed on the word.

She yelped and waited, but strangely it was not so very painful to hear it.

She remembered Penny saying to her once, 'You're afraid of someone loving you too much, so you push them away.'

'Not in this place,' Manon said to Roy, putting her hand over his mouth to quieten him.

'This is our place.' His hand shrugged hers off and gesticulated around the small room. The light seeping round the edge of his jacket was pale now. A new day was approaching. 'This room has always been ours. I pretended it was my office, but it was never my office. It was always the place where I had lost my virginity.'

'You were a virgin?' she asked, rolling off him and lying next to him.

'What did you think?'

'Not that you were a virgin,' she said, coyly.

'We were so good together,' he said, running a finger down her breastbone.

'Why did you not move away from here?' she asked, suddenly shy about talking about sex.

He sat up, and sighed, as if he didn't want to talk about his life since that day but knew that it was inevitable.

'Why would we move? We couldn't afford to. I stayed out of this room as much as I could.'

She noticed how careful he was not to use Penny's name.

He slumped back down to the floor beside her. They both lay staring at the ceiling. She tried to cover herself with her dress. He put an arm behind her neck and drew her into the warmth of his chest. She felt so comfortable there that she allowed herself to ask the question she had always banned from her consciousness.

'How would our lives have been, do you think?'

'If you had let me love you?' he asked.

'Yes.'

'I don't know. I don't know if there's any point in talking about it.'

'Of course not,' she said, quickly.

Could she have settled into Oxford life and

become a don's wife? Or a don herself? Would she have made him happy? Would he her? And the most unanswerable question of all. If all their lives had followed different paths, would Penny still have died?

Nobody knew why Penny had cancer. It was not in her family. She had not smoked. People talked about chance X-rays in the atmosphere randomly hitting cells and making them cancerous. But if that was what had happened, then it was only logical to think that anything could have changed events. A phone call, a supermarket queue. Even if her life had been different by just a second, the lethal ray might not have found its target.

But the unrelenting chain of guilt would never bring her back. It would not change anything except the future.

'Why didn't you tell Penny about us?' Roy suddenly asked, as if he had been having similar thoughts.

'Why didn't you?'

He thought for a moment.

'At first I kept it secret because I somehow knew that Ursula wouldn't like it, and, I suppose, because it kept it alive. If it was a secret then it was a possibility. If I had told anyone they would have said, don't be so stupid, forget about it, and then it wouldn't be there any more.'

He paused, then went on:

'I didn't meet up with Penny until several years later, and we were just friends to begin with. It was irrelevant. I did consider telling her when we started sleeping together, but because

I hadn't told her all the time we were friends, I thought it would look as if I had been hiding it for a reason, or that it was significant to us. It would have made it more than it was...'

He looked at Manon.

'Why didn't you tell her?' he asked.

She had been frightened of her own feelings, and terrified because she knew that he had fallen in love with her. Keeping it secret was the nearest she could get to persuading herself that it had not happened, because if it had happened, then it would destroy him. Just as loving her had destroyed Carl.

She thought for a long time before answering him, and when she spoke the words were only half-truthful.

'I dared not admit that I could feel so much. I thought it would go away,' she said. She looked at him, his cornflower blue eyes, his chopped corn hair.

'But it didn't,' she said.

Chapter 35

The lights of the service station were like the palm trees of an oasis to a desert traveller. Annie was hot, sweating profusely and so out of breath that her lungs felt as if they were full of sand. The last couple of hundred yards were downhill. Annie freewheeled gratefully down the dual carriageway. Ian was sitting on his bike at the entrance to the services. He waved at her. Unwilling to negotiate the roundabout, Annie got off her bike and pushed it across the road.

'Bad news, I'm afraid,' Ian said, 'It's closed.'

'Closed? It was always open all night...'

'Apparently, the nearest all-night one is Cherwell Valley.'

'Where's Cherwell Valley?'

'Fifteen minutes away.'

'Fifteen minutes by car?'

He nodded.

'I can't believe it,' Annie felt close to tears. 'The only thing that has kept me going is the thought of one of those huge cooked breakfasts drenched in fat that turns to little white circles on the plate which you mop up with piles of white toast...'

She slumped over the handlebars. 'I once knew a bloke with a car and we came out here once and filched loads of sachets of brown sauce and teaspoons and things. I think I even got away with a sugar shaker...'

'No wonder they had to close,' Ian joked.

'There must be something open,' Annie said, looking round desperately.

'The petrol bit is.'

He had clearly done a full reconnaissance while waiting for her to arrive.

The bright white light of the kiosk was intensely unflattering and accentuated the black pinpricks of stubble on Ian's white chin, but Ursula was right, he did not have a moustache.

Annie knew that her own face was shiny and

pink after all the unaccustomed exercise, especially around the nose, which had in the past couple of years begun to behave like a beacon whenever she was hot, cold or drunk. She reached into her bag, and, as surreptitiously as she could, flicked open a compact and dabbed at her nose with powder, then reapplied her lipstick, checking with a quick grimace that there was none on her teeth.

'So your mother is an Avon lady?' Ian said, watching her hasty beauty routine. 'I didn't know that they really existed.'

'What do you mean by that?' Annie asked, snapping the compact shut.

'Well, I thought they were just an advertising gimmick. You know, like the Michelin Man.'

'He was made of spare tyres and had no idea how to make the best of himself,' Annie said, 'the complete antithesis of an Avon lady. What are we having?'

'Twix, Mars, Lion Bar?'

'Fine, and what do you want?' she asked. 'Will you get me a Diet Coke?'

'Diet?' Ian said, looking at the array of chocolate.

'Of course.'

'Well, this is nice,' Annie said, with heavy sarcasm, as they sat down on some grass near the exit. The artificial light of the signs made it feel a bit like being in the studio. She tore the wrapper off her Mars Bar.

'I'm going to start a diet on Monday,' she said, before taking a large bite.

'You don't need to diet,' he said.

'Sweet of you,' she smiled at him. 'Anyway, I do need to load myself up with carbohydrate if I'm going to pedal all the way back to town. You assured me it was flat,' she said in an accusatory tone.

'I don't think I ever came here on a bike,' he said.

'Now he tells me.'

'Anyway, it'll be downhill all the way back.'

'No, it won't. When you had this mad idea of becoming bicycle thieves, I had momentarily forgotten the two laws of cycling in Oxford.'

'Which are?'

'One, whichever road you take, it is always uphill, and two, the wind is always against you. So even though you'd expect the wind to be behind us on the way back, it will definitely have changed direction while we were here.'

A blast of laughter.

She struggled to her feet and marched over to the kiosk again, returning after a few minutes with a Wispa.

'I had to sign an autograph,' she told him.

'Must be quite tiresome being famous.' His face was a picture of mock sympathy.

'Only when they insist I'm the one from *East-Enders*.'

'Oh.'

'You must get bothered all the time too,' she said, 'when people hear that you're a doctor. Do they start telling you about their ailments?'

'Sometimes,' he said cautiously.

'Must be awful having to hear about someone's fungal toe at a dinner party.'

'I don't seem to do as many dinner parties as you do,' he said.

'No, well, not surprising in the circumstances,' she said, then, thinking that might sound rude, she added, 'I meant with having children and everything.'

'You ever thought of having any?'

'What?'

She didn't know whether he meant dinner parties or children.

'Children. Have you ever wanted children?'

'How do you know I haven't got any?'

It was the first time she had seen him looking surprised.

'I suppose from your show, and – how can I put it tactfully? – most women your age who have had children...' He stared appreciatively at her chest.

'That is an outrageously sexist thing to say,' she protested, but she felt a little secret thrill nevertheless. It was a bit like the time two years before when she came third in a viewer poll of best legs in television. It wasn't the same as winning a BAFTA (she imagined, because she had never won one), but it was pretty damn close. She knew that it wasn't politically correct to like people admiring her legs (Ursula had been appalled), but Annie wasn't offended enough to refuse to go on a daytime television programme to pick the winning entry form out of a giant stiletto shoe and announce the name of the lucky viewer who had won a year's supply of Sheer and Silky 15 denier tights. Unfortunately her random choice had been a man, but the producer loved that even more.

'You shouldn't assume anything,' Annie said, hoping that in the neon her red nose would equalize the blush she was trying to suppress, 'but as it happens I haven't got children.'

'Do you want some?'

That was a bit intrusive.

'Mind your own business,' she snapped, then, thinking that made her sound like a typical thirty-something with a biological clock, she added, 'Actually, I don't think I do.'

'Are you an only child?'

She began to feel slightly irritated by his probing. Just because they were sitting on a motorway verge together at, she looked at her watch, half-past two in the morning, didn't mean he had a right to her life story, did it?

'Yeah,' she said. Then she couldn't resist the urge to elaborate.

'In a way, I'm glad, because I couldn't bear the idea of competing for my mum's affection, but it also means I have to look after her,' she said. 'She's going a bit barmy even though she's quite young, and ... oh well, you don't want to hear all this. Mothers with Alzheimer's are probably worse than fungal toes as far as you're concerned.'

'Not at all,' he said, and his saucy grin changed instantly to a look of real concern. She could see he would be a lovely doctor.

'I'm thinking of having her move in with me,' she said for the second time that day. Say it a third time, she thought, and it might as well have happened.

'Why?'

'She's getting so forgetful, I keep expecting the call that says she can't find her way home.'

'But you wouldn't be able to look after her yourself, would you?'

'I'd probably hire a nurse.'

She didn't really want to venture any further into the practicalities.

'Can I say one thing?' he asked.

'Yes,' she said, eager for any professional advice.

'Don't do it out of any misplaced feeling of duty. It can be pretty miserable for the carer, you know, and I'm not sure how much difference it makes to the sufferer. Alzheimer's patients need round the clock attention. It can be a thankless task.'

'She's not incontintent or anything,' Annie said.

'No.'

The equivocation in his voice made it sound like 'not yet'. Suddenly she was rather frightened by what he was saying.

'She did everything for me,' she said.

'Of course she did. She's your mother.'

'I'm her daughter.'

'Not the same. Let me ask you something. Think of your mother in her right mind. Would she have wanted you to give up your life in order to look after her if she lost her mind.'

'Absolutely!' Annie said with a laugh, but she realized that she was speaking about the interfering mother in her show. The last thing Marjorie would have wanted was to get in Annie's way.

Ian looked at the sky.

'If we're going to get back by dawn, we'd better be off,' he said.

Away from the neon, it was still quite dark and the road was quiet. Very few people were mad enough to be out at this time. None on bikes. The night air felt damp in her lungs. Annie wished that she was tucked up asleep in a nice warm bed. She pedalled as fast as she could, but the bike was like the exercise bike she occasionally sat on at the gym which had all sorts of computer-animated scenery on the screen, but never actually went anywhere. The difference was that at the gym you could program the bike for an easy ride and read a glossy magazine while you pedalled, whereas on the road you were forced to get off and push at every slight incline.

Ian would get far ahead, then get off and wait for her to catch him up.

It reminded her of the holiday she had been on with Rick who was the love of her life before Max. They had spent a week on Crete. The way to get around the island, he had said, was on motor scooters. She had gone along with the plan without really thinking about it. It looked like fun, but the reality of entrusting yourself to a machine that had the power to run away from you if you twisted the handlebar a little too quickly, as it did when she first started the engine and tried to get on, was a little different.

The man from the hire shop caught the bike as it spluttered off without her. She picked herself up and bravely got back on, but her confidence had gone. Rick sped off ahead looking back at her and steering the bike with one hand at the same time, but she could only manage a snail's pace. For the rest of the day Rick would ride a few miles ahead then stop and have a cigarette while he waited for her to catch up. At first he found her pathetic crawl along the half-made roads amusing, but after a few stops he became impatient, and by the end of the hot sweaty day he had descended into a silent sulk from which he never quite emerged. Despite the sunburn, she had tried to make up for it in bed that night, but his disappointment in her was immutable. The next year, he had taken the woman he was going to marry to Greece, and Annie had wondered whether the motor scooter ordeal was a kind of test-drive for marriageability which she had dismally failed.

By the time they reached North Oxford, she was tired and hot and had a strong presentiment that the strain she was feeling in her calf muscles was nothing to the pain she would suffer the next day. It was getting light. Dawn was chasing them and catching up.

'Shit,' she said, puffing up behind Ian's stationary bike.

'Come on,' he said, 'the last haul. It really is downhill from here.'

'It's all very well,' she muttered. 'You have a nice rest while I catch you up – no wonder you're finding it easier. And your bike's got more gears.'

'Swap?' he offered.

'All right.'

They swapped bikes, but the seat was too high on his.

'I don't have a spanner,' he said, patting his pockets as if there might be a toolkit about his person.

'Call yourself a man!' she said.

'Come on. You can't give up now,' he said, swapping the bikes back again, 'I'll give you a start. As soon as you disappear from view I'll start pedalling and the last one to Magdalen Bridge pays for breakfast.'

Unable to resist a challenge, Annie set off pedalling as hard as she could, but within seconds he caught her up and rode along beside her, and even though she could see that he was only pretending to struggle to keep up with her, she was still determined to win.

Suddenly the greying light began to flash like a stroboscope. They both craned their necks, saw the police car coming up behind them and Ian pulled easily in front of her to make space for it to speed past. Instead the police car began to slow down and stopped about a hundred yards down the road in front of them.

It was only when a uniformed officer got out and began walking towards them that either of them realized what was happening.

'Oh God,' Annie said, putting both feet down flat, 'we're going to be done for theft. I can't believe it. My career is over.'

In her mind she could see a little box entitled 'On yer bike!' under the main story on the front of Monday's *Mirror*. There was never much news on the weekend and there was nothing they liked better than a minor celebrity embarrassment.

'Let me handle this,' Ian whispered, giving her his bike to hold, then striding forward manfully.

'Can I help you officer?' he said.

'Do you realize your lights aren't working, sir?'

'I'm terribly sorry, officer.'

'Indeed, you don't seem to have any lights...'

'Let me explain, you see, the thing is,' Annie said, coming up behind him, 'we were only borrowing them. It was a kind of dare. I'd never seen the sunrise on May the 1st and he had only done it with an alarm clock, and we had to keep ourselves awake, so...'

Ian stepped back hard on her foot.

'Can I ask if you've been drinking sir?'

The policeman continued to address Ian.

'A couple glasses of wine at dinner, officer.'

The policeman looked suspiciously at Annie, as though he was trying to call up a computer-generated image of a suspect rather than the publicity photo of a sitcom star. From experience, she knew that it would take about a minute for his brain to click through the options and finally remember where he had seen her before. She knew that there was a wonderfully witty line waiting to be said to him, but she couldn't think what it was. Seconds of silence felt like hours spent staring at the screen of her word processor when she was blocked. Then, like a miraculous piece of inspiration, the policeman's radio began talking to him. He continued to stare at them, ignoring the nonsensical blasts of buzz, and then he cautioned them humourlessly, as if they were students who spent their lives performing dangerous pranks:

'I'm going to let you off with a warning on this occasion, but I don't want to see you without lights again and I shall remind you that it is an offence to be drunk in charge of a pedal cycle.'

'Now just a minute...' Annie began to protest, but Ian interrupted.

'That's very kind of you, officer. Thank you for being so understanding. We'll walk back to town, shall we?'

'If you wouldn't mind, sir.'

The policeman looked at Ian, then at her. Annie opened her mouth to say something, but Ian was quicker.

'Come on darling, let's do as the officer says, shall we?' he said, taking her arm. He and the officer exchanged a look of sympathy as if it were part of a man's suffering to put up with silly women. The policeman gave her another frown, and then turned and walked away.

'Be quiet!' Ian hissed under his breath.

'What a bloody nerve!'

Ian smiled and waved as the police car drove away. Then, as soon as it disappeared from view they both got back on their bikes and began to pedal along side by side at a leisurely pace.

'I don't believe that drunk in charge of a pedal cycle is really a proper charge,' Annie said.

'I think it is.'

'So, would they breathalyse you?'

'I don't know. I remember a friend of mine had a friend who was done for it. He was cycling on the pavement and this police car was crawling along beside him, but he was so wrecked that he thought that they were having a race...'

'That happened to a friend of a friend of mine too,' Annie said.

'Perhaps it was the same one?'

'I think it was probably one of those apocryphal Oxford stories.'

'Like the one about the philosophy student who went to his final exam and the question was "Is this a question?" and he wrote, "If it is, then this is the answer"?'

'Yeah, and the one about the student who telephoned his college on Christmas Day and said "Is that Jesus?" and when the porter said yes, he said "Happy Birthday!"'

They shrieked with laughter as they pedalled past their old college.

'Hey, have you noticed something,' Annie shouted.

'No, what?' he asked.

'It's light. We've missed the bloody dawn again. And it was all your fault for chatting to that bloody policeman ... "oh thank you so much, officer, you've been so understanding, officer..."' She put a finger in her mouth and pretended to puke.

'If I'd let you deal with it, we'd have been charged with theft by now,' Ian defended himself.

'I thought he was bound to have a report of the theft. I was only trying to offer our mitigating circumstances straight away.'

'Don't you remember the guys we stole the bikes from? Did they really look as if they would have gone straight to the police?'

'Oh all right,' Annie conceded, as they pedalled the last stretch of St Giles. 'So since you're so clever, what are we going to do with them now?'

'Put them back where we found them,' Ian suggested.

Cornmarket was deserted. They rested the two bikes against the lamppost outside McDonald's.

'They're going to think it was one hell of a trip they were on when they find them again,' Annie said with a smile, which turned instantly into a wince of pain.

'What's the problem?' Ian asked.

'My leg has cramped,' she said, bending over to rub her calf. 'Jesus, it feels as if it's seized up.'

Ian helped her sit down on the pavement. He slipped off her shoe and bent her foot towards him from the ankle.

'Ow!' Annie cried.

'Better?'

'Worse,' she said.

'Wait here,' Ian instructed.

He disappeared up the road. Sitting on the cold pavement, she fought tears of pain and exhaustion. The chilly air was suddenly full of the incessant chirping of the dawn chorus.

'Oh shut up!' she shouted.

Where was Ian? What was he doing leaving her crippled like this? Had he gone to get his doctor's bag. How serious could cramp in your leg be? she asked herself, feeling her muscles tearing as she tried to stand up again. She hit the pavement hard with the palm of her hand in frustration, swore out loud, then stopped to listen. Amid the mocking twittering of birds there was a metallic clinking and trundling noise drawing closer which she could not place but which sounded strangely familiar. Then, from the cobbled side street that led down the back of the Oxford Union, Ian reappeared pushing an empty Marks and Spencer shopping trolley.

'Madame, your carriage awaits,' he announced with a bow.

He let go of the trolley to help her up. It rolled away to one side.

'Hmm, not exactly the Rolls-Royce of shopping trolleys, but it was the only one I could find.'

He hoisted her up and lifted her into the trolley as if she were weightless, then stood back to look at her.

'All you need now is a ballgown.'

She began to giggle, then to laugh, as he pushed her all the way back to the Randolph Hotel.

Chapter 36

The light round the edges of the impromptu curtain was bright and golden. Roy sat up quickly. Alone. Manon had left him again.

He lay down, feeling guilty because it was the first time since Penny became too ill to share a bed with him that he had woken up without a moment of surprise that she was not there beside him. There was always a split second when he was tempted by the thought that nothing had happened, that his wife was simply sleeping in the children's room as she did when they were ill or frightened, that he was not alone.

He gazed at the corona of light around the window until his focus was lost in tears that rolled down the sides of his cheeks and dripped silently into the carpet. He wondered whether there would ever come a time when he would greet the new day free from dread.

Manon had gone. He was more resigned than disappointed. The intensity of sex the night before had made him as certain of his love for her as the first time, but it was an illusion, a spell that she cast.

Perhaps Ursula had been right to say, as she had one weekend when she was visiting with George just a baby, that Manon was a siren, calling men to their doom. He tried to think why Manon would have been the subject under discussion, since they rarely mentioned her. On the odd occasions when one of her letters dropped through the door, Penny would smile and put it in a pocket to read it later when she was alone.

It must have been just after Lily was born, he thought, and Penny was telling Ursula of her choice of godmother. It was an awkward conversation in which he had realized that even though Ursula was already godmother to their first child, she was still jealous of the honour to Manon. She had always wanted Penny to be her best friend. Women could be very possessive about such things. He remembered his sister's increasingly hurt face as Penny had defended Manon.

It was then that he had found out about the boy who had killed himself. It had finally given him a reason why Manon had behaved as she did. As the women chattered on, he remembered the pale, fearful face staring back at him the last time he had seen her in the Piazza Navona, and began to understand.

Manon was sitting on the edge of the bath wearing Roy's shirt as a dressing gown. The first rays of sunshine had already taken the chill out of the air, but she was shivering, from sex and love and loss of sleep, and the giddy mix of elation and fear that follow. In this pleasant white room with the door locked behind her, she could believe she was in a transitional capsule between the grey continuum of the past, and whatever would become her future. She wanted her life to be as simple and light as the sky outside the curtainless bathroom window which was the palest duck-egg blue. But she feared that when she opened the bathroom door, it would all become complicated again. She felt safe sitting staring at the door handle, wishing and wanting all on her own.

Her first instinct on waking had been to flee, but she knew she could not do that to him again, or to herself.

All the pent-up anger that had made her so tense in his company had gone. It was as if she had been walking along a beach on a bleak winter day with the wind blowing so strongly that her head and face had become numb, then suddenly the wind had dropped and a few thin rays of sunshine had begun to warm her features back to life.

She smiled at the physical memory of making love with him, then frowned. If she was going to have a future with Roy, he would have to know about the baby. Sooner or later the question of contraception which had eluded them in passion would occur to him because he was a decent man. She could either not tell him and have the abortion, or risk everything by telling him. Or there was a third choice: to encourage a relationship and announce the pregnancy as soon as it was feasible, playing around with the dates when the baby was born. It was a seductive thought.

Manon stood up suddenly and grasped the door handle.

Roy heard the click of the bathroom door. He held his breath as footsteps padded across the landing.

'I was dying for a wee,' Manon said, lying back down beside him, 'I seem to want to go all the time now. I think it must be something to do with being pregnant.'

In one mad second of joy that she was still there, he thought she meant with him. Women knew sometimes, didn't they, straight away?

'You're pregnant?' he repeated.

'Yes,' she said.

She found herself smiling at him. It was such a relief to tell someone, such a relief not to have given in to the temptation of deception.

'How many weeks?' Roy asked.

'I don't know. Two or three?'

He stared at her as if he was about to cry. The rims of his eyes were red, she suddenly noticed, as if he *had* been crying.

'What's the matter?' she asked him.

Then he did cry. And she put her arms around his shaking chest and held him tightly, so sorry for upsetting him.

'I'm sorry, I'm sorry … it's all been…' he tried to excuse the unmanly display of weeping.

'It's all right. I know,' she said softly into his hair.

His fast, dry shaking sobs became slower wretched gasps, and then he became calmer. 'I'm sorry,' he said, looking up like a child. 'You haven't got a tissue, have you?'

She got up from the floor and went back to the bathroom, returning with a wodge of toilet roll.

He blew his nose with an unexpectedly noisy blast which made them both laugh.

'These are new,' he said, gently pushing the shirt off her shoulders, touching first the bluebird on her shoulder, then the heart tattoo on her outer thigh.

'Not very new,' she said.

'This will have to go.' He touched the ring through her belly button.

She shrank away and pulled the shirt back on.

'I thought you said you weren't with someone,' Roy said, very casually, as if he was now going to pretend that it didn't matter to him.

'I'm not really with him.'

'What is his name?' he asked, as if they were having a perfectly normal conversation.

Her natural inclination was to deflect his efforts to extract further information. She did not want to talk about Frank, but she realized she must.

'Frank,' she said. 'He's one of the regulars at the club.'

'Very trendy?'

'A film producer.'

'I see.'

What do you see? she wanted to ask him. It was the response of a jaded tutor to a student's excuse for failing to produce an essay.

'Are you in love with him?' Roy asked.

'He's married, very married. He fascinates me, but I don't like him very much,' she said.

'Then why?'

He pushed back the hair from his head in a gesture she remembered from long ago. It made her think of Huckleberry Finn, and she almost expected him to say 'Aw shucks!'

'I didn't mean to get pregnant, if that's what you mean.'

'Oh.'

He thought of the methodical way Penny had gone about the process of conceiving Saskia: no alcohol or soft cheese, and folic acid tablets on the bathroom shelf for weeks before. When it did not happen the first month after the ceremonial throwing-away of her cap, there had been a test to tell when she was ovulating. He didn't know that grown women became pregnant by accident any more.

'The condom broke. I even got myself the morning-after pill, but I'd taken it before and it made me sick. I didn't think there was much of a risk,' Manon explained.

'But why did you sleep with him?'

She looked up. The plaintive tone of his question sent a tremor of terror through her that made her shrink like a snail poked with a stick by an inquisitive child.

'Roy, I have slept with a lot of men.'

'I know that, but why him, if you did not like him much?' he asked, trying to convince himself as much as her that his question was an entirely reasonable one. He could not be jealous of someone he did not know.

'He's attractive, very sure of himself,' she began.

'Very unlikely to kill himself over you?' Roy interrupted with cruel directness.

She was startled.

361

'I did not know that you knew about that.'

'I didn't, until quite recently.'

'Penny told you?'

'It just came up in conversation.'

She wanted to know when, but she knew it wasn't important. Was that really the reason she had been attracted to Frank, she wondered. Was that why she had felt safe with Rodolfo? Had everyone been able to see that except her?

'When's the baby due?' Roy asked softly.

Baby.

'I don't know. I only did a test yesterday, no, Friday. I haven't decided what to do.' She found she could not say the word abortion. 'I can't even give it a home.'

'Why did you tell me?' Roy asked.

'I don't know.'

In the bathroom it had seemed absolutely necessary to tell him, and now it seemed complete stupidity to have involved him at all. It made it look as though she was asking him to do something about it. She couldn't believe that everything had gone wrong so quickly.

Roy's mind was churning with questions he was frightened to ask. Was she asking him to be the father? Was this to be the beginning of a life together? Did she want to be with him? Did she want to have the baby? He pictured her face again as Lily and Saskia hurtled towards her and thought that he knew the answer to that one.

'If you are asking me to be the baby's father, I would be delighted to oblige,' he said. His nervousness made the statement sound pompous,

362

like something from a Victorian novel.

'Sorry,' he said, 'I sound like a complete prat.'

'No, it's a very generous thing to say, and chivalrous...'

'Nobody need know that I'm not the child's biological father,' he interrupted, to show that he meant it. 'Not that it matters anyway.'

'Doesn't it?' she asked.

'It's the person who's there who counts,' he said. 'I still call myself a Marxist, so I must believe it's your environment that makes you what you are.' He paused. 'Hell, Manon, you know that I love you, don't you?'

The bright boyish innocent smile again.

Manon got up off the floor and stretched up on tiptoes to take his jacket from the curtain rail. Light flooded into the room. She turned round. Roy raised his forearm to shade his eye. She smiled at him. He stretched out both arms to her. She knelt down between his legs and he half sat up and hugged her chest down onto his. They held each other tightly for many minutes in the pool of sunlight. Her cheek was pressed against his and she could feel that he couldn't stop smiling.

So this was it, her future. It was simple and light after all. In this empty room in this empty house, it felt as if they were the only people in the world.

Then his grasp loosened very slightly, and he began to kiss her face, and she could feel his erection hard against her tummy, and suddenly she began to panic.

Things didn't work out like this. It was crazy

to think that they could just become a family. It wasn't real life. She hardly knew Roy, she realized, and he knew her even less, and they were not the only people in the world.

She drew her head away from his. He was looking at her as if he expected her to say, Fine, that's settled, Let's live happily ever after.

'I love you,' he said, trying to pull her towards him again, disappointed when she made herself rigid to resist him.

She rolled off him and onto her back a little way away from him. 'You wouldn't love me if you knew me,' she said, looking at the ceiling.

He sighed.

'You said that before, a long time ago,' he said, putting his arm under her shoulder and drawing her stiff body close to him again. 'Explain.'

'Frank paid me money to sleep with him,' she blurted in a rush of wretched self-incrimination. 'He knew someone who had known me years ago in Cannes, and he knew that's what I did then...'

Now she looked at Roy, wanting him to see that she was telling him the truth.

'When I left Oxford, I fucked strangers for money.'

The words were brutally honest and cold. She saw his face turn white, and wanted to take them back, but they were said now. It was too late.

'Not on the street,' she said, trying to soften the information, 'not in some terrible cramped room with a leopardskin bedspread and pink net curtains or anything. I worked the good hotels.'

'Why?' he asked, stunned.

364

'Because we needed the money. Because it was easier for me to get it than for my mother.'

He had imagined many lives for Manon, but never this one, and yet there was something specific and familiar about the description of the tawdry tart's apartment Then he remembered a story in Manon's collection which was set in that very room. She had been describing her mother's flat.

'My mother was an alcoholic and a drug addict, and by the time I understood that, her body was so fucked up it was too late to do anything about it except keep her supplied. I did modelling, which is only really the sanitized end of the whole business, and, God, if you're being ordered to pose this way and that all day by egotistical men, 5,000 francs for a fuck seems like such a breeze.'

She looked at the side of his face to see his reaction. He was punch drunk.

'Far easier than taking the Civil Service exams anyway!' she said, with a short ironic laugh.

'And when your mother died?' he asked, as if he hoped that would be an end to it.

'When she died, I left Paris. I went south and worked the resorts. I was never a full-time hooker. I always wanted to believe that it wasn't my real job. I became a croupier. I was very good at it. That's how I met Rodolfo.'

'Did he know?'

'I made the mistake of telling him before he found out for himself. At first, when he loved me, he saw me as a victim, and in his big-hearted Italian way he wanted to take me away from all that. I think he thought I would be his Sophia Loren, plucked from the streets and turned into a star, or something like that. Then, when he didn't love me so much, he said I was born a whore. Neither version had much to do with the truth.'

She saw the alarm on Roy's face. It was strangely reassuring to know that he now despised her.

'He began to give me wildly lavish presents when he wanted sex, and I know it sounds silly, but I found that more cheapening than anything I had done before. But perhaps I was just kidding myself. Perhaps I was prostituting myself all along. He had almost limitless wealth, you see, and when I decided to go with him I thought his money would make me free.'

'You did not love him?' Roy asked, shocked.

'You're such a romantic, Roy.'

She allowed herself a smile which faded as he did not return it. She picked at the carpet as if searching for a lost speck of dust.

'I don't know if it was love,' she said. 'He was offering me a home. A lovely home. I had never really had a home before. I went willingly and happily.'

'You ended up a prisoner in a *palazzo*.'

'Almost. I escaped.' Again she tried to smile at him but he would not look at her.

'Did Penny know all this?' he asked.

'Some.'

'What did she think?'

'She worried about my safety. She thought I should value myself more.'

366

'You should.'

The advice sounded final, as if she was nothing to do with him any more.

'She made me promise that I would not do it again, but she didn't need to because I don't hate myself now quite as much as I did,' she offered.

There was a long pause. Several times Roy looked as if he was about to say something but stopped.

'And Frank?' he eventually asked.

'Frank didn't know that I had changed,' she protested, resenting him for remembering Frank's name and picking her logic apart. How could she explain to this innocent man about £1,000 hidden in a Lulu Guinness bag?

'I see,' Roy said again.

'Now you hate me,' she said.

'I don't hate you,' he said, too quickly.

His grip had relaxed on her arm and it did not tighten for a moment to show that he meant it. She lay perfectly still, craving that absent squeeze, feeling exposed without it.

The silence felt unending.

'Come on,' he said at last, 'I want to be back before the girls wake up.'

He put his shirt on.

Did Mrs Harris's curtain twitch? He couldn't be sure, but he felt suddenly ashamed of what had happened in Penny's house.

In the candid morning light, he noticed for the first time that Manon's face had aged in the years that had passed since they first met. There were fine lines around her eyes. She was a woman, not a girl, not an evanescent wisp of fantasy that slipped away as soon as you tried to clutch it.

'I'll get the bus,' she said, putting her clothes on and peering at the floor as if she might have left something behind.

'No. The girls would love to see you.' He looked at her.

'I can see them some other time. I have to get back.'

He knew he must be honest about his ambivalence otherwise she would be gone again, for ever this time.

He grasped her forearms. She looked up at him. He thought of all the times he had imagined those pale green eyes and wondered what was going on in her mind and how it had never crossed his mind to think...

'Look,' he said, abruptly, 'I feel as if we have thrown our lives up in the air and they're still up there and we don't know where they're going to land. We have to wait for them to come down. Don't go just yet.'

Her instinct was to catch her falling life, bundle it up and run away with it, but she felt so tired.

'Come on,' he said again, sensing her giving in.

Downstairs, in the middle of the living room, her red rose flowerbasket bag sat on the beige fitted carpet like a fresh bouquet on a grave. She went to pick it up. Then the room was empty again, and there was no evidence that anyone had been there.

'Well, this really is goodbye,' Roy said, as he

opened the front door.

She looked down the hall to the kitchen at the back, seeing them all for a ghost of a moment sitting at the table around the remnants of one of Penny's pasta dishes, laughing, and Penny asking, in that slightly shocked way she had when things got a little raucous, 'What will become of us?'

The dampness of the dew chilled their flesh as they stepped into the street. He put his dinner jacket around her shoulders. They walked through the maze of little terraced streets that separated the flotsam and jetsam of bohemian Jericho from the respectable burghers of North Oxford. A shivering girl in an oversized dinner jacket, a man in formal dress and shirt sleeves. She imagined that they must look like exhausted revellers returning from a May Ball, not an unusual sight on a cloudless summer morning in Oxford.

As they neared the junction with Woodstock Road, another couple, the man also dressed in evening wear, the woman in jeans, sailed past the end of the road on bikes, their laughter pealing through the still silence.

'Was that Annie?' Roy asked, pausing, interrupting the metronome tap of their footsteps on the pavement.

'Can't have been. She was with a man.'

She realized the sentence was ridiculous when Roy raised his eyebrows comically.

'She's coming to lunch,' he said, 'with Ursula. Please come?'

He was working hard at keeping it going so that they would not leave each other in confusion.

'What will we tell Geraldine about where we spent the night?' she asked as they crossed the road to where Roy's car was parked outside St Gertrude's. Next to it was a small sports car she had not noticed the day before. Its polished silver paint gleamed in the sunshine.

'She won't ask,' Roy replied confidently, but she could tell that he was as uncertain as she was.

Chapter 37

Ursula was sitting in the Examination Schools preparing to turn over her first finals exam when she became aware that the invigilator was walking up the aisle between the long rows of desk towards her.

'Candidates for the University Examinations must wear full subfusc,' he said, staring at her chest and she was suddenly aware that she was wearing no clothes at all...

Ursula woke up.

There was a loud thumping on the door.

'Yes?' she said cautiously, struggling to think who would have reason to knock at the door. The police? Why should the police be here? What was going on?

'I've got your husband on the phone,' said the voice.

Why would Barry have called the police?

She stood up uncertainly. The full rush of her hangover pulsated through her head, making her reel. She sat down again, looking forlornly round the room for the beige dress she had been wearing the previous evening. First she saw Annie's black dress crumpled on the floor, then she saw Liam sleeping in the bed. There was a dribble of saliva dangling from the side of his mouth. The moment of readjustment was instant and bitter. Guilt hammered against the inside of her skull.

'Just a minute,' she said to the door, trying to collect herself, 'who is it?'

'It's the porter,' he replied. 'Shall I tell him to call back when you've had a chance to sort yourself out?'

The clear implication was that he knew what she was up to.

'What's the time?' she called.

'It's nearly nine o'clock. He says he would have left it, but he's at the hospital and he didn't want you calling and finding nobody at home.'

'Hospital?' she shrieked. The fuzz of alcohol suddenly evaporated from her body leaving only the clarity of fear in her brain.

'Which hospital, why didn't he call my mobile?'

She snatched up her bag and saw that the phone was switched off. Who had switched it off? She was about to round on Liam, who was beginning to stir irritably, as if inconvenienced by the noise, then she remembered the moment that she herself had switched it off in haste when

371

Annie had caught her talking to him in Brown's.

Frantically she pulled on her casual clothes, Marks and Spencer khaki slacks and a matching top; then, running her fingers through her hair, she opened the door. Behind her, Liam turned over again, pulling the blankets over his head.

'Come on!' she said to the porter, as if he was the one who had been keeping them waiting.

They ran down the stairs and across the quad. She was at the lodge before he was and snatched up the receiver.

'Barry?'

'We're at Casualty. Hang on, I've got to put some more money in...'

'Which hospital?' she screamed at him, in case his money ran out.

'It's OK, that's another pound's worth.'

'What's happened?'

'It's George. His temperature went right up and he got a bit of a rash. I called the GP, he couldn't come for hours, so I decided to bring him here.'

Meningitis, she thought. My punishment is meningitis.

'Oh God!'

'We've seen a doctor...'

Ursula held her breath. There were sinking moments when the responsibility of having a child was so awful you did not think you would be strong enough to cope with it.

'...and you'll never guess what, it's chickenpox!' Barry said.

'Chickenpox?' she repeated, 'you mean as well?'

'As well as what? It's just chickenpox.'

'Have you seen a consultant?'

'No, I think she was a registrar.'

'Insist on a consultant.' Ursula's mind raced on, thinking of all the newspaper stories about mis-diagnosis, children who had been brought to hospital only to be sent home to die twenty-four hours later. Whole episodes of *ER*...

'Ursula, it's OK. It's chickenpox. They're none too thrilled at us bringing an infectious child in anyway.'

'Have you done the glass test?' she asked him, trying to summon up all the medical knowledge she had gained from anxiously watching *Panorama* specials.

'What?'

'Have you pressed a glass down his arm and seen if the rash goes away?'

'No? Would a can of Coke do? There's a machine.'

'Barry, you can't see through a can of Coke, can you?' She tried to keep herself calm. 'Is he listless, not himself?'

'A bit, but I think he's missing you.'

A sharp intake of guilt.

'Is he there? Shall I say hello to him?'

'Here, George, do you want to say hello to Mummy? Oh. He says he's busy playing with the train.'

Her heart seemed to start beating again. Children in the advanced stages of meningitis did not get preoccupied with trains, did they?

'Where are the others?' she asked.

'I've got them all here. It was a bit early in the

morning to wake your mother.'

'What does the rash look like?'

'Lots of spots,' Barry said, 'more and more of them by the minute. Look, I'd better be getting them home.'

'I'm coming back straight away,' she said.

'There's no need.'

'Of course I will,' she said.

'Are you sure?' he asked, and she could hear the relief in his voice.

Poor Barry, she thought, suddenly realizing how frightened he must have been to take the child to Casualty. She pictured the four of them, all in their pyjamas, waiting anxiously in the inhospitable pale green waiting area. The last time they had been up to A and E was when Chris had caught his foot in an animal trap on a night hike with the Cubs. Barry had held the bloodied limb in position for the X-ray, talking bravely to his son all the while, but when it was over, he had promptly fainted on the hard lino floor of the radiography room. Afterwards he had blamed the weight of the lead waistcoat they made him wear, but she had witnessed the greyness of apprehension on his face.

'We'll be OK,' he said, 'really.'

'No, of course I'm coming, darling,' she said.

'I'm sorry,' he said, 'were you having a nice time?'

'Not really,' she said, 'it was only going to be a picnic with the children today. I can do that any time. Anyway I saw them yesterday, briefly, so I don't suppose Roy would mind.'

She realized she was babbling. Stop talking,

she told herself. Do not incriminate yourself.

'I'll get the first train I can. I'm going back to my room and turning my mobile back on. I seem to have switched it off by mistake,' she explained. 'Call me when you get home.'

'Money's running out again,' he said.

'Big kiss,' she said into the dead phone.

It felt so normal talking to him that she had almost managed to block out the world of deception she had created for herself but it returned as soon as she replaced the receiver. She didn't know how to behave with the porter. She told herself it did not matter. Right now, all that mattered was George. She thought of the alabaster roundness of his sleeping face and a great welling of love rose inside her.

'One of my children is ill,' she told the porter, which wiped the knowing smirk off his face.

'I am sorry. Anything I can do to help?'

Don't tell anyone about the man in my room, she wanted to say, but knew that it would only add fuel to his speculations. Don't volunteer information: she reminded herself of the advice she gave her clients. The right of silence had been undermined recently, but it was still usually the best way of protecting yourself.

'No, thank you. We'll be leaving right away.'

For all he knew she might be divorced, or separated. Loads of people were. She tossed her head casually, feeling herself going red. She had always been useless at dissembling.

'Of course,' the porter said, in his irritating, knowing way.

Oh, for heaven's sake, she told herself as she

hurried back across the quad, it's no good blaming the porter.

In her haste, she had left her key inside her room. She knocked.

'Go away!' Liam growled.

'It's me, let me in,' she said.

After a moment or two, he came to the door.

'What's going on?' he asked, looking at her expectantly.

'What?' She glanced behind her to see what he was getting at.

'When I saw you gone, I thought you might have nipped out for coffee and croissants. There's a Raymond Blanc pâtisserie next to Brown's...'

'George has been in Casualty,' she said, pushing past him and starting to gather up her belongings.

'Which one is he?' he said.

'My youngest,' she said, picking up her mobile phone and switching it on only to hear the sharp bleep that said the battery was about to run out. Swearing she threw it back into the bag.

'Your son George? I thought you...'

'You thought what?' she asked impatiently.

'I thought you meant the television programme,' he laughed and tried to put his arms around her. She shrugged him off.

'Why would I race out at–' she looked at her watch '–nine in the morning, to get the latest on a long-running soap?' The words shot out aggressively.

He held up his hands in his defence. She realized that it was the first time he had seen her behaving like an angry grown-up woman rather than a simpering adolescent.

'Excuse me!' He put sarcastic emphasis on the second word.

'I've got to go back,' she said.

'Nothing infectious, is it?' he asked, shifting away from her.

She looked at him with undisguised contempt, then rifled through her handbag and produced a timetable.

'You're going back now?' he asked.

'Yes!' she screamed at him. Why was he being so thick? He had not even asked what was wrong with George.

'Is there anywhere I could shower?' he asked.

'No. There isn't time.' Her eyes tried to make sense of the blur of numbers in front of her. 'It's Sunday, isn't it? There's one in forty minutes.'

'Let me drive you,' Liam offered half-heartedly.

'Thank you, no,' she said.

'To the station at least?'

A brief image of herself as a student puffing frantically up the road to the station flew through her mind. It was always a longer walk than you expected.

'All right then,' she said. 'I have to stop off at the Randolph first.'

She took one look back at the shabby room as she closed the door, wondering whether she would be able to shut away what had happened there as easily.

'I could do with a coffee...' Liam looked longingly at the Maison Blanc as they drove past it.

377

It would only take five minutes and he was saving her time by driving her to the station, she told herself.

'OK, then,' she relented.

He pulled up opposite.

'I don't think you're allowed to park here,' she told him.

'I doubt if there are any traffic wardens about at this ungodly hour of the Sabbath,' he replied.

The pâtisserie smelt of buttery pastry.

He ordered two cappuccinos, and they perched on high stools waiting for the scalding coffee to cool. She went to the counter to get a bottle of fizzy mineral water and took a sip from the neck. The bubbles seemed to reactivate the champagne from the night before.

Liam's eyes travelled along the rows of gleaming chocolate mousse cakes and tartlets of downy crimson raspberries dusted with icing sugar. His face was like a child's trying to weigh up the advantages of each indulgence against the next. Eventually he chose a palmier, then was unable to resist an almond croissant to take away as well.

'Can I get you something?' he asked, breaking the rounded heart of flaking pastry and popping a little piece into his mouth.

She imagined the sensation of the sweet pastry melting to butter on her alcohol-soured tongue.

'No,' she said, 'no thank you.'

There was something quintessentially French about the smell of fine baking, the mirrored walls, the perfection of the presentation of everything from simple sandwiches to long clear tubes of pink and white sugared almonds.

When Liam had talked of a weekend away, a weekend she had never seriously thought that they would share, she had imagined Paris, because that was where lovers went, and here they were, she thought, in a little bit of Paris transported to the centre of Oxford. She watched him eating, a few crumbly flakes of palmier clinging to his unshaven chin, but she could not reclaim the overwhelming excitement that the Paris fantasy had always given her. This morning he seemed an entirely separate being from her, just a good-looking man eating a pastry at the same table. Before, she had felt as if their souls were intertwined.

'Come on,' she said, 'we'd better go.'

He got the assistant to pour his coffee into a polystyrene cup which Ursula held for him as he drove down St Giles. At the Randolph Hotel, she left him drinking the scalding coffee in the car then walked quickly through the lobby and up the stairs, taking them two at a time, and ran down the corridor to Annie's room.

A DO NOT DISTURB notice dangled from the door handle.

Ursula knocked, then looked at her watch. Half an hour had passed since she had talked to Barry. Come on! She knocked again, harder.

Annie opened the door looking cross and bleary-eyed.

'Oh, it's you!' she said.

'George is ill, I'm going home. Can I have my dress? I've got yours in my bag. I'll have it cleaned and send it to you.'

379

She would buy another one, she thought.

'Of course,' Annie said, waking up a little. 'Is it serious?'

'Chickenpox. But it's horrible to be ill without your mum, isn't it? Look, I've got to run, I've got a train to catch.' She wondered if Annie was sleepy enough not to ask questions.

'Can't I drive you home? I'm sure it would be quicker.'

Ursula just looked at her.

'You're right. It probably wouldn't,' Annie admitted.

'Thanks for the offer, though,' Ursula said. She knew how much Annie hated driving.

Annie went inside and got the dress. Then she stepped forward and gave her friend a long, tight hug.

'Hey, I hope Georgie's OK. Ring me, won't you, and let me know?'

'Of course I will,' Ursula said, squeezing her back, drawing strength from the embrace, then breaking away. 'Look, will you say sorry to Roy for me? Tell him I'll call later. My mobile's not charged, you see.'

'Yes, of course.'

'And, Annie, you won't tell anyone about last night, will you? Promise?'

'Of course not,' Annie said, her face suddenly brightening into a salacious smile as she remembered. 'How was it, by the way?'

'He didn't turn up,' Ursula said.

'Oh. I'm sorry. Bastard. Actually, probably just as well in the circumstances.'

'Yes.' Ursula didn't trust herself to say more.

'Call me,' Annie said, closing the door.

'Thanks.'

Ursula walked down the stairs and past reception with the linen dress under her arm.

'OK?' Liam asked as she opened the passenger door.

'OK,' she said.

'I saved you a bit of croissant,' he said, 'it's very good.'

He handed her the paper bag that he was using as a plate. It was covered in flakes of pastry and toasted almonds crusted with icing sugar. She put a piece into her mouth. It was sweet and fatty and tasted like the apotheosis of everything sinful in her life. Shameful and delicious at the same time. She looked sideways at her companion. If in the future she ever thought about her affair with Liam, she knew she would remember this moment, the taste of sugar and almonds, the slight leathery smell of the interior of his car, and the overwhelming feeling of having done wrong.

'How long before your train?' he asked, as he drew up at the station.

'About seven minutes.'

He switched off the engine.

She wished she had said two minutes and then they would not have been obliged to talk.

'What will you do?' she asked him politely.

'I thought I might go out to Woodstock. Have lunch at the Bear.'

'Look, I'd better get going. I need to buy a paper to read.'

'OK, then.'

She gathered up her overnight bag and her handbag from the floor. And then she looked at him. He was staring through the windscreen, not looking at her. This was it. This was the last time she would see him, unless they happened to bump into each other in court, where they would nod professionally at one another and turn away, and she would probably manage to go over on her heel as she attempted to walk nonchalantly away from him.

She wondered if it would have been different if Barry had not phoned, but she couldn't help thinking that in a way she had had a lucky escape. In the cold light of day, Liam's love-making felt as humiliating as it had the previous evening, and she could not believe that they would have found themselves this morning in perfectly harmonious sexual union. Her body felt so tender she could hardly bear the thought of being touched. But still, seeing the end of it all so stark in front of her, she was struggling to bite back tears. The affair, which she had never quite believed in, had proved her right by not really happening after all.

As she opened the passenger door, he smiled at her and she could see the relief in his eyes. He was clearly finding this as difficult as she was, although she suspected for different reasons. She closed the door again. His face fell.

'What was it that you saw in me?' she asked, determined to know, because if she did not now, she never would.

'What do you mean?'

'What was it that you found attractive?' she persevered.

He thought for a moment.

'Your eyes,' he said.

'My eyes?'

'They're an incredible colour, both startling, and startled. Your gorgeous hair...' he reached over and pushed a lock of it behind her ear.

'...and I suppose, your innocence. For an intelligent woman you are so very innocent,' he said, smiling at her.

She didn't know whether to feel flattered or patronized.

'They're not real,' she said, suddenly, 'my eyes. They're contact lenses.'

For a moment he looked slightly disconcerted but said nothing. He did not ask what she had seen in him. It was obvious. He was clearly used to daft middle-aged women falling for him.

She opened the car door again, and looked back at him one last time, 'Bye then,' she said, pulling herself out of the car and slamming the door without hearing his response.

He accelerated away, and she watched the car as it circled the car park then roared towards the exit.

She thought of Meryl Streep in *Bridges of Madison County* watching Clint Eastwood's van disappearing down the long farm track at the end of their illicit weekend together.

But instead of thinking, 'I am giving him up for my family,' Ursula was asking herself, 'What on earth can I have been thinking of?'

Chapter 38

Annie could hardly believe her eyes. Unless Oxford minicab drivers had suddenly taken to ferrying their passengers around in metallic grey two-seater sports models, she had just seen Ursula getting into her lover's car and driving off at speed.

Annie let the curtain drop back in front of her face. Outside, in the scant privacy of Beaumont Street, both her virginal ex-flatmates were carrying on illicit affairs, while the one who had been renowned for her promiscuity looked on from the window of her chaste single room.

When Ian had tipped her out of the shopping trolley onto the steps of the Randolph earlier that morning, there had been a moment when she knew that if she held onto his hand for one millisecond longer than she needed to get her balance, they would end up in bed together. In the space of twelve hours her relationship with him had gone from not even remembering who he was, through tolerating him for politeness' sake, right the way to beginning to fantasize about what would have happened if she had noticed him when they were at university. Her initial assessment that he would be a boring lay had changed in the light of his laughter, his unneurotic appetite for chocolate in the middle of the night, and particularly his remembering what she had said about the shopping trolley. Now she thought that he might well be a considerate and inventive lover, but somehow that made it all the more difficult to think about going to bed with him. There was too much at stake. She didn't want to spoil their larky night together with all that 'I'll call you' stuff in the morning.

That, and the fact that the torn muscle in her left calf made her leg feel as if it were trapped in a vice, had made her gently withdraw her hand from his.

Annie got back into bed, pulled the cover right over her head and tried to go back to sleep, but the image of Ursula ducking into the stubby little sports car tormented her with its intrigue. For one thing, what self-respecting middle-aged man would drive such a car? Secondly, it was so unlike Ursula to lie. Ursula had many qualities, but she simply did not have the imagination to invent a child with chickenpox as a reason to bunk off from her obligations as a friend and aunt.

Annie turned over onto her front, but unconsciousness continued to elude her. If she was going to go to lunch with Roy and the girls, she thought, she would have to buy them presents. She was clearly famed for the presents she sent them because just the day before, as they were leaving to go punting, Lily had suddenly registered who she was, and demanded to know whether she had brought her anything. It had been a sweet moment for Annie, flanked by Ursula and Manon, and she the only one not a godmother.

Annie stuck her left arm out from under the sheet and squinted at her watch. She had no idea how far it was to Penny's parents' village, but she found it impossible to drive with a map on the steering wheel as some men did, and she wasn't very good at navigating even with the car parked in a lay-by and both hands and eyes free to work out how the lines on the page translated into the scenery around her. If she didn't get a move on, she would not even get there for lunch.

By the time she had showered and dressed, breakfast downstairs was over, but they were serving morning coffee in the lounge. She discovered Ian behind the *Observer*, which slightly surprised her because she would have had him down as a *Sunday Telegraph* kind of man, although she did not really know what that meant. Of the great pile of newspapers she lugged back from the newsagent's every Sunday lunchtime the only one she ever read was the *Mail on Sunday*. Most of the people she knew who called themselves *Guardian* readers spent the tube journey to work craning over the person in the next seat's shoulder to read the *Sun*.

There was a rather forlorn-looking Danish pastry on a plate beside his cup.

'Do you fancy a fry-up in the covered market?' she greeted him.

'Good morning! Are you quite determined to harden my arteries?' he asked.

'I beg your pardon?'

'Pounds of chocolate and a fry-up in less than twelve hours?'

'Well, I'm going on a diet tomorrow, so might as well get in as much as I can today. Perhaps the café in the covered market does muesli or something healthy these days?'

'Perhaps,' he said, standing up.

'Not that we'd want to eat it or anything,' she added.

'Course not,' he said smiling.

They both avoided greeting each other with a kiss.

It was better this way, she thought, walking along the street beside him feeling tremendously comfortable in his company. He was wearing blue jeans and a red polo shirt, the sort of determinedly casual outfit that man-of-the-people Tony Blair usually chose to wear for his refugee-camp walkabouts. Like Blair, Ian looked heavier when he was casually dressed than he did in black tie.

Usually she fancied skinny men, like Max, whose bum was so small he could probably wear a pair of Mick Jagger's jeans. If Ian wanted to borrow a pop star's clothes then he might have to go to Meat Loaf, she thought, although he wasn't really that fat, but her brain was so tired through lack of sleep that she couldn't seem to conjure up a medium-build pop star with a slight weight problem, except Gary Barlow, and the younger generation didn't seem to wear jeans any more. Anyway, it didn't really matter because if Ian ever had to borrow someone famous's Levis, then Tony Blair's would be the perfect fit.

Sometimes she wondered how it was that she never seemed to have time to get her head around profoundly important issues like the politics of the Balkans, the peace process in Northern Ireland or global warming, but could still manage quantities of energetic thought on irrelevant hypotheses about total trivia.

She lifted her face to the sun. They walked past Thorntons, the second-hand bookshop, past the bank where she had pleaded so often for an extension on her overdraft, past the paperback bookshop where, just as they were turning the corner into Turl Street, she caught sight of the pair of them reflected in the window. Beside Ian, she looked very slim. Practically sylph-like, she thought. It was almost as good as being with a much older man who made you feel about twenty-three.

The Taj Mahal restaurant, where she had once been so drunk she had mistaken a month's supply of birth control pills in her wallet for her credit card and attempted to pay the bill with it, had changed its name to Simla Pinks. There was one of those menus in a glass case outside that described the entire history of the dish as well as listing every ingredient down to the last sprig of coriander. It came as rather a shock to see that something in this fossilized city had changed with the times.

The covered market was comfortingly the same as it had always been. The café had the same black-and-white lino floor and the same red-and-white checked covers on the tables and the menu was still formed from little white capital letters on a black pegboard. They ordered bacon sandwiches and tea.

'So what are we going to do today?' Ian asked.

He wasn't one of those dreadful people who said we when they meant you and she was mildly surprised that he assumed they were going to spend the day together.

'Duty calls for me, I'm afraid,' she sighed, martyrishly. 'I've got to go and see my god-children, well they're not really my godchildren, but I sort of think of them like that because Penny told me that if she'd had a third, I would definitely have been its godmother. I know that it shouldn't bother me so much,' she admitted, seeing his effort not to laugh at her tortuous explanation, 'and it doesn't really matter whether I'm their godmother or not, since I don't believe in God anyway, but I could under-stand her choosing Ursula, because she was Roy's sister too, but Manon...' She raised her eyebrows.

'Who's Manon?'

'The extremely beautiful, dark-haired one. She was wearing black last night,' Annie said.

'Almost everyone was wearing black,' he said.

'True,' she acknowledged, then added im-patiently, 'oh, you'd know her if you saw her. She's stunning. I'm talking supermodel, but irritatingly, not as tall. Have you ever seen a supermodel in real life? As a matter of fact, they look a bit odd, like giants, but not fat, if you know what I mean.'

This time he laughed out loud.

'Are you always so garrulous when you're hungover? Most people are quiet.'

'I don't think I am hungover, Tired? Yes. Almost unable to move because of muscle strain? Yes. But I think I sweated all the champagne out on the Tour de Oxon last night. Am I giving you a headache?' she suddenly asked.

'A bit.'

'Well, you deserve it for making me cycle all that way,' she told him.

'Are they in Oxford?'

'Who?' she asked.

'Your godchildren.'

'Not any more. Of course, they would have to move miles away the day before I come to lunch.'

'They probably didn't do it just to spite you,' he reasoned.

She smiled at him.

'It's just I hate driving,' she explained.

'What car have you got?' he asked.

'A Ferrari,' she told him.

A loud blast of laughter.

'Right,' he said, disbelievingly.

'No, really. I have got a Ferrari. What's so funny about that?'

'Well, one, I've seen you on a bike, and two, you've just told me you hate driving. How could anyone with a Ferrari hate driving?'

'It's a long story.'

What had been so comical about her performance on the bike?

'What car do you drive?' she asked with barely

390

feigned interest.

'Pretty boring doctor's family car,' he admitted. 'A Volvo.'

She looked suitably bored, then suddenly sat up straight.

'What sort of man drives one of those funny little cars that had all those adverts on television a while back?' she suddenly demanded, remembering the metallic grey Sports car below her hotel window earlier.

'Fiat Cinquecento?'

'No, that was the yellow one, wasn't it? No, I mean that silly, sporty one that looks a bit like a toy, you know,' she urged impatiently.

Men could always remember the names manufacturers gave to cars even the ones which were so ridiculous she would be embarrassed to say them out loud in a showroom.

'A Tigra?'

'That's it!'

'What kind of man drives a Tigra?' he said, thoughtfully, 'A wanker!'

She laughed.

'What?'

'It's just the way you said it. Made it sound like the name of a car too. I think I'll be able to use that somewhere.' She took her notebook out of her red handbag, wrote down the date then CAR NAME – WANKER, WANKA, WANCAR?

'Is everything research for you?' he asked.

'Absolutely,' she said, snapping the notebook shut, 'no secret's safe with me, I'm afraid. Sometimes I don't even know I'm using things that have happened. I wake up with this great idea, I think, wow, what a fantastic imagination I've got, I write it into an episode, and then Ursula points out that it happened five years ago, and actually, she'd have preferred me not to tell the whole world.'

He laughed.

'So, this lunch today...' he said.

He was clearly fishing for an invitation. What was to stop her taking him along? It might be quite fun. She was about to ask when she had a fleeting memory of Penny's mother's disapproving face. She always seemed to time her 'poppings in' to Joshua Street to coincide with the moment Annie emerged from her bedroom at noon with a new man behind her.

So what? She was nearly forty now, for heaven's sake, Annie thought, and she hadn't bonked Ian anyway. Of course the irony was that because she was forty, Penny's mother would think there was something wrong with her if she hadn't bonked him, but at twenty there was a lot wrong if she had. Sex wasn't approved of in Joshua Street. Even Penny, who had been sleeping with Vin since she was sixteen, very rarely dared to do it in the comfort of her own home. Ursula never did (how times changed), and nobody really knew about Manon or dared to ask. And that was a point. Manon. Had she really gone home the night before as she had pretended? It was awfully late for a goodnight snog outside the Ashmolean. Had she stayed the night?

It was mainly the possibility of Ian meeting Manon that made her decide not to invite him along. She was bored with introducing Manon to her male friends and then having them drool on about how bloody marvellous she was. She'd had enough of that when Manon stayed on her return from Italy. It was two years ago now, but still there were men who asked whether her French friend was still staying with her, and declined an invitation to come back for coffee when they discovered that she was not.

'What are you going to do?' she asked Ian.

'Oh, I don't know,' he said, 'it seems a pity to waste the best part of the day on a train. I'll probably have a walk, a leisurely lunch by the river.'

'I thought you had a Volvo,' she said.

'Not with me. It's being serviced. Anyway it's a long drive up from Broadstairs.'

'Broadstairs?'

'Yes.'

'You live in Broadstairs?'

'Yes.'

'Oh.'

The only time she'd been to Broadstairs was on a school trip. She had seen the Dickens House and been sick in the coach on the way back to London after smoking her first cigarette in the shelter of the harbour wall. She couldn't think about Broadstairs without thinking about the flavour of regurgitated salt and vinegar crisps and Number Six. She'd never been able to eat that flavour again, but the aversion therapy oddly hadn't extended to cigarettes.

The fact that Ian lived in Broadstairs made it almost more impossible for them to see each other again than the fact that he was married, she thought. It was so far away, and it just wasn't the sort of place where you did that. It was provincial. He was a provincial doctor, she was a metropolitan media personality. Even though shambling bookshop owners could fall in love with film stars in romantic movies, it didn't happen like that in real life.

Anyway, she wasn't in love with him, she reminded herself, and he certainly wasn't with her. Oxford made you do mad things for a weekend, and then you went back to your life.

As a matter of fact, she thought, she could write a movie about that very thing. She could see Hugh Grant pushing Julia Roberts along in a shopping trolley on the posters already. Dreaming Spires. It was such an obvious theme for a romantic comedy, but had anyone actually done it?

'I suppose this is where we part, then,' she said as they came out of the gloom of the covered market into hot sunshine. 'I have to get some presents for the girls.'

'There was a jewellery shop back there,' he said, pointing inside again.

'Oh, really?'

They went back in together and he showed her a tiny boutique they had passed without her noticing which sold exactly the sort of jewellery she would have coveted as a child.

'How did you know about this?' she asked him.

'It's having a daughter,' he said. 'I was looking round yesterday afternoon, during the thunderburst. I usually buy Zoe something, but this would not be quite sophisticated enough for her these days.'

How sweet he was, Annie thought, falling upon a couple of little silver chains with sparkly cubic zirconium pendant hearts. They were expensive enough not to give the girls a rash, but not so dear that it would matter too much if they lost them.

'And perhaps a little bag to put them in?' Annie said, as they emerged again. 'The thing I loved most as a child was the idea of a present with another present inside it, didn't you?'

He pointed her in the direction of Next, where she found two miniature straw carrier bags in the shape of orange and pink daisies, and then, as they were passing Laura Ashley she could not resist buying them each a dress and hat.

'My goodness, you are a good godmother.'

His patience with all the shopping made her feel warm all over.

'Listen,' she said in the lobby of the Randolph, not wanting to say a final goodbye, 'I could give you a lift back to London. Or,' she decided to make it an irresistible offer, 'you could give me a lift.'

She paused long enough for him to work out what she meant, then had the pleasure of seeing his eyes light up like a little boy's.

'Drive a Ferrari?'

'Yes!'

'What about insurance?'

'Oh, it's fine for anyone over twenty-five or something. I'm sure they infinitely prefer to underwrite the risk on you than me.'

'Wow,' he said.

'OK,' she said, looking at her watch, 'rendez-vous outside at four o'clock.'

Chapter 39

Roy knew logically that nothing Manon had told him should matter. He had known that she had lovers: how could she not in almost twenty years? He had seen her in Rome with Rodolfo, and he had felt then that she had sold herself to him. So why did it matter? It was only her body that she had sold.

She made love to him with her entire being. It was that feeling of totality that made her like no-one else he had known. When he climaxed inside her it felt as though he was on the perimeter of humanity where love was so intense it was almost terror.

But was that how she was with everyone? Was that the 10,000 franc fuck? Did you get less for 5,000 – a quick detached blow job, and nothing more before she saw the colour of your cash?

If he asked, would she tell him? If she told him, would he believe her? She must be very experienced at telling men what they wanted to hear. He realized that he probably would not believe her unless everything she said fell in with his worst suspicions.

Yet she had told him. She had told him something that he would never have found out. She must have thought that there was a chance that he would understand, not just react like a character in a Hardy novel.

He was gripping the steering wheel so tight, his knuckles were white.

'What are you thinking?' she asked him quietly, as they turned off the main road down the winding country lane.

'Nothing,' he lied.

'Oh, I can't bear this,' she said.

'Have you ever told anyone what you told me except for Penny?' he asked, feeling betrayed by Penny too for keeping this knowledge about Manon to herself.

'Rodolfo. I should have learned from experience,' Manon said, bitterly.

'I am not like Rodolfo,' he protested, glaring into her face.

She raised her eyebrows just a fraction.

'Why did you tell me?' he asked, looking back at the road.

'Would you rather not have known?'

'Yes ... no...'

'Did you not suspect, when you read my stories?'

'No!'

He looked across again, and could almost hear her thinking that he spent his life studying the lives of writers. How could he not have known?

'Perhaps I did not want to know,' he admitted.

'Oh Roy,' she said, with a sad ironic smile, 'I think that really you are just like Rodolfo. You think that there is a type of woman who is a prostitute, but prostitutes are not born, they are made. I should have thought that you above all...'

'Or they choose,' he interrupted. 'For a beautiful woman with a first from Oxford University there are other ways of making money. For heaven's sake, Manon!'

'Do smokers choose to smoke?' she asked, 'or do they try something and then find that they can't stop?'

'They still have a choice,' he said.

'All right, so I chose it. If I admit that, does it make it worse? Would it be better for me to be a passive victim? Would that be preferable?' she enquired, sharply.

'Of course not!' he shouted, 'but the risk of disease apart from anything else...'

'I haven't got AIDS, if that's what's worrying you.'

'No! I don't know!' he shouted at her, 'I just don't know what to think.'

'And I don't care what you think!' she said, suddenly angry. 'You seem to think that I did what I did as a personal affront to you. It had nothing to do with you. Nothing.'

'It does now though.'

'No, I don't think so.'

Had her telling him been a test for him, he wondered, a test that he had failed abysmally?

'Oh, I don't know why I allowed myself to come back here with you,' she said, stamping a foot on the floor of the car. He noticed that her accent always became more French when she gave vent to her emotions. He found it very endearing.

'I'm sorry,' he said.

'Would you please take me back to Oxford now?' she asked.

'Not now, the girls will be waking up. I've got to be there. I'll take you after lunch,' he told her.

She looked away, staring stiffly out of the window as she had when driving in the other direction the day before. In the furious air between them, he could almost taste her disappointment in him.

During the night, when he had thought about bringing her back here in the morning, he had imagined them walking up the flagstone path towards the stone rectory like a couple of newly-weds, and the children running out to greet them. It was an image, he now realized with shame, that bore a striking resemblance to the scene in *The Sound of Music* when Maria and the Captain return from honeymoon. It was one of the few videos that Geraldine allowed the children to watch when they were staying with her, although he never could see why Austrian versus German nationalism was deemed more suitable than *101 Dalmatians*.

Their progress up the vicarage path now was as far from that celluloid fantasy as it could be. For a moment, it seemed as though Manon would stay in the car with her arms folded and leave him to explain away her presence, and then as he neared the front door, she jumped out and ran ahead of him, as if eager to put her version of events first.

They found the girls eating cereal at the kitchen table. In the quotidian atmosphere of a family kitchen, he felt grounded again.

'Where's Grandma?' he asked.

'Having a bath,' said Saskia.

'In fact, Grandpa is in church,' Lily announced, spooning most of a spoonful of Rice Krispies into her mouth. Milk dribbled down her chin and he snatched at a piece of kitchen paper to wipe it before it dropped onto her Sunday dress.

Manon's reappearance drew no comment. He was grateful for their innocence. And Geraldine who later emerged in a fuchsia-coloured suit and a white straw hat appeared far more flustered about getting to the church in time for the first service than she was about the uninvited guest at breakfast.

'You go on,' Manon told her. 'I'll tidy the girls up and bring them over.'

Geraldine smiled gratefully and hurried out of the door just as the church bells began to peal.

'Are you coming to church with us, Manon?' Saskia asked.

'Yes.'

'Can we sit at the back like we did with Mummy?' Lily asked.

'She wants to count the hats,' Saskia explained.

'Grandma always makes us sit at the front,' Lily complained, 'and then I can't see anything, and it's a long way if I want to go for a wee.'

'OK, we'll sit at the back,' Manon agreed.

'In fact, Daddy's agnostic,' Lily told her, as if their father's lack of enthusiasm needed explaining.

'What does that mean?' Manon asked mischievously.

'It means he doesn't believe in God, or Jesus or miracles, or *anything*,' Lily told her in amazement.

'No, no, it means...' Roy tried to defend himself.

'Poor Daddy,' Saskia said, wearily, 'life is so much easier when you believe in miracles, isn't it, Manon?'

Manon looked at Roy, wondering whether he too had heard Penny's voice.

He avoided her gaze, instead laughing and kissing Saskia on the forehead.

'I think it must be,' he acknowledged, ruefully.

From the bathroom window, he watched them trotting off together, Manon still in her black dress, the girls in the pretty cotton pinafores he had made them change out of the day before. They looked odd together, a slightly surreal tableau of urban sophistication and rustic simplicity. He watched Manon crouch down to inspect the daisy Saskia picked her from the lawn, then she stroked a buttercup against Lily's chin.

'Do you like butter, yes you do!' he knew she was asking, because Lily, who was standing very still while Manon performed the experiment, suddenly shrieked *'I do!'* as if it were a hugely interesting discovery, even though she ate butter with bread happily every day of her life.

He had never understood what that buttercup thing was all about. It was one of those girls' rituals that boys couldn't see the point of and girls couldn't explain, a bit like all the non-sensical hopscotch rhymes that Saskia had already learned at nursery school.

As they ambled through the old graveyard, the girls each took one of Manon's hands, and then the three of them disappeared into the blackness of the church porch as the bells suddenly ceased.

He stood in an ankle-deep bath, taking spongefuls of water and squeezing them over his body, trying to remember whether the cottage they were buying had a shower. If it did not, he would have one plumbed in. You could lose yourself in a shower, a power shower. He did not like baths. All that wallowing gave you too much time to think. He scrubbed at his skin with a loofah.

He dried his hair roughly with a towel, then pulled on crumpled khaki shorts and a black T-shirt. Geraldine would be after him with an iron, he thought, catching sight of himself. In the unfamiliar long mirror on the back of the bathroom door, it was like glimpsing another person.

Too young to have all this responsibility.

The thought surfaced from his mind so clearly he could almost hear it.

It was the sort of thing that his mother would say. Indeed she had said it when he told her he was getting married, and again when he informed her about Penny's first pregnancy. Too young to be a widower, she had said, when Penny died. He had taken shelter under the protection of his mother's pronouncement. He was so used to being looked after by her, then Ursula and then Penny, that the notion of looking after someone else came reluctantly.

Perhaps Manon had been right to tell him that her life was nothing to do with him. It was not fair to be disappointed in her for turning out not to be the person he had imagined. Perhaps his hostility was simply an excuse to relieve himself of the prospect of taking on more responsibility, when he couldn't cope with what he had already. Perhaps when he thought this morning that she had run away again, he had been transferring his own subconscious wishes onto her.

Roy leaned forward and opened the bathroom door, suddenly annoyed with his own reflection.

In the garden shed he found Trevor's barbecue, a bag of charcoal and some firelighters. He set the barbecue up on the patio and it lit straight away, which was something he had never achieved before and that made him feel absurdly triumphant. He went inside to look in the fridge. There were several packets of organic sausages and a large clingfilmed bowl of marinating chicken pieces. On the vegetable shelf was a tray of wooden kebab sticks threaded with pieces of red pepper, mushrooms and cherry tomatoes.

It was good for the girls to eat fresh food. He had lost count of the times he had taken them to

McDonald's because they refused to eat the undercooked pasta or leathery omelettes he had prepared for them, but he knew that they both were proud owners of the entire McDonald's World Snoopy collection, and were impatient for the next promotion.

There were few occasions when they talked openly about missing their mother, but her absence was ever present at mealtimes. When he asked them what the difference was between the chips he put in the oven and those that Mummy cooked, the reply was always the same.

'Mummy's tasted nicer.'

He found mealtimes debilitating, but for some reason barbecue was different. Daddies were supposed to do barbecues and even sausages that were burnt on the outside and still cold and pink in the middle were pronounced delicious.

He wondered whether it was too early to start the cooking. He decided to anyway. He needed something to do to stop himself thinking.

He was manoeuvring a chicken thigh onto the grill when a loud, 'Yoohoo!' a couple of yards behind him made him jump. The tongs snapped shut, the chicken slithered between the wires and onto the charcoal with a subdued sizzle.

'I've been ringing the doorbell for hours!' said Annie coming round the side of the house, ducking under the hanging basket of petunias outside the kitchen door.

It was the first occasion he had ever felt positively glad to see her. There was no peace to think when Annie was around.

'Took far less time to get here than I thought,'

she said. 'Where is everyone?'

'At church,' he replied.

'Church? Oh well.' She inspected the containers of raw food, then stole a cherry tomato and popped it into her mouth. 'Apparently they're wonderful at preventing cancer,' she said, 'so I try to have one for every cig I smoke. Oops, sorry!'

'It's OK. I don't know why nobody's supposed to say the word,' he said.

'It's because illness is contagious. I don't mean literally. What I mean is, well, you don't want to name cancer, because if you talk about it, it means it exists, and if it exists then there's a possibility that you might get it.'

Roy raised an eyebrow sceptically.

'That's why people go on about standing up to it,' Annie continued. 'The reasoning goes like this: if you're brave enough, then the cancer will take fright and go away. So, conversely, it's your fault if you die. And if it's your fault, not the illness's, then that's quite comforting for anyone else who might get it. Do you see?'

'That's an interesting view of the psychology,' he said.

'Of course I don't think that: rationally I don't anyway. But I'm as bad as anyone else when it, comes to talking about it. That's a long way round of saying sorry I've been so useless, by the way,' she said, looking at him through big round apologetic eyes.

'What do you mean?' he enquired.

'Well, you haven't exactly seen much of me since Penny was ill, have you?'

'No, but we never did before,' he said.

Annie had been feeling so guilty, she had forgotten about that. Their lives had gone their separate ways long before Penny's illness. First Penny had been in Africa, and then when Annie was a waitress and Penny a teacher, they didn't seem to have much in common any more. Whenever she had visited Joshua Street, Penny would enthuse about the latest ragrolling techniques and stencilling, and Annie would give slightly exaggerated accounts of snorting cocaine and dancing at the Fridge. Annie was always in love with a different man, Penny pined chastely for Vin, then met up with Roy.

Actually, it was no wonder she hadn't asked her to be godmother, Annie thought.

Her face brightened. She put a half-pepper in her mouth and crunched.

'Healthy food. Fantastic! I've been eating like a student since I got here. I couldn't make myself a cup of coffee, could I? I'm knackered. Only about two hours' sleep, woken up by your bloody sister.'

'Where is Ursula?' Roy said as if he had only just registered her absence. 'I thought you were giving her a lift.'

'No, she popped in on her way to the station to get ... to tell me to tell you that she wouldn't be coming because Georgie got ill in the night. Only chickenpox, apparently, but she wanted to be with him. And her mobile's run out of juice.'

As she said it, Annie thought it sounded a really pathetic excuse. Had Ursula deliberately invented a minor illness to stop Roy running to the phone to find out what his nephew's condition was? Had she lied about her mobile so that no-one would try to ring?

'Oh well.' Roy didn't appear very bothered.

'So it's just me,' Annie said brightly.

'And Manon,' he said, casting his eyes down. A distinct blush rose from his neck to his hairline.

'Manon,' she said thoughtfully, 'And I thought she said she was going back to London. Oh well, my mistake!'

The knowingness in her tone made him look up, but she was walking purposefully onto the lawn.

'Anything I can do?' Annie asked rhetorically, lying down across the full length of the yellow-and-white swing seat.

One of the reasons her relationship with Roy would never have worked was that she could never think of a thing to say to him, she remembered. Roy was the sort of person who liked to do a proper critical test of any theory you happened to make up on the spur of the moment to fill the silence. His seriousness made her gabble. In fact she had never been able to see what Penny had seen in him, except that he was probably a good gene mix for the father of her children. Penny was so organized she thought about things like that, and she had always been unfashionably keen to have children. Actually, after Vin, anyone would have been a refreshing change, Annie thought. Vin took up so much space in a room. He was a lad before lad behaviour became acceptable in a post-modern sort of way.

She tried to imagine Roy and Manon on their own. Did they talk or did they just stare meaningfully at each other exchanging silent intellectual thoughts?

Annie reached into her bag and lit up a cigarette, her first of the day. Roy looked over at her when he smelt the smoke, frowned, but did not say anything. She looked at her watch. Less than twenty-four hours ago she had considered him the perfect partner for the rest of her life, and now she was wondering how she would tolerate getting through the next couple of hours in his company.

'Good morning Annie, I'm afraid we don't allow smoking in the house or the garden.' Geraldine's voice was commanding the moment she emerged round the side of the house.

Startled, Annie squashed the cigarette out on the lawn, put the butt back into the packet and scuffed the grass with her foot to disperse the ashes. She caught Roy's eye. His look said, I have to put up with this all the time. It annoyed her. Why had he not told her she mustn't smoke? He was a coward. There was only one sort of man worse than a domineering man and that was a weak man, she thought. She had definitely had a lucky escape with Roy.

'The girls have gone to put flowers on Penny's grave,' Geraldine announced.

'I thought I might go later.' Annie said the first thing that came into her mind. She tried to remember the name of Penny's father. Trevor. That was it. She was about to ask where Trevor was when the thought occurred to her that he might be dead. People's parents were always dying these days.

'Hello, by the way!' she said, trying to make a joke out of the not-very-good start they had got off to.

'Come along and help me scrub some potatoes,' Geraldine ordered. 'I thought we'd have new potatoes with fresh mint, Roy,' she added. 'They eat so many chips.'

'Fine,' he agreed.

Annie walked desultorily inside. She had only attended Brownies once in her childhood, and that was because the Brown Owl had been a woman very much like Geraldine.

'Just a minute!'

As Annie was about to plunge her hands into the bowlful of cold, earthy water and recently dug potatoes, Geraldine grabbed her wrists and inspected the long red nails. For a moment Annie thought she was going to be told to get the polish off immediately, just as she had been by Miss Greer during the Oxbridge entrance examination at school.

'We don't want to spoil that, do we?' Geraldine said kindly, reminding Annie that she had been Penny's mother, after all. 'Why don't I do the scrubbing and you pick some mint for me?'

Annie scuttled back into the garden. Scanning the herbaceous borders with increasing desperation she hissed at Roy.

'How would I recognize mint?'

Chapter 40

On the see-saw, Lily and Saskia balanced almost perfectly.

'Hold on tight, Lily,' Manon said, as Saskia bounced her up and down increasingly forcefully. 'Slow down, Sas, she's much littler than you, remember?'

Saskia gave her kid sister a sceptical glance. Lily was a little shorter, but what she lacked in height, she made up in weight.

'Younger, I mean,' Manon corrected herself.

Lily wasn't fat, but she was solid, just like her father, Manon couldn't help herself thinking.

Since Geraldine had been in charge of buying the girls clothes, Manon had noticed that they were usually dressed in identical outfits. She wondered if their grandmother simply couldn't be bothered to choose different outfits for each child, or whether it was a subconscious effort to make them look more alike. Oddly, it had the reverse effect of emphasizing their differences. Saskia was willowy with flyaway blond hair; her sister was sturdy with short dark curls and a determined expression.

Perhaps Lily asked to be dressed like her big sister. When Manon was little, her mother had sewn dresses and skirts for her from the pieces of material she had left over from making her own clothes, and she had loved the feeling of stepping out of the door into the world dressed the same as her beautiful mother. When they returned to Paris and her mother was working for the couturier, she had sometimes sneaked out tiny scraps of fabric for Manon to make into clothes for her dolls. But at boarding school, Manon's idiosyncratic home-made clothes had drawn ridicule. She remembered her mother's horror when she returned in the holidays, inspecting the machined hems of the cheap little garments she had purchased with her pocket money in Chelsea Girl.

'Doesn't anyone at this expensive English school teach you about style?' she had asked, genuinely bewildered.

Some older children wanted to go on the see-saw.

'Come on!' Manon said, 'let's give them a turn.'

'No,' said Lily, 'it's my see-saw.'

'No, it's everyone's see-saw,' Saskia said with the sactimoniousness of a five-year-old. She slipped off and Lily banged down to the ground.

Lily began to cry.

'Come on, Lily,' Manon said, lifting her off and giving her a cuddle.

Lily held tightly on to her.

'You won't leave again, will you, Manon?' she asked.

'I'll be leaving later this afternoon, but I'll be back soon. I promise.'

'Cross your heart and hope to die?'

The phrase was too old for her, Manon

thought. It must have been something Saskia picked up in nursery school.

'Yes,' she said.

'You have to say it,' Lily insisted.

'Cross my heart and hope to die,' Manon replied reluctantly.

'Mummy died,' Lily said.

'Yes.'

She could see the child trying to work out why the promise was a good thing to say then, but she resisted the temptation to elaborate. She had learned to answer only what was asked and not to try too hard to explain, because it only became more confusing.

Saskia had gone to talk to some bigger girls who were sitting in a line on the swings. She was beginning to be able to meet people through conversation. Lily was still at the stage where, if she liked the look of someone, usually a boy, she would mimic everything he did in parallel, which sometimes led to some very silly behaviour, but usually achieved the end that she desired. She was pretending to dig sand next to the sandpit where there was a small boy with a shovel.

Manon left her to her flirtation and wandered to a bench within earshot of the swings, interested to hear the first overtures of friendship developing.

'We've just moved to this village,' Saskia was explaining.

'Is that your mummy?' the older girl asked, giving Manon a cool look.

Manon pretended not to hear. The girl was

wearing a cropped top and cargo pants and her ears were pierced with two holes each. In a couple of years, Manon thought, she would be the one who offered them all cigarettes.

'No. My mummy is dead,' Saskia replied, with perfect equanimity.

'Is that your dad's new girlfriend, then?'

For all their sophistication, they couldn't be more than eight or nine. How did they know about things like that?

'No. She's my mummy's friend....'

'Is she your auntie or something?'

'No,' she could see Saskia struggling, then finding a resolution, 'she's like a godmother, but without the god bit,' she said, which finally seemed to satisfy them.

'See ya, then.' The leader of the pack skulked off.

Saskia stared at the still-rocking swing as if she was wondering whether it was permitted to get on now.

'I want to go on the swing.' Lily raced over, having failed to get the attention of the boy in the sandpit.

Manon put her on. The thick heavy chains were too big for her fat little fingers.

'Do you want me to put you in that other one?' Manon asked, pointing.

'No! That's for babies!' Lily declared, adding immediately, 'I don't like this park much.'

'Well, why don't we go and see where Mr Jeremy Fisher lives?' Manon improvised.

'We're going to see where Mr Jeremy Fisher lives,' Lily called in a singsong voice.

'He doesn't live here,' Saskia replied, authoritatively.

'Perhaps he does, in the stream,' Manon suggested, holding onto a straining Lily as they waited for Saskia to catch up.

'He lives in a lily pond in the Lake District.'

'That's very clever of you, Sas, how do you know that?'

'Daddy told me.'

'Did he read you that story?' Manon asked.

The thought of Roy reading Beatrix Potter with a child on each knee momentarily made her forgot how cross she was with him.

'I can read on my own.'

The encounter with the older girls seemed to have made Saskia grumpy.

'Shall we pick some flowers for Mummy now?' Manon asked, taking Saskia's hand.

'Yes please!'

The child smiled with relief. She was such a good girl normally and such an obedient sensible personality that it was sometimes easy to forget how much she must miss Penny, whom she could remember more clearly than Lily could.

Both girls had recently been on a day organized by a charity for bereaved children and returned with bottles of coloured sand that they had carefully filled. Each layer of colour was supposed to help them recall a happy time they had spent with their mother, and Saskia's recollections were agonizingly specific, like the sugar pink of the icing Penny had used to decorate her fourth birthday cake, and the blue of the swimming pool where she used to take them swimming. Lily's memories changed all the time, often echoing the things she had heard Saskia describe. Very quickly, her layers of sand had mixed together because she couldn't resist shaking the bottle up to see what would happen. Saskia's bottle was right beside her bed, in pristine condition, and nobody else was permitted to touch it.

'Where's the best place for picking flowers?' Manon asked, 'do you know?'

'Grandma's garden!' Lily shrieked.

'No, we're not allowed to,' Saskia said.

'How about the meadow? There were some lovely flowers there...' Manon thought quickly.

'But they're only weeds,' Saskia said.

'Another name for weeds is wild flowers,' Manon said. 'Mummy loved wild flowers, and when she was a little girl she used to pick flowers there herself.'

She didn't know that it was true but it was a harmless enough lie.

'Did she?' Saskia's eyes lit up at the thought of doing something that Penny had done.

'When I'm died and Mummy is a little girl she will pick flowers too!' Lily added authoritatively.

She had an endearing habit of reversing the roles of adults and children, so that whenever an adult said to her, 'when you're grown up...' she would immediately reply, 'yes, and when you are little...' as if the cycle of life went round in a simple form of reincarnation.

Saskia picked a bunch of buttercups, red campion and cow parsley and Manon found her a few purple aquilegia that had seeded them-

415

selves from one of the neighbouring gardens. They sat in the long grass while Manon showed her how to braid three blades together to make a garland to tie her posy. Meanwhile Lily dashed around pulling the heads off daisies and little purple rockery flowers that had woven themselves in the stone walls of the churchyard. Then they walked round the side of the church, to the new graveyard where their mother was buried.

The grave had settled now and there was just a simple grey stone on a flat rectangle of lawn. Manon bent down and removed the bunch of pink roses that someone – Geraldine or Roy – must have placed there the day before, which had already browned in the heat. Then she stood back a little distance and watched the girls.

Saskia stooped reverently to put her offering down on the exact spot where the roses had been. Then she stood back from the grave and mouthed each letter of the inscription silently, spelling out words she knew by heart. Lily, on her hands and knees, studded her flowers all round the edge of the plot, pressing the fragile little blooms hard into the mown grass with her thumbs, her tongue stuck out onto her chin in concentration.

They were so different. Did it ever occur to Roy how different they were? Did he ever wonder where the brown eyes and the curls came from when his hair was thick and golden like straw, and Penny's was fair and fine as a baby's?

Penny told Manon about her last encounter with Vin the day after her thirty-eighth birthday party and it was only then that Manon had understood why she was so keen for her to become a god-mother.

It was late afternoon. They were up in Penny's bedroom. Roy was taking the girls for a walk. They both heard the front door bang behind him and the squeaking of the double buggy as he pushed it down Joshua Street. Then, almost immediately, the story began to spill from Penny's lips. It was as if she had been waiting to tell her, anxious that her time was running out.

'I saw Vin again...' Penny began, her voice wavering slightly.

Almost ten years after they had parted company in Africa, Vin had returned to Oxford for a conference about world debt. After a boozy lunch with some of the other speakers, he had found himself, so he said, in Jericho wondering what had become of Penny's house in Joshua Street. Penny had been drawing the curtains in the upstairs front room for Saskia's afternoon nap when she saw him standing on the pavement looking up. He waved. She let him in.

They talked politely while she made him tea. He was divorced, no children. She told him proudly that she was married with a baby girl. On cue, Saskia cried. She brought her down and breastfed her.

'Why did you do that?' Manon had interrupted, anticipating what was going to come next. Vin had never looked at a woman's face first.

'I suppose because I'd known him all my life. It didn't seem so odd,' Penny had replied, then, as Manon stared at her, 'oh hell, I never stopped loving him, you know, and I could see he fancied me with my big tits, and I just wanted to make him feel bad for leaving, for rejecting everything I could have given him.'

Saskia had fallen asleep and when Penny had returned her to her cot and come back downstairs, Vin had knelt before her, throwing his arms around her waist with his head on her stomach.

'He told me he had been a fool. I felt sorry for him. I kissed the top of his head...'

'Penny!'

'Not you, Manon. Everyone's always thought I was perfect, but not you. You're not allowed to be shocked.'

'I'm sorry.'

'And then, well...' Penny had actually smiled at the memory.

'What?' Manon had asked.

'The sexual attraction had never gone away. It doesn't, does it, not with your first love?'

In the early evening shadows, Manon had felt herself reddening. Go on, tell her. It's the right time. But she had not.

'Anyway, I was randy as hell. Prolactin, you know, the hormone you get when you're feeding, does that to me, but it seemed to have the opposite effect on Roy,' Penny had added with a trace of naughtiness in her voice.

'So?'

'So nine months later...'

'No!' said Manon.

For a moment she was too shocked to say anything.

'I thought that stuff stopped you getting pregnant,' she eventually said.

'So did I. Wrong. Lily's the proof.'

'You don't seem to regret it.'

'I can't because Lily is so wonderful. You will look after her, won't you?' Penny asked.

'Of course I will. Does Vin know?'

'No, I never saw him again, and I don't expect I will now,' she said with a bitter laugh. 'I don't want to. It was like a proper ending. I knew he just wanted a fuck, and that's what I wanted too. There was something very honest and equal about it.'

It wasn't like Penny to use foul language. Her bluff nonchalance seemed false to Manon, as if it were masking something else.

'Does Roy know?' she asked.

'No.'

'Are you going to tell him?'

'No. He loves Lily. He thinks that she's like him, and Sas is like me. And it's true. She is. He wouldn't love her any less, but he would be hurt. I don't want to hurt him.'

It all sounded very logical. Too logical.

'Don't you feel bad about it?' Manon asked.

'It's horrible to have a secret from the person you trust most in the world,' Penny said carefully. 'Look, I know it sounds corny, but it didn't mean anything with Vin. It didn't mean anything to do with me and Roy. If anything it made us stronger. I felt as if I had finally acknowledged that Vin wasn't what I wanted. He wasn't the love of my life. He was the love of my youth.'

She looked at Manon, pleading for her endorsement. Manon didn't know what to say.

'If Roy asked, I don't think I'd lie,' Penny went on, 'but he won't ask. So it's a white lie, isn't it? I think there must be lots of children like Lily in the world, don't you?'

'I suppose so.'

Manon was too stunned to give her the affirmation that she wanted.

'Manon, you can't be shocked.'

'What about Lily? Don't you think she has a right to know?' Manon asked.

'Maybe. When she grows up. That's why I'm telling you. You tell her if you think she needs to know.'

'Penny, that's not fair!'

'No, I know it's not fair, but what else can I do? I can't leave her an envelope at a solicitor's to be opened when she's eighteen or something, can I? She might not want to know. She might be having a bad day. It's horrible enough that she's losing me when she's three years old. I don't want her to have to hate me too when she's eighteen.'

It was clear that Penny had thought all the options through.

'It just isn't like you,' Manon said, unable to deal with the shock.

Penny's laughter was sunshine in the suddenly gloomy room.

'Oh, but it is. It's *so* like me. The one time in my life I'm adventurous and wicked and it's with my old boyfriend ... please ... anyway I'm suffering for it now, aren't I?'

'What do you mean?' Manon asked.

'You mean apart from the fact that my punishment is cancer?'

And only then had her voice cracked, her blithe façade collapsing into uncontrollable sobs.

'Oh, love, Penny, of course it's not. It's nothing to do with that,' Manon had said, leaning across to comfort her.

'Well, why then? Why? Why? Why?'

Manon sniffed back tears. She didn't want to cry in front of the children.

She thought of Penny's face reeling into consciousness for the last time and staring at her blankly, as if she did not recognize her, and then her smile, her last dimply smile.

'You will be a friend to my girls, Manon, won't you?'

'" ... beloved daughter wife and mother",'

Saskia read out loud.

'" July 23rd 1959 to December 19th 1997
Rest in Peace".'

Friend. It should say friend too, Manon thought, as the words on the stone blurred behind her tears. She thought of the sea of women's faces the previous evening listening to the Elgar, each transported to their own individual memory of her.

Rest in Peace.

Are you peaceful, Penny? Can you see that your girls miss you, but they are healthy. They are fine. Am I looking after them as you wished?

Rest in Peace.

There *was* a sense of peace there. Even Lily was quiet as she persisted in her determined adornment of the grave. The air smelt of cut grass and there was the sort of rural summer silence that might only be interrupted by a blackbird's song, or the gentle thwack of a cricket ball on a willow bat. It was so very different from the angrily dark and muddy churchyard where Penny had been buried.

Manon stared at Saskia's little bouquet. The colours were bright in the almost-white sunshine illuminating the grave. Manon's eyes were clear, so clear they felt cold, and she was suddenly aware of a peculiar sensation of recognition. The flowers were the same as those that Frank had offered her on Friday evening, but that bouquet had been so artificial in its artlessness that she had left it to wilt on the wooden boards of the cloakroom floor. She looked again. Now the flowers on the grave were a simple bunch fashioned by a child's hands.

Lack of sleep was playing tricks on her.

A sudden breeze swished though the leaves of the line of poplar trees that marked the edge of the cemetery. If she were superstitious, she thought, startled, she might almost believe that Penny was trying to tell her something.

Life is so much easier when you believe in miracles, she thought.

'I'm hungry,' Saskia said.

'I'm *starving*!' shouted Lily, jumping up.

'Come on, then, let's go home,' Manon said.

Chapter 41

They *must* have had sex, Annie thought. Roy was studiously concentrating on the blackening pieces of flesh on the barbecue. A rare, pink shadow floated across Manon's face as she smiled at Annie, then remembered the agreed rendezvous in the Randolph which she had failed to keep.

God, she was beautiful, Annie thought, with her heart-shaped face and eyes so pale that men could see their dreams there.

But where had they done it, Annie wondered. Surely not right under the nose of Brown Owl? It had been a warm night, but they were getting beyond doing it in a secluded bit of garden, weren't they? Which left the car. What sort of car did Roy have anyway?

Annie recalled a boyfriend at Magdalen who had been keen on trying sex in all sorts of different locations. The punt had been fine when moored, but slightly distracting when drifting; the chapel would have been deliciously sinful if he had been able to manage an erection there; all she remembered of the cloisters was the smell of dog on the picnic rug he brought along for them to lie on. They had eventually been caught *in flagrante* on high table in the dining hall in the middle of the afternoon, and his gibbering panic and eagerness to cast the blame on her had spelled the end of that relationship. She had spotted him on television at the last election losing a safe Tory seat, and she had wondered if he had had anyone on the benches of the House of Commons.

'Come and say hello to Annie,' Manon encouraged the girls, who were staring at her shyly from the patio.

'Hello Annie,' Saskia said politely.

'Have you brought us any presents today?' asked Lily.

'Manners, Lily,' Geraldine reprimanded from the kitchen window.

'It's OK,' Annie called, 'I promised them yesterday I would.'

'Nevertheless,' Geraldine said, disappearing from view.

'Nevertheless!' Annie mimicked, sticking her tongue out in Geraldine's direction. Both little girls shrieked with laughter. She was quite gratified to think that she might have empowered them to be cheeky to their grandma.

'Come and see what I've got you,' she said, stretching out her hands so that they could pull her out of the swing seat.

Roy's car had to be the nondescript navy blue saloon parked in the road at the front. She peered in the window as they passed, looking for evidence of the previous night's frolics. There were two children's seats strapped side by side in the back and crisp packets all over the floor. It looked unlikely.

'I like your car, Annie,' Saskia remarked.

'In fact, it looks like a toy,' Lily said.

'You're right, it does,' Annie agreed, bending down to the passenger seat and pulling out two large cardboard carrier bags each containing several smaller bags.

'Now whose is which? Take them back to the garden and open them there,' she instructed, wanting the generosity of the presents to be witnessed by Geraldine. Lily's was really too big for her to carry, but she dragged it along manfully.

Geraldine was drawn into the garden by the yelps of joy as the little girls pulled out treasure after treasure.

'Really, you shouldn't give them so many things,' she scolded Annie.

'I know,' Annie replied with a satisfying smirk.

'Where's Ursula?' Geraldine asked.

'George has chickenpox and her mobile's run out,' Annie said, bored with acting out Ursula's apologies all over again.

'She's gone home?' Manon asked, surprised.

'So she says,' Annie gave her a conspiratorial wink.

Only then did Manon remember the plan for adultery hatched between them the evening before What a peculiar night it had been.

Annie yawned histrionically and lounged back in the swing seat.

'Did you manage to make me that coffee, Roy?' she asked.

'Sorry!' he replied.

'I'll put the kettle on,' Geraldine called wearily from the kitchen as if they were all children incapable of doing anything for themselves. She

425

was standing at the sink beside the open window pretending to be busy, and eavesdropping on everything that was said.

The little girls had stripped down to their knickers and were trying on their clothes. Manon went to sit beside Annie.

'Two hours' sleep. I'm knackered,' said Annie.

'What did you do?' Manon asked.

'Waded about in a fountain, stole bikes, narrowly avoided arrest, that sort of thing.'

Manon laughed indulgently.

The trouble with being a comedienne was that people assumed you were joking all the time, Annie thought.

'No really...'

'Then it *was* you we saw on a bike whizzing past college this morning?' Manon asked.

'So, tell me, what were you doing up so early? I thought you were going back to town,' Annie said, jumping on the fact that Manon had just revealed more than she had perhaps intended.

'I was,' Manon said, smiling sweetly.

'Jesus Christ, I was meant to be the promiscuous one and I'm the only one who didn't get laid,' Annie exclaimed.

Manon said nothing, but she didn't deny it, Annie thought.

An arm was holding a mug of coffee for her out of the kitchen window. Annie jumped up to go and get it.

'I'd prefer it if you didn't take the name of the Lord in vain in front of the children, Annie,' Geraldine said.

'I'm sorry,' Annie said. 'I'm sure they didn't

hear.' Geraldine sniffed and went back to some non-existent washing up. Returning to the swing seat, Annie contorted her face into a grotesque expression of contrition.

For someone who had been intending to seduce and marry Roy, Annie seemed remarkably indifferent towards him this morning, Manon thought. Usually it was quite clear when Annie fancied someone, like the chap she had been sitting next to at dinner. Had he been the man in the penguin suit on the other bike, she wondered.

'When are you going to make your move with Roy?' she couldn't resist whispering.

'Change of plan,' said Annie. 'I forgot how loud he makes me feel, and anyway, I hate the countryside.'

Manon smiled.

'No, really, I do. I mean, smell it!'

Both women sniffed the air.

'I don't know what you mean,' Manon said. 'It smells fresh.'

'But there's always a kind of background note of manure, even when it doesn't actually stink of the stuff.'

Manon sniffed again.

'You see what I mean?' Annie asked.

Roy looked up when he heard their laughter.

'Look at me, Daddy!' Lily said.

She was wearing every item of clothing that Annie had bought her, all unbuttoned and askew. The little straw handbag in the shape of a daisy was perched on her head.

'You look lovely, Lily,' he said.

'Daddy swing me round!'

'Say the magic word,' he said for Geraldine's benefit.

'Abracadabra!' said Lily.

Roy chuckled.

'No, I meant the word you say when you want something,' he said.

'Daddy, please will you swing me round?' said Lily charmingly.

'Well, OK, then, just once.'

He put down his tongs, ran over to her and took her outstretched hands.

Her eyes shone with joy as her body flew in horizontal circles round and round and as she began to laugh, Roy's face lit up, the pressure to be happy suddenly too powerful for him to resist. Nobody could be cross or gloomy when they heard Lily laugh, Manon thought, watching him and loving the way that his face looked. She remembered the day before when they had watched Lily running in the sunshine after her fall in the river. Love for his child had animated his face then too, and Manon had known that compared to that, his love for her was nothing. And that had made it safe for her fall in love with him all over again.

'This would make a fantastic croquet lawn,' Annie said, wondering what they were going to do until her planned escape straight after lunch. She didn't think it would be acceptable to leave before that, although the indefinable thread of attraction between Roy and Manon was making her feel like a gooseberry. One moment, the air was filled with the invisible mist of an unresolved quarrel, the next, they were smiling their secrets at each other.

'Anyone fancy a spot of croquet before lunch?' she called.

'I'm very good at croquet,' Lily volunteered, as she and Roy toppled over together.

'Oh good, you can be on my team then,' Annie told her. 'Roy?'

'I'll help you set it up.' He pulled himself up and went to the shed, returning with a proper croquet set in a wooden box as well as a plastic version from the Early Learning Centre that the children used. He banged the hoops in the correct formation and then retreated to the protection of his barbecue.

'OK, so it's Manon and Saskia against me and Lily,' Annie said. 'Toss to start? Oh, damn, I put my bag in the car. Have you got any coins?'

'Why don't you just go first?' Manon said.

'Oh, if you're sure. Come on Lily, show them what you're made of. We're red.'

Lily swiped at a green plastic ball and missed.

'Oh well, wrong ball, but never mind,' Annie said. 'Your turn, Saskia, you're yellow.'

Lily swiped again.

'Not you, Lily, it's Saskia's go,' Annie told her.

'Oh I don't want to play stupid croquet then!' Lily hurled her plastic mallet to the ground and began to cry.

'Come on, sweetie,' Annie said, trying to pick her up, but Lily screamed even louder. 'Oh don't be such a bloody crybaby!' Annie tried another tactic. Then as the screaming continued, she said, 'Well, if you're going to scream at least get out of Saskia's way.'

Manon came to the rescue.

'Why don't you and I play together, Lily, and Saskia can play with Annie?'

'You realize that means my team gets an extra go?' Annie asked, and without waiting for an answer, she took Saskia aside for a team talk.

'Do you think you might like to try my mallet? You get more power with it,' she coaxed.

Wielding the mallet like a golf club, Saskia managed to move Annie's red ball about a foot.

'Not like that!' Annie shouted, exasperated.

'Your turn, Lily!' Manon said.

Lily got to her feet and hit the green ball into a flowerbed.

'Good shot!' Manon called.

'Hang on a minute, are you playing with two balls or one?' Annie asked.

'All of them if Lily has her way,' Manon said, adding under her breath, 'she's only three.'

'You can't allow a three-year-old to determine the rules,' Annie replied. She took a shot. The red ball went through the hoop.

'Now, we're off,' she said with satisfaction, then took Manon's ball and roqueted her far into the border.

'Sorry!' she called unconvincingly, and went to take her other go.

'Lunch is almost ready!' Geraldine called, shaking out a large blanket and spreading it on the ground between the centre post and the final hoop.

'Well, that's the end of that then,' Annie said,

sitting down on it grumpily. 'Since we're the only ones who got through a hoop, I think we scored a moral victory anyway.'

Manon and Roy were unable to stop themselves laughing at her competitiveness.

'Well, what's the point unless you're going to play properly?' she asked, exasperated.

'They're just children,' Roy said.

'I thought children were meant to like games,' Annie said.

'Come and wash your hands,' Geraldine said.

Automatically, Manon put a hand on each of the girls' heads and turned them towards the house.

Annie watched them go in then stood up.

'I'm going for a short walk,' she said to Roy.

The sharp sour hit of Marlboro against the back of her throat tasted exquisitely pleasurable. She began to walk along the road, then after a minute or two she heard light footsteps running to catch up with her. She dared not turn round in case it was one of the girls and she would have to put the cigarette out again. She quickened her pace, then realized that the footsteps were too fast for a small child.

'Wait!' said Manon, breathlessly.

Annie stopped.

'Are you going to visit Penny's grave?'

'No, actually I was just having a ciggie.'

'Oh. Look, do you mind if I ask you a favour?' Manon said.

'Ask away!'

'Can you give me a lift back to London?'

'Err...'

'It's just that I came by bus, and it seems a bit stupid to ask Roy to drive me back to Oxford.'

Manon's expression said, please don't make me explain further.

'I'd love to, really I would, but it's just that I promised someone else, and I've only got two seats,' Annie said.

'Who?' Manon asked.

Annie felt herself blushing, she wasn't sure why.

'But, look, I can get you back to the bus station, no problem,' Annie suggested.

Manon's face broke into a blissful smile.

'That would be perfect.'

'Except I want to leave here straight after lunch,' Annie continued. 'It's worse than the reunion. It's actually worse than being back at school.'

'Fine by me,' Manon agreed readily.

'So, are you going to tell me what happened last night?' Annie couldn't resist asking, as they walked a little further from the house, feeling that their friendship had just crossed a significant barrier.

'I'll tell you later,' Manon agreed with a rueful smile, 'and are you going to tell me?'

'Later,' Annie said, thinking that she had probably got the better deal.

'OK. Shall we go back?'

Annie took a long drag, then stubbed the cigarette out on the road.

'I think I will just pop to see Penny's grave,' she said.

'It's over there, you can either go round the road to the church entrance, or climb over this wall and go through the meadow. The grave's round the other side.'

'Do tell Geraldine where I am. I couldn't bear her to think I'd just nipped out for a fag.'

'Of course not,' Manon smiled again.

'And save me a burnt offering.'

Chapter 42

Should she tell Barry?

Ursula took out her compact, looked at herself in the mirror, then looked away and back again quickly, trying to catch herself out. Did she look different? Every time she looked, her eyes seemed to be a more virulent green and her hair a brassier shade of chestnut. She was a fake. Liam had fancied a woman who was not her at all.

Would Barry notice?

She stood up and walked along the fast-moving train, stopping and reaching to grab the knobs on every other seat to steady herself. Why did they not put knobs on every seat, instead of making you take great leaps, she wondered, as the train clattered over points and her hips crashed against another passenger's copy of the *News of the World*.

In the toilet, she rocked from side to side, her hands poised for a moment when she would be able to whip out a contact lens without stabbing her eye with a fingernail. When she had them both removed, she tipped her head back and dripped in some saline solution. Most of it ran down her cheeks, some dropped directly to the unpleasantly puddled floor. She did not think that the other spillages there had been caused by contact lens solution. She felt so lumpy and anxious, she couldn't be sure if she needed to wee or not, and just as she had decided that she might as well try, the train slowed, and she knew that you weren't meant to go while the train was in a station. It was one of the things you were told as a child, but never quite understood. It had given her an unhealthy fear of going to the toilet on trains, because she had imagined guards opening the door to check what was happening every time the train stopped. She sat holding herself in until the train started again, and then the pathetic dribble of urine that emerged was hardly worth waiting for. Dehydration, she thought. There was no toilet paper. She was very aware of the fact that she had not washed herself. Liam's request for a shower had infuriated her in her panic to leave, but now she thought it would have been sensible to shower herself, even if it had meant missing the first train.

Did she smell?

Ursula sniffed her armpits.

Had the experience of adultery changed her in indefinable ways she could not detect? As soon as she reached home she would run upstairs, lock herself in the bathroom and scrub every trace of Liam away.

'No time to shower,' she rehearsed saying into the small mirror above the dirty basin.

But she wouldn't be able to do that, she realized, on the walk back to her seat, because George would need a cuddle, and an application of calamine lotion. She tried to envisage the bathroom cabinet, picturing a half-full glass bottle of pink stuff behind the cotton buds and the packet of disposable razors that fell out whenever she opened that side of the cupboard.

She wished she had remembered to tell Barry to put George in a bath with bicarbonate of soda in it. It was helpful for the itching. There was bound to be some in the kitchen, but perhaps it would be worth stopping off for a fresh supply at a chemist's on the way home in the taxi. Except it was Sunday, she reminded herself. Better to get home and take over, then Barry go and find a twenty-four-hour chemist. Hopefully then she could settle George in front of a video, Chris and Luke could play on the computer and she would have a chance to scrub the odour of betrayal from her. And wash out her knickers.

The rattling progress of the drinks trolley sounded as loud as a clanking dustcart. She bought a fizzy mineral water. Her third that day and yet still she wasn't weeing. Her body had become a sponge.

'Anything to eat?' asked the lady in charge of the trolley.

Ursula was simultaneously nauseous and starving hungry. She perused the labels on the sandwiches. There was only chicken tikka. She didn't think she could arrive home unwashed and tasting of curry.

The woman opposite bought a coffee and a packet of cheese and onion crisps then picked up her magazine again. The sound of crunching was like someone stamping on brown paper bags, and a slight synthetic onion smell wafted over, making Ursula glad about her decision to avoid food.

I betrayed my husband and my best friend screamed the headline of the magazine.

The woman opposite was obviously an avid reader, because most of the month's glossies were fanned out on the table between them.

How does be really see your body? asked the cover of the unopened *Cosmopolitan. The you-can-do-it experiment that proves he desires you more than you think...*

'Do you mind if I have a look?' Ursula asked.

The woman lowered her copy of *Panache.*

'Go ahead.'

The feature asked boyfriends to draw a picture of their girlfriend's body. All the women were young enough to be her daughter, Ursula thought. It was a long time since she had read *Cosmopolitan,* and it seemed to be aimed at younger women now. Or was that just like thinking that policemen were younger? The women, all of whom were stick thin, had drawn themselves unflatteringly, and then, rather sweetly, their boyfriends had drawn them with the body image that they hoped would satisfy their girlfriends' anxieties.

Ursula remembered the painting that her

oldest son Chris had brought home one winter's day during his second term at nursery school. It was more considered than his usual primitive abstract and it was the first time she had seen him attempt to draw people. She had been delighted with the two figures.

'That Daddy!' Chris had told her proudly pointing at a face with two spokes sticking out of it horizontally, which she guessed were arms, and two vertically which were legs.

'And that's the snowman!' she said, because they had made one together the previous weekend.

'No, that you, Mummy,' Chris had told her, impatient with her inability to see something so obvious.

How would Barry draw her body? Sometimes Ursula wondered whether he had even noticed that she had lost four stone in the last year. But he had loved her through all her metamorphoses. He had loved her when she was technically obese, he had loved her in pregnancy when her breasts were so distended under the stretched white skin they looked like blue cheese. He had even loved her when her hair had come out disastrously tangerine instead of strawberry blond. She knew that had looked horrible because no one, not even her secretary, had remarked on the glaringly obvious change, and when she had finally screamed at Barry, 'Well, what do you think?' he had replied, 'I wasn't going to say anything because I thought it might be a mistake.'

Barry wasn't good at compliments like he

wasn't good at gifts. But just as he never forgot to hand over generous quantities of vouchers on anniversaries, birthdays and at Christmas, so he had always been there with generous supplies of love. Even when her eyes were a nondescript brownish colour.

It was very easy to take someone nice for granted.

It was very easy to despise someone for being stupid enough to love a fat, mousy woman.

Ursula put the magazine down and stared out of the window, seeing nothing. Her brain felt like a soft mush of guilt which was being prodded occasionally by an electric knitting needle to provoke images of her wrongdoing.

She tried to focus on something different. Closing her eyes, she attempted to remember the contents of the briefs she was preparing at work. There was a kid with no previous record who had been caught with a small amount of cocaine and a large amount of cash, who had been charged with intent to supply as well as possession. The case was going to turn on where the money came from and she knew that the boy was too stupid to make up anything plausible. It seemed so unfair that he would probably go down because he had little imagination and lived in a council flat and therefore needed to explain why he had five hundred pounds. It occurred to her that a student at Oxford in a similar predicament would probably not even face questioning about the money. Oxford always twisted reality, she thought.

Her other client about to face a jury was a childminder accused of shaking a child. Her only defence would be to try to shift the blame to the parents. Ursula was not looking forward to that. The child was alive, but brain-damaged, which made it more likely that her client would get off, because it was going to be quite difficult for the prosecution to prove that the damage had been caused by a shaking that no-one had witnessed. But Ursula knew that she would feel uneasy about an acquittal on those grounds. After all this time in the law, she had still never quite hardened herself not to care about the truth of the case.

In her idealistic youth, she had thought guilt or innocence essentially a matter of politics. She and Roy had learned Marxism from the cradle. Their father was an old-fashioned left-winger who believed that theft was mostly a perfectly justifiable redistribution of wealth, and that the only real crime was capitalism. When she decided to become a lawyer, she had seen herself as someone who would fight from within for a finer justice system and a better society, and yet now most of her work seemed to consist of running defences that fitted the facts but might have nothing to do with the truth of what had happened. If the police weren't so imperfect, she would have felt morally outraged by some of the acquittals she had engineered.

The woman opposite put her magazine down on the table and picked up her coffee. Ursula's eye was drawn to the headline on the letters page.

439

Should I tell him about my affair?

I've been happily married for seven years, but recently, at a business conference I made the mistake of sleeping with a colleague. It didn't mean anything, but I cannot seem to stop feeling guilty. Should I tell my husband? I cannot bear to risk losing him, but...

The bold type ran out at that point and, without her lenses in, Ursula could not read any further.

Should she tell Barry what had happened?

Her first instinct was a light-hearted confession. Pass it off as another foolish situation that she had got herself into through alcohol, like being drunk at the office party. She was 98 per cent sure that they would laugh together about it, and he would forgive her. Perhaps if she introduced the subject by telling him about Annie's speech and the feeling that they all shared that they had to live a little, before reaching forty...

Ursula imagined him listening to her excuses. The 2 per cent chance that he wouldn't understand nagged at her.

He would set about examining the evidence as he always did, and then he would begin his gentle, but ordered, cross-examination. Even if she lied to him about having invited Liam down to Oxford, claiming that she had just bumped into him there, it wouldn't be possible to claim that he had been at the dinner because there were too many witnesses.

So why had he been in Oxford, and what was

it that had made her meet up with him later?

All these questions would have to be answered, drawing her deeper and deeper into a web of lies.

Perhaps she should tell him that Penny's death had taken away her reason. It was true in a way because if Penny had been around then it certainly would not have happened. She could have talked in confidence to Penny about fancying Liam. Penny would not have goaded her on like Annie. Penny would have taken her through it all reasonably, and she would have ended up wondering how she could ever even have thought of doing something so stupid. Penny had been a real friend.

She closed her eyes again and tried to imagine what advice Penny would give to her now. She tried to clear her brain for any message that Penny might want to pass on. Please, Penny! She imagined Penny's face, but all she could hear her saying was 'Don't tell him', which wasn't at all what Penny would have said.

Then suddenly Ursula remembered that she and Barry had talked about adultery only recently. She had mentioned that her secretary was in a state because she had just discovered that her husband was having an affair.

'It's not the sex, *per se,* that she minds,' she had explained, 'it's the fact that she thought everything was one way, and then it turned out it wasn't.'

'Wasn't she upset about the sex too?' Barry enquired neutrally.

'Well, I don't think that she was exactly surprised. I don't think she's ever been that keen.'

'But surely you can't separate the two, can you?'

'What do you mean?'

'Well, would she have been OK if he had said, look, I fancy some sex so would you mind if I did it with someone who enjoys it?'

It was the sort of statement that would sound funny if anyone else had said it.

'I don't know,' Ursula replied, wishing then that she had never brought the subject up. Had she been testing him even then?

'Sex is a private act and so privacy is essentially part of it, isn't it?' Barry argued.

'So it always involves betrayal, does it?'

'I wouldn't put it that strongly,' he said. 'Like most things in a relationship, it's negotiable.'

'What do you mean?'

'Well, I'm sure that very often one partner suspects something is up, but decides to turn a blind eye to it. I assume that's how Hillary Clinton dealt with Bill's peccadillo, hoping that it would blow over,' he smiled wryly, 'so to speak.'

Perhaps Barry himself had given her the answer, Ursula thought now.

She must not tell him. If he suspected, then he would turn a blind eye, and they would continue as normal.

But it wouldn't be normal, because she hated secrets. She didn't even really like surprises very much and it would eat her up to conceal something from Barry every day of their life together.

Far better, surely, just to say what had

442

happened. Plead guilty, with mid-life crisis and death of best friend as mitigation. Punishment would be a few days in solitary, then a bit of rehabilitation in the shape of a weekend away, somewhere nice, with a golf course, and vintage claret at dinner, all on her.

The weekend in Oxford had been like virtual reality, she would explain, where she had been allowed to try out another sort of life and find that it was not to her taste at all.

But then he would ask why she had needed to try it in the first place. And there would be more lies involved in answering that without hurting him.

Even the truth was going to end in lies. Her life was going to be irrevocably changed by what she had done. There was no good way to explain it, reverse it, or forget it because it would be there for ever.

Lose ten pounds in a week, an advert next to the letters page promised.

Don't bother, Ursula thought. When you are slim you are attractive and that creates all sorts of problems. A fat woman is a happy woman because at least she knows her limitations. A fat woman doesn't even bother to fantasize about making love to a stranger on a tropical beach, she just goes straight for the Bounty ice cream.

She wondered if she had let herself be so fat for so long because it was easier that way. There were far fewer surprises when you were fat. Maybe that was why people always said you looked well.

The train was pulling into the station and suddenly Ursula's stomach was full of butterflies, as if she were going for an interview, not just going home. She stood up and took a deep breath.

'Do you want to take this? I've finished with it now.' The woman offered her the copy of *Panache*.

Did she want to read the agony aunt's advice?

'No thanks,' Ursula said. 'I have to decide on my own,' she added, as if her travelling companion had been party to her thoughts throughout the journey.

Chapter 43

There were paper plates with chicken bones, dollops of barbecue ketchup and a few escaped fronds of frisee lettuce strewn over the picnic rug. The little girls had finished eating and were playing Ring-a-Ring-a-Roses with Manon on the lawn.

'God, paper plates are useless, aren't they?' Annie remarked, thinking that she had hit upon a subject that everyone was likely to agree on, but forgetting that she wasn't supposed to swear.

'Not if you're the one doing the washing up,' Geraldine retorted.

'Oh no, they're absolutely wonderful for that. What I meant was when you're trying to cut things up, they kind of give way. The number of sausages I've lost in my life because of paper plates!'

Roy was staring at the girls, but she thought she saw a glimmer of a smile pass across his features.

'What job are you doing, these days, Annie?' Penny's father asked.

He had changed his vicar's robes for a pair of ancient colonial shorts, which on anyone else would have looked rather Gap khaki and stylish, but he had an old man's spindly, white hairy legs, and he was still sporting his dog collar over a crisply ironed pale blue shirt. On his feet were a pair of the kind of white and pink rubber flip-flops she could remember in baskets outside the Southend branch of Woolworth's when she was a child.

'Oh Trevor, don't be so silly, she has her own television show,' Geraldine said.

She had two tones of voice, Annie thought, ordering and scolding.

'Well, well, well,' Trevor said, 'we used to watch a bit of television when the children were younger ... chap who died recently, did the animal noises, what was his name?'

'Johnny Morris?' Annie suggested.

'That's the one. Marvellously funny, eh?'

'A master,' Annie agreed.

It crossed her mind that the loss of his daughter had turned him prematurely senile. She remembered him as a tall, upright sort of man, but he seemed to have shrunk. Maybe that was why Geraldine had become so bossy, she thought, because someone had to hold it all

445

together. In this sort of village, the vicar must be a person of some regard. At what age did the Church of England pension vicars off, or did they just die when it was the right time?

'Well, that was so delicious! Do let me help you with the washing up ... oops, silly me,' she said, looking at her paper plate, 'there isn't any!'

'Coffee, anyone?' Roy intervened. 'I'll put the kettle on, shall I?'

'That would be kind,' Geraldine said.

He jumped up and went to the kitchen, returning a few moments later with a big black bin liner into which he began to collect the debris of lunch. Annie dropped her own plate in the bag, then stood up.

'Must be getting along now, but so nice to see you all again,' she said, standing up.

'Aren't you staying for coffee?' Geraldine asked.

'Fraid I'm late already,' Annie told her, glancing at her watch. 'Manon!' she shouted, 'we're off! I'm giving Manon a lift back to the bus station,' she explained. 'Thanks so much for lunch. It was so very ... al fresco!'

'But I was going to take her later,' Roy stammered after her.

'Well, I've saved you the journey then.'

'But it wouldn't be any trouble.'

'Well, you'd better sort it out among yourselves,' Annie said, mischievously. 'She asked me.'

'Oh.'

They both turned and looked in Manon's direction. She shook Trevor's hand and kissed

Geraldine on the cheek, then she knelt down on the lawn with her arms outstretched. Saskia and Lily raced to either side of her, and the three of them gave each other a great long hug. Then she kissed each of them on the cheek, and stood up.

'See you soon, see you soon,' they called after her.

She waved, and then as she turned to Roy, her face lost its smile.

'Bye,' she said.

'Right,' he said, 'bye. See you soon?'

'I'll call and let you know when I can next come to see the children,' she replied carefully.

'Right,' he said, pushing hair back from his face.

They looked at each other for a moment, and then both of them turned to Annie.

'Well, thanks for coming,' Roy said, leaning forward to kiss her politely on each cheek.

'My pleasure,' said Annie. 'Are we off?'

'Yes,' said Manon.

Annie noticed that Roy made no attempt to kiss Manon.

Definitely slept together, she thought.

'Do you think it's possible for someone to change?' Manon asked, after a few moments' silence as they drove away from the village.

'Do you mean, has Roy changed, or will he change?' Annie asked, impatient with the abstract way Manon approached things.

Manon laughed. It was a short, light laugh that Annie had always taken for superciliousness, but now she sensed it might be due to nerves.

'I wasn't talking about Roy,' she said.

'Well, who the fuck were you bloody well talking about?' Annie asked. 'Excuse me,' she added, 'but I've got all these swear words in my throat that I've been biting back for the last couple of hours.'

Manon laughed again.

'I was wondering whether I was capable of changing,' Manon said. 'Sometimes it is so much easier not to, isn't it?'

'You're talking in riddles.' Annie crawled the car round a corner. 'God, I loathe these country lanes. They're so narrow.'

She hated driving when she couldn't see what might be approaching from the opposite direction. Sometimes she found herself gripping the wheel really tightly and closing her eyes, as if she were on some really fast ride at a fair, and not in control of a powerful car.

'I was wondering whether I could ask your advice,' Manon began again.

'Ask away!' Annie relaxed enough to touch the accelerator. The car's speed lurched to about 30 m.p.h.

'You've read my stories. Do you think I could make a living out of writing, if I really worked at it?'

'You're kidding?'

Manon's face fell.

'Of course you could, you silly cow,' Annie said. 'I'm sure your publishers have given you a whacking great commission for a novel, haven't they?'

'No.'

'What?'

'They asked me if I wanted to be commissioned. I said no. I didn't really know what they meant. They said to let them know if anyone else made me an offer.'

'You don't understand the word commission? What kind of useless agent have you got?'

'I haven't got an agent,' Manon said.

'Oh, for God's sake, hello, is there anyone in there?' Annie pointed at Manon's head. The car swerved alarmingly. She put both hands back on the steering wheel.

'You've had the sort of reviews normally only accorded to books that have already been bestsellers in the States. And you're beautiful. Every publisher in London would kill to get a novel from you. For God's sake!' she practically screamed.

'Do you know any agents?' Manon asked.

'You must know agents. The Compton Club is oozing with them.'

'I'm the hat check girl.'

'You're a bloody moron,' said Annie. 'Tell you what, I'll ask Holly.'

'Holly?'

'My new best friend. Very tall, red hair. She's always in the club. Used to be an agent, but then she became a film producer. You know the movie *Jane and Mabel?*'

'I didn't see it, but obviously, I've heard about it.'

'She's the producer. She's hot and she knows everyone here and in LA. She used to work at Louis Gold. I'll ask her who you should get.'

'Would you?' Manon sounded ridiculously grateful.

'Get a grip,' said Annie, a little embarrassed. 'It does my image no end of good to be known as a friend of yours.'

'Why?' Manon asked, bewildered.

'Because you're class. You've got lit. cred.', she said, pleased with the term. 'You have to be careful how you say that,' she added, 'and everyone wants to get into your knickers. Which reminds me,' Annie continued, 'what happened last night to make you miss the last bus?'

'They run all night.'

'So?'

The pause was so long that if Annie hadn't been concerned with turning right at the T junction onto the main road she would not have succeeded in remaining quiet. Annie could not stand silence.

'Roy and I went to Joshua Street,' Manon said eventually.

'A walk down Memory Lane?'

'Sort of.'

'And then?'

'And then we came back to Geraldine and Trevor's.'

Annie waited, then realized that was all Manon was intending to say. She wasn't going to get away with that. Not with ten miles still to go.

'Hang on, what happened in between walking down Joshua Street and seeing me on my bike in the early morning?'

'We went into Joshua Street,' Manon admitted.

'You broke in?' Annie asked, shocked.

'No. Roy still had the keys.'

'You slept there?'

'Yes.'

'Together?'

Manon turned and looked at her.

'Yes,' she said simply, suddenly unable to see the point of pretending otherwise. They were all grown-ups now. Ursula would no doubt find out, but she didn't think that she was in much of a position to criticize.

'It's not the first time, is it?' Annie said.

'No. How did you know?'

Annie was about to tell her about seeing them kiss outside the Ashmolean, but decided it would make her look as if she had been spying on them.

'I just have an intuition about these things,' she replied, enigmatically.

'You don't mind?' Manon asked.

'Why should I mind? Oh, I was only joking about fancying Roy myself, if that's what you mean.'

'I thought so,' Manon said.

Then Annie fell quiet and it was so strange to be with her and not to hear the sound of her voice that Manon began to feel uncomfortable.

'You didn't while Penny was alive?' Annie finally asked.

'No. Well, technically yes, on the last day of finals.'

'Jesus H. Christ!' said Annie. 'What does the H. stand for, by the way? I've never known...'

'When you were all out,' Manon said. She wondered why it was so difficult to admit to a simple act of love that had taken place so long ago.

'Did Penny know?' Annie demanded.

'I never told her,' Manon said.

'And Roy didn't tell her, did he?'

'I don't think so,' Manon said.

'He must always have been in love with you,' Annie announced.

She was very loud, but she was also very perceptive, Manon thought.

'Poor Penny,' Annie said.

'No, he loved Penny. He was just infatuated with me,' Manon said.

'That sounds like a nice difference, but it's still pretty difficult to understand: for her, I mean,' Annie said.

'I think Penny was one of the few people who might have done,' Manon said carefully.

There was a long pause.

'Oh well, you knew her better than I ever did,' Annie admitted.

Manon said nothing.

'Secrets are awful, aren't they?' Annie moved on again, 'they kind of have a momentum of their own. I can never be bothered with them. Nowadays, when people start a sentence with "Can I tell you something in confidence" I just say no.'

She was about to tell Manon about Ursula driving away in her lover's car, but for some reason held back.

'So are you and Roy going to be an item now?' she decided to ask.

'No,' Manon said categorically. 'I think this

weekend has taught me a lot about letting the past go.'

Annie turned this information over in her head. Then she said,

'I went on a two-week therapy course on a Greek island once. I couldn't stand all the angst exchange with humourless bearded men whose real problem was they couldn't get a shag. I'm so bloody competitive I kept having to make my life sound much worse than theirs. After a couple of days, I kind of decanted to the local taverna and found an alternative source of therapy called Stavros, but that's another story. Anyway, on the last day, at sunset, the leader of the course made us all pick up a stone and pretend that it held everything that we wanted to get rid of in our lives, then hurl it into the sea. And even though I'd thought the rest of it was complete mumbo-jumbo, I invested that stone with so much insecurity and jealousy and inadequacy, and I found myself throwing it out to sea really hard as if I really hated it, and when it went plop into the wine-dark Aegean, I felt much better...'

Manon waited, turning over in her mind the image of Annie, silhouetted at sunset, throwing away her problems like an Olympian shot putter.

'And did it change your life?' she finally asked.

'Not really,' Annie said.

They were approaching the ring road which divided the countryside from the leafy suburbs of North Oxford.

'I would like to change,' Manon said, quietly.

453

'Why? I'd give anything to be you,' Annie admitted.

'No. No, you wouldn't. What you mean is that you'd like to look like me, but it isn't as easy as you think looking like I do. I know that sounds crap,' she said quickly, anticipating a shrewish remark.

'So, what's so difficult about it,' Annie said, between clenched teeth. She missed the turnoff to Summertown and had to go round the roundabout again.

'People, men mostly, think that they know you. They think that you are their fantasy. They sort of think that they have created you because you look so much like their ideal. It's true,' she noticed Annie's raised eyebrow, 'even if they're total strangers sitting opposite you in the tube and they don't even know what language you speak, they think they know you. Sometimes you have to behave in peculiar ways to prove them wrong because you feel your body has become everyone else's property.'

Annie tried to work out what she was talking about.

'Peculiar ways?' she repeated. 'What do you mean, like getting tattoed?'

'I suppose so,' Manon said.

'Drugs?'

Annie had always half hoped that Manon's slim figure might be due to heroin addiction.

'I avoided that because of my mother.'

'Prostitution?' Annie joked. Manon said nothing.

'Jesus!' said Annie.

They passed the yellow brick building that had been the Careers Advisory Centre.

'When you think of yourself, I mean your actual self, where do you think you are?' Manon suddenly asked her.

'In my stomach, mainly, and in my breasts and vagina, and, I don't know, all over the bloody place,' said Annie. 'What about you?'

'I think of myself as something very small trying to hide inside my head.'

'Really?'

There was another moment's silence, then Annie said, 'A bit like at the club!' Annie said. 'You hide in the coat cupboard, while I eat and drink and laugh too much upstairs.'

'Exactly!' Manon exclaimed, delighted.

They smiled at each other.

'Jesus, you're fucked up,' Annie said, 'and I don't suppose that seeing a shrink would do you much good, because you're shrunk enough. You want to get out of that head of yours and live.'

Manon laughed.

'I think I've been trying to pretend that I don't exist,' she said. Then added, as if she had to say it out loud to make it true, 'but this weekend, I've decided that I want to exist.'

'Hoorah!' Annie cheered.

'I'm probably going to need some help,' Manon said, a little nervously.

'You know where I am.'

As long as she didn't want to sleep in her spare room again, Annie thought.

'I think it's time I did all that career stuff, don't you?' Manon asked in a self-mocking tone as if she were tired of talking about herself so seriously.

'It's more fashionable to give it up now,' Annie warned.

'I've never been very fashionable.'

Annie looked at her companion's plain black dress, and then at her own ponyskin mules, cargo pants and cotton twinset. She was a fashion victim and Manon was effortlessly stylish. The acid flows of jealousy that had frozen temporarily as they talked, began to melt into her thoughts again.

'Downshifting,' she said.

'I don't think I've got much further down to shift,' said Manon.

'So what are you going to write?' Annie asked, trying to persevere with their new friendship.

'What should I write?' Manon asked her as they stopped at a pedestrian crossing.

'Well, if you want to make money you have to write about a single thirty-something who can't get laid. That's what sells. In fact those books sell so many that they create their own audience. All the single thirty-somethings are now so busy reading books about single thirty-somethings who can't get laid, that they haven't got time to go and get laid ... but there again, it's all going to change soon.'

'Why?'

'Demographics,' said Annie knowledgeably. 'I read this article. Apparently there is soon going to be a surplus of single thirty-something men who can't get laid, and not just because all the women prefer a good book, so maybe you should anticipate the trend and write a novel about a love-lorn lad with a slight weight problem.'

'I think I'm probably better at writing about people who do get laid,' Manon said.

'Yes, you are, aren't you?' Annie let the clutch up a little hastily and stalled.

'Now, tell me,' she put on a silly voice as she started the engine again, 'Is your work at all autobiographical?'

Then Manon really laughed so that the air in the car reverberated with good humour.

'Jesus H. Christ!' said Annie, 'everyone thought I was the tart and you were the serene ice maiden, and look what became of us!'

Ian was standing outside the Randolph. He smiled broadly as he caught sight of the car. Annie couldn't help smiling in response.

'This is where we go our separate ways,' she told Manon, indicating right at the lights at the end of St Giles.

'I thought it would be him,' Manon said. 'He looks nice.'

'All I'm doing is giving him a lift back into town,' Annie said, blushing. 'Actually, he's giving me a lift because I'm letting him drive. You know, boys and fast cars...'

'Hmm.'

'Hmm, what? He's happily married to Chloe Colefax and he's a provincial doctor,' Annie said, as if that settled the matter.

'Chloe Colefax?'

'Read zoology, rowed for the college, was the

457

token scientist on the *University Challenge* team but didn't answer a single question. Oh you're hopeless! She was the one who used to tie her blouses in a knot round her waist to make her tits look bigger.'

'Oh her,' said Manon.

'Anyway, he's not really my type, is he? Too nice. Marks and Spencer polo shirt, probably owns a pair of sandals.' She looked sideways at Manon's expression.

'He likes you,' Manon said.

'No he doesn't. Well, not like that. Does he? Why do you say that?'

The car behind beeped. Infuriatingly the lights had changed to green.

'I saw him looking at you at the dinner,' Manon said, 'and you were riding bicycles at dawn.'

'That was just to keep ourselves awake,' Annie said, drawing up just past him without indicating.

The man in the car behind wound down his window and shouted something nasty at her.

'One of these days you'll probably read in the paper that I've been the victim of a road rage murder,' Annie said melodramatically.

Manon laughed.

'Thanks for the lift,' she said.

Suddenly Annie wished that she would just get out of the car and disappear. She didn't want to have to introduce her to Ian.

'Look, call me if you need any help with an agent,' she said.

'Thank you,' Manon said, 'thanks for your support.'

'Yeah, all right,' Annie said, seeing Ian nearing in her rearview mirror. 'Call me anyway. Let's have a drink?'

'OK, I will,' Manon said.

She opened the door and sinuously wound herself out of the low-slung seat up onto the raised pavement. Annie ducked down so that her head was practically resting on the passenger's seat to be able to see the exchange between her and Ian, but they were both too tall.

'Hello,' she heard him say.

'Hello and goodbye,' Manon replied in her sexy French accent, with a little laugh.

Annie was furious. How dare she flirt with him. How dare she? Then suddenly Ian's face was right in front of hers as he bent down to look inside the car.

'Hello there!'

'Hi! Er, I was just moving over to let you get in,' she explained, wriggling her body with difficulty over the gearstick.

'Shall I get in the driver's side?'

'Well, I don't want you on my lap.'

She watched his quite substantial legs walking round the front of the car.

'I've booked us tea somewhere nice,' he said, lowering his bum in. The suspension seemed to sag under his weight.

'Oh good!' she said, 'I've had nothing to eat today except a charred chicken drumstick.'

'And a bacon sarnie,' he said, starting the ignition and looking as if he were about to have an orgasm.

'I'd forgotten the sarnie,' she said. 'Oh well,

never mind. Diet tomorrow.'

He indicated and pulled the car smoothly out into the road.

'Who was that?' he asked.

Jealous acid streamed through her veins.

'Manon.'

'Oh that was Manon, was it?' he said, smiling. 'The one who always looked as if she was in mourning. I thought you said she was so beautiful?'

'Isn't she?'

'A bit scrawny and tragic for me, I'm afraid,' he said.

'She's got mystique,' Annie said, trying to catch him out.

'Life's a bit short for too much of that, don't you think?' he asked, winking at her.

'I suppose so,' Annie admitted, settling back into her seat and thinking what an amazingly alkaline effect Ian had on the bloodstream.

Manon boarded the coach and chose a window seat near the back. She closed her eyes so that she could think better, and when she opened them again, the coach was pulling up Headington Hill, leaving Oxford behind. She turned round, wanting to see the dreaming spires as she said goodbye to them finally but forgetting that there was no rear window on this type of coach, only a toilet and the place where the hostess left the drinks trolley.

She turned frontwards again. A middle-aged man with a mobile phone who was occupying the two seats on the other side of the aisle smiled at her. She closed her eyes again, blocking him out.

There was one obvious way of getting some money. At least until the pregnancy started to show. How long did it take for that to happen? Two months, three months? She calculated she could probably earn at least ten, maybe twenty thousand pounds before that, if she wanted to.

Then she forced herself to imagine a client's penis thumping against the neck of her womb and it made her feel sick and frightened. You could not afford to be frightened alone with a man you did not know. Fear had a scent, an invisible vapour that mixed with arousal and turned it into violence. She was not going to do that. She put her hands on her tummy and rested them there and was suffused with a feeling of well-being.

She opened her eyes and suddenly knew that she had just quit prostitution. Even though she had not done it for many years, it had always been there in the very back of her conscious-ness, like an ex-smoker's craving for nicotine. Just one trick won't matter, if I'm desperate. Addicts never quite lost the desire to abuse themselves and so they trained themselves never to accept a taste of their addiction. But she knew now she was no longer an addict. And now she understood why people spoke of relief as a liquid that flooded or seeped, because she began to be aware of each part of her body again slowly filling with the fluid of sensation after the catatonia of long paralysis.

Chapter 44

The familiarity of their street calmed Ursula's racing heartbeat. Each house was set back from the road, each had its own plot of land. Theirs had four bedrooms, two reception rooms and a conservatory. They had been poor students when they met at the Royal College of Law. They had come a long way together. They had done something with their lives, she thought, as she walked up the path to the door.

It opened before she had a chance to pull her keys out of her bag.

'Welcome back!' Barry said.

'You haven't shaved!'

'Haven't I?' Barry put his hand to his chin, 'so I haven't!'

The grey stubble on his chin made him look so vulnerable she wanted to hug him. Barry always shaved. He must have been very preoccupied to forget.

'You look a bit rough yourself,' he said.

'Not half as rough as I feel. I didn't have time to shower. How's George?'

'He's watching Thomas the Tank Engine on video. I'm afraid we're having a bit of a Thomas fest today.' He opened the door to the living room where the entire box of Brio train set had been tipped onto the floor.

'And we're a bit self-conscious about our

spots,' he whispered.

George was wearing his Thomas the Tank Engine T-shirt and shorts, and the familiar theme tune was um pom pomming the beginning of another episode.

She picked her way across the bits of wooden track and stooped to kiss him.

'Can I have some Thomas crips?' he asked her.

'If we've got some of course you can.'

'Trouble is, we haven't, and Daddy won't go to the shop to get me any. He says that ordinary crips are the same.'

'Oh, I see. Well, they are.'

'No, Thomas ones taste really yummy!'

'I'll see what I can do,' she said.

'Can I have a Thomas cake?'

'I don't think it's your birthday, is it?'

'Mummy, chickenpox is not really ill, is it?'

'Not really, no,' she agreed, thinking that a white lie would do more to build his confidence than a discussion about what constituted illness. Clowns are not really clowns, she thought.

'I've got quite a lot of pots, haven't I?' George said. His language was well developed but he still could not pronounce an s before a consonant.

She looked at his little blistered face contorted into the strange expression he made when he was trying hard not to cry. It was difficult to believe when they were like this that they would ever regain the smooth child's skin.

'Yes. I think you've got even more than Luke had when he had chickenpox.'

'I've got even more than Luke!' George shouted triumphantly.

'Now, why didn't I think of saying that?' Barry asked her as she came out into the kitchen.

'He seems fine,' she said.

'I told you we were OK.'

'I know. I'm sorry.'

'Don't be sorry. It's nice to have you back.'

'It's lovely to be back,' she said, sinking down onto a kitchen chair and looking fondly at the detritus of lunch left on the table.

There was an individual portion of frozen lasagne microwaved and half eaten, and one of cannelloni that had barely been touched; a triangular heel of a loaf of bread that some inexpert hand had hacked sloping slices from; a half-pound of butter still partly in its wrapping and covered with crumbs. She liked the mess. It was tangible evidence that she had been missed. Automatically, she began to collect up the plates.

'Don't you do it. I just haven't had a chance to clear this lot up yet,' Barry apologized.

'No, it's fine,' she said, smiling.

The look of surprise on his face made her feel ashamed of how cross she must normally be. Well, someone in the household had to be organized, she told herself, or they would live in complete chaos.

'Why don't you go and have your shower, and I'll make you a cup of tea?' Barry said.

'Where are the others?'

'They're upstairs.'

She climbed the stairs and opened the boys' door. 'Hello, Mum,' they both said, neither of them looking up from the computer.

'Are you all right?'

'Fine.'

In the bathroom, she turned on the taps and cleaned her teeth while the bath was filling, staring at herself in the mirror. Then the steam misted the mirror over, and she spat out the toothpaste.

Barry brought her tea and sat on the edge of the bath.

Should she tell him?

If he had been away for a weekend and come back smelling of sex, would she want to know?

'I got very drunk last night,' she said.

'Yes, your eyes are a bit bloodshot.'

'I slept in my contact lenses.'

'I see.'

She thought he knew that she was trying to tell him something. She half expected him to say, like Celia Johnson's husband in *Brief Encounter*, 'You've been away a long time.'

But he did not. Instead he asked, 'Did you enjoy yourself?'

'Not much,' she said hastily, cupping her hands full of water and splashing it over her face, unable to look at him.

'Maybe we should try to go away ourselves for a night or two. The boys are old enough, aren't they? Your mother would come and keep an eye on them.'

'When George is better?' she said.

'Of course.'

She wouldn't want to know if Barry had had a one-night fling, she told herself. Once it was admitted it would have to be dealt with. It

465

would get in the way of the life of the family. It would be an act of pure selfishness to tell him. Completely irresponsible. Her affair wasn't really an affair, she told herself.

'I'd like that,' she looked at him, trying to make her smile let him know that she was grateful.

'Well,' he said, looking at his watch, 'if I leave now, I might get to M & S before it closes.'

'M & S?'

'Thomas the Tank Engine crisps...'

'Oh, of course.'

'Shall I get us something nice for tonight?' he asked.

'Mmm,' she said, lying back so that the water slooshed up and down like a wave pool, 'I fancy Chinese.'

'You always do when you've been drinking,' he said.

'Do I?' She never ceased to be surprised when he knew something about her that she did not. 'How about some duck and pancakes, and, hey, what about those mascarpone cream things for dessert?'

'It's a long time since you've eaten dessert, little bear.'

She wondered whether she had just given herself away...

'Well, you only live once,' she said.

Chapter 45

'So where are you taking me?' Annie asked as they turned off the M40.

'The Manoir aux Quat' Saisons,' Ian replied, taking his eyes off the road for a second to witness her reaction.

'Oh,' she said.

'Don't you like it?'

'It's not that ... no, it's fine, really lovely...'

'What's the problem?' he asked, crestfallen that she was clearly not as excited by his surprise as he was.

'Nothing, really,' she smiled at him, trying belatedly to look thrilled.

He wound the low red car expertly round the country road.

'You've been here before,' he said, as he pulled into the gravel drive and switched off the ignition. Neither of them opened their door.

'The last time I came here was with Penny,' she admitted.

'Oh, God I am so sorry!'

'How could you have known?' she asked.

They sat in silence for a few moments staring through the windscreen at the hedge in front of them.

'The thing is, I was completely hopeless when she was ill,' Annie said quietly. 'I kept making excuses not to come to see her and then finally

467

I brought her out to lunch here and I was so nervous, I couldn't seem to say a single sentence without the word die in it. You know... I've been dying to see what this place is like, the *foie gras* is to die for, and then the waiter was particularly snooty at the end, implying I didn't know the difference between cognac and armagnac, so when he brought the bill I told him I'd rather die than come here again.'

Ian let out a bark of a laugh.

'Sorry,' he said.

'Actually Penny thought it was funny too,' Annie said. 'We decided to go for a walk round the garden afterwards, and she asked for her jacket. "I don't want to die of cold, do I?" she said.'

Annie kept staring forwards.

'And then she couldn't walk very far. She was clinging on to me, she was really frail. And I remember thinking, hey, this is the first time I've ever supported you. It's the wrong way round.'

Tears began to drip down her cheeks.

'Hey,' said Ian, trying to put his arms round her shoulders, but finding it difficult in the cramped interior of the car.

'...I really miss her, you know, because she was the only person who understood that underneath all this loudness and confidence there's an incredibly insecure person,' Annie said, pulling away from him, wiping her eyes with her forearm.

'I'm sure there are other people who understand,' Ian said.

Annie cried for several minutes, then sniffed

several times.

'You mean I come over as an insecure person?' she asked. 'Does it show that I'm a screaming bag of neuroses?' she demanded with an alarmed look.

'No, well, sort of. I think it's a very winning combination of strength and vulnerability,' he improvised.

'Oh, you're just saying that,' she smiled, not believing him, but appreciating the effort.

'Shall we just go back to London?' he asked.

The journey would only take half an hour with him driving, she thought, and then she would have to face the rest of the day alone.

'No, let's have tea. Really. It was a lovely idea. Especially since I've got to start this damn diet tomorrow,' she said, 'and I hear that the lemon tart is to ... second to none.'

They opened their doors and got out, then smiled at each other across the roof of the car.

'What is the difference between armagnac and cognac anyway?' he asked her.

The waiter clearly recognized Annie, but she thought that he must have seen her show because he behaved with impeccable servility. They decided to sit on the terrace, drinking Earl Grey tea and eating deliciously eggy lemon tart with tiny silver pastry forks.

'The herb garden is through there,' Annie told him, pointing at a gap in the hedge. 'They grow most of their own vegetables.'

'Are you a cook?' he asked.

'What do you think?' she asked, trying to do a

Delia Smith sort of smile.

'I think not,' he said.

'Why?' she asked, miffed.

'Well, partly because you said so in your speech last night.'

'Oh, right. Are you?'

'Given a pound of mince and a jar of pasta sauce I can whip up a passable spaghetti bolognese.'

'Does anyone eat spaghetti bolognese any more?' she asked. 'I thought that was what students made because they were poor and it went a long way.'

'Kids eat it,' he explained.

'Oh, right. Of course.' She suddenly looked downcast.

'What?' he asked.

'I don't want children,' she said. 'I only realized that today. They drive me completely crazy. I'm just too selfish. But it's an odd thing to learn about yourself, isn't it?'

'They are a huge responsibility,' Ian said. 'My two are almost grown up now but still when the receptionist at the surgery tells me that Chloe's on the phone, my heart stops for a moment thinking she's going to tell me that something's happened to one of them.'

'It's not totally selfish of me, I suppose,' Annie continued, 'because I don't want to be a burden to anyone when I'm old.'

'I've got to ask you something,' Ian said, pressing the last buttery crumbs onto the pad of his thumb and putting it into his mouth.

'Go ahead,' she said.

470

'I was wondering if there's a man in your life?' He tried to make it sound like a purely academic question.

Annie looked at the side of his face as he pretended to be very interested in the antics of a family of ducks on the lawn. He was a lovely, funny, kind man, she thought. The kind of man who could be your friend, or your husband, but he couldn't be your lover, even if you wanted a lover, which you did not. It wasn't that he couldn't do that flirting stuff, because actually he was quite good at it. Instead of telling you how marvellous he was, his technique was to listen to you and surprise you by remembering what you'd said. It wasn't even that he didn't look the part, because his smiling eyes and comfortable body were really very sexy. The trouble was, she could already feel herself becoming fond of him, and it was disaster to be fond of a lover. Affairs really only worked when you knew you would chuck him immediately if you sensed the remotest possibility of him leaving his wife.

'The short answer is no,' she told him, 'but it's about to change.'

'Oh?'

'Apparently it's all a matter of the birth rate,' Annie said, 'I read an article recently. You see, women tend to get together with men a bit older than they are so if the birth rate's rising then you're fucked. Or more accurately, you're not...'

'Just a minute, you're going too fast...'

'Well, if there were 500,000 babies born in the year you were born and 400,000 three years

471

before then there are approximately 50,000 fewer men to go around, but if the birth rate's rising then there are more. And the best thing about it is that men won't be able to be bastards, because they'll be at the mercy of women's whims because there'll be more of us! Ha, ha!'

'But surely you'll have to go for younger men if that's the case?' Ian asked, clearly struggling with the statistics.

'And you see that as a problem?' she asked, wiping the crumbs from her mouth with a pink napkin. Her lips left a red imprint on the ironed damask. She looked at it with satisfaction.

'That'll take them several washes to remove,' she said. 'God, I'm so common, sometimes, aren't I?'

'Oh well, you seem to have got that sorted out then,' he said.

'I just have to be patient,' Annie said. 'Admittedly, not one of my best virtues.'

'All good things come to those who wait,' he said, trying to look cheerful.

'So I'm told.'

'Well, I suppose that we'd better be getting back,' he said.

'Yes.'

He paid the bill.

He drove a bit like Max had done that first day they had gone Ferrari hunting. She didn't mind going fast when someone else was driving.

'OK?' he shouted at her as the speedometer wavered around 100 m.p.h.

'Listen,' she yelled back, 'if we get stopped, is

it me that gets the ticket or you?'

'Me,' he said.

'In that case, fine!'

He smiled.

She put on a CD.

'Tragedy!' sang the Bee Gees. She joined in, singing at the top of her voice and hardly noticed the turn-off to her mother's suburb.

'Which exit?' he asked, as the car shot up onto the elevated section of the A40 by the BBC.

'The Paddington one.'

They sped over the rooftops of Notting Hill, then turned off and she directed him back along Westbourne Grove, pointing out the best Indian restaurant, then up Pembridge Villas and into her street. He parked expertly in a space which she would have considered far too small to accommodate the length of the car, but left at least two feet at either end.

'The tube's just up there,' she said, as he handed her her keys. 'Shall I walk you?'

'No, I'll be fine. I enjoyed that,' he said. His face had a shiny post-coital kind of redness about it.

'I'm sure my car appreciated it,' she said.

'Well, thanks,' he said, shifting awkwardly from foot to foot, 'for a great time, last night, this morning ... the whole weekend. It was great getting to know you.'

'Yeah, likewise,' she said.

'Come and see me in Broadstairs, if you fancy a break any time. The beach is good. Sea air...'

'Yeah. Thanks,' she said.

'Well, here I am.' She scampered up the steps

to the front door of the large white early Victorian house.

'Second-floor flat, if you're in the neighbourhood,' she said, and immediately regretted it.

'Right,' he said, still dawdling at the foot of the steps.

It would have been normal to exchange a kiss after the weekend they had just spent together, she thought, but it was too late now to go down the steps again. She put her key into the lock.

'Oh well,' she said, with a shrug, wishing he would walk away. She couldn't just leave him standing outside on the pavement, but she could not now invite him up. It would give the whole thing too much significance.

'Say hello to Chloe for me, when she gets back,' she said.

'I will.'

'When will that be?' she asked.

'Not sure. We gave up keeping tabs on each other some time ago.'

'Oh,' she felt stung by the implied rebuke, 'what a tremendously trusting relationship you must have,' she said.

He laughed.

'Yes, since the divorce! Anyway, cheers!'

He started walking briskly down the street.

'Oh fuck,' she muttered, letting herself in, 'fuck, fuck, fuck, fuck!' she shouted, closing the door with her bum, and staying for several long seconds with her back flat against the heavy wooden panels, her feet surrounded by junk mail that had come through the communal letterbox.

Then she opened the door again, just in time

to see him turn the corner of the street into Pembridge Villas. He was walking briskly, looking from side to side at the terrace of white stucco-fronted houses. He didn't even glance back at her.

Chapter 46

Manon got off the coach at Baker Street, then caught the tube to King's Cross and walked through the council estates towards her flat.

There was an enclosed park with a tiny zoo opposite the end of her street. The notice on the gate stated: NO ADULTS UNLESS ACCOM-PANIED BY A CHILD.

The sign had always made her smile, but she had never really looked inside the park gates. Now she peered through at the sandpit and the climbing frames and listened to the random shrieks of children playing.

We will be able to play here, she thought, putting her hand on her tummy again. Each time she let herself imagine the baby she felt stronger. It was like the feeling after a long illness when you wake up one morning knowing suddenly that you are going to be well again.

The Italian restaurant at the end of the street served the best pasta she had eaten outside Italy. One of the waitresses was sitting at a table outside smoking. There was an empty espresso cup in front of her. She waved her cigarette in greeting. Manon smiled. She could not decide whether she was hungry or tired.

'I may be in later,' she told the waitress.

The proprietor shouted 'Ciao bella!' from the dark interior of the restaurant.

The street was very quiet. During the week, the pubs put tables outside and after work drinkers spilled out onto the street in a cloud of beery fumes, but on Sundays there was no-one around.

The flat was cool and dark after the insistent heat and brightness of the city pavements. She ran a glass of water and lay flat on top of the bed. Her body felt heavy and tired, but her mind was racing as if trying to compensate for all the time she had wasted.

Tomorrow, she thought, making a mental list, she would go to the library and read everything she could find on pregnancy, then she would register with a doctor. She would ring Annie and get the number of her friend Holly. After that she would ring her publisher and suggest that they have that lunch he was always promising her. Then she would buy a typewriter. Suddenly, she jumped up and knelt down beside her bed, frantically searching for the roll of notes she had stuffed under the mattress. They were still there. Holding them tightly in her hand, she lay down again. She would find out where the council offices were and ask about getting a council flat. The government was always talking about girls getting pregnant in order to get themselves a flat, which must mean that single mothers jumped the queue.

It wouldn't be easy, she told herself. It was a

gamble. But the one thing in her life she had always been good at was gambling. She closed her eyes and tried to relax. The combination of fear and euphoria made her shivery.

She got up and went to run a bath. She pulled the black jersey dress over her head and studied her body in the mirror on the back of the door for a long time. Then she looked down, unfastened the ring that pierced her tummy button and smoothed her hands over her abdomen.

Chapter 47

The girls were both asleep by seven o'clock, exhausted by the heat and excitement of the day. Roy bent to kiss each of them. Lily was still holding the little straw bag in the shape of a daisy that Annie had given her. As she relinquished consciousness, it slipped from the determined grip of her small fingers and fell with a rustle to the floor. He plugged the night light into the socket nearest to Saskia's bed, knowing that it reassured her to see the sand bottle of memories on her bedside table if she woke during the night.

Downstairs, Geraldine was buzzing around the kitchen, finding surfaces to wipe and bowls to clingfilm and shut in the fridge even when everything looked perfectly clean and tidy.

'Where's Trevor?' Roy asked her, sitting down.

'Gone to a harvest festival planning meeting,

or so he says,' Geraldine said.

Roy was surprised by the sharpness of her tone
He raised an eyebrow.

'I'm well aware that there are at least half a
dozen widows in the parish who'd like to get
their hands on him,' she told him, half smiling,
half perfectly serious.

He laughed, embarrassed, and then he
thought how unfair it was to assume that older
people stopped having sexual feelings when it
became increasingly difficult to imagine them in
bed together.

'Cup of tea?' she asked.

'Yes. Yes, that would be lovely,' he said, sitting
down at the table. 'Anything I can do?'

'No, everything's done,' she said. She poured
them both cups of strong tea, put a few rich tea
fingers on a plate in front of him and a copy of
that morning's *Observer* in such pristine condition it looked as if she had ironed it.

'Thank you,' he said, touched that she had
remembered which Sunday newspaper he read.
Her thoughtfulness made him more inclined to
chat than to read it. The *Sunday Telegraph* was
Trevor's paper of choice. He read it messily in
the living room after lunch and Geraldine would
rush around as soon as he left for evening
service tidying all the sections together to be
placed neatly in the recycling bin in the corner
of the kitchen.

'It was a lovely afternoon, wasn't it?' Roy said.

After Manon and Annie had left, he had put
up the paddling pool in the garden and the
children spent the rest of the day jumping in and

out of the water with their grandfather.

'Yes. The garden's perfect for children. It's too much for the two of us really, but days like this make all the work worthwhile.'

'Will you still live here when Trevor retires?' Roy asked, suddenly a little anxious about the prospect of living in the village without his in-laws around.

'We used to think that we'd retire to the cottage, but hopefully it'll pay for somewhere small around here,' she told him, allaying his fears, 'If we can be useful.'

They had put all their savings into a cottage in a village near the North Yorkshire Moor near where Trevor had been born.

'You were very clever to buy property,' Roy told her.

'Well, it's lovely to live in a place like this, but we always knew we would have to give it up one day. Trevor's a Yorkshireman, so he was all for investing whatever we had in bricks and mortar. Better than any pension plan really. Penny had Joshua Street when she needed it...' Her voice trailed off as she was lost in thoughts of her beloved daughter. 'Of course, we only had enough for a deposit on Joshua Street, but the girls' rent just about paid for the mortgage, and then Penny took it over when she was earning, and then you, and now it's almost paid up, isn't it?'

'Five more years, I think,' he said. 'I was sad to say goodbye to Joshua Street,' he added, flushing slightly at the memory of what had happened there the previous night.

'Yes, it served its purpose well, even if the first occupants were a bit of a motley collection,' Geraldine remembered fondly. 'None of them had a penny more than their grants, which is why I think she chose them. But look at them all today!'

'Yes,' he said. I'm sorry that Ursula couldn't come,' he added, feeling vaguely annoyed that he had to excuse his sister yet again.

'She rang, didn't I say? Oh dear. Her little one has chickenpox. It's not serious, but she was happier going home. I told her she was quite right. She says they'll try to come down in the summer holidays.'

Geraldine smiled her approval and pointed at his untouched cup of tea. 'Perhaps you'd prefer something stronger?' she asked, as he stared through the kitchen window into the darkening garden.

'I'm sure we have some gin. Not so sure about the tonic, but there's orange?'

'No. Thanks. I'm pretty wiped out after last night,' he said, adding quickly, 'I drank quite a lot and we had to wander round for ages until I thought I was sober enough to drive.'

'Oh, for goodness sake, Roy, I wasn't born yesterday,' Geraldine said.

He hadn't really expected her to believe him, but he certainly hadn't thought she would challenge the perfectly reasonable version of events he had made up to fit the facts and cause as little offence as possible.

'What do you mean?' he asked, wrong-footed.

'Well, of course, I could never prove it, but I'd

be most surprised to learn that you and Manon simply wandered round Oxford until you were sober enough to drive,' she said, with a little laugh.

'You don't seem very concerned,' he said.

'Roy, you're a grown man. I expect you to be a good father to my grandchildren. I don't expect you to remain faithful to my daughter all your life.' Her voice was suddenly gruff. She stood up, turned her back to him and ran the kitchen tap to do some non-existent washing up.

He did not know what to say.

The silence was filled with her missing her daughter and his guilt. Then suddenly she turned to him and said, 'You might as well know that Penny told me that I wasn't to give you a hard time if you wanted to be with Manon. I don't mind saying that I was horrified at the time. But I think now that I probably misjudged everyone. My daughter was very wise, you know.'

He was like a sailor on the deck of a ship in a stormy sea lifted into sudden hope, then thrown into the depths of despair. Had Penny really said such a thing? Had she known all along?

Geraldine sniffed.

'There was never anything between us when Penny and I were together.'

'Oh Roy, do you think if I didn't know that, I'd be telling you this?'

'I ... I ... I don't know!'

He didn't know anything any more. He didn't know how to cope, he didn't know whether he was in love, he didn't know whether he was doing the right thing, or thinking the right thoughts. He felt as if he had lost himself, as if he had shattered into a thousand pieces. Suddenly he was crying in great gasping sobs, unable to do anything about it, even though the last person in the world he wanted to see him cry was Geraldine.

'Poor boy,' she said, putting a hand on his shaking shoulders, 'poor Roy.'

'When did Penny say that?' he asked finally.

Geraldine sat down again opposite him.

'Near the end. When she knew I wouldn't argue with her because she was so ill,' Geraldine let out a small rueful laugh. 'And Manon was coming up from London every day, and it was obvious how good she was with the children. I think that Penny thought that Manon would be able to tell them how she was better than we could. She told me that Manon knew her better than anyone else. That made me sad, but it doesn't now, not so much. I can now see some of the qualities in Manon that Penny could see...'

'Manon's had an odd life,' Roy said.

'Yes. She frightened me when she was younger. She seemed so sophisticated. She cast a spell on people. I was afraid she would spirit my daughter away too. But I think that that was more to do with me not wanting to lose Penny.' Geraldine wiped away a solitary tear. 'Ah, Roy! I loved her so much, I feared from the day she was born that I would lose her. Sometimes, I think I made it happen because I prayed so much that it would not...'

He felt strangely as if she had not told anyone that before.

How brave she was and how relentlessly honest. just like Penny, he thought, surprised that he should now be able to see in Geraldine virtues he thought Penny possessed in spite of her mother, rather than because of her.

He reached out across the table and held her hand.

They looked at each other for a moment. Then she withdrew her hand, pretending to search for a handkerchief up her sleeve.

'Would you mind if I went for a walk?' he heard himself asking.

' Of course not.'

'The girls are both asleep. If they ask for me, tell them I'll be back soon.'

'They'll be fine.'

She smiled again, relieved, he thought, at the change of subject.

'I just need to collect myself.'

'Of course you do.'

'I won't be very long.'

'Be as long as you need,' she told him.

'Thank you,' he said, stooping to give her a kiss. Her skin smelt slightly of dried roses, 'thank you for everything you do.'

'It's nice to have family around,' she told him, blushing slightly, embarrassed by the softness of their exchange: 'it's good to be useful when you're older.'

The days were beginning to draw in. If he had been out at this time only a few evenings before, it would still have been dusk, but it was quite dark, and the sky above was brilliant with stars.

He walked along the lane past the meadow towards the village pub.

There were people in the garden sitting at wooden tables and as he drew closer he could smell the yeasty vapour of beer and hear the murmur of summer evening conversation. The windows of the pub were like pumpkin lanterns of warm orange light. He stood for a few moments unseen in the shadows, tempted to venture into the warm smoky embrace of the bar.

There was a young couple at the table nearest to where he was standing. The girl had long hair and was holding a bottle of lager in her right hand, the boy was drinking a pint of beer. Underneath the table, their hands were stroking each other's wrists. He stared at them, then the girl turned and saw him. He looked away, and began walking quickly back towards the rectory.

It was getting slightly chilly. He thought about going in for a jumper, but decided not to. The key to the car jingled in the pocket of his shorts. He slid it into the door of the car and climbed in. It wouldn't take much more than an hour to drive to London at this time of night, he thought, turning on the ignition.

In the rearview mirror as he pulled away, he thought he saw Geraldine's silhouette at the staircase window, on her way upstairs to check the children, or perhaps watching him. But maybe it was just a trick of the light, he thought, switching his headlights to full beam, or a friendly ghost.

Chapter 48

'I can't believe I'm the only one of us that didn't get laid,' Annie said.

There was a sharp intake of breath.

'What?'

'Sometimes one of the boys picks up the phone upstairs,' Ursula said.

'Oh, sorry,' Annie said. Surely Ursula's children were too young to know what getting laid meant, or did she think of Barry as one of the boys?

'You promised you wouldn't mention it.'

'I thought you said he didn't turn up,' Annie reminded her.

Ursula's silence proved her guilt.

'How is George, by the way?' Annie asked, wandering restlessly round the flat with her cordless phone. She shut the doors to each of her cupboards, then went into the kitchen and threw open the fridge.

'Spotty but fine,' Ursula said, 'thank you.'

The choice was champagne or Diet Coke. She took out a can and opened it, took a slurp, swallowed and said, 'So, I spend the whole weekend thinking how brilliantly restrained I'm being with a married man and it turns out that he's divorced.'

'Really?' Ursula said, 'for how long?'

'No idea. He only announced it as we were

saying goodbye. It was a bit too late to be interested by then.' She took another slurp but some of it missed her mouth and soaked into her white T-shirt.

'I thought he wasn't your type,' Ursula said.

'I think I've been going for the wrong type.'

Annie took a sponge from beside the sink and ran water on it then dabbed at her front.

'Are you in the shower or something?' Ursula asked.

'No, just trying to get something off my T-shirt.' Annie held the cordless phone under her chin and scrubbed. Now the T-shirt had Diet Coke, washing-up water and little flecks of orange sponge on it. She gave up and walked back into the living room.

'You see, I've always gone for small bums, and that just makes me feel huge, so from now on I've decided I'm not going to look at a man unless I could comfortably wear his jeans. I'd never eaten a guilt-free bacon sandwich until I met Ian.'

'Oh, then it must be love,' Ursula said, sarcastically.

'How's Barry?' Annie shot back, lying down on the sofa.

The room was rather hot. She thought she had better look into getting air conditioning if this weather was going to go on, or a ceiling fan. A ceiling fan would be good, she thought. And some palms in terracotta pots.

'He's in the kitchen cooking me supper,' Ursula said smugly.

'Very Marco Pierre White.'

'Marks and Spencer actually,' Ursula said.

Barry was probably a bit Marks and Spencer in the bedroom too, Annie thought, imagining Ursula's husband in a pair of pyjamas. Did Ian wear pyjamas? She didn't think so.

'I've never had sex with a doctor,' Annie ruminated. 'Do you think it feels like you're having a smear? Open a little wider, now relax, good, that's it, well done?'

'Probably,' said Ursula.

'At least he'd know where all your bits are,' Annie said.

'Yes, but that's not what makes good sex, is it?' Ursula replied. 'You can be as proficient as you like, but in the end good sex is about a willingness to give another person pleasure, don't you think?'

'I hope your boys aren't listening,' Annie said.

Another sharp intake of breath.

'Although it would probably do them good to hear it,' Annie said.

Ursula remained silent.

'At least the world didn't end,' Annie said.

'What?'

'Nostradamus said it was going to this weekend.'

'Oh.'

There was a short silence.

'Anyway, I've blown it,' said Annie.

'Why don't you call him?' Ursula suggested.

'Haven't got his number,' said Annie.

'Oh, for heaven's sake, that couldn't be too hard to find.'

'Oh, I don't think there's any point. We're from

different worlds, aren't we?' Annie said, airily. 'Do I honestly want to be a provincial doctor's wife in Kent?'

'You haven't even got to first kiss yet. Anyway, that's not a very feminist hypothesis, is it?'

'Well, he wouldn't fit into my world, would he?'

'It might finish off your series if you suddenly retreated into married bliss,' Ursula observed shrewishly.

'Yes, there aren't a lot of laughs in marriage, are there?' Annie retaliated, wishing that she and Ursula weren't always so competitive. She had rung up for a good old self-pitying moan, but they never could resist a sniping contest.

'Anyway,' she said, 'I don't want children. An afternoon with your nieces once a year is quite enough in that department.'

'How are they?'

'They seemed happy enough. I'm just not very interested in children, I think.'

'Is he, though?' Ursula returned her to the subject of Ian.

'He seems very fond of those he's got. They would probably hate me...'

'I'm sure they wouldn't.'

'...although, of course, there might be quite a good series in that. You know, famous metropolitan television personality decides to downshift and become a provincial doctor's wife, giving up the bitchy media world she has come to despise, only to find that she's met her match with her new stepdaughter...'

'Aren't you getting a little ahead of yourself? I

mean, how about suggesting you have dinner together for a start?'

'Or lunch? Isn't the Whitstable Oysterage somewhere round there?'

'Trust you to think of oysters,' said Ursula.

'Oh, there's no point,' Annie sighed. 'We'd bore each other to tears before they brought the main course.'

'But you got on so well.'

'But that was Oxford. Oxford's like that, isn't it? It gives you a false idea of what you are.'

'It does,' Ursula sighed heavily.

'Didn't you have a good time?' Annie couldn't resist asking.

'Not really,' Ursula said.

'I'm sorry.'

'I'm not. It's made me see how happy I really am.'

'Oh God, not you too! Manon's been banging on all afternoon about changing her life. Everyone in the world had a life-enhancing bloody watershed of a weekend and all I learned about myself was that my body is not up to cycling back from the Woodstock roundabout ... and there's the doorbell. All I need now is some bloody Jehovah's witness telling me that the world is about to end after all...'

She got up from the sofa and went to the window. Whoever it was had either gone, or was standing underneath the porch. Usually friends of hers stood on the steps looking up at the window, because they knew that the intercom was broken. The doorbell rang again. She waited. It rang again. Very persistent Jehovah's witnesses, she thought.

'Listen Ursy, I'll just deal with this and call you back,' she said, and pressed the disconnect button.

Her left leg hurt too much to contemplate the idea of running downstairs to open the door, but she was paranoid enough about stalkers not to simply buzz them in. She heaved up the heavy sash window and leaned out.

'Hello?'

Her visitor took a step back. It wasn't a head she recognized, but it had a good covering of greying hair, then he tipped his head back to look up at her.

'Hello!' Ian called.

'Oh!'

'I got as far as Faversham,' he shouted up.

'Haversham?'

'Faversham!'

'I don't know what you're talking about.'

'It's a town in Kent.'

'Oh!' she said, as if that made everything clear, 'hang on, I'll buzz you in.'

She went to the entryphone, buzzed, then turned and looked at herself in the huge mantel mirror. Hair everywhere, a white T-shirt with a grubby wet patch on it. Too late to do anything about it because she could hear him taking the steps two by two.

'Come in!' she said, opening the door, 'I was just about to change.'

She pointed at the sofa, then ran into her bedroom, grabbed a clean T-shirt from her separates beach hut cupboard and pulled it on.

He was standing looking out of the window.

'I got as far as Faversham,' he began again.

'So you keep saying, but it means nothing to me,' she interrupted.

'It's where the fast trains stop. You have to change there sometimes.'

Was he a closet trainspotter or something?

'So?' she asked.

'What I'm saying is that I didn't get all the way home. If I had got all the way home then I wouldn't have come back. You know how it is, back to reality and all that. I was almost there, but at Faversham I decided that it might be crazy, but it might be crazier not to...'

'You're making no sense at all. How about some champagne?'

'Oh, yes. That would be nice.'

She suddenly realized that he was tremendously nervous. It was rather sweet, she thought, taking the champagne from the fridge, then breaking a fingernail trying to get the wire off.

'Damn!'

She banged the bottle down on the counter then picked it up and angrily twisted the cork out without getting glasses ready. The champagne foamed down the front of her T-shirt.

There weren't any more clean white T-shirts. She pulled on a black one and when she came back into the living room he looked at her oddly as if he thought something had changed, but couldn't make out what it was.

'Cheers!' she said, holding out a glass.

'Cheers!' he replied, smiling.

'So what was it that you wanted to say?' she

asked, with as much composure as she could manage.

'Are you free for dinner?' he asked.

'Yes, but I want to know what it was first,' she said.

'That was it.'

'What?'

'I wanted to know whether you were free for dinner,' he smiled a little more confidently. 'I wondered whether you would like to have dinner with me?'

'That's it?'

What she had envisaged, she realized, when he had looked up at her from the steps, was something more along the lines of I'm just a provincial doctor standing here asking a famous television personality to love him.

But dinner was a start.

'And there's another thing,' he said.

'Yes?' she smiled sweetly.

'Can I use your loo? I'm dying for a wee.'

She could feel the smile settling on her face becoming more of a rictus as she tried to cover her disappointment.

'In there.'

She pointed at the bathroom door.

She slumped down on the sofa, half tempted to put on *Meat Loafs Greatest Hits*. It was beginning to get dark outside. Where would she take him? she wondered. 192, or the tapas bar on the Portobello Road? No doubt he would suggest a curry at the Indian she'd pointed out. They would have nothing to talk about and then she'd have to put him up in her spare room and in the morning they would have an embarrassed breakfast and that would be that. She drained her glass of champagne.

'Do you mind if I ask you something?' he asked, coming back into the living room.

'Ask away,' she said.

'Why have you got a wedding dress on your bathroom floor?'

It took her a couple of seconds to understand what he was referring to.

'It's not a wedding dress,' she told him, laughing weakly, 'it's a dress with a hooped petticoat. They only had ivory left because of launch of Scarlett ... oh doesn't matter...'

The great mass of ivory silk on the floor of her bathroom was a fitting metaphor for her life, she thought. Grubby, torn, nothing whatsoever to do with weddings, and soaked with champagne.

'There was this party,' she tried to explain, 'and I'd always wanted to wear a dress with one of those huge skirts that sort of bobs along on its own, and, well, anyway,' she wiped a tear away from her eye. Why on earth did she keep crying in front of him? 'Well, anyway, it was a bit of a disaster, really...'

He knelt down in front of her.

She thought he was about to say 'there, there', and if he had, she knew she would have hit him.

'Put it on,' he said, quietly.

'What?'

'Put it on,' he insisted, 'I want to see you in it.'

'Oh, you're just saying that.'

'Put it on.'

'All right, I bloody will,' she said defiantly.

She got up and went into the bathroom and stepped into the dress. 'I need some help with the hooks,' she called, walking back into the living room.

In the huge mantel mirror above the fireplace she caught sight of herself. Her hair was all over the place and her lipstick was slightly smudged. Her cheeks had bright spot of pinkness from the first glass of champagne. She was holding up the stiff corset of the dress by pressing her elbows into her sides. She looked, she thought, like a courtesan at the end of a hard night.

She turned and offered her back to him.

His fingers fiddled with the hooks and then stopped. She waited silently, holding her breath, feeling his hand hovering an inch away from her spine.

'Your skin is like a peach,' he said.

'What orange and pink with a sort of dust on it?' she asked.

'No, it's smooth and creamy and ... yes...' he put both his hands on her shoulders and sighed, 'very soft.'

'So more like a Mr Whippy ice cream then,' she said, nervously. He had large hands, they felt heavy resting there.

'Except warmer,' he said, and then he laughed his bark of a laugh, which cut through the incredible sexual tension that had descended on them and made her turn to face him.

'The trouble is,' he said, running a finger from the bottom of her earlobe down her neck and along the top of her bare shoulder, 'there doesn't seem to be a great deal of point doing up all these hooks just to undo them again...'

'You could rip them apart, rather than going to all the trouble of actually undoing them,' she reasoned.

'True,' he said, leaning forward and kissing her very, very lightly on her mouth.

If she had been a soft ice cream, Annie thought, she would just have melted.

'Wait a minute,' she said, 'I have to hold out until at least our second date.'

'But you've been holding out nearly twenty years,' he protested.

'But do you think that counts? Because I didn't even notice you then,' she said.

'It counts.'

He kissed her again, for longer this time.

'I don't want to have children,' she said, breaking away.

'Suits me,' he said.

They kissed again. This time she let the dress fall to the floor.

He stood back and stared at her wearing only her knickers.

'You are gorgeous,' he said, like a hungry child looking at a table laden with party food unable to decide what to try first.

'Do you think we should join the Euro?' she suddenly demanded.

'Yes.'

'Are you a Woody Allen fan?'

'Can't stand him.'

'Do you like my show?'

There was a definite hesitation.

'Not as much as the real thing,' he said.

'Is that a nice way of saying no?' she asked.

'It's a qualified way of saying yes.'

'Oh, so what's wrong with it?'

'I think Annie should move on.'

'You think there's been one series too many?'

'Yes.'

'So, what should happen to her?' Annie asked.

He gave the question serious consideration.

'I think Annie should find someone who loves her, fuck him senseless, and see how she feels in the morning...'

'Hmmm,' said Annie thoughtfully, 'it might just work, but I don't know about leaving the ending so open...'